SLAYING *the* NAGA KING

JESSICA M. BUTLER

Editor: Maggie Myers

Cover Art: Natalie Bernard

Proofreaders: Nic Page, Cassie G. Rachel Theus Cass

To the love of my life who, upon hearing what I intended to write about, said "Snakes...why'd it have to be snakes?"
I, of course, answered "I know."
And when he asked me why not something more realistic, I said in the gruffest graveliest voice I could "I'm a romantic fantasy writer, Jim, not a realist."

And if you got those movie references, you're my kind of person, and thus this book is also dedicated to you.

P.S. Variations of that quote are literally the only time I call my husband Jim. He is totally a James.

I

DESPERATE TIMES

Could you outrun a nightmare?

Or carry someone you loved out of its path?

Probably not. But you could always run toward it. Or try your best to prepare for its coming. Especially when it came every night to torment the people you loved.

Rhea noted the long slanting path of orange light that filtered through the oak branches over the windows of their tiny tree home.

Less than six hours before the next attack.

Unless the time changed.

Please, she prayed, *don't let the time change. No extension or addition. If anything, it could just go away.*

She adjusted the coarse sheet of paper on the low table and resumed sketching. Fatigue burned her eyes. What she wouldn't give for a night and day of peace. This breakneck pace had only intensified. It could not last forever.

But no one—not them, not the elders, not the Paras, not the entirety of all the worlds' leaders combined—seemed any closer to finding an answer.

She rubbed her forehead and stared down at the dark lines on the page. They wavered a little, some of the markings less strong than others.

Usually, drawing comforted her. Now, though, she felt only the desire to finish her illustrations so she could turn them in to her clients and get paid. She shook her head. Pity purchases. No doubt about that. But pity purchases purchased food as well as any other money.

It seemed like such a small thing. Like she was just staking out space for them to survive. To get through. To give Tiehro and Salanca, her spirit family, time to rest and hopefully to fight off this psychic plague or curse.

The pencil slipped between her fingers.

Fight it off...for how long?

The rest of the month?

The rest of the year?

The rest of their lives?

She set her jaw, tightening her grip over the pale wood. The lead scraped over the page with uneven pressure as she willed herself to sketch faster. There was no way to know for certain. And she needed to do something—to find some way to hope. She had to do something, or she was going to go mad herself. And then what good would she be?

A large firm hand grasped her shoulder. "You should be resting right now," Tiehro said, his gravelly voice hoarser than usual.

She kept her focus on the page though she knew what she'd see if she glanced up—straight purple-black hair tangled and mussed over his filed-down horns, his amethyst eyes bloodshot and watery, and his jet-black eagle wings tucked firmly against his back and yet showing traces of molting. She pushed the anger at their situation down. It wouldn't accomplish anything good.

"I don't think you slept long enough."

"Funny thing about sleep. When you want it, it never comes." He nudged her again then stepped back. "You should at least close your eyes for a bit."

"If I rest now, I won't get these done. If I don't get these done, I can't deliver them to my clients. If I don't deliver them to my clients, we don't get paid. If we don't get paid, we can't afford food. If we can't afford food, we have to hunt or gather. In which case, none of us will be sleeping then either. And as drawing is significantly safer than hunting, I think this is the best choice."

He staggered and caught himself on the coarse wall.

Her focus snapped to him. "It's getting worse?"

He held his hand over his eyes. His mouth twitched. "Just clumsy."

She set her jaw. He'd not only had to battle the nightmares but aura migraines and double vision. It had gotten so bad that as of last week, he couldn't fly.

Setting the pencil and paper aside, she stood. "If you aren't careful, you're going to drop out of this tree. And then where will you be?"

"On the ground, most likely," he said dryly. "A fall from this height wouldn't kill anyone though. Not unless they landed on a knife. Or a besred. You don't still keep that little blade in your shirt, do you? You might want to take that out in case you fall."

Of course she did. She always kept that little blade for sharpening her pencils. It was wrapped in rubber and stuck between her breasts, but it was never at risk of stabbing her. Even if it did, it wouldn't do much damage.

"At least we don't live on Ecekom where even the rocks want to eat you." She tried to smile, but it wavered. "I think we need to talk about moving, Tiehro."

They'd spent what remained of their savings to move to this little hut situated in the trees over an hour's walk from Dohahtee and any other place with people and commerce. All in the desperate hope that distance from others in the psychic races would protect them. It hadn't.

And if Tiehro and Salanca followed the path of so many others of their races before them, there would come a point when they would not wake from the nightmares. When they would simply be trapped. To her knowledge, no one had woken up from those comas yet. Perhaps they never would. If one fell, she might be able to manage to keep that one alive. But if both fell?

He didn't look up at her.

She forced her voice to be stronger. "I think we need to move back to where there are people who can help us. We won't be able to do this alone."

Tiehro stiffened. He straightened his shoulders and then gave her the most casual smile he could manage, the tightness in his expression wavering with his pain. "It'll be fine, Bunny. We'll find a way. Not planning on collapsing any time soon. This house is for you. To make sure you aren't without something."

The floorboards creaked beneath her feet. All for her. Part of her hated this little house, even though she knew they wanted her to have it with good intentions.

"I know you're concerned about—"

He scoffed. "No. It isn't that." His eyes darted toward her, his expression slightly guilty as if he were trying to construct a poor half-truth. "I will not enter that place until I have no choice. I will not be near it until there is no choice. I might even rather die. If I fall here, I fall. You owe me nothing. I don't expect you to drag my comatose husk to their door." As his words sharpened, he winced. "I'm sorry," he said, softer this time. "Just the paranoia."

Rubbing the back of her neck, she tried to seem as calm and confident as before. He'd never been paranoid or suspicious before, but, even so, she wouldn't blame him for fearing Dohahtee. The psychic quarantine quarters were unpleasant for anyone to consider. Her own pulse quickened in fear at the thought of going that far underground with so many. But she was certain that his reaction was largely because he didn't want this house to be taken from her. Moving to Dohahtee and paying for lodgings would likely require losing this house, small as it was. And then she would be homeless and without prospects once Tiehro and Salanca left on their own important journeys. Both off on their way to grand purposes and plans while she was left to putter around this place.

"If you want to go stay in Dohahtee, that isn't a bad idea," he continued. He crossed to the cracked basin on the far side of the room. The little cooking area was small enough that if he spread out his wings, he would easily fill it. "I can take care of this house. You could see about taking out credit against my name. If they'll give it."

"I'm not leaving either of you unless it's to do something that helps. But they do have medicines there and physicians who might be able to give you relief."

"The relief isn't worth the risk," he said. "Mark my words. We go in there. Only some of us come out. The rest—chopped up probably."

"They wouldn't do that—"

"None of us know what they would do. There are stories. Some of which are true. And it only takes one or two." He dragged his hand over his face, then blinked slowly. With a shuddering sigh, he picked up the squat stone kettle and checked the water within. "We wouldn't know until it's too late. We just—we have to find another solution. And we will, Bunny. But it won't involve selling this house. This house belongs to us—to you."

If she hadn't been worried before, she'd be worried now. He only used their childhood nicknames when he was deeply troubled.

She hugged her arms around her middle, her fingers curling against her coral tunic. "Is there anything we could do to make Dohahtee feel safe and keep this house?"

He laughed ruefully. "If only it were that simple."

A weak smile pulled at his mouth. It didn't even come close to reaching his eyes. "It'll be fine. I promise. We're going to find a solution for this. The Paras and the council and everyone will figure out something. It's been a few weeks anyway. They're probably this close to finding the answer." He held his thumb and index finger a fraction apart. "Just wait and see, Bunny. Everything is good."

Her heart broke. "All right, Chickadee."

His smile pulled a little higher as he set the kettle on the stove.

Tears stung the backs of her eyes, and she released a slow breath, trying to regain control of herself. "They probably won't call you that when you join your new sodiwa." This particularly sodiwa was especially elite, dedicated to enhancing the skills of all its members.

"If—"

"There are no ifs." Sniffling, she rubbed her hand over her eyes, then crossed to the cupboard. Inside the deep shelves sat a variety of clay pots, covered baskets, and slim tins. "We both could use some tea. Salanca, too, once she gets back."

He peered out past the fur curtains that had been wedged up over the window frame to let the air in. "She's been gone too long. Should have been back over an hour ago."

"She said that was the earliest she'd be back. She's probably just following her lead."

Shaking his head, he kept his hand tight over the handle of the kettle. "Still...if she isn't back in the hour, we should go find her."

"Stop worrying." Salanca pushed through the door, her gait uneven for two steps and her Neyeb betrothal necklace twisted about. She shot him an almost playful glare though her face was pale and beaded with sweat. Her long brown-black braid was damp, and her cheeks had heavy red streaks. "If I was going to die, I'd do it with far more dignity and far fewer dramatics."

"Or both." Rhea hurried to her.

These two both struggling to stay on their feet and battling bouts of dizziness made her even less enthused with staying in a house thirty feet above the ground.

Shooing Rhea back, Salanca shook her head, her heavy grey cloak swinging with the movement and flashing the embroidered and beaded designs within. "No need for dying today, my loves. I have what we need. Everything is going to be fine now."

Rhea set her lips in a tight line, not certain she believed this. Salanca was always coming up with crazy plans and strange schemes of one sort or another.

"How?" Tiehro demanded, hand still on the kettle.

Salanca gripped Rhea's shoulder, her eyes so bloodshot they looked almost fully red. "The Paras—the council—the elders—none of them are doing a damn thing that works. Only a matter of time before this takes everyone, including them. They're evacuating the cities even now, and all of the shifter cadres have been asked to go out and start searching for the fallen and get them to care facilities."

"I didn't ask *why* we needed to do something," Tiehro grumbled.

Rhea tried to tug her to the sleeping pelts on the opposite side of the little house. The thin patchwork curtains that provided a little privacy had been pushed almost entirely out of the way. "Let's get a little rest before tonight, all right?"

Salanca's grip tightened as she dug her feet into the wood floor.

Tiehro strode over and lifted her up, his arm around her waist. "You aren't going to fix anything by getting sicker."

"Don't pick me up, you big crow." She smacked his arm. "Don't you understand? I actually have the solution. We need to dream walk and thought-project. It's going to take all three of us though. You both have to help me."

Frowning, he set her down in the center of the room on the edge of the woven red rug. "What? Where did you go exactly?"

"Ah, ah. I have my secrets for a reason." Salanca wagged her finger at him, but she smiled nonetheless. Reaching into her cloak, she removed two items from the deep pocket on her right. A squat bottle with dark-purple liquid and a black glass bowl with a series of strange marks etched into it. "I found an incantation to apply in conjunction with dream walking and thought-projection. We will ask to be shown either the source or solution to the problem."

"Either? Why not just one?" Tiehro asked, his frown deepening. "Doesn't this open us up to confusion?"

"Because we don't know what is or isn't connected to another person. There has to be someone that we reach for this. Besides, how hard would it be to sort out which one it is? It's safer this way. Trust me. I've worked it all out. You just need to do what I say."

Rhea hugged herself, uneasy. Salanca never needed help

with mindreading. Her dream walking and dream weaving abilities were at such a profound level even as a child that a Neyeb elder lovingly referred to her as the Tapir when he had brought her to the home. In the past months, Salanca had been expanding those skills into more arcane pursuits.

A prickle of unease curled up Rhea's spine. "What exactly would we be doing?"

"Excellent question." Salanca pushed the table to the back of the room and kicked the rug aside. "It's very simple. We make the preparations and drink this special serum that will intensify our abilities. I will make the connection and send us forward to the source or solution. Tiehro will bolster it, ground it, and project it into Rhea's mind, and Rhea will interact with whoever it is and bring back the report."

"Salanca, we have no idea where this person is or if they even exist," Tiehro responded. "And if it is so simple, why wouldn't the Paras have done it or even the Council of Elders?"

"Because they didn't have this." She tapped her fingers on the black glass bowl. "Trust me. All right? Besides, it would take time to get it to them, and then you know how much time it would take for them to determine what could be done and how and whether it would be wise. And I don't know about you, Tiehro, but I don't want to go back into those dreams."

"I don't either," he said tightly, "but I don't want either of you hurt. This puts Rhea at tremendous risk. She is the one whose mind will be connected to this person."

"If there's a problem, she can end the connection, and we will pull her back. We'll pull her back regardless if it takes too long." She placed her hand on his arm, her fingers curling over his dark-green sleeve. "The only reason this is not dangerous is because it is the combination of our specific abilities.

Because of you, we have far stronger power and focus. That is what your new sodiwa wants from you, yes? Because of me, that power and focus can be focused in the right place. And because of Rhea, we will see beyond the veil and understand what is happening without having to diminish either of our focuses. This is so perfect. It is as if we were destined to do this."

Rhea tightened her arms over her chest. "This isn't part of the Forbidden Arts, right?"

"Dream walking and thought-projection form the foundation for so much of the Neyeb and Tiablo traditions," Salanca responded. "Without them, we would lack most of our abilities. There's nothing forbidden in using them."

"But what happens if Rhea is exposed and bound to someone evil?" Tiehro snapped. "You and I will be safe. She's the one who will be seen. There's too much we don't know. My strength and focus have been waning."

"It's better than nothing," Salanca responded.

"It could damage or kill you! Either of you. What if the answer is beyond our reach? What if it takes us beyond my ability to ground and yours to channel? I would rather die than see either of you harmed."

"Tiehro..." Salanca started, pinching the bridge of her nose as if she didn't know where to begin.

If this remained unchecked, one day her family would collapse and never wake again.

Rhea hugged herself tighter. "I'll do it."

"See!" Salanca gestured toward her, her face brightening though her expression seemed rather crazed with her bloodshot eyes. She scooted back the low table and then grabbed the seat cushions. "Now you have to help, Tiehro. It'll be far more dangerous if it's just Rhea and me."

A muscle jumped in his jaw as he looked between them,

arms folded tight over his chest. "All right. But no unnecessary risks."

Salanca scoffed as if such a thing was unimaginable. She then instructed them to help her finish moving the furniture to give them plenty of space in the center of the room. After that, they put the sitting cushions in a triangle on the floor, and each sat.

She uncorked the vial with the purple liquid and offered it to Rhea. "Each of us needs to drink this. It enhances our abilities."

The glass bottle weighed heavy in Rhea's hand. She turned it over, watching the dark liquid slosh within. It smelled like tart raspberries.

"You remember how to cut the connection in dream walking and thought-projecttion, yes?" Tiehro asked softly, his gaze fixed on her. "Always look for the walls."

She nodded. One of the advantages of having a Neyeb spirit sister and Tiablo spirit brother. "I remember."

Drawing in a full breath, she took a mouthful. At first, it tasted only like raspberries. Then it became muddy. Then once again, it became like raspberries, the final note turning to something far more acidic and similar to a bitter red wine.

She grimaced. Already her mouth was uncomfortably dry. "I don't suppose we can drink anything else?" She passed it to Tiehro as she wiped her mouth.

"Afraid not." Salanca held out her hand as Tiehro took his swig and pulled a dramatically perturbed expression. "Don't be such a child about it."

"That's disgusting." He handed it to her anyway.

Salanca lifted the bottle as if toasting them and then tipped a mouthful past her lips. Shaking her head, she then poured the remnant into the black glass bowl. That bright sweet scent filled the air. "It isn't really when you consider what this could require."

Carefully, she placed the bowl between them and then removed a knife from the sheath on her sash.

Rhea opened her mouth to say something, but the words died on her tongue. Was she—was she doing what she thought?

Salanca slit a line across her palm, then dripped the dark blood into the bowl. After setting the knife aside, she removed small pouches from the pocket of her dark-blue skirt. She emptied those contents into the bowl as well. Herbs. Hair. Chopped bark.

"What are you doing?" Tiehro's eyes widened. He lifted his hand. "You said this wasn't from the Forbidden Arts."

"Not all of it." Salanca bit her lower lip as she wrung more blood out into the bowl. "Most of it isn't at all. So don't even worry about it. The only reason this little tiny part is forbidden is because of the pain and harm to me, but I'm more than willing to pay it. It isn't nearly as bad as you might think."

Rhea opened her mouth to speak, the hair on the back of her neck prickling up. The Forbidden Arts were forbidden because of how dangerous they were and because they relied on the pain and suffering of others.

"Whose suffering is this drawing on?" she said, struggling to form the words.

"Only mine. I know what I'm doing. But do not waste my time with more questions. This is our only opportunity. I'm paying the price regardless. Let's at least have a chance at solving this problem, all right? If you don't do what you're told though, you make it dangerous for all of us."

Tiehro's eyes flashed with confusion, anger, and fear. Reaching over, he gripped Rhea's hand and squeezed it tight.

The edges of her vision had already started to blur, and an intense humming filled her ears, strong enough it was as if it wanted to drag her into the floor and down into the earth below.

Vaguely, she heard him say something. The words danced around her consciousness. The dryness of her mouth and the cotton sensation in her ears absorbed so much of her focus, she scarcely felt Salanca take her hand. A vague panic rose within her. The colors intensified around her, bleeding out into a pool of inky black that absorbed the entirety of her vision.

Strings danced in front of her face, plucking and going taut. Wind stirred, then swept faster around her. It tugged at her hair, nearly pulling it free from its clasp.

She was floating in darkness, but those strings plucked. They sang with little cries and muted whispers. Water surged and trickled and splashed somewhere in the distance, all at once as loud as if she stood in the tidal path of the ocean and then somehow as quiet as if a small creek chuckled beyond the forest and over a hill.

Nothing held her hands now. She floated freely through the air, blinking and trying to focus. Though she could not see, she knew she was moving. Somehow. Somewhere.

Glass shattered somewhere to her right. Rocks snapped and cracked. She spun, her hair whipping into her face. Energy sparked, and thunder boomed. Something like lightning tore through the air, lighting up an enormous cave.

The air changed, turning cold for a breath.

Purple light shimmered around her, brilliant and undulating. A more intense shade than the puffs of fog that appeared over Tiehro and Salanca when the nightmares trapped them.

Something pulled her away, out from the open air and onto black stone. Veins of the same purple light branched out across the walls and ceiling, brimming and pulsing with jagged energy.

Was this what had caused the attacks? The plague? The curse?

As she moved farther away from it, it looked like an actual tear in the air itself. Purple light enflamed with blue and silver veins arced and stretched at intervals like a dying heartbeat and a raging lightning storm at once. Beneath it was a mass of purple light with amethyst and silver streaks bubbling and churning.

Where even was this? What defining features were within this cave that she could even recall?

She stretched her hand out and opened her mouth to call Tiehro and Salanca, but her voice stuck in her throat. They were close, but she had moved beyond them somehow. The veil they'd mentioned—whatever that was—was thick. The air had gone thicker too, all the sound and energy fuzzing in her ears as if there were thousands of bees clustered around her head.

But she wasn't alone. The air clung to her, crackling with energy and tension.

This had to be the source. Was there also a solution?

A perpetrator—she fell back.

Wait. No.

He stood—well, not exactly. He was half snake. Really more than half by the length of those coils. From the waist up, he looked like a man. He held a long-handled weapon of some sort as he swayed back and forth, his features blurred in a mass of indigo, turquoise, green, and cerulean. A naga?

He lunged at something in the shadows with a snarl.

Everything went black.

2

IN HIS MIND

Rhea looked around slowly as the darkness receded, blinking to moisten her dry eyes. They burned a little even now. Wherever she was, she had arrived, whether at the source or the person who could help them fix it.

The hazy heaviness still filled her ears, not so intense as before yet more compelling. The more she listened to it, the more it droned, lulling her into a peaceful state, willing her to forget and simply exist in this place.

Wherever it was.

She pressed her eyes shut for a moment. No. No lulling away. Time to figure out what was going on. She could do this.

She was here to find the source or the solution. Salanca had formed the connection. Tiehro was strengthening it. She just had to observe and return.

She cracked her eyelids open and tried to take everything in.

Hmm. Not quite what she'd expected.

No longer did she hover above a cavern floor. No, now she

was in a relatively small but luxurious chamber. Thick shiny satin turquoise cushions sat on striped rugs. Small sculptures rested in shelves cut directly into the wall. Each time she tried to focus on the little carvings, they seemed to dissolve or move. The dark stone of the walls seemed more purple at some points, then more a deep grey, then charcoal. Sometimes indigo if she didn't focus on them at all.

A wardrobe with serpents, dragons, and other creatures carved into its frame in brilliant detail filled another cubby directly carved into the wall. The floor itself was smoothed dark stone.

As she turned, she observed a large bed pressed up against the wall, rich with bright silk sheets, padded blankets, and thick pillows.

All right. So this was a bedroom. What next? She squinted. Was anyone even here?

The covers on the bed stirred. Then a man sat up, frowning as he looked at her. "Hello?"

Oh.

Hello indeed. Her mouth went dry as she struggled to find words. It wasn't that she had never seen a man without his shirt or a handsome man half-naked, but he stole her breath just by sitting there. His powerfully sculpted shoulders and ridged abdominals left no doubt regarding his strength. Yet the striking planes of his face outdid those, his bold features highlighted all the more by tapered lines that curled at his forehead and cheeks as well as over his biceps and shoulders like inky tiger stripes. His hair was a rich blue, somewhere between cobalt, indigo, and black. Most of it had been bundled back into a series of braids with the odd silver bead and large blue and turquoise feathers worked in.

His eyes though. Those seized her completely—deep jade green with a hint of gold around the pupils and scattered throughout, highlighted with speckles of indigo and spots of light-peridot. A complex mixture of caution, sadness, grief, and loneliness overshadowed by a heavy brow. Over the years, she had sketched, painted, and drawn many portraits and often delighted in the depiction of eyes, capturing personality and nature in a single still image. His would have challenged a master artist.

The man pulled a hunting knife out from under his pillow, pushed the thick shining blankets off, and stepped out of the bed, scowling. His long flowing turquoise trousers hitched up on his right leg, revealing additional stripes along his ankle and calf. "What are you?"

"Can you see me?" She folded her arms over herself, suddenly self-conscious. She hadn't really thought about whether anyone could see her. "Can you hear me? I'm here to help, not harm."

"Yes," he said slowly. He lowered the knife, and his expression became less hostile. "Somewhat. You're like a diamond of light. What are you?"

Salanca had said it would be obvious whether someone was the source or the solution. What was she missing? Was it possible that he was something else?

She pressed her hands over her heart, a thought flowing to her lips before she even processed it. "I think you're in great trouble."

He scoffed, but the faintest of smiles appeared over his full lips. "You think?"

"Well, many are. There's some sort of plague or curse or attack that keeps happening. It's pouring out through the worlds. And something started it. My family and I used an—something to try to find the source or the solution to this, and before it brought me here, it showed me a naga."

A terrifying naga. She'd read about them in stories. A shiver coursed through her.

"Then it brought me here. So you're connected somehow. And my gut tells me you're in trouble too."

"Your gut." He blinked slowly, then sat on the foot of the bed. Its black frame rested almost on the floor, low enough she couldn't slip a shoe under it. "This is...rather confusing. I am struggling to keep up. I hate nagas. And snakes. Let's move this conversation back." He pressed his hands together and gestured toward her. "What are you exactly?"

She slipped closer to him, her pulse throbbing faster. "Just an Awdawm. An artist. An Awdawm artist."

His smile returned, broader this time. Oh. It made her heart stutter, and as it reached his eyes, they shone with rich green depths that she could get lost in if she didn't pay attention. Thank Elonumato he couldn't actually see her expression.

"Awdawms can't do this," he said, his tone now far more amiable. "Not unless something has changed."

"Usually not. But my family includes a gifted Neyeb and Tiablo."

One of whom got access to something arcane and was probably among the Forbidden Arts and was probably going to cause a lot of problems for all of them.

"So that does change things a little," she said.

"And you came here..."

"To get answers."

He brushed the back of one knuckle against his cheek. "I don't have any to give. I am as confused as you."

"Let's start with your name and where you live? Your world's name? Where are we?"

He scowled once more, then shook his head. "No. Even if this is only a dream, some things are too dangerous. There is power in names, and I cannot guarantee we would not be overheard."

She sat at the other end of the bed. "All right then. But we'll still need something to call one another. What should I call you?"

He scoffed again, a slightly more mirthful tone in his voice. "I don't even know. Bitter. Or Sour perhaps."

"What about Chicory?"

He laughed. "Why that?"

Because his eyes were the color of jade chicory.

She shrugged, then realized he might not be able to see the movement. "Because chicory can be bitter, but it is still important."

The left side of his mouth tweaked up. "Well, I suppose that is not so bad. Other than your name, which you should not tell me in a place like this, what should I call you? Sweet, perhaps?"

She wrinkled her nose. "No. I'm not really that Sweet. And not Sugar either. Or Honey."

The only reason she tolerated Bunny from her family was because they had called her that when they were children. Or they were Killoth who just managed to make it seem charming rather than insulting.

"That's all right. I prefer salty to sweet anyway. Or salty sweet."

"Then Salt works." It really didn't fit, but the fact that he liked it suddenly made it more palatable. "Or Salt-Sweet."

Heat warmed her cheeks. Were they flirting? She really shouldn't be flirting.

No. Wait.

This wasn't flirting. She was gaining information. Yes. That's what it was. She straightened her shoulders.

"Well, Salt-Sweet. I should warn you that I don't know

how long I can make this haven last. I don't know how safe it is for you here. I don't even know that I'll remember this conversation when I wake."

"You're dreaming now?" It did feel rather like a dream.

"I don't really know. Perhaps? Most of me, anyway." His gaze drifted to the door as he tapped the back of his knuckle to his cheek. "Part of me is out there...fighting."

"Fighting what?" Her throat tightened as her fingers bunched into fists. "Is it the nagas?"

"Everything," he sighed. His eyelids slid shut. He rubbed his palm over his eye. "Everything all at once. It's bad here. And getting worse by the day. The fighting never ends. Eventually, we will lose. Unless we find answers." His gaze grew distant as if he struggled to speak. "I don't—I don't think there are any real answers left."

She edged closer. "Where is 'here?' Can you at least tell me that?"

"Beneath..." He drew his hand over his brow and then tilted his head. "Wait. You said that your friends—they aren't here with me. With my people. They're in other worlds? This has reached other worlds too? This cursed plague?"

"Yes. And eventually they're trapped in comas. Once they're in the comas, they don't wake up. Some of them are dying. Can you help us?"

"I did not know. This—this wasn't..." He stared off at the wall. "You should be careful, Salt-Sweet. This isn't—I don't even understand all that is happening here. I am so sorry that it has spilled into the other worlds. My people—we've done all we can to prevent that, but it's getting out of hand. I have to protect them. If that means I must sacrifice myself, then—"

"Sacrifice yourself?" She moved in front of him. "Chicory, tell me how to help you. I can take whatever message you want taken to anyone who will listen. I will find a way to speak to the Paras if you want."

"The Paras?" He blinked, his brow furrowing more as he avoided looking directly at her.

"Do you not know what they are? They're the leaders who oversee all use of the Tue-Rah and the worlds but not the leaders of individual nations. They are trying to find a solution to this problem with world and national leaders. If you can give me something to tell them, I'll take the message to them right away—"

He grimaced, doubling forward. "You need to go. Please. Go. I don't want you to see this, Salt-Sweet. No one...no one should see this."

Heavy thuds sounded outside. As if a great force lashed at the door with heavy blows.

"Wait. See what?" She edged closer. Energy shimmered around him, blurring her vision. "Chicory, what's wrong? Please. Tell me! I'm going to get help, but you have to tell me what's going on here."

Something cracked. A loud crackling series of pops followed as if glass were exploding. Something wet struck her face.

She pulled back, holding up her hands to shield her face.

The world tumbled, spun, and burned. She struck something flat and hard, and the wind was driven from her lungs.

"Rhea?" Tiehro's voice sounded far away and muffled, but it grew steadily closer. The spinning sensation continued as strong hands seized her at the shoulders. "Rhea, follow my voice back."

It didn't even take conscious thought. It was as if someone had just swept her into a current and now pulled her along. The air turned cold and thin, the intense scent of blood, berries, and smoke singeing her nostrils. Gasping, she started, her fingers digging into the wooden floor.

Tiehro and Salanca loomed over her, staring, concern on their faces. Tiehro's shoulders slumped with relief. He covered his face, releasing a jagged sigh.

Salanca's face brightened. "You made it back. I knew you would!" she cried, dragging her up into a hug. "Tiehro, make the tea now. Rhea, deep breaths. Collect your thoughts. Then tell me everything. Don't try to talk just yet though. You probably won't be able to for a little while longer. Just a side effect. Nothing permanent."

Rhea blinked slowly, her mind still spinning. She'd made it back. Somehow.

Her hands hung heavy at her sides, her movements clumsy.

Tiehro shifted her up onto one of the cushions and gave her water to drink. Her chest ached as if hollow. Chicory's face filled her mind. Poor Chicory. Sweet Chicory. Trapped in a cavern and battling the nagas. The thoughts tumbled and tangled in her mind, but one thing that remained clear was how much he needed her and how much she needed to get back to him.

3

BROKEN PIECES

Rhea's thoughts tangled and snarled in a confusing mass. She couldn't stop thinking about Chicory. Chicory up against the nagas and trapped in a cavern with strange purple lights. How long had she been with Chicory?

Someone had pulled down the pelt curtains and lit one of the small oil lamps on the wall. No sunlight streamed along the edges.

Tiehro placed a blanket around her shoulders, cautioned her again to be still, and then prepared the tea while Salanca bustled about in various tasks. She spoke happily about how well it had gone and took care not to step on Rhea, arms gesturing with delight in between putting matters right. She swept up the broken black glass and dumped it into their garbage pail.

"Good thing it worked," she said. "Because we can't do that again without the bowl."

"What makes you so certain it worked?" Tiehro poured the hot water into the mugs. "She hasn't been able to say anything yet, and unless there was something verifiable, we will have no way of knowing its truth. I couldn't ground even slightly. It took all I had just to channel the energy through."

"It worked. Trust me." Salanca laughed. She tapped the dust pan on the edge of the black pail. "It won't take much longer for the side effects to wear off."

"You don't know that for certain either," Tiehro said dourly.

Rhea dropped her gaze to the floor. Her jaws ached so much she could scarcely move them except to take a deeper breath. Whatever the cost, she agreed with Salanca. It had been worth it to save and protect her family and all those other people.

A twinge spiraled through her.

Not just that though.

Heat blossomed across her shoulders and up her neck into her cheeks.

It wasn't that she didn't care about her family or all the other people suffering. There was just—there was just something about Chicory that intoxicated her thoughts even in that brief contact.

She paused then, realizing what Salanca had said.

"Can't. Do. It. Again?" She struggled to form each word, her lips dry and painfully tight.

Polph, her jaw still hurt. She'd had no idea how many muscles it took or how much movement within her mouth required even one word. Thankfully, it was easing fast.

Salanca nodded as she tucked the broom away in the little curtained nook. "Afraid not." She cut her eyes back at her, her brow furrowing. "You did learn what we needed to know, right?"

Rhea shrugged, her chest tightening further.

"Did you learn anything?" Salanca pressed, her voice

growing more cautious.

She nodded.

"Good! We'll be able to use it then. Because I know we got to the right place."

Rhea hoped so, but she wasn't certain.

Tiehro lit two more candles and placed them on the shelves. The amber flames danced to life, creating shadows that waltzed on the walls. Usually it was a homey sight, but now it reminded her of the strange purple light that trembled and pulsed through the stones like an infection in the cavern.

Had she learned enough?

There was no name of the place that she could recall. No particular details that would help guide them to where they needed to be.

She worked her mouth, eager to restore movement to it. It wasn't going to be long before Tiehro and Salanca needed her to keep them safe.

Tiehro handed her a large brown mug with roses painted on it. The pear-scented steam caressed her face and eased her tight muscles just with its heat. He handed Salanca a mug with buttercups painted on its side and kept the one with lavender spires for himself.

"You feeling any better, Rhea?" he asked gently.

At moments like this, he seemed far more his old self. No trace of the paranoia in his eyes. Only the mild concern that he always exhibited when she and Salanca were up to something he considered risky.

She managed a tight smile that was smaller than she felt, then lifted the mug and took a sip. The hot fruity and floral notes struck her tongue and spread throughout her like a soothing song.

Salanca sighed and then took in a long breath of the steam. "Tiehro, no one makes it better than you."

He managed his own small smile in response, his thumb rubbing the side of the clay mug. "At least I remain skilled at something."

"Bit of an understatement there." Salanca turned her gaze back to Rhea. Excitement shone in her face. "If you're feeling up to it, can you tell us what happened? What did you see?"

Rhea took a deep breath, then another sip of tea. She tried to steady herself, but her insides remained all jittery and jumbled. "Could you see anything? Either of you?" she asked, forming her words slowly. Her jaw didn't feel so tight now. Improvement there.

"Nothing but darkness," Salanca responded.

"It was the same for me," Tiehro said. "It was as I feared. And part of what made this so dangerous. I couldn't ground enough to tell you about the place or interpret anything except that, if it exists, it is far from here. You're sure you're all right? Both of you?"

"I'm as good as I can be given what's happened," Salanca answered.

Rhea nodded, rubbing her arms. Chicory's face remained emblazoned in her mind, vivid as if he sat across from her.

She rubbed her jaw and then began to speak carefully. "I did find someone there. And I think I saw the problem. Or at least what is causing it."

Salanca leaned forward, gripping her mug with both hands. "Tell us everything. No detail is too small."

Rhea's cheeks warmed, more excitement rising within her as she recounted what had happened, first about the cavern and the light, then about Chicory.

Both listened in silence. After she reached the part about the rippling light, Tiehro rose and paced at the back of the room, his steps silent on the wooden floor except for the one squeaky floorboard that always complained.

Salanca remained on her cushion, her hands wrapped around her own mug of tea, the steam framing her face. Contemplation furrowed her features, especially when she mentioned the naga. "Are nagas—nagas aren't real."

"There was definitely one there, and Chicory definitely said that they were fighting. He also said that he hated nagas."

Rhea shuddered. The blurred image of the naga with the weapon standing before the purple light returned to her mind, sending another frightened shiver down her spine. Even without seeing its face, she could imagine the horrors it would wreak about the poor people present.

Tiehro halted, his hands behind his back. He mouthed the word, then tilted his head. His brow furrowed so tightly that his eyebrows seemed to merge.

"There are stories, myths about nagas." Salanca tapped her fingers against the mug. "But they aren't on any of the inhabited worlds. They aren't one of the Eight Races. If nagas are responsible, then that means—" She blinked. "That means—"

"If that is true, that means that the rumors that there are other races out there beyond the Eight are true. That there are inhabited worlds beyond the ones we are allowed to access," Tiehro said. "If it is true."

"And that they are unfriendly," Rhea added. The sorrow and terror she'd seen in Chicory's face. The way he had contorted before he sent her away. "He was so afraid."

Tiehro's throat bobbed. "Myths say nagas possess magic of certain types. But psychic attacks? Across the worlds? Expanding and growing with time? There is nothing in any lore I know that says that."

"Maybe they made whatever caused that purple light. It looked like a wound in the air and the stone itself," Rhea suggested. "Almost like there was a sea of it beneath."

Salanca stood. She hugged herself. "You see, we were right to do what we did," she said, fixing Tiehro with a fierce gaze. "But we need more."

"Maybe we can repair the bowl," Rhea suggested. "Now that Chicory knows me, he might be able to focus better in the dreams. Maybe there are other things he could tell me."

Her heart leaped at the hope that she might be able to see him again. Her jaw still ached from the magic, and her body did not feel as naturally light as usual. But it had all been worth it.

"That's beyond hopeless, though if you want to try, you're more than welcome to. I'd have to find more of the serum as well, and that is just as hard to come by." Salanca tapped her index finger to her lips as she now paced. Her footsteps were whispers across the wood, her long dark skirt rustling. "Besides, what we need is proof. Proof of location. Proof of person. Proof of nagas."

"The Council of Elders will laugh us into the streets or request our commitment if we go to them and say that these psychic attacks are the result of nagas," Tiehro said. "Especially after what was done."

"Well, especially given—" Salanca shrugged, then gestured from the pail to Rhea.

Rhea straightened her shoulders, her nerves tightening. "Just because I'm an Awdawm doesn't mean that the Council won't listen to me."

"No," Tiehro said softly, his gaze fixed hard on Salanca. "But there will be questions about how we gained the information. Especially if contact was made with an individual on one of the Separated Worlds. The Forbidden Arts are forbidden for many reasons, just as the Separated Worlds are separated for many reasons."

"That doesn't take away the fact that it worked. If they are not even considering that the answer to this plague lies on—"

"We don't know that they aren't, Salanca," Tiehro responded. "If this is real, they could already be taking steps with better information and greater accuracy."

"Regardless, we did what we had to do. And we're going to find an answer."

Rhea dropped her gaze to the mug. The light-amber liquid usually brought her comfort. It was their favorite tea, all three of them, and it had brought them joy on so many occasions. Now it tasted weak and bland, unable to wash away the ashy acrid bile.

"They are in trouble as well," she said.

"I feel like there's something neither of you are hearing," Tiehro said, louder this time. He dragged his hand through his hair, stopping at his shorn horns. "Rhea, I know it felt real. What Salanca used is not only forbidden, it is unreliable and can be dangerous. Especially when we failed to fully do our part. All the chemicals and components aside, there was no way to ground you. No way to ensure where you were. If you were in this Chicory's mind, there is no way to tell what portion. Who is this Chicory? You could have been in a dream that had no bearing on who he is. You could have been in a lie. You could have been in a place that reflected what you wanted to see. I cannot attest to whether you were actually there, and neither can Salanca. The whole practical point in this would be to find a location and see whether what you found was there. But if our two clues are purple light that fractures out and nagas causing the problems? Who would listen to us? Why would they listen to us?"

A heaviness stole over Rhea. "He seemed real."

Tiehro's brow furrowed, his expression softening. "I'm sure he did."

"I couldn't have imagined him. Not someone like that. He was too real."

He cast a sharp look at Salanca who flinched. Then he returned his focus to Rhea and crouched beside her. "Bunny, you had temporary lockjaw. You seized. You were unconscious for hours. Motionless for most of it. You were breathing improperly. Things—things happen. A mind like yours is exceptionally creative to start with. Someone like you could create someone who seems that real."

Oh. That was why he had been so angry. It didn't feel real that she had been in that much danger. She rubbed her jaw. It had hurt. Her whole body had hurt and felt strange. But now the hollowness within her ached more than those sensations.

Chicory was real. Right? He—he had to be.

If he wasn't real, how could the thought of his non-existence already hurt so much?

"I'm sorry," Tiehro continued, even gentler now. "I can tell that he means something to you already. And if there is a way to prove his existence, then I will help. I give my word. But—" He hitched, a spasm of pain spreading over his features. His hands flew to his temples as his wings tightened against his back.

All the aching and sorrow faded to the back as Rhea stood. No matter the truth of Chicory or the nagas, the psychic attacks were returning.

"It's almost time, isn't it?" she asked.

Salanca's features tightened as well. She set the mug down and crossed to the cupboard. "I lost track of time. We need to hurry."

Rhea's hand shook a little as she set her own mug down. Answers found or not, they still had to get through this next attack. After that, they could sort out what was real, what wasn't, and what needed to be done in response.

4

NIGHT TERRORS AND LATE VISITORS

U sually, it took almost an hour to prepare for the psychic attacks. In the past weeks, they had put together a system, a series of techniques and steps designed to limit the suffering and terror that the night attacks brought.

But the attempt to find the source and the length of Rhea's recovery cut into that. She staggered a little as she tucked the washed sheets over the pelt beds. Cotton was far easier to clean than fur. Tiehro went to the kitchen at once and began measuring out dried herbs and bark while Salanca brought up more water from the covered well at the base of the tree. She filled the kettle again as well as the canteens and a pot. No one wanted to walk far immediately after the dreams. Indeed, most nights of late, they simply collapsed from exhaustion after a few panting moments awake, barely able to drink the tea Rhea made them.

Once the beds were made, Rhea tested the ropes fastened in the walls. She then swept the floor again, checking for anything sharp that they might cut themselves on.

Time moved too fast now. The air took on a sharp tang. So much to do.

Tiehro took the handful of dried herbs and bark dry, then washed it down with water. Salanca took hers steeped. By the time she was sipping, he'd had to lay down. He thrashed on the pelt, his long legs kicking at the curtain as he started up, staring about as if he heard something. His eyes became white-rimmed, his breaths shallow and fast.

Rhea sat beside him, in between his bed and Salanca's. "There's nothing out there," she said in the most soothing tone she could manage.

He nodded each time, then fell back. A vein pulsed in his throat. "You should bind me down now," he said after the third time. "It may take me sooner."

This part never got easier. The soft ropes were intended to keep them from hurting themselves. Tiehro requested it after he had accidentally struck Rhea, blackening her eye and cutting her cheek with one of his sprouted claws. If he'd had his way, they would have been tied so tight he lost circulation. She adjusted them and tried to soothe him, but the waiting terror already gnawed at his mind.

Salanca hated to be bound. She insisted it made the nightmares worse. So far, it hadn't been necessary. Rhea prayed it never would be.

Chin high, Salanca sat on her bed. She folded her knees to her chest, skirt tucked tight about her. "It will be all right, Tiehro," she said firmly. "We are both strong, and Rhea is faithful. We will survive. We are strong."

Rhea reached over to place her hand on Salanca's rounded shoulder. "You are."

Salanca pressed her lips together so hard they almost disappeared into her mouth.

Hints of purple fog appeared in the room. Nothing they

had ever done—nowhere they had ever gone had been able to keep those trailing purple clouds from seeking them out.

Salanca set her jaw, balled her hands into fists, and drove her fists against the pallet. Then she stretched out.

The purple fog darted about the room, coiling and expanding as if something made it grow. Something they had never figured out, though they had tried everything they could think of.

Rhea held her breath, her hands on each of their shoulders. It wasn't the same as living the nightmares, but for the next hour or three or however long this torment lasted, she had to make sure neither Tiehro or Salanca harmed themselves.

The fog spiraled up still farther, then parted, its coloration deceptively pretty. For two heartbeats, it hung in the air like a set of wings. Then, it snapped down and poured into Tiehro's and Salanca's airways.

Both went rigid, their eyes flying open wide for one moment, before they went limp.

What followed in their minds, she didn't know. Neither spoke about the dreams in specifics. Only that they were dreadful.

Somewhere in the distance, a scream pierced the air.

Normally, that would have alarmed Rhea. Now it was simply part of the night.

Tiehro shuddered. His fingers curled tight against his palms as his body stiffened.

Salanca twitched, a sharp moan escaping her sometimes along with a gasp.

Rhea remained kneeling between them, her hand on both of their chests or their arms. As the night passed, the intensity would ebb and flow. She prayed that this night would be one in which the nightmares were swift and light.

But now she had more questions. Deep questions.

Was this naga magic that tormented her family?

Chicory—if he was real—had said he was fighting. He'd started to spasm too. The way that the muscles knotted in his throat reminded her of Tiehro's now. Not simply pain but fear as well.

Tears stung her eyes and rolled down her cheeks.

Most nights she took comfort in singing small songs that they'd heard and hummed as children. Tonight she struggled. No night was ever easy. But this one was nearly unbearable.

She rocked back and forth as she tried to whisper words of comfort and pass the time while guarding them against hurting one another or themselves. The lullaby she forced out over an hour in was so inadequate.

What if there was no cure to this? What if this plague simply took everyone with abilities to see beyond or connect beyond the physical realm? All the Neyeb and their mindreading, all the Tiablos and their illusions, all the Machat and their visions of the future, all the Bealorns and their beast talk.

She couldn't even imagine a world with only humans, shapeshifters, healers, poisoners, and elementals.

And who said it would stop?

How much longer before all of them went mad as well?

Especially if she could create someone like Chicory with nothing but her thoughts.

Was a tormented man with stunning green eyes the best hope her mind could conjure up?

Would she have envisioned nagas though? It wasn't as if nagas had been an important part of her childhood. She'd heard a few stories. Especially about the Separated Worlds. The ones not accessible by the Tue-Rah. The ones that might exist with people and beings and entities that were not yet ready to come interact with them.

But she'd never feared them deeply. Not any more than any other monster.

The only thing she'd really feared was being alone, and that was because it was far more likely.

Salanca cried out softly. Her face twisted, her hands flying up to cover her mouth. Her fingernails started to dig into her skin. Sweat beaded her forehead.

Gently, Rhea pulled her hands back. "It will pass, Salanca. It will pass."

Her sister was clever and scared. They all were. They had to find a solution to this. Though the ache in her jaw and the stiffness in her body remained, she couldn't bring herself to even be a little angry with Salanca. And she should. Especially given the risk.

All she actually felt was sadness—sadness and longing.

She cast her eyes up to the curtained windows and the candle on the shelf. It had burned down past the third black mark. Time crawled.

Still the nightmares continued, trapping her poor family in unrelenting torment. She sang, hummed, prayed, and rocked, keeping her vigil as the night crawled forward.

These periods of trembling and crying were better than the comas. There was always that. That was one small thing for which to be grateful.

In the comas, there was nothing to watch for except waking and trying your best to feed and care for the physical needs of an unresponsive patient. The victims couldn't even tremble or cry out. They simply lay there as if dead. Regardless of what else, this at least confirmed they lived.

Tiehro screamed out, struggling against the bonds. Garbled names and words flowed from his mouth, too distorted for her to understand.

She leaned over him. "It's all right," she soothed. "You're

not alone. Remember that you aren't alone. You're loved, and you are safe."

"Always," he gasped. "Always." His body went limp, then twitched.

The night wore on.

After two and three-quarter hours, both Tiehro and Salanca stilled. Then, after a few painful moments as she watched and waited, fearing the worst, they woke.

Rhea breathed with relief even though neither wanted to talk. They drank the tea she gave them followed by the water. Mercifully, they also ate a little of the nut bread with smiley faces cut into the spongy substance before collapsing back on the pallets. She scarcely had time to strip the sheets off and put down fresh ones before they were ready to actually sleep again.

In the beginning of all this, they had all sat up together, she and Salanca whispering back and forth about what was going on and Tiehro usually silent. Sometimes none of them slept. But now the exhaustion was too much. No matter how bad the dreams, Salanca and Tiehro had to rest.

All the energy that had come from their attempt to find the source and solution had bled away into the cool night, and once they were settled, Rhea moved to the cushions and sat with her own cooling mug, her thoughts disjointed. The candles and torches burned, yet their flames seemed muted, the light duller and thicker.

Then a low whistle pierced the air. A merging of a call between a night lark's trill and a grey-winged pootoo's lament, followed by a tapping on her mind. As if there could be any question about who it was. A faint smile pulled at her lips as some of the heaviness fell away.

Standing, she picked up the small stack of commissioned sketches. It took six steps to cross to the door and step out onto the porch. The crisp night air was cooler than usual for spring, but at least her breath didn't frost.

The porch itself opened to allow a sturdy ladder up. The sides lacked rails. Down below stood Killoth, a slim Neyeb man who had become her friend over the past few months, formally appearing to purchase sketches of various subjects but really coming because he wanted to learn about Salanca, his betrothed. They were nulaamed to one another, their marriage arranged at their birth. Now that they neared the date, Killoth had started trying to learn as much as he could, even though he and Salanca were not to meet until the day they married. He wore his coordinating Neyeb betrothal necklace proudly.

He always came after the attacks lately. Not because he endured them. Somehow he was one of the few Neyeb who seemed to be immune. Maybe the only one. He was also one of the few Neyeb who was capable of assassinations. Perhaps that tied into it? Regardless, once a week he came under some pretense but always to ensure Salanca was well and nothing was needed.

"You picked a good time," she said, forcing cheer into her voice. "The attack has passed, and everyone is resting now as peacefully as possible."

A warm smile spread over his tanned face. He climbed up the ladder with graceful ease, his long black hair bound back and swinging with the movement. "Good to hear."

She sat down on the edge of the porch, sketches in hand. Reaching out, she steadied herself against one of the branches. Bits of coarse brown bark scraped off, sticking to her coral tunic but glancing right off her brown trousers. "Yes. About as good as could be expected."

If tonight went as most nights when Killoth came, they'd spend a couple hours chatting about life in general as he coyly sought answers to questions regarding Salanca: what she liked, what she didn't, what made her smile.

But as Killoth hopped up beside her, he paused. His onyx-brown eyes widened. "What's this, Bunny?"

"What's what?" She frowned. He was the only other person other than Salanca or Tiehro who she let call her that. Unlike those two, he only used it as a term of endearment.

He held up his finger, squinting a little as he studied her. "Something important happened. You're...brighter."

She almost laughed at that. "Brighter?"

He nodded. "Did you meet someone?" He waggled his straight black brows at her. "Who are you falling for, Bunny? Do you need me to investigate him? I can find out all his secrets and get him evaluated in any way you wish."

This time she did laugh. And it felt good. Then she shook her head at him and dropped her legs over the side of the porch. "No. I don't think it's anything."

"Something happened though." He sniffed the air. "Smells like colburn berries."

Was that what had been in the vial? She frowned a little, contemplating what else to say. "Do you know much about the Forbidden Arts?"

"They are forbidden. So I have never practiced them, but I know a fair bit about them. It is helpful for assassins to know of such things. Why?"

"How do you feel about people who practice it?"

"It depends entirely on what is being done with it. Sometimes the pain and suffering they require is asked only of the caster. Other times, it is far more expansive. But they have been gathered up and put away because the risk is deemed too great." Concern crept into his voice. "Have you been trying your hand at it, Rhea?"

She chewed on her lip. "Let's just say that today a couple of my friends and I decided to try to find the source or the solution to what had been causing this plague." She then summarized what had happened, not mentioning Salanca or Tiehro specifically, though she knew he'd probably guessed it already.

Killoth's expression relaxed into something more akin to gentle amusement as she concluded. "Ah. I see. It's not so bad as I might have feared. I wish I had known you three were going to do that. I might have been able to find another Neyeb to help and that would have ensured it worked. Whoever came up with this plan was actually quite clever, though there are a few risks about it. You're certain there's nothing you can verify?"

"Nothing that I know how to verify." She continued to worry her lower lip.

"You really like this Chicory."

Heat rose up her spine and bled into her cheeks. "It's nothing. He seems sweet. And distraught. And nobody deserves to be destroyed by nagas."

"Hmm." He turned his gaze to the horizon as he peered through the branches. The silver half moon was still high in the sky, the night far from over. "I see. Well, odd as it is, I'm glad you found someone, Rhea. I'd love for you to be happy. Happier than me if that's possible."

"He may not even be real. Let's not get ahead of ourselves."

"Still, he's made you happy for a little bit. Seems like a good start. If you find out more and need my help, you tell me. You've certainly done more than enough for Salanca and me. Maybe I can find you some information on nagas. That might start giving some clues that would lead to a place where we can verify the situation enough to move forward."

She dug her fingers into her palms, the tension tightening within her. "Could I ask you something?"

"Whatever you like."

"Can you look into my thoughts and see if it is—if he is real?"

Killoth hesitated, then smiled a little. "I can try." He put out his hands and lifted them near her face, palms facing her. The elmis stood out along the base of his palms and his wrists, dark sensory patches that resembled thick freckles and allowed him to read minds and sense thoughts. "Think about this Chicory."

That took next to no focus. Chicory's face leaped back into her mind, bright and vivid. Those gorgeous expressive deep-green eyes. His kind voice. The way he studied her. A bit of a smile pressed against her lips. Oh, if it was possible for him to be real—she bit her tongue.

Killoth drew back. His brow remained creased, his eyes now a little sadder. "I can't tell, Rhea," he said quietly. "I'm sorry. It isn't my area of expertise. He certainly is...bright. Your perception of him is clear."

"That means something, doesn't it?" Hope and fear twisted in her gut.

"If he is indeed on another world that is separated from ours and not one of the worlds that we are to access, then that would make him challenging to find. Challenging to find even his thread. But if he is your creation, then he would also feel similar because you do have such a clear imagination. I have never known anyone to sketch and draw with such realism and with only internal references. Your memory for images and your ability to see patterns is uncanny."

She shook her head, tears rising to her eyes. "That's nothing. Patterns are easy. Everything is simple shapes when you get down to it. And you just put the images in my mind so clearly that of course—"

"It's a gift, Bunny. Though you might not see it as having much value, it is a gift. And your mind is rich with possibilities."

"How do I find out if he's real or not?"

"I don't know. If you tell me what it was that was used in this incantation, I might be able to find the proper components. There are many who owe me favors or who would like me to be in their debt. Perhaps we could recreate it with at least one, perhaps two other members to ensure that it went through without the same problems."

"It was a dark glass bowl. It had markings on it."

He gestured toward her once more. "Would you let me see?"

She nodded eagerly. He could access whatever memories or thoughts or mental connections she had if it would mean there was a chance to learn the truth about Chicory.

He repeated the same movements, then asked her to think of the items. This time, she did feel the pressure of his mind against hers. A light raking and pressing that grew a little uncomfortable, then passed.

His fingers grazed her cheek. He leaned back. "Well, that's a little more complicated."

She opened her eyes. "What do you mean?"

"Did Salanca say how or where she found those items?" Killoth fluttered his fingers against his palms, then cracked his knuckles. His onyx eyes glinted with curiosity.

"No. And she doesn't really like to be pressed on where she finds items like that."

"Fascinating."

"She also said it was the only one."

"Well, on that, she is incorrect. I might actually know where to go."

"How much would it cost me to hire you?"

He chuckled, glancing at her sidelong. "You could never even hope to afford me, Bunny. But fortunately for you, I like you, and I am greatly in your debt. Consider it a favor between friends."

She dropped her gaze to her hands. Though she had certainly helped him a fair bit in these past weeks, it was far from equal. If she didn't need to know whether Chicory was real and whether he needed help so much, she would have refused the offer. But for now, she was willing to play along with this little lie.

"It'll take me awhile to get them. Maybe a few weeks. Hard to say. And I wouldn't recommend you take that journey again until at least a full moon cycle passes. Drink lots of water. But, that said, this won't help you tell whether he's real or not unless he gives you something you can verify. Like a location where you can find him. But dream or not, if you focus on him as you meditate, there might be a strong enough connection between the two of you and enough of the residue that you can find him."

"Salanca said we could only do it with the bowl and the vial."

He shrugged. "Well, her goal was to get Tiehro grounded and herself situated and then to ensure you could observe. How she handled this would theoretically have allowed you to actually pinpoint roughly where this source or solution is. What I'm about to do won't get you there. All it will do is play on the connection that was established between the two of you. If there is one. The weakness to this is that if your own imagination is the one that created this Chicory, then you still may find him."

"All I have to do is think of him?"

"Think of him. Use the name you agreed on with him. Talk to him in your mind. You aren't actually telepathic, but your thoughts still have weight. I could feel something there."

"Just not enough to be able to tell if he's real." She hugged herself. "I feel so torn on believing he is. If he is real, he is in terrible danger. If he isn't—"

Killoth smiled a little. "Love is a complicated thing, Bunny."

Heat sprang into her cheeks. "I don't love him. I don't even know him. He might not even be—" She closed her eyes. Oh, polph. Chicory's face filled her mind's eye. Her heart swelled with emotion.

"You Awdawms." He chuckled. "Yes, you could love him. Love has no requirement for time. You just don't know if it's safe to love him. That's the part that actually takes time. And I have no answers for you on that point. Whether he is real or not, safe or not, what you feel is what you feel. And what you feel will change. If you are fortunate, that love will flourish and turn into something richer, deeper, scarred, and beautiful."

"Must it be scarred?"

"All love is eventually."

It was funny how simply he offered this. As if it was the most natural thing in the world and not as if she were some errant child daydreaming ridiculous fancies.

"Thank you." She tucked her hair back behind her ear. "Do you know if there's any harm that will come from our doing this?"

"The incantation itself causes stress on the mind and body of all involved, but not the deadly sort," he responded. "Unless there was an additional price paid for the vial and the bowl, the primary price that the one initiating it would pay would be an intensification of nightmares and dread. But it's possible that whoever chose to initiate this assumed that they were already at the worst of what those could be, which is possible as well. All in all, not the worst by any means."

"So why is it forbidden?"

"Sometimes incantations like that are forbidden because of the cumulative damage that they do if used in rapid succession. What's remarkable is that, if this was real, it means you were successful on the first attempt."

"That's unusual?"

He nodded. "When you are dealing with a connection to a Separated World, yes. Exceptionally. The fact that your friends couldn't ground or gather more insight is not surprising. That's far more often the typical situation the first time. And with each time that specific incantation is used, the price increases. So when we do this again, someone else must initiate and bear the cost. If it turns out that this is real, the next question is why were you successful in reaching this man so swiftly and clearly. Because that does not happen without reason either. Unless you are holding out on me and you are secretly a powerful sorceress."

That laugh wasn't quite as strong, but it was just as welcome. She shook her head at him. "I feel confused about the whole thing. Based on what you're saying then, it's more likely it's something I created."

"If I were in your place, Bunny, I wouldn't let that stop me from nourishing the dream. It gives you hope. Something to look forward to perhaps. And stranger things than this have been true. Let's not count Chicory out just yet." He shrugged. "And if it does turn out that nagas are invading one of the worlds and sending out psychic attacks, that is something that needs to be addressed sooner rather than later."

"It won't be easy for me to forget him regardless." She

sighed, then handed him the sketches he'd purchased. "I'll have the next batch ready for you next week."

"Excellent." He then placed a small pouch on the porch. It likely held at least seven silver coins. Perhaps more.

She picked it up and dangled it in his face. "And, Killoth, I know you're coming here because you want to learn more about Salanca and because you want to make sure she has good days. But you don't have to buy illustrations from me too."

He scoffed, tucked the drawings under his arm, and then hopped over to the ladder. "I don't know what you're talking about, Awdawm. So suspicious, you." He cleared his throat. "Of course, if you happen to know of something that any Neyeb in your vicinity would need to make their day better—"

"You mean Salanca."

"Perhaps. But it would be helpful if I knew what tea would be most appreciated?"

"Magnolia roses, lavender spires, and pear with white tea are her favorites right now."

"Ah!" He struck his forehead. "You realize how perfect this is? I have too much pear with white tea as it is." He opened the pack at his side, fished out a small bundle, and set it down.

"You know eventually, Salanca is going to get suspicious that the tin of tea she has never gets low."

"I doubt that. You're a good friend. You handle the purchases, do you not?"

"Yes."

"Well, just keep putting it in there. She doesn't need to know it's me. It's better if she doesn't, really. Just see if there are ways to make it brighten her day."

She leaned back, resting her elbow on the plank porch. "You know, for an assassin, you're unusually thoughtful."

"You don't know many assassins, Bunny. I assure you,

most of us are this way. Next time I'll bring some more dried pumpkin slices." He started to step down, then stopped, his expression growing somber. "And, please..." He placed his hand on her arm. "If something goes wrong—if Salanca is taken—send for me at once." He slipped a few psychic stones into her pocket. "All you must do is grip it and think hard on my name. It will call to me."

She put her hand to her pocket. These stones were valuable and had many uses. His generosity soothed her spirit.

"We won't be moving again before this is cured. I don't think any of us have the strength left. But if Tiehro or Salanca do fall into the coma—" She swallowed hard, not even wanting to imagine it. It was hard enough to watch them suffer in nightmares. "If they do, we're going to Dohahtee."

"They're good people there," Killoth acknowledged, "but send for me nonetheless. There will be some manner in which I can help. I'm certain of it. Even if it's the winged one. I'll help you with him too. Chickaful? That was what you called him."

Tiehro would be so annoyed if Killoth ever called him Chickaful. "You mean Chickadee. And probably best to just call him by his real name: Tiehro."

He snapped his fingers. "Yes. Well, if Chickadee falls, you summon me then. I'll be here within a day."

Footsteps sounded below. A deep but gruff male voice called up. "Are you through with your important side task that will take no more than five minutes?"

Killoth scoffed as he leaned his elbow on the ladder rungs. "Vawtrians are so impatient. Must come from being able to shift shapes. They forget how time works."

"Killoth."

Rhea smiled a little. She wasn't sure who the Vawtrian was, and she only glimpsed him a couple times previously. All

SLAYING THE NAGA KING - 2023

she really knew was that Killoth enjoyed tormenting him. She half-expected him to take the descent at a painfully slow rate.

"I'll see you later, Killoth." She leaned forward, catching a glimpse of the shifter's black boots. "I'm sorry for the delay, Vawtrian."

"I don't want apologies," he responded. "I want to leave."

Killoth slid down the ladder. Once he landed, he turned to face his friend. "You want a hug?"

"No." He started to walk away.

"What do you know about nagas?" Killoth followed after him.

"Nagas? Why do you want to know about nagas?"

"You know, if they do ask you to be an arbiter, you really can't be this surly about ordinary questions."

Rhea returned to the relative peace inside the treehouse. It still stunk of sweat and adrenaline, but the scent had lessened. And morning would bring new opportunities. Perhaps even answers.

5

SKETCHES AND LIBRARIES

Usually, Rhea went to sleep as soon as Tiehro and Salanca were settled and she finished her business with Killoth if it was a night he checked in. But tonight her mind refused to calm. She swept the floor again, worked on more of the medical diagrams, and contemplated Killoth's words. Interspersed through that were flashes of Chicory—his face, his eyes, his voice. Whether it was better to believe that he was real and in trouble or fictional and fine.

She did not sleep at all, and her attempts to meditate resulted in only darkness. No response. No voice. No drawing in. Nothing but the spiraling of her own mind and twisted thoughts.

No Chicory.

Nothing except the memory of him.

It was mid-morning before Tiehro and Salanca stirred. Tiehro moved stiffly, favoring his right side. He accepted the tea she gave him with murmured thanks and went out to drink it on the porch, face turned toward the east despite the fact that you could scarcely see anything of the sunrise through the thick green leaves and ever-swaying branches of the towering oaks and imposing elms.

Salanca simply held the tea and sat with her back to the wall and knees up to her chest, staring down at the mug in silence. Occasionally, she released a shuddering breath. Her grip on the mug remained white-knuckled for more than an hour.

What did they dream about in that state? Were Salanca's worse than usual now because of the incantation, or was it simply just the relentlessness of these attacks?

Rhea finished working on one of the last sketches, the scritch-scratch of the pencil on the paper sometimes gratingly loud. Neither Salanca nor Tiehro commented on it, but she tried to soften her strokes anyway. Even the bird song outside remained muted as if the sparrows, wrens, and robins understood that today was a weary day.

A weary day but a full one. She needed to deliver the sketches to Hotah, and that meant walking to Dohahtee. At least it was a good clear day for the trip. She'd purchase some supplies as well.

Tiehro strode in from the porch, his large eagle-like wings remained tucked along his back. He had taken the time to comb and style his hair while out there so that it did not reveal the filed-down horns and so he looked less like a "harbinger of doom" as he liked to put it.

"Is your headache better this morning?" she asked, glancing up from her sketches.

He lifted a shoulder as he picked up the square blue kettle and filled it with water from the pitcher. "Enough. The nightmares don't help it though."

For a moment, it seemed as if a flare of purple light appeared before his face.

He shook his head, then pinched the bridge of his nose. "Until the nightmares end, it's rather moot."

"I can juice some more sooln berries, if you'd like?"

"No. I'm fine."

"He's lying." Salanca stood. "It's getting worse. Not just for him. For everyone."

He set the kettle on their small stove. "Sal—"

"Why lie about it? In a month, we'll probably be incapacitated. Actually, probably dead. Incapacitation will come sooner."

"That's a dire way to look at it." Tiehro continued to rub his forehead, his fingers circling around the edges of his filed-down horns. "But I am sorry you are suffering as well."

"And nothing else can be done?" Rhea asked.

"Not until we find the answer at the source. I've been thinking about it." Salanca kept her eyes covered. "What we found wasn't even close to enough, and there's no chance of making it better." She scrubbed at her face, focusing on her eyes with particular aggression. "The nightmares are getting worse. I got stuck in the darkness this time. It lasted until the dream's end."

"Might be best not to talk about them. It isn't as if we don't have to spend enough time with them," Tiehro said.

"Talk about them. Don't talk about them. It doesn't mean that they won't come back and haunt us."

"Must you shout?" he asked.

"I'm not shouting." Salanca covered her face with both hands, wincing. "It's just...I can't do anything. I can't believe that that whole spell was such a failure."

"I'm going to Dohahtee today." Rhea sharpened her pencil. The small curls of wood and lead fell onto the little tray as she slid the blade over the wood. She then wrapped the blade up and tucked it in her breast band. "Hotah needs those drawings. He's a little too busy to come get them, but that means I can also visit the library. See what I can find out about nagas and their abilities. If any of them include anything like this, well—I guess we'll take it from there."

"I'll go with you to Dohahtee today," he said.

She nearly dropped the pencil. "What?"

"It wouldn't be unwise for all of us to request examination after last night, and it's best that you don't go alone. So long as we don't have to go—as long as we don't have to go underground, I can bear it. Unless you'd rather go alone."

"No. I'd be glad for the company." Rhea looked to Salanca. "Do you want to go?"

Salanca nodded. "It'll be better than staying here all day. I have business in Dohahtee anyway."

It did not take long before all three were ready to walk to Dohahtee. They kept an easy pace between them. Salanca's mood brightened within the first few minutes as if the rich golden sunlight evaporated the heaviness and fears. Tiehro remained his steady self, though he walked with more strength today than he had for a while. There seemed to be a greater purpose in his manner.

They had nearly reached the edge of the forest when he turned to look at her. "Do you feel like we're abandoning you, Rhea?"

That was abrupt. And certainly not what she had expected.

Salanca's brow scrunched. "Why would she think that? You don't feel like we're abandoning you, right, Bunny?" She stepped in front of her, her dark honey-brown eyes searching hers.

Rhea held up both hands, her striped bag swinging on her shoulder. "Don't read my thoughts."

51

That was one of the earliest and most important rules. One which, fortunately, Salanca usually followed.

"I wouldn't." Her brow tweaked a little more. "I'm getting married and starting the next level of my training, and Tiehro is joining a powerful sodiwa when all this is over. Those are good things. You know—"

"I do. And I'm happy for both of you. I don't know what I'm going to do with myself, but I don't have to know right now." She lifted her shoulders, then quickened the pace. The grasslands up ahead would be easier to walk through.

"Even so," Tiehro said, matching his pace to hers. "I was thinking that it's possible that Chicory came about because you are lonely. Even though you're happy for us, and I do believe that, it isn't easy. We are leaving you behind, no matter how we try to phrase it differently. This isn't a simple transition."

No. It wasn't.

She avoided looking at either of them, so she smiled. "Life is full of adventures and change."

But when whatever caused these psychic attacks concluded, her little family would at last be scattered. All to good things. Good things that meant she would be alone.

A deep pang coiled in her stomach and tightened her breaths. Yet another compelling reason she might have created Chicory. It wasn't as if Awdawms never created imaginary friends to soothe themselves, though most stopped that after childhood.

"I can't believe you'd say that," Salanca responded, glaring at him. "Rhea is the best and truest person I've ever known. She wouldn't wish ill on us just because we are going elsewhere."

"I didn't say she would. But we are leaving. I would feel hurt if I were the one staying behind."

She blinked away the tears that formed in her eyes. "I don't think we should keep talking about this. I'm fine. Everything's fine. It'll be fine."

Salanca gripped her hand. "No matter what happens, our friendship won't change. You will always be my sister, and he will always be our brother. You know this, don't you?"

"Of course I do. We'll find somewhere to meet and catch up about all our adventures."

"Yes." Salanca's expression brightened. She wrapped her arm around Rhea's shoulders and squeezed. "A little vendor or a pastry shop or a tea shop if we're particularly fancy. Who knows? Maybe you should work in one of those. They could certainly use someone like you to keep their costs down for pear tea and all the rest."

Rhea smiled a little. If ever there was proof that Salanca respected their boundaries, it was that she didn't even have an inkling of a clue about Killoth's little gifts that he brought simply to make life a little better for her. She wasn't sure if she would be able to withstand the temptation of reading someone's mind, especially if she was curious about something. But in that and many other ways, Salanca had been a true friend.

"We should meet where there will be a festival of some sort," Tiehro said contemplatively. "Lots of possibilities. Lots to explore. Lots of food and drink."

"Perhaps your sodiwa will host one," Salanca suggested.

"My sodiwa's focus is on other pursuits," he responded.

It was a great honor that they had asked him to join. Rhea still felt fuzzy on what they were exactly. Something like a clan or the shapeshifter cadres but with a particular concentration on certain skills and dedicated focuses. Regardless, he would leave and learn and master his skills far beyond what he could ever do while with the two of them. His self-taught methods had been impressive enough to catch the attention of Tiablo superiors, and there was still so far for him to go. Salanca, too, was going to go on to do great and powerful things. Every Neyeb elder and council member who encountered her tended to comment on just how strong she was. The power practically rippled off her, her aura dancing with potential.

And as for Rhea herself?

She almost laughed. Well, she had an imagination that might be strong enough to fool herself into believing that the most wonderful man who ever existed was trapped in another world far away and under attack from nagas.

All feelings aside, that was likely the greatest proof for why Chicory could not be real.

He was too good to be true, her feelings too intense to be real or grounded.

And as far as gifts went, her imagination was not particularly wonderful. Just strong enough to fool her, and everyone knew how easy it was to fool the willing.

They continued to walk into the deeper switch grass. The mauve- and pink-topped grasses had not yet reached their full height though they were already well past Rhea's thighs. They'd keep growing as spring rolled into summer until they were up past her waist.

Rabbits bounded about and dove into burrows hidden in the little mounds of earth. A few ground squirrels with black-tipped tails chirped out warning calls. Whether at them or the jewel-colored winged serpents or the ten-inch grey and brown pterosaurs, who could say?

It was a good day for walking. Especially if they didn't keep talking about Chicory or the plague or anything else.

Fortunately, the subject of where to meet after all of them went their separate ways had captured Salanca's attention and even Tiehro seemed more cheerful and willing to go along with the topic.

"It will have to be a place where we can talk late into the night like we do now—or like we used to do." Salanca frowned as she plucked a piece of grass. "So that also means comfortable seats."

"Yes. Because we'll be there a long time," Tiehro added.

Yes. They would. She was probably going to spend most of it listening. The years would likely pass quietly for her. And that wasn't dreadful. There were far worse fates than mindlessly passing days without purpose or meaning.

Her heart twinged again.

She was going to miss them so much when they were gone. But there would now be a relief in it as well because it would mean that this plague had ended.

They reached Dohahtee close to midday.

People bustled about their regular tasks, but the swept streets had an empty feel to them as if most of the inhabitants were gone even though there were people about. It was especially odd to see the Bealorns so quiet. Children sat beneath the trees or rested on roots, their expressions haggard and seeming far older than their years. Even the animals that they had bonded to were quiet. The poor beasts likely understood what was happening far less; they probably had to be restrained to keep them from causing harm when their masters lapsed into the deep unrelenting nightmares.

Streamers trailed limply from the shaggy red-barked boldan trees; a few beaded glass lanterns still hung from the branches. Family banners and scarves dangled at odd angles, some more tattered than usual. Probably there from the last attempt at a party or a feast. The vendors didn't call out from their carts or their stalls. Not even the ones with savory steam wafting up from green or yellow boxes.

One older woman with silver-streaked hair and a heavy woven shawl sat on a stool as she fried up strips of dough. Her two terror birds—one dark blue, the other silver and black—stood behind her. The blue one nuzzled her and made a low croaking sound. She scratched that one beneath the throat and rubbed the other on the head.

The Unatos were easy enough to spot, even if one did not know their distinct tattoos and clothing style. They walked with swift focus, eyes straight ahead. No trace of cologne or perfume on any of them today. They were the healers and venom masters, and this plague had tested their abilities beyond their strength.

No Unato children played outside. They were probably helping. Most of the Awdawms would be as well. There was a certain irony in the fact that it was the races most affected by the plague who engaged the most in common activities. Those not in leadership trudged along as much as they could, making bread or casting visions or weaving rugs. All trying their best to create some semblance of normality and keep the home and city rolling.

It had to be horrid to be in an entire city where this happened. It had been bad enough being in a small town. Hearing the wails and screeches. The shattering dishes as someone flailed. The pleas of mourning family and friends when someone fell into the coma and went death still.

No. Staggering and weary as these people might be, this was the better choice. In the early days, they had been able to help with gathering herbs, grating bark, and cooking food. Finding purpose in small ways.

But fatigue took its nightly bite with no reprieve. And they were becoming more and more like the undead even in the waking world. Filling up time from one nightmare to the next and praying that they wouldn't be the next to fall.

Everyone had been diminished here. They'd lost coloring, strength, and vigor. Once bright eyes were now dull, steps heavy. And the absence of laughter or playful games lent it all a morbid air.

A gryphon swooped down, carrying a prone form in its claws. Its grey-brown wings swept out as it slowed, then placed the motionless body on the ground. With one more twist, the gryphon moved back and dropped back into the shape of a woman.

"Hurry!" she shouted, hands around her mouth. "We found a caravan. More than half fell in the night. My cadre is bringing the rest, but this man was bitten by a rock rattler."

Two Unatos trotted up, both in embroidered dark-blue robes and their hair bound tightly to their heads. They had matching ivy and bone leaf tattoos curling from the backs of their necks to their cheekbones.

Tiehro slowed his pace, his breaths tightening. "How do they find room for all of them?" he whispered.

It wasn't a question any of them had an answer to.

One of the ward leaders arrived and spoke to the Vawtrian woman who had arrived as a gryphon. She spoke in swift but quiet tones, her voice cut off by panicked wolf howls in the distance.

Salanca cast a glance over her shoulder, then shuddered. "His wolves are terrified for him. They might not be able to control them." Her brow tweaked. "Sounds like red wolves. At least five. They shouldn't be out in the daylight."

"Let's get to the library then," Rhea said.

Tiehro lightly placed a hand on each of their shoulders as if to ensure they weren't going to collapse or disappear. His broad palm was clammy.

Rope ladders and wooden staircases led up to the various levels of the tree city. Each of the central boldan or sequoias towered far above them. The city went up at least ten levels here. In some other parts, it went as high as fourteen.

The library was near to the center of the city and to what was known as the Heart, the sacred central portion set aside for celebrations, reunions, festivals, and feasts. It had been stripped of its ornamentation until the plague was cured. At which point, a new holiday and feast would be created to commemorate it.

Whenever she came here, she met Hotah in one of the external study chambers, simple rooms with no more than a wooden table, wooden chairs, and wood walls. Not even a lamp on the inside.

Hotah arrived only seconds after them.

Rhea lifted her hand in greeting.

The massive Unato looked imposing enough to be a warrior, and his preference for boxing to take the edge off his nerves seemed obvious. His massive shoulders nearly filled any doorway he entered, and he often had to stoop to avoid scraping his head. Usually, half his head was shaved, but today all of his hair had been removed except for his thick eyebrows. Not only that, but he wore the heavy belt of a ward overseer over his black garments.

"You were promoted?" she asked, stepping forward to grip his forearm in greeting. His arm was so thick she could barely get her fingers halfway around.

He returned the gesture, his fingertips digging into the soft skin of her arm. "All in my cohort have been assigned their own ward now. We can no longer be young. But even so —" His throat bobbed. "Our kumar has sent out the call for more help, but we are swiftly approaching the point where there are none left. Kumar Talutah of Chepi has offered to start building a faster road system with any who are willing to assist. The Bealorns Nidawi are gathering and training terror birds and other fast creatures to assist in moving the supplies through."

The list could go on and on, she was certain. Everyone was doing what they could to stop this force. And yet there was no hope in Hotah's jet-black eyes. Despite all the good his leader and others were attempting, it was not going to be enough. Everyone knew that. And yet here Hotah was, purchasing the medical illustrations and plant diagrams as he had in months before.

"You have a good kumar. He seems kind."

"More so than many. And you are more than welcome to join us with your friends in Dohahtee." He nodded toward Salanca and Tiehro. "Guest lodgings have been set aside, and they are above the ground, so they should be safe. As safe as any can be." He removed a small bag of coins and handed it to her.

He always paid double for medical drawings, biological illustrations, and stylized portraits. He insisted it was because the extra silver ensured extra quality, but it was common knowledge he had had the same deal with many artists, perhaps because of what had happened to that one young artist years ago. Everyone had a different account of what happened as well as different speculation for why the young physician-in-training—now ward overseer—would care so much.

"Thank you. I need to give some of this back to you though. We need examinations."

Hotah glanced between them. "All is not well?" His squared brow creased with concern.

"We drank some colburn berry juice with other things we don't know for sure," Salanca interjected, stepping forward. She kept her arms folded over her chest.

"Why would you do that?" He frowned.

"To see if it would help us strengthen our abilities and fight off the nightmares."

Rhea remained silent. Hopefully that was enough of the truth. Acknowledging that they had participated in anything involving the Forbidden Arts could easily result in far more stringent punishments.

Hotah scoffed, but he examined each of them in turn, including Tiehro though the Tiablo tensed as soon as Hotah put his hands near him.

"I see nothing beyond exhaustion and the usual ailments for this time, but you should not do that again. There is nothing to indicate that colburn berry juice will do anything to assist in fighting this," Hotah said, stepping back. He rested one hand in the deep paneled pocket beneath his belt and gestured with his other. "You should know though, those lapsing into comas now are showing greater difficulty breathing. I fear that in time, the nightmare attacks themselves will advance to the point that those who are awake may be seized even in the daylight. We will make room for you and settle the bill later."

"How can you care for all who have need?" Tiehro asked. "How is this even possible? There are thousands now. Every day, more and more fall."

Hotah shook his head. "Everyone is assisting as they can. What we have to offer is not the best, but we are not the only ones offering it. Kumar Sucheii has asked for additional geo Shivennans to come in and build more passages below."

"Passages that cannot be furnished." Tiehro lifted his chin, his voice tight. "More are dying, aren't they?"

Grief dampened Hotah's eyes. "Yes. We can't stop it. Nothing has worked to rouse the sleepers once they succumb. The Neyeb attendants, before they collapsed, said that the sleep is a torment. They struggle to get through, to speak with the dreamers and offer any hope. And many cannot endure long in that state. We keep them warm. Give them food and water. We do all that we can. Still...they perish."

Tiehro closed his eyes. Even Salanca paled.

Rhea swallowed hard. "And nothing can be done? Still? Not even a possibility of stopping it?"

Hotah removed a large oiled leather pouch of musty-scented herbs from within his cloak. "Some think it will help stave off the comas. It sharpens the senses. Makes it easier to handle the wearing of the terror upon the body." He handed them to her as his gaze passed between the three of them. "I am sorry there is not more I can do."

"You've done more than enough," Salanca said softly. "Thank you. On our behalf and all those whom you have helped."

"Yes," Tiehro murmured. "I don't suppose you can tell us how long we actually have before—" He cleared his throat. "Before the paralysis and the coma?"

"It's impossible to say. It could be a few days. It could be weeks. It could be never. We may even find a way to beat this in its entirety." He turned his focus to Rhea. "I have more drawings I require." He offered her a list with notations as well as a bone that had been wrapped in a clear material and cut into cross-sections. "If you are willing."

"Yes." Rhea accepted them and slipped them carefully into her large drawing bag.

"The offer remains open. I'll personally see to it that you three have a place to stay if you change your minds," he said. He then bowed his head and strode away, his steps heavy but swift.

Salanca straightened the ties on her cloak. "I have my own matters to tend to," she said. "I will meet you both back at the house."

Tiehro caught hold of her wrist. "You're going alone? Did you not hear what the physician said about when the comas might claim victims? It could attack you while you are gone."

"I'm fine, Chickadee," she said, a little of the old strength returning to the smile on her face. "I'll be back to the house long before the next attack, and he said that it *might* come. Not that it has already come. All right?"

She tugged free and darted off before either of them could answer, her booted steps quick and light.

Rhea bit the inside of her lip. She hoped her sister was right about that.

She and Tiehro made their way into the receiving area of the library. The Unato scholar who managed the inquiry desk regarded them with grave curiosity. Like many of the Unatos, she had full sleeves of tattoos up her muscular arms and across her clavicle and throat. Hers were of books, writing implements, and birds, including numerous owls.

As they spoke, the librarian tilted her head, but she then nodded. It probably wasn't even close to the strangest request she had received. She helped them gather several dusty lore books and a few thinner ones with almost see-through pages. "These should help you get started. Nagas aren't a topic of much research or interest lately."

"This is good," she said. "Thank you."

She and Tiehro carried the books to one of the tables in a tucked-away nook. Owls perched on wooden rods nestled in between the shelves and shrouded with cloth and wood. Guardians to protect the books at night, most likely, but also a soothing presence in the day.

Tiehro lifted the first book. "My mind is going in circles on this. I feel as if I can believe it for one moment, then I can't for another. But if there is a race of nagas, we should assume that they are people like any other. That would mean that there are good and bad. And remember that myths are often drawn on the more memorable events which are more likely to be intense in one direction or the other." His eyes glazed. He dipped his head forward again and held his temples.

"Yes, and I am not saying that all nagas are evil." Rhea pulled the first of the books down. It puffed up a small cloud of dust that smelled more like old wood than old parchment. "But Chicory is afraid of these naga. He said that we have to be careful. That our words might be used against us."

"That's just good advice when you're dealing with someone else's mind." He winced, then leaned back in the chair. "Just—you realize that if naga are real, then this changes a fair bit."

"Yes, it means that the Eight Races aren't alone. But there have been many people who have wondered that over the years."

"It could mean that this is an act of war; these attacks might be a weapon," he murmured. "For that alone, I pray this is not real."

Her blood chilled, and she slowed from her reading. "Yes. And—if this is how they plan to fight us, we're in trouble. Which is why I have to prepare for the worst of them." She put her finger on the index and began scanning for sections that could help. "You don't need to be here though. Go rest. I've got this."

"No." He removed a thick blue bound book with three sigils engraved along the spine. "I can help you gather information at least." As he opened it, he covered one eye with his fingers and squinted down at the words, his nose inches from the yellowed page.

She gave him one of her sketchbooks and pencils for notes and set up to take her own as well.

Tiehro turned one of the books around to show her a picture. "What did he look like?"

"Big. Green and blue." She tapped one of the watercolor and ink images. It depicted a large muscular snake-man. "But I don't remember if he had a cowl..."

The sinister glint in this image's eyes and the long curving fangs and jagged shoulder scales certainly appeared monstrous enough. But she didn't remember those.

"Did the naga have any defining features? Any weapons?"

She shook her head, then frowned. It was so blurred she could scarcely recall more than the general perception. "Some sort of weapon like a spear or a trident. Just jot down anything that seems like it might be relevant."

Even as she said it though, she knew that was almost asking too much. How was this going to help?

In truth, she did not know. Nor did she know what else to do.

And the more she read, the more she found herself hoping that there was no such thing as nagas despite wishing with all her heart that Chicory was real.

6

SEEKING KNOWLEDGE

Tiehro and Rhea combed through all the books available to them and made their notes until the mid-afternoon gong sounded. Within hours, it would be time for the evening meal here, but they needed to go.

They purchased bean soup, fry bread, tangy palja dip, and almond sweet balls. Enough for both of them and Salanca when she returned as well as some other supplies. Tiehro seemed in a calmer humor than the day before, observing that he might even be able to hunt again. Rhea chided him. They could make do with the fish caught in the trap. It was far more important to get through whatever this plague was.

That led to talking of what they had learned. Both their sets of notes had been carefully slipped within her worn bag, next to the requirements for Hotah's new illustrations and the bone. It did not seem so terrifying now that they walked in the bold orange sunlight across the grassy field. Deer bounded away, dipping in and out of the grass with their white-backed tails bobbing like flags.

Most of what they had discovered was similar.

Nagas did indeed have magic. Powerful magic that was said to cross all manner of boundaries and knowledge. Some of them even had distinctive markings and traits that indicated more about their type and culture in these lore books.

They had exceptional skills, similar in some respects to Tiablos and Vawtrians. They could change their features to mimic others. They could change their voices. Steal them in some cases as well as chosen victims' faces. And if you looked into their eyes, they could hypnotize you.

But nothing in the books spoke about psychic attacks or great projections that could stretch out into multiple worlds and lay low entire races. Tiehro found that encouraging.

"There will be some other answer then," he said as they reached their little house in the trees. "Unless this is something in the Forbidden Arts that they have tapped into or something we haven't heard of."

The truth was they could just be chasing nothing. The bean soup was good though. And between Killoth's and Hotah's generous payments and their own stores, they would be able to get by for a few weeks. They were exceptionally fortunate. She prayed they continued to be. That somehow they made it through and these attacks would end.

Salanca stumbled in shortly before the sun set. She refused to say what it was she had been doing, but she seemed more encouraged than before.

They took more time to prepare for the night's attack, preparing the strange concoction that Hotah had given them.

And then it was time.

Sitting in the dim light, guarding her friends, Rhea struggled against the weight of her fatigue and confusion. Desire and fear warred within her while exhaustion tugged at her eyelids.

Mercifully, the night passed quieter than usual. The nightmares did not last quite as long either. And once they passed and after she made sure Tiehro and Salanca had all they needed, she crawled onto her own pelts.

She closed her eyes to meditate. The darkness engulfed her.

Chicory.

Maybe it would be better to just stop. To no longer search for him.

But...was he there?

The Neyeb spoke of threads and the connections. Salanca had said that everyone had a thread. Everyone was connected. It was just that Neyeb knew how to see and touch those threads to form the connections.

There was nothing except the darkness and a faint burning as her eyes rejoiced in the comfort of rest.

Nothing but darkness.

No stirring of emotion. No call or cry. Nothing.

Sighing, she shook her head. Why was she wasting her time? Chicory was a figment of her imagination, brought upon by a potent combination of fermented fruit and bad herbs and an overactive imagination. It didn't matter that she needed him.

She shifted her position so that she was laying down and then pulled the blanket up over her shoulders. The coarse material grated beneath her fingers. Her head pressed into the thin pillow. Sometimes she could control her dreams. It was another artistic ability that she appreciated. If she tried, she might be able to create a dream with him. But that—the fact that this might be all that she might have—that stung.

She grimaced, not certain why this hurt so much. No. She'd dream instead of walking down by a river and finding those clays that some artists used to paint.

She stirred, suddenly aware of cool light fabric over her arm.

That wasn't right.

Her sheets and the blanket were rather thick.

She opened her eyes, then froze.

The bed wasn't hers. The sleek sheets were turquoise and almost like silk. She had never had silk in her life. The last time she had seen silk sheets was when she had been interviewed to possibly sketch diagrams of a wealthy Unato's sculptures.

Something stirred beside her.

Gasping, she pulled back. Chicory?

A man lay on the other side of the bed, resting on his side. A bright turquoise feather protruded at an awkward angle from his mass of hair. He blinked as he studied her.

"You're...were you here before?" He tilted his head on the pillow. Confusion filled his face, though he did not appear alarmed.

"Yes. Do you remember me?" She sat up, startled at how much it meant to her that he did remember.

"Yes..." he said slowly. "Yes...I do remember you." His face brightened as if a memory reached him. "Salt-Sweet?"

Her heart leaped. It was as beautiful as if he had said her actual name. The only thing better was the way that he smiled.

"Are you a dream?" She covered her mouth, her voice trembling. This had to be a dream. It couldn't be anything else.

Yet somehow—these sheets felt real. The air smelled like —like jasmine, green tea, musk, stone, and sweat. That wasn't what the house smelled like.

"You are the dream, I think," he responded. That slow smile spread over his face as he stared at her from the bed.

"You couldn't—this couldn't be anything else, could it? Is it so bad if this is a dream?"

"I'd rather it be real," she whispered. "Real if it meant you were out here somewhere. Not that you are in danger."

He shook his head. Reaching out, his hand came close to brushing her cheek but stopped. "I wish you were real as well. Your visit was the one good thing to happen to me in...I don't know how long. Time is so strange here."

"You don't seem bothered that I'm back."

"Should I be?" His brow tweaked as he sat up, his strong shoulders rolling with the motion. Once more he was sleeping without his shirt. He laughed a little. "Maybe I should. These are my dreams and my thoughts. But—" He closed his eyes. "It's nice to hear a friendly voice. And you called me Chicory. It's been a long time since someone has called me by a name they created for fun and affection."

He sounded so lonely. It stabbed straight through her.

"Maybe I can help," she whispered.

"I don't think anyone can. You should be careful even speaking to me. Dream or not."

"Are you trapped, Chicory? Are you in trouble?"

Could a dream think he was a dream and not be?

"Trapped?" He laughed again, the sound still warm but sadder now. "I suppose you could say that." He squinted as if he struggled to make her out. "Far from my best, I am afraid. All of this is far from any of our best. All the snakes."

"The nagas?"

He glanced around as if distracted.

"Who else would harm you? Are there others coming to you maybe? Like me?"

"No. There are none like you. In truth, I wonder how you found me." His thick mass of hair and beads and feathers slid over his shoulder as if it was a single chunk rather than

69

dozens of individually fashioned pieces. "Tell me how you came to be here. I'll try to remember this time."

"First, can you tell me the world you are on? Please. I think it's safe for us to talk."

"We call her Serroth. It probably doesn't matter. Though I'm still not sure."

"What's happening to you there?"

"Monsters," he said quietly. He hooked his arm over his pillow. "Taking us apart. Over half are gone. Can't even eat in peace. All so much worse than the stories. I cannot protect my people from this. I cannot protect them from anything."

"Your people? You are a leader?"

He managed a wry laugh as he rolled onto his back. Those gorgeous deep-green eyes of his focused on the coarse domed ceiling above. "A king. Long may I live. As above so below, forever here amid the underglow." He pantomimed a flourish as if he were presenting someone in a royal court. "I can't save anyone here. Not even myself. And they want blood. So much blood."

"Why?" she whispered.

He tapped the back of his knuckle to his cheek. "They think it will fix the problem. Just the guilty they want. But we are all guilty. We weren't even supposed to be here, though it was love that brought us here." He blinked, his eyes shining with emotion. "Love and good intentions can wreak such horror."

She repeated the name Serroth. That she would remember.

"And the nagas?" she asked.

He shuddered. "Monsters. I have feared them since I was a child. Bloodthirsty and feral. In their minds exists only rage. At least in what I've seen." His eyelids slid shut. "I've tried to cut out the serpent's heart. It bleeds and screams. But it accomplishes nothing but rage and vengeance." His hand clutched his heart as if in sympathetic pain. "And I don't know what it wants. It must want something."

"The naga?"

"There is something in it that seems intelligent. Cunning. How else could it have known so well what we feared and understand how to make it reality? Everyone. It knows us all. Under our skins and in our minds." He turned his face toward her. "You are the only peace in this nightmare."

Her heart thundered faster. "Chicory—"

The entire room shuddered. He faded, the color leaving him as if he had suddenly turned into one of her pencil sketches. His body went rigid as he drove his head back against the pillow.

She started, scrunching her eyelids shut as energy jolted through her. When she opened them, she was no longer in the small but luxurious bedroom. She lay on the pelts with the patchwork curtain swaying near her face, smelling like adrenaline, bean soup, old fry bread, pear tea, and wax candles.

Unlike the last time, her jaw did not hurt, nor did her heart race for anything more than her feelings for him. For someone who might not even be real.

Oh, polph.

She draped her elbow over her eyes. Dreams. That's what they were. Probably. She'd dreamed of him because she had wanted to see him. A jagged sob rose within her. How could she already miss him? Especially when he didn't exist.

But she had a name this time. Serroth. If he was real, she'd find the truth, and she would find a way to get to him. Bloodthirsty nagas or not.

7

NO CHOICE

No one had ever heard of a world named Serroth. Salanca once again reminded Rhea that if it was one of the Separated Worlds or one that had been cut off, then they might not know it, not that it didn't exist at all. Tiehro agreed, but the caution in his face warned her he thought it was more likely she was dreaming and lonely.

All of those things could be true.

They could all be true, and Chicory could exist.

She just—just didn't know. And that was a torment in and of itself.

One torment among many.

The days trudged on. The lack of answers was as consistent as the nightly attacks. Killoth continued to come at least once a week with news of the worlds and information on nagas as he found it. The word he brought from the other nations and worlds was far from encouraging. While there were rumors of nagas and others even more unusual, none of those contained anything even remotely connected to these psychic attacks. The one terrifying tale circulating about was that one of the Paras had lapsed into the coma as well. More and more of the leaders of the psychic races were also falling into the endless sleep.

Hotah gave her additional teas and herbs to try to keep her little family going, but the nightmare toll wore on all of them. Streaks of silver formed in Tiehro's purple-black hair. Killoth brought what he could to help, but little did.

The one joy she had was seeing Chicory. She didn't find him every time she slept, but more times than not, he was there. Even if she could not reach him in meditation. Even if she could prove nothing. Even if, as time passed, she became more and more convinced he was nothing more than a creation of her mind.

Dream or not, he comforted her, and her presence brought him joy, which made her happy for a time. She lay beside him on the bed, both whispering back and forth about nothing in particular. He still would not say his true name, and he often grew hazy when she pressed him for details as if he either could not remember them or didn't want to speak about them. He struggled to remember much of what she said. But some details followed through. Like the fact that she cut little happy faces into her brother's and sister's morning toast or made smiles out of fruit after hard nights to remind them it was going to be all right like they had when they had been children.

More than once, she had to explain how it was that she was even speaking with him or how she had come to find him. Sometimes he blinked in and out, disappearing for a time, then reappearing just a few seconds later, panting and staring up at the ceiling. He was always fuzzier on his memory at those points.

"Tell me again," he said when she found him once more in the bed. "I know you've told me before. Just—the words aren't staying."

She smiled, even though typically she didn't like having to repeat herself. It was midsummer now. She'd told him why and how so many times already. Just more confirmation that he was only a creation of her own mind and needed to be bolstered to continue. But if this was what it took to continue the connection, then it truly was better than nothing.

She rested on the pillow next to him as close as she could be. "My family and I are trying to understand the source of this illness that is spreading through the worlds. Salanca commanded it to take me to the source."

"The source of what?"

"The problem, I suppose. Or the solution. Either way, it brought me here. To you."

Always to him.

"Hmm." His brow knit. "I am the source. Or the solution." For a moment, grief filled his face. "It's true then. Or maybe it will be if I don't—but that can't be it. That's so barbaric." He shook his head. His hair rustled with the movement, sliding entirely off his shoulders. Sometimes there were more beads than usual woven into his hair. Today there were more than three dozen. "They meant no harm. But if the Rift demands blood, what else can be done? Surely something. There has to be something." His eyelids slid shut as he pressed his hand to his face. "There must be something else. And you said this before. I am certain you did. My memory—here it is so warped. It is so hard to recall." He held his head.

She sat up and reached for him. As always, her hand passed through him. She could lay in the bed and rest under the covers with her head on the pillow, but her mind could never accept her actually touching him. "It's all right."

He shook his head.

A sudden flare rose within her. Sometimes when he spoke, the sincerity and tenderness was too much to ignore. They'd had parts of this conversation more than once, but she had to press again. Even if it ended the dream.

"Please," she whispered, her fingers curling against the silk sheets. "If you're real, please, please just give me a sign. Something I can work with. Something I can use."

He tilted his head. "Something you can use? What can you use?"

"To help you. To reach you. If you're real."

His gaze grew sorrowful. "What?" His shoulders drooped. "You question me too, Salt-Sweet?"

"Chicory." She stared into his eyes. Those beautiful soulful eyes. "I don't question you. I just—if I can help. I want to."

He dragged his hand through his hair once more. "Forgive me." He closed his eyes. "You are my reprieve. My calm. I should not take this out on you. Sometimes—sometimes reality intrudes even here in this sacred place."

"There's nothing to forgive, Chicory. This is all—I'm sorry for how hard it is. How hard everything is."

She stared down at her hands. Even in dreams, they were accurate with the little burn scars on the back and whatever minor cuts and scrapes she had picked up from the day. Aside from not being able to touch him, this place did feel real. And its realness comforted her.

"You are..." She bit her lip, closing her eyes. "I wish that I knew how to make this better, but I keep dragging my own issues in here. I don't know how to keep this a happy place for us."

"Gentle Salt-Sweet," he said softly. He sat back on the bed as he studied her face. He lifted his curled finger as if to touch her, then drew back, tapping his knuckle to his cheek.

"This is not your burden. You've already done more than enough."

The heaviness intensified over her, the hum filling her ears again. "Chicory—"

He gasped, lurching forward. All the color streamed out of him as he then unraveled, vanishing into smoke.

She covered her face. Soon she would wake as well.

For all her previous abilities in controlling her dreams, these had never truly cooperated. But at least she knew the signals. Much as she disliked them.

The dream receded now. As consciousness seeped back into her body, she hated knowing how much the day would hold and how much it would feel as if they were making no progress—just marginally keeping from collapsing.

Daylight streamed through the now tacked-up curtains. A gentle breeze, full of the scents of maturing switch grass, damp earth, and dew-drenched leaves ruffled the fur on the pelts.

She remained beneath the covers, staring at the warped wooden floor. More than ever, her heart ached. Her fingers curled against the coarse sheets as tears welled up in her eyes.

If Chicory was not real, why did her mind construct him to break her heart so?

Was it simply a representation of the helplessness she felt? It certainly wasn't hard to imagine that. The helpless terror in his eyes mirrored what she felt most nights. What she saw in her family's faces as they battled the grueling litany of night-mares and weariness. As it was for all of them, there were no answers—only a painful ache that hollowed her out.

No matter how she felt, it was time to get up. Just because she didn't feel like she could keep going didn't mean she couldn't.

She frowned then, realizing that the sunlight was far richer and darker, the air heavier and warmer than she expected. Wait. Oh no.

Salanca was cooking something. A large omelet made with duck eggs, tul mushrooms, spring onions, and pink-topped chives.

"I overslept!" Rhea started up. "I didn't—"

Salanca shook her head, her expression contemplative. "Decided to let you sleep. Isn't much that can be done anyway."

"It's—late afternoon." She stood slowly, her body stiffer than usual. How had she slept that long? Even if they hadn't awakened her, she should have woken on her own.

Oh. Her back hurt. She'd slept wrong.

"Tiehro found the eggs while trying to hunt. Brought back half. Thought it would be nice." Salanca picked up two of the plates, her hand twitching.

Rhea darted in to scoop the third. "Well, it's very nice. I'll take care of clean up afterward."

Salanca managed a small smile. The past years had aged her significantly, putting years on her face and shoulders. "Always there for everyone."

Tiehro strode in. He, too, looked far older now, his gaze more hollow and thicker streaks of silver in his long purple-black hair. Still he smiled, and it only wavered a little bit at the end. "Good afternoon."

"What's good about it? Still no closer to answers," Salanca responded glumly. She set the plates down hard. They rattled on the tabletop. "They've given up on us."

"Something is blocking them." Tiehro sat at the table. His knees brushed its underside as he leaned his elbow on the tabletop and rested his chin on his palm. "They wouldn't have given up. It's over half the worlds' populations and more than half of the leadership. They're saying it's starting to impact Vawtrians and Shivennans too. By the time it's over, it may only be Unatos and Awdawms standing and those other few who have been found immune."

"They will find a cure," Rhea said as firmly as she could.

Killoth thought he was close to finding the components so that they could attempt to ground and find the source or solution. But some part of her despaired that it would yield nothing.

"What does it even do to Vawtrians and Shivennans?" Salanca asked, frowning. She poked the omelet with her wooden fork. "I think it's just rumors. Nothing I've heard makes it make sense."

Tiehro twitched his shoulder. "How much does these days? It sounds like it is only happening in prolonged exposure to the fog."

Conversation stilled. It brought with it a weary uncomfortable silence. What was even left to be said? This was not sustainable.

"Maybe we should all take a walk down to the river and try to enjoy the quiet in the day," she suggested.

Salanca remained dour, her gaze fixed on the omelet. She hadn't even eaten a third of it. "If we enjoy it, it only passes faster until the next torment. I don't even know where to look anymore. I don't—I don't know what to do."

"We pray. We hope. We endure until we can't," Tiehro responded.

If only she had something to offer her family. She frowned. "Salanca, your hand. Are you all right? It's shaking."

Salanca frowned. As she drew her hand up, the tremors worsened. She opened her mouth to speak, then hitched to the side. The trembling clawed through her arm as her eyes rolled back, allowing her only a strangled gurgle.

Tiehro started up.

"Salanca!" Rhea stood, reaching for her.

Salanca's body twisted and seized, moving beyond her grasp. Her foot caught the table and jarred it as she collapsed over the chair. The plates slid off, one shattering across the floor. Tea spilled onto the cushions.

Tiehro staggered around the table, then caught hold of her as Rhea tried to stop her from hitting her head on the floor.

"Salanca!" Rhea cried.

Salanca's body twitched and contorted as if she had been struck by some great energy. But by the time they got her away from anything that might hurt her, she had gone still.

Still and unconscious.

Tiehro placed his hand along her throat as Rhea checked her wrist.

"She's breathing, but her pulse is weak," she said, looking up at him. "Why won't she wake up?"

Tiehro stood. He raked his hand through his hair and then crossed to the cupboard. After rifling through, he found a jar of ginger and peppermint tea. Bringing this back, he put it directly beneath her nose.

Though Salanca breathed, she did not move. Her nostrils didn't even curl or flare as if she recognized the scent. Was her pulse weakening? How had she declined this fast?

Rhea steadied her voice. Dread pooled within her. "We have to get her to Hotah. He'll know what to do, or at least be able to help her until someone does."

Tiehro shook his head, his jaw set. "They'll put her underground. They'll take her into the dark—"

"Tiehro." She looked him in the eye, matching his intensity. There was no time for paranoia of any sort. "I've never seen a seizure like this, and neither have you. We don't know what we're doing. If she has another or if she falls and hits her head, what then? I know you're afraid, but this is her best hope. This might be something else entirely, and she's weaker than either of us want."

Though she did not say it, it was also the only chance she had if Tiehro also fell. She couldn't move both of them alone. She couldn't even move Tiehro alone. With Salanca's help, she might have managed it.

Conflict warred in his eyes, a muscle jumping in his jaw.

"It's reasonable, Tiehro. You know this. You know Hotah has done nothing but help us. It's the nightmares that make this feel terrifying. But they aren't going to kill her. We might accidentally. Especially if—especially when the fog comes tonight. No one ever said anything about seizures like this. If something else happens, we can't make the trip by night. We can't risk waiting till morning like we planned for this."

Jaw still tight, he bowed his head. "I'll pack some things," he said hoarsely. "We're going to be there for a while."

Probably so. But better than forever.

She smoothed the hair back from Salanca's face as she glanced around the tiny little home. Oh, please, Elonumato, let all of them be able to leave Dohahtee. Even if they didn't come back here. Even if they all parted ways and she came back alone to only her dreams and drawings.

It did not take long to gather up the few items they would need for their trip to Dohahtee. In the event one of them had not awakened from the nightmares, the plan was to wait until morning, then one—probably Rhea—would run to Dohahtee and get a cart or something to help them transport the sleeper to safety. That could no longer be risked. Especially given how weak Tiehro looked now. If he collapsed too—well—that would mean she'd have to leave both of them and risk nothing worse happening.

Rhea seized one of the psychic stones Killoth had lent her and sent one terrified pulsing word through: Salanca. He would understand.

She turned back and thrust the other stones into her pocket, her chest aching and tight.

Salanca did not stir. Not even when a silver fly landed on her cheek. Her skin paled further though. Not simply as if the blood was draining away but as if all life was too. Already her hands were cold, her fingers clenched to her palms. They placed her body in the pulley system and lowered her to the ground. Then Rhea carried the bags while Tiehro carried Salanca.

They made their way through the forest and to the grassy plain, steps slower and heavier than usual.

Rhea halted multiple times to give Tiehro the chance to catch up. "Do you need help carrying her?"

"No. Just a little dizzy." Tiehro kept his words clipped. Sweat shone on his neck and shoulders, his muscles tense through his dark-blue tunic with the silver embroidered doves and ravens.

After the third time, she slowed her pace and walked alongside him. Sometimes she put her hand out to steady him. It wasn't just taking twice as long. It was taking three, maybe four times. The shadows stretched out long across the grass, and Dohahtee's welcoming trees seemed to be miles and miles away as darkness spread across the eastern sky.

Wolf howls to the north warned of the coming night. With it, these gentle grasslands and quiet forests turned far more dangerous. Especially with one person unconscious and another soon to be unconscious when the attacks happened. She couldn't defend them out on the grasslands.

She turned to face Tiehro. "Here. Let me carry her legs. You carry her by the arms. We might be able to go faster." It would let her help to steady him as well.

He only nodded this time. His muscles twitched a little, his pace uneven. But when she grabbed Salanca's ankles and started to trot backward, he started moving a little easier.

The sun continued to set as the dusk larks called out. Their trills and evening song chilled Rhea. She quickened the pace as she twisted over all the possible reasons Salanca might have seized. And at such a strange time as well. No one seized like that. Were they carrying her right? What if they were making it worse?

Someone shouted out behind them.

Tiehro lifted his head as if acknowledging someone. "We need help!" he shouted, his hoarse voice strained.

Rhea glanced over her shoulder. Two figures ran out from the tree city, one leading a grey llama. She almost gasped with relief. Thank Elonumato.

Two women ran up to them, one Awdawm and one Unato. The Unato hurried to Salanca and began examining her as Tiehro and Rhea held her.

"She just seized and then went unconscious," Rhea explained. "We can't wake her up. Have you seen anything like this?"

The two newcomers exchanged glances, then the Unato shook her head.

The Awdawm stroked the llama's nose. "We'll get her to the city."

"Get her on the llama. We'll take her back as swiftly as we can. Can you both walk the rest of the way, or do we need to send someone for you?" the Unato woman asked.

"We can walk," Tiehro responded.

"Yes, just get her to someone who can help, please," Rhea

said. She hugged herself tight, her muscles tense. Her arms shook, and tears filled her eyes as they carried Salanca away.

Tiehro put his arm around her shoulders. "It's all right, Bunny. It's going to get better."

Maybe. But somehow—she didn't know if she believed that.

8

TRAPPED

When Tiehro and Rhea reached Dohahtee, an Awdawm man in a colorful striped robe with cotton trousers approached them. "Your friend— the Neyeb—she has been taken below."

"Do you know which physician she is with?" Rhea asked, her arms still wrapped tight around herself.

"Hotah asked that she be placed in his care. He said that I should tell you he will look after her. Do you both intend to stay?" His gaze lingered on Tiehro as if guessing that they would have little choice given he was a Tiablo.

She nodded, aware of how tense Tiehro was beside her. "If there is room. I do have some money."

"That can be dealt with later. Come. Let me show you where you will be staying." He gave them a warm smile, then gestured for them to follow.

If Dohahtee had seemed quiet before, it was even quieter now. The torches along the main road guarded against the darkness, but the few people who were out and about kept close to the trees or the walkways, hurrying about their busi-

84

ness. The air had taken on a startling bite considering the usual heat of summer. She shivered from more than the coolness.

The Awdawm led them on the stone walkway first, taking them to the eastern side of the city, then up steep wooden stairs to the third level. Whispered conversation wisped about, snatches of statements and hints of emotion catching on the slow breeze. Tiehro kept his gaze straight ahead, his pace steady but his hands clenched into fists. Sweat still glistened on his neck and face.

Was it possible that Salanca's seizure and collapse had more to do with the incantation they had attempted? It seemed rather far removed, but sometimes those side effects could take time. Did that mean Tiehro was at risk next? Maybe it had accelerated the psychic attacks?

She prayed Tiehro did not fall next. That he never fell. And that Salanca woke soon. And everyone else.

The Awdawm stepped off the rope bridge walkway and onto the wooden platform. Rhea had scarcely noticed walking across it. She had been so caught in her own thoughts. Was this it? A bright yellow door with a wooden handle had been fashioned into the tree that supported this platform.

He gave a flourish with his hand and twisted the wooden knob. "You are welcome to stay here as long as you have need."

Tiehro murmured his thanks as he stepped through, ducking his head to avoid cracking it on the frame.

Rhea thanked the Awdawm as well. "When we're finished, can we...can we..." Emotion knotted in her throat.

"Yes. The healing chambers are due north. Impossible to miss. They're cut directly into the mountain with multiple points of access. Hotah's ward is on the northern face though. It will have the three speckled turquoise leaves on its marker. Anyone can show you the way if you can't find it."

"Thank you." She stepped inside then, her insides twisting.

The little guest home that had been set up for them was simple but cozy with beds built into the wall. Four could sleep in here, beneath red and yellow blankets striped with black, brown, and white. The pillows were thick and soft, easy to sink into. The attendant had suggested that Tiehro should rest in one of the lower bunks. Cloth had been wrapped around the wooden bed frames in colorful strips that resembled an autumn sunset.

Black and white sand art and weavings depicting various Unato healing symbols and venom marks adorned the walls. Two sets of deep cupboards as well as two closets built into the wall provided some storage, though between the two of them, Tiehro's and Rhea's belongings fit in half of one.

A rectangular maple table in the center of the room could host six. It had been stained and marred as well as burned in a few places. Most likely it was older than all of them combined. The curve-backed chairs were probably older still, one seemingly made of walnut, another perhaps of pine, and two of oak with spatterings of paint and warpings on the spindles.

A yellow floral cactus sat in the window, emitting a pungent but clean scent similar to the bubbling soap the Unato used to scrub the floors. It masked all scents of sweat and body odor, which was good considering. Though tonight perhaps it would be tested. And in the nights to come.

She placed the bags on the table. "I'm going to check on Salanca. I know how you feel about—"

"I'm going to see her as well." Tiehro sat heavily in one of the chairs. "It doesn't matter. The dread—the fear. It doesn't matter. If there's a chance she can hear us, then she needs to hear us." He rested his face in his hand, then released a long slow breath. "Everything will be all right."

She dropped her gaze to the wood floor, the bright-blue planks abrasively cheerful. More than anything, she wanted Tiehro to be right.

"We should probably go sooner rather than later, Chickadee," she said softly. "Especially if—"

She gestured toward the window, not wanting to actually say that they needed to get him back before the attacks. She could only imagine how terrifying it would be for that to happen underground with dozens, perhaps hundreds of other psychic individuals, all reacting in terror even if they couldn't move. They had to impact one another. Even if all was silent.

She had never doubted Tiehro's bravery, but his willingness to go below solidified it.

They left the little place that was to be their refuge and made their way through the night-darkened city. Once she had stayed here overnight, and it had been hard to sleep there with so much happening even in the middle of the night. Those Bealorns who were bonded to nocturnal creatures tended to keep night hours, and they also tended to be a bright-spirited and often chaotic bunch.

But there was none of that tonight. No snatches of song, no telling of tales, no performing of feats. Barely even hauling or cleaning. And it was not as if Dohahtee slept. It was as if it waited, watching and trembling. As if something more was about to strike, and everyone knew that it was coming.

As the Awdawm said, it was easy to find this infirmary. The small mountain jutted up out of the forest, and the trees climbed its smooth summit. But the people of Dohahtee had cut into its sides to construct an enormous underground hospital.

As they drew near, a voice spoke just beyond the cavern

wall. "This is dangerous," one said. "These nightmares have become different. They are creating a force, a life all their own. Even if the ill are separated, as they connect, they grow stronger. Their auras intensify. Their fields grow stronger. Eventually, we will not be able to suppress it. Soon even those without such abilities may be trapped. And who knows what it may yet become."

"Regardless, we're running out of time. Someone has to find an answer," another responded.

"And quickly—" the speaker broke off, then peeked out.

Rhea pretended she hadn't been listening. If she were to guess, Tiehro's face remained blank. She lifted her hand in greeting. The two men straightened, one frowning while the other flushed. "Could you tell us where to find Hotah and our friend, the Neyeb, who was just brought in?"

The speaker they had just heard, a man with three eyebrow rings, continued to frown, but he pointed to the large hallway that stretched beyond them. "He's on the seventh level."

Reaching back, he pressed a button. A couple bells rang dully, and something cracked and rolled, sounding like a dry walnut running down a clay shaft.

Now that she listened, she caught other faint but similar sounds throughout the walls. She stepped under the overhang.

Hotah was already striding up the hall, drying his hands on a white towel. His expression was mostly solemn though he managed a flicker of a smile. "Your friend has been taken below, and we have done what we can for now. The seizures— we haven't seen anything exactly like that aftermath yet, and she started to convulse again. We are trying to discern what led to them. But she is resting and safe. You want to see her?"

"Please. Yes." She started forward, then glanced back.

Tiehro remained pale, his breaths tight. The terror of entering that place, even if it was intended for healing, clung to him like a shroud.

When she reached for his hand, he pulled her into a tight hug. She embraced him back. His heart hammered against her ear.

"You don't have to go down there," she whispered. "I'll go make sure she's—"

"No. For either of you, I'd do this. I can't—I won't abandon her. I just...I need to breathe." He drew in another shaking breath. His eyes remained white-rimmed, but he nodded. "Let's go."

Hotah studied him for a moment before stepping forward with a slight gesture to indicate they were to follow him. Walking alongside Tiehro and taking his hand in hers, Rhea did as instructed.

The infirmaries had been cut into the earth and stone, but large charcoal sachets with incense and other pleasant-scented plants like lemongrass and junipers kept it from smelling oppressive or damp. It was almost pleasant. Especially with the warm torchlight dancing on the walls.

Their brightness faded as they descended farther and farther into the earth. Hotah slowed his pace as they passed some of the corridors, casting a cautious eye over them as if to ensure all was as it should be.

Rhea matched her pace to his. What had him uneasy? Disease didn't make people act that way. Had there been other signs or warnings about what this involved?

"Something wrong?" Tiehro asked, caution in his voice.

"Other than the obvious?" Hotah said in what seemed like an attempt at gruff humor. He ducked his head then. His skin had paled beneath the elaborate and elegant designs painted from his throat to his temples. The torchlight did not make him look any healthier or stronger. "We're almost there. Keep close."

There weren't staircases, but the path did slant downward, leading to separate levels. Down, down, down they went. It felt as if they could walk forever. This place was massive. More and more Unatos and Awdawms hurried about, some carrying baskets, others pushing carts. Everyone had places to go, and they moved there in near silence.

At the seventh level, Hotah guided them off the path and down a broad hallway lit with more torches fastened with iron. He led them through the fourth door on the right.

Rhea halted, staring in shocked horror at the rows and rows of beds. There were hundreds. Maybe thousands.

Her stomach fell. She'd heard about the numbers. Guessed it was worse than what was said. But to see all these people laying here in this cut cavern with faint circles of pale light to keep the darkness at bay—it looked more like a cavern of death than a place of healing.

Where was Salanca even? The beds were lined up, each one with crisp white sheets. The patients lay beneath those sheets like bodies waiting to be embalmed. Even more eerie was that they were positioned in sections. In one section, all lay on their back. In another, all lay on their right sides. In another, all on their left. Most likely to prevent sores from forming and guide in the necessary rotation. But it unnerved her nonetheless.

Tiehro stared with wide eyes as well.

Hotah slowed his pace. "Your friend is this way." He gestured toward a section of beds on the right.

How could Hotah keep track of all this? How could any of them? There were so many levels. So many rooms. Each one was probably as big as this one.

She followed along slower, dazed.

Amid the beds moved various attendants. Mostly Unato and several Awdawms. No wonder they hardly saw any Unato out on the streets. They were all probably in here, working. They wore turquoise robes in this place, unlike in other healing houses Rhea had visited in other cities. Perhaps to help them stand out in the dim light. Perhaps intended to bring some cheer? And yet it struck her that they looked more like blue spirits hovering over those near to death. They worked in pairs, tending to each patient and ensuring that they received broth, water, and whatever else was needed for comfort and health. At least as much as could be given in a few minutes.

Still Hotah moved forward. Tiehro nudged her to keep up.

Hotah cut across another line and then gestured to one body in particular.

She covered her mouth. The Unatos were doing all they could. They did this to help those who were suffering. But it was still so alarming to see her friend there, motionless and pale against the sheets. No longer did she wear the rich amethyst and soft ecru dress with the beaded panels. Her clothing had been changed to a short-sleeved cotton shift that was a few shades darker than the sheets.

She looked dead. As if all she waited for now was the building of the stone pyre and the weeping flowers.

"Can she hear us?" Rhea whispered, her voice tight in her throat. "Even a little bit?"

"Not at this stage." Hotah strode to the end of the bed. His expression remained neutral. "There is still precious little we can do for any of them aside from feed them, keep them clean, and at the proper temperature while we search for the cure. At one point, it seemed as if it was possible for them to hear us. A few of the Neyeb who did not succumb were even able to weave better dreams for the ill. But lately it has gotten worse."

Tiehro glanced around. "They say that it is dangerous for the psychic races to be too close together. Up above, those two were talking about it. How is this—"

Hotah's gaze dropped momentarily. The briefest flash of sorrow filled his dark eyes. But when he spoke, his voice was calm and professional. "While there are concerns that they might worsen through proximity, it would be far worse for them to starve or die from exposure to the elements. And we do not have the resources to tend to everyone in separate locations. Not on this scale." He indicated the door. "With that said, Tiablo, I would recommend you consider leaving the cavern. Once you are back on the surface, you should be far enough removed. The stones help to block the psychic fields. You are a brave man, but what you are feeling here is not just yourself."

Rhea still held Tiehro's hand. If things did not change, soon he would be here as well. His palm sweat against hers, his grip not quite as strong as at the surface.

As she glanced up, she froze.

No.

Her heart hammered faster. Her mouth dried.

That—that was not supposed to be here.

Tiehro stiffened, his fingers digging into her hand and Salanca's blanket.

The Ki Valo Nakar.

The moon-eyed entity circled the bed of a sleeping man. It moved as if it were part of the shadows, determined and cunning but silent and easy to miss until you caught a glimpse. Its host was a young Neyeb man, and it had shrunk its form to accommodate his. Sometimes glimpses of the much longer centipede-like body beneath the heavy cloak broke through just as the face at times seemed more skeletal. The long claws on its hands and the great antlers cast such distinctive shadows even in the dimness that she couldn't look away. Then it tilted its head, those massive moon eyes fixed upon the body, unblinking and unwavering. A light formed within the man's chest. Its claws twitched.

Rhea covered her mouth. Was this—was it cutting out the souls of the sleepers? Here in front of them?

Hotah did not even look in its direction. Nor did any of the other attendants.

She swallowed hard. "You see it?" She glanced at Tiehro.

Tiehro nodded. "Is it so bad that the Ki Valo Nakar walks this place unhindered?"

Hotah nodded as he bound a strip of blue silk around Salanca's wrist. "They say it takes only those who wish to go. And from the little we have been able to learn, the pain and sorrow of those trapped within these comas is a horror to behold. The Ki Valo Nakar brings relief."

"By killing them," Tiehro said.

"Do you know that for certain, Hotah?" she asked.

She had never been fond of entities like the Ki Valo Nakar, despite the insistence that they all served vital purposes within the communities and worlds. Watching it now as it drew out the shining orb of a soul from that poor man's chest —how could anyone know? There were stories about how it and others like it had chosen their own path at times. Gone against what they were created to do and picked their own dangerous and devastating courses.

"Elonumato knows." Hotah finished fastening the silk to Salanca's wrist. "And there is nothing that can be done to stop it unless the host defies it."

"Or someone has the right weapon to kill the host," Tiehro muttered.

"Few are strong enough or quick enough," Hotah said.

"So you just trust," she said. It wasn't a question. That was the answer. Of course they did. The Ki Valo Nakar was of the Neyeb, and it walked freely among all the races. Her stomach twisted.

"I don't recommend that you watch," Hotah said gently. "It is unnerving to say the least. We can only do what we can. And there is nothing that you or anyone else can do about it. If it chooses to take a soul, few could even cause it to turn its head. It is simply another form of death. And death is very active here. In some cases, it is more a mercy than a cruelty."

Perhaps. Yet her skin crawled nonetheless.

She stepped back, then crouched beside Salanca's ear. "Please," she whispered as she smoothed her sister's hair back. "Please don't let go. We're going to get you out. I promise. We're going to find a way."

The truth that Salanca couldn't hear them hung heavy over her, but she'd have said those words again if she could force them out. They choked her now.

Salanca did not stir. Her face had gone paler still, the small freckle at the left corner of her mouth seeming all the darker and more livid against her skin.

It was hard to move away. Hotah placed his hand on her shoulder and guided her back, reminding her how important it was that they not spend too much time underground. She kept her gaze on the stone floor. They had to find a solution here.

As they reached the surface, a clamor reached them. The attendants argued with someone, telling him that he could not enter, that it wasn't safe.

"Please step away from this place. You have no business here."

"I have to see her! You can't keep me from her."

Rhea's ears pricked up. Killoth?

9

THE HOSTILE GROOM

Hotah quickened his pace, moving in front of them as they left the hall.

"This Neyeb insists on seeing the visitors," the gruff attendant with the eyebrow rings said. He used the staff to block a slim figure in brown leathers. "He refuses to accept the risk, and he has no business going below."

"Killoth!" Rhea exclaimed.

Killoth turned so fast that his bound black hair swung over his shoulder. His lean face at once brightened and then twisted. "Rhea, tell them. I have to see her!"

"You know this one?" Hotah asked, his brow creasing.

"Salanca's his betrothed. They're nulaamed," Rhea said.

At the same time, Killoth said, "Salanca is my wife."

She ducked her head, shame flaring through her. She should have thought of that. "I'm sorry," she murmured.

Tiehro put a hand on her shoulder as if to comfort her.

Hotah frowned. "Your eyes didn't flash red."

Killoth remained tense, his focus honed on Hotah. "It doesn't matter. She is my wife in soul and spirit. More impor-

95

tantly, I am immune. I have every right to see her, and there is no risk to me. Please. The only nightmare I am trapped in is this one where I can't help her."

"The ceremony between you and your betrothed has not happened yet?" Hotah asked, resting one hand on his head. His shoulders remained tight.

"No." Killoth's jaw worked. "But I would give my life for her—"

"It doesn't matter. She is not your wife yet. There are laws, and I am bound to uphold them. You cannot just come in here and expect that you will receive an exception."

"Let me see her."

Hotah shook his head. "You may appeal to our leader, the kumar, if you so choose, but we honor the Neyeb laws. That woman is your betrothed. You are nulaamed. There is nothing that you can offer that is sufficient to break the bonds of tradition."

"I am one of the strongest mindreaders in existence," he snarled. "I have abilities that may allow me to reach her even if she is alone."

"Abilities?"

Killoth's jaw tightened.

Was he going to admit it? He had only done so reluctantly with her, admitting to being one of the very few Neyeb assassins who had ever lived. It also wasn't something that was wise to share.

That particular skill set came with the ability to cut through most mental barriers with ease as well as exceptionally powerful boundaries, barriers, and shields. It might actually be the reason he had been immune.

Hotah's broad squared brow creased even more. Then he nodded slowly as if Killoth had said something.

Killoth lifted his hands, gesturing toward the passage. "If

you won't let me down to see her, then at least let my friends come and take her back to their home. They're the Shrieking Chimera Cadre. You have so many to tend to here. It would be a small matter for them to take her to the cadre houses. Please."

Hotah set his hands on his belt, then shook his head. "Neyeb, you must remember that there is far more at stake in this than your beloved. I realize that that may truly be hard, but it does not change the truth of the matter. And I know of that cadre. I know of the work they are doing and what they have been assigned to. You should be proud of them."

"They are my friends. Practically family. I am exceptionally proud of them, and I am willing to entrust the one I love most in all the worlds to their care."

"But they do not need the burden that comes from caring for a comatose psychic," Hotah responded. His voice took on a sterner note. "You know as well as I how dangerous this is for your people. And what is it that Vawtrians around the globe—around all the worlds—are being asked to do?"

Killoth pressed his lips in a tight line.

Hotah's gaze narrowed. "Answer the question."

A snarl formed over his lips. "They are seeking out those who have fallen and bringing them to safety."

"Not all are so lucky as your betrothed to have friends or family like these two." Hotah motioned to Tiehro and Rhea. "Even now, there could be dozens—hundreds who are dying of exposure, starvation, and thirst. Do you truly believe that these Vawtrians need the exceptional task of caring for your beloved in addition to rescuing all the rest?"

Killoth ground his teeth even harder, his gaze now fixed on the wall rather than the physician. "I understand."

"Good."

Rhea stepped closer, her cheeks still hot with embarrassment. "I'm sorry," she whispered. "I didn't think—"

He shook his head at her. "It isn't your fault. I could have told you what I was going to say, but I didn't."

"I'll stay with her as much as I can," she whispered. "As soon as Tiehro is back and safe. But they say that there is nothing else that can be done. They cannot even hear us when we speak. But maybe she'll wake—"

"No one has woken yet," Killoth said sharply. His face remained drawn. "We do not know what they can and cannot hear or feel at this point."

True. She ducked her head as she pulled away. It wasn't wise to try to lie to a Neyeb to comfort them. She should have known better. Could she find any more ways to make this day harder?

She released a tight breath, then crossed back to Tiehro. "Are you all right?"

He stared over his shoulder back into the hallway. "I don't like leaving her down there," he whispered. "Not when the Ki Valo Nakar walks."

"No. But we need to get you to a safe place because the attacks are going to come again."

Hotah had started to write down notes on the pad of paper. The other two attendants had resumed tending to their own matters.

Killoth approached again. "I apologize for my shortsightedness," he said, speaking with a stronger clearer manner. "These are strange times."

"They are indeed." Hotah offered a gracious nod in response, his tone easier. "And we all realize how hard this must be on all of you. I hope you understand that we must honor the Neyeb laws. Even though it must be difficult, especially in your situation."

"I am certain that we can all recognize how challenging it has been. You and your people spend so much time caring for the rest of us. It is exceptional."

"We are among the masters of healing. It is our duty as given by Elonumato." He gave Killoth an almost pitying look. "Go and rest, Neyeb. You may stay with your friends if you wish. Let us hope that your beloved wakes soon and your bonding can be all that you hope for and more."

"I imagine that you have had to make many modifications and adjustments in your time here," Killoth continued, the mild nod he gave the only indication that he had heard what he said. "Compromises and the like."

Rhea raised an eyebrow. That edge to his voice wasn't one she particularly liked when it was directed at her. Watching him in action against someone else, though, was fascinating.

Hotah glanced up though he continued to make notations, the reed pen scratching across the paper and leaving its trail of dark-red ink. "Of course."

"Then you will understand that in this case, it is an acceptable compromise for me to be at my beloved's bedside. Tradition or not."

Hotah sighed. He pinched his brow as he stopped writing. "We have agreed to honor the—"

"Yes. But in this case, it may be the difference between her life and death. Is tradition more important than that? I am one of the most powerful of my kind. I am skilled at breaking through barriers. I could reach her and learn what is happening within her mind. Give her hope. Remind her that she is not forgotten. And that could be invaluable. You said you don't know exactly what these people are feeling right now. You don't know what they are experiencing in the darkness of their minds beyond some vague assumptions concluded days, even weeks ago. Wouldn't it be helpful if you had information?"

Hotah narrowed his eyes at him. The trap was sprung already. Even if Killoth wasn't through making his pitch. "There are other Neyeb—"

"There are none like me as there are truly none like Salanca. And I don't think you have a single one left in your force or team. You are running out of people who can care for these victims. You let me help her, and I will help you with all of your patients. I will share every scrap of knowledge I find, and that in turn may at least help you in providing for their actual needs rather than leaving you to guess. Most importantly, the laws against a nulaamed couple interacting forbid skin-on-skin contact among other specific requirements that I can vow I will not violate."

Hotah closed his eyes as if weighing this, then sighed. "Can you swear that you will not touch her?"

"I don't need to touch her. All I need is to be close enough to feel the presence of the attack upon her. Please. I do not beg. But I am begging you, noble physician. Let me be in her presence, and let me help her find her way back to us."

"It's best if this one is not down here any longer than necessary," one of the physicians said, her voice calm and clear as she came up beside Rhea and Tiehro. "He does not look so well."

No. Tiehro had gone a little green around the eyes, and his pallor had intensified.

"As if that makes any difference now." He tried to smile.

Rhea looked back to Killoth, her hand still gripping Tiehro's sleeve. "Are you—"

Killoth waved her away. "You've done all you could." His expression tightened as he faced the attendants. "Please.

Show me Salanca. I vow that I will remain here after that for so long as it takes to help every patient in this place."

"Very well. But you will answer for any harm that comes to her and if your people object to this."

Killoth shook his head. "I doubt many of them are in any condition to do any such thing," he muttered.

Rhea lifted her hand to wave to him, then returned her focus to Tiehro. "Ready?"

He indicated Killoth who was already starting down the hall. "As much as anyone ever could be in this place."

10

A DANGEROUS PROPOSAL

They made it back to the guest home in time, but Tiehro struggled through the nightmares more than ever. It brought Rhea to tears just to listen to him. Along with it was the worsening sense of hopelessness and helplessness.

When he roused, she wiped her eyes and cried more with relief. She then gave him black tea with honey and cinnamon. At least he was going to stay conscious for a while longer. At least she wasn't going to lose all of her family at once. Even though it struck her now that it was inevitable.

He moved from the bed to the small settee in the eastern corner of the room. A few more dark feathers lay on the wood floor as he walked. Bald patches had formed along his wings in several sections. He didn't walk with that easy confidence anymore. His left leg hitched as well.

She brushed her hand over his arm. "Chickadee..."

He offered a tight smile in response. "Just feeling the weight of the attacks. It's fine. It'll pass. It always does."

Until at some point, it wouldn't.

102

His throat bobbed as if he was thinking of Salanca too.

She placed her hand on his shoulder. "She'll come out of it. You know she will. And Killoth is there to help her. If there's anyone who can figure out a way, I'm sure it's him."

He managed a small nod and then took a sip of the tea. "Of course." He tweaked her chin, and his smile shook. "You know whether I am able to join my sodiwa or something else happens to me, I am not going to forget you. No matter how long or short. You'll always be my sister."

No, they were not going to have the death talk. That was what this was leading up to.

She forced a smile and tried to make her voice sound easy. "Yes. And you will always be my brother." She tugged a strand of his hair, then tucked it back behind his ear. "And you are going to get to go to your sodiwa. You're going to learn to be one of the best illusionists who walked or floated any of the worlds."

He tried to smile. "It is strange for that to be my skill, and yet...in the dreams, it is useless. Which isn't how it usually is."

He had never spoken about the nightmares in detail. And she had only tried to ask once.

Somewhere the courage to ask returned. She bit her lower lip. "When you fall into the dreams during the attacks...what happens?"

He hesitated, then stretched out on the black settee, sinking into the heavy cushions. "It used to be many things at first. Almost too much to take. But now? It's darkness. The worst kind of darkness. A darkness that is so thick you hear your own heart and feel your own blood. And you know your time is running out. There is no connection. No path. It's just...the other nightmares are easier than that. Because at least then there is something. Something to focus on fearing. When the darkness comes, you don't know if you are sitting or standing or falling or...anything. You can't even form images or shapes or forms for more than a few seconds. And your own voice...your own voice is not your own. I know that it is only a matter of minutes, but it stretches on as if it is eternity."

She shivered. Fear was dreadful. But nothingness—that was equally bad. Perhaps worse.

Picking up the blanket, she wrapped it around her shoulders as she listened. The silence grew heavier.

His gaze dropped to a spot on the wall. A muscle in his jaw worked. "In the end, it really isn't so much terror of death. Death might be a relief. And it isn't simply darkness. It is darkness with knowledge. Knowledge that I am trapped. Trapped in darkness. And screaming. Sometimes there is nothing except the darkness. Other times, it is as if I am aware of the sun over me, burning my flesh. Then I am aware of its absence. Sometimes I am stung. But I can never—I can never see. And I can't hear. My ears are stopped up. It's a constant dull roar with pressure that won't break, and that makes it feel as if there is someone constantly near."

"Is anyone ever near?" she whispered.

He shook his head, then paused. His eyelids slid shut. "Sometimes there is a voice. It says that this is where I end and that all have forgotten me. That we all always die alone and eventually almost all are forgotten on this side of reality."

She frowned, alarmed at the cold words and the pain in his voice. "That's—that's dark."

What an insightful thing to say. And she had no idea what to even suggest.

She swallowed, hoping her next words would be more comforting. "But it isn't really true. Sometimes people die with their families and friends around them."

"In the end, we are alone, but more importantly, when that voice speaks, I have no doubt that it speaks true. That

that is somehow where I wind up. Because when it speaks, it is as if it is speaking almost the full truth."

"Almost?"

"Enough that I have to take it seriously," he responded. "I don't even know how one goes about protecting oneself from a fate like that. Perhaps it is in the near future. Perhaps it is later. But...I can think of few greater torments than that. And try as I might, I cannot find a way to break the monotony and torment of that darkness. It feels like an eternity. It would shred anyone's sanity if left in there long enough."

"Do you think that's what Salanca is experiencing now? It sounded more like night terrors and bad things."

"I don't know. I hope not. When you're running for your life, at least there's the chance for you to escape somewhere or to find relief. There's something to do. In the darkness—in *that* darkness—there is nothing but sorrow and grief. Even prayer feels futile because time itself means nothing in there."

"I—I don't know what to do to help," she whispered.

He laughed, his gravelly voice even lower as he drew his hand over his eyes once more. "Oh, Bunny, there's nothing you can do about it. I don't think there's anything anyone can do about it except Elonumato maybe. Not even the Paras."

"I wouldn't go that far." A dark head popped up through the window. Killoth hauled himself up.

"You don't knock?" Tiehro asked, his brow lifting.

"Too many concerned people along the traditional routes." Killoth sat on the windowsill. He had paled significantly as well, the contrast between his hair and his usually tanned skin now stark.

"Is Salanca..." Rhea tried to find the words.

Killoth shook his head. "Any more tea?" He pushed off the sill and landed lightly. His boots made only the faintest thud as he landed.

"Killoth?" Her voice shook.

He picked up the tea kettle and poured himself a small black mug, not adding any honey or spices. "She...she's not responsive. I couldn't reach her. At all."

"Did you feel what she was feeling...?" Tiehro remained seated on the back of the settee, body rigid as if he had already prepared himself for the truth.

"She's afraid." Killoth remained silent for another few breaths, the heaviness in his words intensifying by the second. "Terrified. Whatever it is, she is trapped. I can't get through that wall. I can't even remind her of who she is and who her people are."

"She can't even feel her bond to her people?" Rhea stared at him in shock.

That was even worse than what she had feared. Even worse than the idea that the comatose psychics might be spilling their nightmares into the others by their presence because then that meant the good connections could not be present even in the background either. How was that possible? Wasn't that a torment all on its own? She had often envied the connection that Neyeb had with their people. The way that they could take comfort in the knowledge that there were others like them, a few gentle or compassionate words just a thought away. To have that and lose it? Maybe that was worse than never having it at all.

"But there are so many of them in there. They can't feel each other at all? Not even a little?"

Killoth shook his head.

Tiehro swore, but it sounded more like a fading cry. He kept his arms banded tight over his chest, his dark wings drooping as well. A feather fell free. "It is a horrible and cursed illness. Whatever causes it must be evil."

"And none of them—none of them at all? Hotah said—"

"Something has happened to Salanca that has isolated her even more. Perhaps...perhaps some of her other activities."

"The Forbidden Arts?" Tiehro demanded. "What we did—"

Killoth waved his hand as if he could bat the words away. "Possibly. Not necessarily. Who knows? That isn't the point!" His breaths sharpened. He then pulled the bag off his shoulder and set it on the table. "What's done is done. It could be something else, I'm certain of it. And it wouldn't matter now anyway. Just—" He dragged his hands through his hair and then stood. "I must be immune to this for a reason." He then struck his hands against the tabletop. "Immune and incapable. So you will have to trust me when I say that this is necessary."

"You want to do something with the Forbidden Arts," Tiehro guessed.

Killoth pulled a plain bronze bowl and two vials of liquid out, one dark purple, the other black. "No. But it builds off what was done before."

"What's the risk then? Why are you so agitated?" Tiehro demanded.

"It is not forbidden, but it is not without risks. And, Rhea—Rhea, I am so sorry. I don't know any other way to accomplish this."

"Then no," Tiehro snapped. "One sister is already trapped and near death. Why should—"

"It's Rhea's decision, and this is about far more than Salanca," Killoth returned, his voice sharpening as well. "The bond that Salanca created—if it is real, then this will solidify it. It will give Rhea clarity and help her know how to reach that person. It may even answer how such a strong bond could be created to begin with. If it is not real, though, you will be trapped. You'll be trapped similar to them. But I can get you out. I swear that I can, Rhea. It may feel like you are in there a long time. It may feel as real as this. But you will not be left behind."

"It's not as simple as that." Tiehro stood. "If this Chicory is an illusion, then she could be trapped with him for what feels like a lifetime. Her thoughts could degrade. The world could fall apart. It could fracture her consciousness! She could be trapped there and think it is real until it destroys her. This is not a game. This is not a dream. We are falling apart, and you would send her in—"

"I have nothing else!" Killoth struck his hand on the table.

Tiehro glared at him. "That doesn't justify it. Do you understand what you are asking? You are putting her at risk. I have practically lost one sister, and I am near to incapacitation myself. But you would ask to take this one who remains and sacrifice her mind as well?"

Killoth rested his elbows on his knees. "If this plague is not resolved, it will take you and Salanca and thousands, millions of others. And frankly in less than three days, you're probably going to be trapped in the same place unless you are very, very lucky. So yes. I am asking your second sister to please possibly sacrifice herself so that this doesn't happen. I would do it myself, but I can't. I don't even understand the full nature of the bond between her and this Chicory. And we can't attempt anything new."

"Besides," Rhea said softly. "It's my choice. And I will take it. It's all right, Tiehro."

"We don't know who this person you are speaking with is. What part of his mind you are speaking to even. He could very well be a monster or a liar. Or both." Tiehro flung his arm toward the window and then to Killoth. "In all my days of studying illusions and dream weaving and thought walking and everything in between, I have never heard of something like this going so smoothly or so simply. Salanca wanted to use something that is placed within the category of the Forbidden Arts. Now you want to do the same."

"It isn't actually forbidden. Just cautioned against without extreme care and great need, and we have satisfied that standard," Killoth responded coolly.

"No, but it does mean there are risks. For all we know, what Salanca did is the reason why you cannot reach her now but can reach other Neyeb," he responded sharply. "I love her. Dearly. But she did things her own way."

"Our only hope now is to end this. Or find the path to end it. We have no other options."

"I agree." Rhea reached out to Tiehro and took hold of his arm. "Please." She almost used his childhood nickname but stopped. "Tiehro, please. For her sake, yours, and even mine. I can do this. I will do this." Her fingers dug into his sleeve. "You are not far behind Sal. And I can't—I can't stand by and lose both of you. Especially not when it asks so little of me. Besides —I might find out once and for all if Chicory is real. And if he is—"

Tiehro clasped her face between his hands. "If he is and he could make you happy, I would bless him, but only if it did not wound you. The thought of you being trapped in your own mind—I cannot bear that thought." Terror rimmed his eyes in white still, but he clasped her close and then stepped back. "It's your choice though. In the end, no matter what I think, it's your choice. Whatever I can do to help you, I will."

"Then understand I have to do this." She picked up the vial and stared at the dark liquid. She needed to save all of them, and if this would help... "What do I do?"

Tiehro stepped farther back, crossing his arms over his chest though he offered no other objections.

Killoth nodded in her direction and then gestured toward

the mug on the table. "You drink it. Then you go to sleep. Which will happen fairly fast. You aren't going to feel so good. Your senses will be far more intense. If he is real and if he wakes, for a brief time, you may even be able to see through his eyes. But you will get answers. Though he may struggle to give them. If this is real, it will be taxing on his mind as well."

"And what is this about getting trapped or—" She hugged herself. "How can I deal with that?"

"If it is false, you collapse in on the reality you have created," Killoth said. "It will present itself an end of sorts. A conclusion, if you will. Sometimes unpleasantly. But I will reach you. And if it is real, you'll know. You'll need to take note of all the details you can. If you can identify a location within the place, we can ask the Tue-Rah to take us there. Even if it isn't the most precise with words, you can show it the image."

"I don't like this," Tiehro responded. "Rhea—"

"I know. But it will be for me too. I need to know if Chicory is real. And if there is something I can do to help you and Salanca and everyone else, then yes, I'll do it."

Killoth had already started to make the mixture. He moved swiftly, his hands trembling a little as he poured the two vials into a mug. He then sprinkled in something that looked like cinnamon but smelled more like mint, then stirred it up. "You should probably choose where you want to rest. It strikes swiftly."

She removed her shoes and then sat with her legs stretched out in front of her on the soft mattress. It still smelled pleasant in here, and the bed was comfortable at least.

As she accepted the mug, she glanced over at Tiehro. "I'll be fine. Just like you."

"That's what I'm afraid of," he murmured.

"Whatever happens, she can be reached," Killoth inter-

SLAYING THE NAGA KING - 2023

jected. He crouched beside her. "I have never met an Awdawm whose mind I couldn't navigate. I'll let you stay in no longer than thirty minutes. Then I'll come for you. All right?"

"All right."

She drank the dark mixture. It, too, tasted like raspberries, but there was no unpleasant aftertaste. Only something more like elderberries and plums. Not even a hint of mint now.

She blinked.

The world started to spin. She barely handed the mug to Tiehro before she collapsed into the softness of the bed.

II

TRUTH OR DELUSION

Rhea blinked slowly, trying to reorient herself. The air around her breathed and lived, the colors far more intense than her mind wanted to accept.

The bedroom had returned, but its scent had become so much more intoxicating and powerful. It was all jasmine, green tea, musk, stone, and sweat as before but also subtle notes of an earthy bakhoor and a gentle amber. Even the walls were more interesting, every grain and streak intricate and present. If she focused on it long enough, she wanted to touch it.

But there was only one person she wanted to see here.

She turned back toward the bed. Chicory's large form beneath the sheets was almost invisible in the soft bed. He sat up as if she had called out his name.

"Salt-Sweet."

A knot of emotion lodged in her throat. His name rose in her mouth as well. There he was. There he was!

He stared at her in awe. "Salt-Sweet, what's wrong? Are you—you're different. What happened?"

Something had changed. It was as if their bond had become so much more intense. As if she actually sat here beside him.

"I can really see you. You're here." Her whole body trembled.

All of her senses were alive, taking in every scrap of information she could. This was real. It had to be real. She brushed her fingertips over the silk coverlet. It was softer and sleeker than any of the times she had ever been here. Warmth reached her.

Outside, heavy thuds announced that something was near. Scales moved over fabric in an almost sleepy fashion, though she could not see anything that would make such a sound. How much time did they have?

He stood from the bed and crossed over to her. "Look at you," he breathed. "Just—just look at you. Yet you're still a dream."

"Chicory, this is real. You're real. I'm real!"

She bit her lip, then lunged forward to grasp his wrists. A delighted and terrified gasp tore from her. Yes! Yes, somehow it was working! He had weight and form and heat. It was true. All of it! All of the good and all of the bad.

He blinked, his mouth falling open. Then he pulled free and seized her hands tight. "I don't—" He swayed on his feet. "Then you're in danger, Salt-Sweet. You have to go. This place —it's so bad. It's getting worse by the day. I can't fix it. But you can escape."

"No. You tell me where you are. No one has heard of your world. Tell me a way to find it. Is it connected to the Tue-Rah?"

"They tried to block it. It isn't safe." He swept her up into his arms, his hand clasping the back of her head as he stared into her eyes. "It isn't...Salt-Sweet, I could be trapped here forever with you."

She gasped, startled at his strength and the realness of his body pressed against hers. His fingers dug lightly into her scalp, sending shivers of pleasure through her. He felt even better than she had hoped.

"We don't have much time. We have to focus. Chicory, is your world one of the Separated Worlds, or is it connected at all to the Tue-Rah?"

"I need to remember you," he said hoarsely, his gaze searching her face. "If you are real—if all of this is real—then you—Salt-Sweet—" His expression twisted, his brow creasing deeply. "You're in danger. You'll be—you're—" He blinked as he struggled to form the words, ducking his head forward. The top of his head pressed against her cheek.

"Chicory, I'm fine, but a lot of other people aren't. You are at the source or the solution. Either way, we have to get there. Someone has to make this stop. There are thousands dying now."

"I will find a way to fix this," he said sharply. "I haven't found the answer yet, but I will. I swear to you that I will."

"You need help. I'll bring my friends. We'll tell the Paras. We can send an army—"

"No!" He released her, horror filling his face. "You can't do that." He held his hands to his temples, his fingers thrust into his dark-blue hair. The beads clacked against one another. "You don't understand. What they would do—"

"They won't—"

"You do not understand," he said again, harsher this time.

"Then help me to understand. I don't have long. Tell me what's going on here because people are dying. My sister is trapped in a psychic coma, and so are thousands of others. We've talked about this. Do you remember any of it?"

"Yes. Somewhat." His tongue flicked at his lips as he looked up at the cracked ceiling. "I know—I know that this has gotten out of hand. They didn't intend it. You have to understand that. And death—it's too much."

"For who?" She cupped her hands around his face and brought his gaze back to hers. "Focus. Please."

His eyelids grew heavy over his eyes. "It came on so fast. Like a tidal wave. Some were washed into its jaws. Couldn't help them. It covered us all. But—just the beginning." He stumbled over the words more, forcing them out.

"The nagas came? I saw the naga in front of this big purple rift."

"The Rift was where it came from." His eyelids slid shut the rest of the way as his grip tightened on her. "It devours, and it does not fill. Can't close it. We keep pouring energy in. But they say blood is what it needs."

"Whose blood? And who is 'they?' The nagas?"

"The nagas. Nagas and bonetrips and minotaurs and fire bones and acid bites and others." He wavered, then stiffened, grabbing hold of her again. His eyes darkened as he held her so tight it hurt. "You have to leave. You can't come back to this place. Even if you aren't real. Even if you are a dream, I will not see you hurt. The hunger never ends. The madness. The tearing. The ripping. The agony. I've held them back this far. They haven't—they haven't gone too far. But we have almost nothing left. Nothing of worth."

A door creaked open. Not near her. It was on the other side of his waking world. Its long creaking voice pierced her mind.

Dread seized her. The air vibrated around her. She looked up into his eyes. "Chicory," she said as sternly as she could manage, not even questioning how she knew this. "You have to wake up. Someone is here to kill you."

He blinked, his breathing going more ragged. "Salt-Sweet..."

He started to vanish, his body fading.

Killoth's words rang through her mind. She stretched out her hand and snagged his wrist. His expression contorted, but she held fast.

Her mind exploded. Hot pain shot up through her arm and into her neck and up through her eyes as heat flared through her. Then, suddenly, she was blinking, staring up at a ceiling. A ceiling very like the one in the dream. Except this one had a much larger crack with many more fractures radiating out from it. The air tasted sharp and bitter, an unpleasant musk heavy upon it as well as a scent like teal incense and amber resin.

Then a green reptilian face loomed over her. Brilliant amber-and-green eyes glowed, the diamond-shaped pupils, intent.

Chicory's voice boomed around her, echoing in her ears and pulsing in her blood. "Steltro—"

The naga snarled, baring long curving fangs, his green cowl flaring out. "If the only way they die is if you die, then so be it, king! I will rule in your stead. I can do what must be done." The flash of a blade lashed forward.

A deep searing pain struck her in the shoulder and part of her chest as if the spear had pierced her. She screamed and fought to hold on as she faded away.

Chicory!

Was he dead?

Mortally wounded?

Her vision blurred. She fought to commit every possible detail to memory, but aside from the greenish-blue of the naga in the dim light, nothing was clear.

Darkness engulfed her as her consciousness seeped away. The pain faded with it.

Something touched her face. A voice called to her softly. Though she tried to reach back for Chicory, the voice grew more insistent, and it tugged her back. "Rhea."

She cringed against the harshness of the torchlight as her eyelids fluttered open.

Killoth leaned over her, his hand along the side of her face. "Rhea, you're back." He breathed with relief.

A low gasp on the other side of the room and a smooshing of the pillows confirmed Tiehro was relieved as well.

Energy surged through her, even as nausea curled within her belly. "I have to go!" she shouted. She sat up so fast her head brushed against the bottom of the upper bunk. Everything crystallized in her mind. She knew precisely what she had to do. "I saw him. He's real! It's all real." She swung her feet over the side of the bed and stood. "Every bit of it."

"Yes?" Killoth's face lit up. He clasped her hand in his, laughing. "You saw? It was real. There really is a place? And you saw it?"

She staggered and caught herself on the bed frame. All the world still seemed bright and vibrant, the air pulsing with possibility. The answer truly had been there all along.

It was the whole reason that the incantation had showed her the naga first.

That had to be the naga king.

"Yes! Chicory and the nagas. I have to go. I am going to kill the naga king! That's how we end this curse!"

12

PLANS TO ASSASSINATE

R hea clutched at her hair, her heart racing. She dipped her head forward.

Chicory had been stabbed in the shoulder. Her own pulsed with the memory, sharp and potent as if she, too, had been stabbed. "We have to hurry. He's wounded! Maybe he fought the one off. We have to go now!"

It had all become so clear. Chicory and his fate—he couldn't be dead. That blade had only pierced his shoulder. Her hand gripped her shoulder, scrunching up the soft fabric of her pale-yellow tunic.

Somehow he had to have gotten away. Perhaps been taken prisoner.

A nagging fear pressed up within her that perhaps that was only what she wanted to believe. How could Chicory have fought off such a powerful reptilian warrior? Especially when he had been caught while resting? Was it the same naga she had seen the first time? Was that the naga king? Or was he king now that—

No. Chicory wasn't dead. Her body tensed just at the thought that he might be.

Somehow—somehow he was going to survive. And she was going to get to him. She was going to save him and her family. Even if it meant she had to kill a ferocious monster. Especially if it had hurt Chicory. But yes, yes! This naga king or interloper or whatever he was, he had to die. That was the answer to all of this! It seemed so clear.

She started to pace around the room before Killoth darted in front of her and gripped her arms. "What then? What did you just say, Bunny?"

"Let go," she said, pushing free. "I'm going to kill the naga king. And any of the others who get in my way."

"Wait. You saw a part of this place? You can hone in on that. This is good. This will work." Killoth held his hands up though he did not touch her again. "You can show it to the Tue-Rah, and it will take us near there."

"I can. I remember it!" She dragged her hand through her hair, gulping in another clear breath. Her mind still buzzed.

"Go back," Tiehro said, standing. He crossed his arms over his broad chest, his head cocked. "Did you just say kill the naga king?"

"Yes." Staggering, she caught herself on the table. Very simple. Simple as simple.

"You?" Tiehro stared at her, jaw agape. "You can't even kill a deer. You don't know how to handle any of the weapons large enough to kill a naga."

"If I have to, yes."

Tiehro rubbed his forehead, then shrugged helplessly. "If they are like the myths, then you have no time for hesitation. But, Bunny, really think about it. Please. The deaths will haunt you. Killing a person isn't easy. Even if you think they're evil."

"Sure it is," Killoth responded dryly, no more humor in his voice or eyes. "You drive the pointed end of the knife or the spear through the heart or the face. Either way, do it fast, and then you don't have to worry about it. And if you find that the nightmares haunt you, I'll help you get those sorted straight away."

Tiehro's mouth flattened into a tight line. "Rhea is an artist. She creates."

"I do." She hugged herself tight. The energy surging through her made her feel like she could climb out of her own skin. Right now she could box an elephant and win probably. "But that doesn't mean I won't fight for the ones I love. That includes you and Salanca. And why shouldn't I? You would do this for me."

"Is there—" Tiehro started.

Killoth cut him off with a wave of his hand. "Going to any one with authority takes more time. We have to move swiftly. If the weapon is sharp enough or the poison toxic enough, even an artist can be a killer. And you, Bunny, you can't do this alone. Fortunately, you don't have to."

"Yeah, all right. Good. Just—this needs to be done."

It was hard to stand still. She couldn't argue that when it came to the experience of killing people, she had less than anyone in the room. She didn't even draw violent sketches or battle commemorations.

Killoth glanced out the window as if marking the time. "There's enough time if we leave at once. I'll go with you to the Tue-Rah, and together we will journey to this land where the nagas have invaded. A mindreader would be helpful."

"I will go as well," Tiehro said.

Though Killoth gave him a startled look, Rhea wasn't surprised at all.

Tiehro shrugged as if it should be obvious. "What can I do in this place other than wait to be taken? I can't reach Salanca.

I can't help anyone. But maybe...maybe I can fight some nagas. What about you, Neyeb? You swore to help these people."

"I did, and I will, but I have down time. I'm supposed to rest." Killoth returned the shrug as if it was ridiculous that he should be sleeping. "As I said, we must leave immediately. But—"

"How do you think we can manage it? It's too dangerous to travel at night alone. Especially if we don't have one of your shifter friends to help protect us." She picked up her bag anyway. She hadn't even unpacked it, but she slipped the strap up over her arm and onto her shoulder. "The red wolves have been far more aggressive."

"I know Berethia."

"Berethia?" Rhea and Tiehro echoed at the same time.

Killoth gestured for them to follow him. "We'll need to be quick. It won't take us long. And we might be able to return before I am due to speak with more trapped minds. In which case, there will be no concerns about our absence." He had already crossed to the door.

They followed along behind him. He did not even glance back as he led them to the western side of the city near the point where they usually entered. When they reached a towering red-barked tree with delicate sigils painted in an interlocking chain up its north side, Killoth darted to the light-turquoise door. He rapped on it swiftly with his knuckles.

Soft footsteps shuffled inside. The door opened quietly, and an older Bealorn woman appeared, wrapped in a heavy striped shawl. "Baby Killoth." The wrinkles in her face creased all the deeper as she embraced him. "What brings you here to my door? My granddaughter is married, but I'm sure she'll still wed you too if you ask sweetly enough. Though I don't think that's why you're here."

"Ahh, you know me well." Killoth kissed her cheek. "This may sound hard to believe. But we're going to fight some nagas and must get to the Temple of Tiacha tonight. Can we borrow—"

"Nagas?" She stroked the fine white hairs along her chin as she raised a thinning eyebrow. "Did they find nagas on one of the Separated Worlds? You have to be careful of them. They steal people's faces and spit venom."

"Yes, Grandmother Berethia. They do, but we have to fight them anyway. It's very important."

"They say if you put walnut oil on your face then nagas can't see you. Or maybe it's lemons. Just a minute."

"No, Grandmother Berethia, it's all right!" Killoth poked his head through the doorway as the woman disappeared from sight. "We don't need—"

"It won't take a second. You cannot fight nagas without the proper supplies."

"Grandmother Berethia—" he turned, then shook his head. "You two wait here. I'll be back."

Rhea tried to hold still. Her muscles remained tense and yet jittery.

"You all right?" Tiehro whispered, staring down at her with obvious concern.

She nodded. "Just focusing. We need to go."

"I'm worried for you."

"Because I won't necessarily be staying in the tree house after you and Salanca go your way like you both planned for me?" She clapped her hand over her mouth. Where had that even come from? "I'm sorry."

He frowned but shook his head. "No. No, Rhea, I'm—I'm sorry. Of course you don't have to stay there. It must feel like we're abandoning you."

She pinched her lips tight. "We don't need to have this

conversation right now. It isn't even that big of a deal. Getting you and Salanca and everyone else healthy is what matters. What happens afterward won't even matter if we don't get that." She rubbed her arm briskly. Her nerves prickled even sharper now.

"You don't have to stay where we can find you easily. You should go wherever you want and pursue your dreams. You deserve happiness as much as either Salanca or I."

"That was so mean. I'm sorry."

It wasn't that she had never been angry at points. It just hadn't been that intense before this. That resentment and sensation of being left out and abandoned—it wasn't right, but it was real within her.

She shook her head again and ground her palm against her temple. "I really am glad you're going to learn how to be a master illusionist. And Killoth is wonderful. He and Salanca will be happy together."

"All of that can be true and you still feel abandoned and like you've lost your family," he said softly. "Just—we'll talk about it later, I'm certain, but know I want you to be happy. You take care of yourself and find a way to be happy, and you'll be doing the same for me. All right? Don't even worry about the house in the trees or caring for anything."

"Let's get this little matter of the cure sorted first." She bit the inside of her lip, her nerves intensifying. That really had just exploded out of her. Shame flared within her, suffocated only by the need to find the answers to everything else.

Killoth backed out of the house as Grandmother Berethia shooed him. He held two vials of liquid, one presumably walnut oil and the other lemon juice.

"You remember if you stab them in the heart, they should be weakened," she said. "If that doesn't kill them, you strike again and again. You don't look in their eyes. You must be careful. You are a sweet boy."

"Yes, Grandmother." Killoth passed Rhea the two vials. "We will be careful."

She motioned for them to follow her as she shuffled around to another door. Inside this darker door was the terror bird stable. They immediately roused, shaking their heads and clattering their massive hook beaks. One uttered a low grunting chirp. Their bright copper eyes lined in black feathers practically glowed in the darkness.

"Ahhh, my babies. Sweet babies. Come here to me." She then uttered a series of vocalizations that were similar to the terror birds but smaller.

Rhea followed, watching intently. Chances were this woman also suffered with the nightmares. Yet she spoke to the terror birds like they were her babies and showed no trace of impatience or frustration with Killoth showing up, asking for favors in the middle of the night to go fight mythical monsters. She wasn't even sure what to say. Thanks seemed insufficient.

"Don't take my babies through the Tue-Rah," Grand-mother Berethia continued. "You get to the temple. Tell them 'delorme, return' or 'delorme, return at dawn' if you don't know if the Tue-Rah will take you where you must be. That way, you can ride them back if necessary, but they do not go to fight the nagas. They are good sweet babies. They don't like snakes."

One with a particularly bright silver streak along its head uttered a low croaking call as if in agreement. It fluttered its small wings to underscore the point.

"We promise we won't take them through," Killoth said. "They are good babies indeed."

She smiled, her dark eyes bright. "You all know how to ride?"

When they nodded their agreement, she set to putting the colorful striped blankets and small saddles on them. It did not take long.

"This is Cha," she said, indicating the one with the extra bright silver stripe. "This is Dah Day." She gestured toward one with bright blue feathers around its eyes. "And this is Mochee." She patted the back of a nearly all-charcoal terror bird.

He ducked his head down to nibble at her shoulder, his great sharp beak clacking harmlessly at the edge of her shawl.

She then embraced each of them, stroking their heads. "You fight the nagas, darling children." Then she kissed each between the eyes and stepped back. "When you come back, you come visit Grandmother Berethia. Tell me how you beat the nagas."

Rhea managed to thank her but reminded herself that she needed to do more when they returned. Killoth gave her an extra long hug in return and promised he'd come to visit and soon he'd be able to introduce her to his actual wife.

As she climbed up onto Dah Day's back, Rhea looked at Killoth. Maybe they should have tried talking to the authorities.

Killoth grinned and tossed a thought back in her direction. "*Nah, Grandmother Berethia is just good like that. You'll have to come back and talk to her some time. Should have thought to introduce her to you before.*"

They made one more stop to gather weapons. Killoth gave her a short sword and belt, while Tiehro opted for two daggers and a series of venom-tipped darts. Then they rode on the backs of the sleek silver, black, and blue terror birds. Their great claws tore into the packed soil with heavy thuds as they sprinted across the moon-drenched grassland to the main road that would take them to the Tue-Rah. The red wolf howls rose through the night, a haunting backdrop to their race to the temple.

She held fast, knees gripping the bird tight. Its long muscular neck reminded her of a serpent. Like a naga. She shuddered, but her blood heated. The incantation had worked the first time. The naga she had first seen had to be who needed to be killed. And she was almost certain that that was the same naga who had attacked Chicory. It was all coming together.

Oh, Chicory. Her heart clenched.

If he was dead, she'd kill every single one of them. Never in her life had she contemplated killing even one person. Now she was fantasizing about an entire group?

What *was* the plan exactly? That figure of the naga in front of the rift remained emblazoned in her mind. It really had shown her the answer. She just hadn't been able to grasp it. And even now she wasn't sure how it all was going to come together. Maybe his blood was what would close the rift. Or maybe he had created a spell. Whatever it was, she had seen the actual place well enough to show the Tue-Rah and ask it to take her there. That had to count for something.

Of course, they also were going to have to get through the Temple of Tiacha first. It was going to be challenging. The guards and attendants of the Tue-Rah protected it zealously.

At least usually.

But with the mysterious illness sweeping over the worlds, the Neyeb guarded ones were especially sparse and the replacements less experienced.

The outlines of the forest around Kuchani and the Temple of Tiacha rose in the darkness. Unlike the Unato and Bealorn cities, the Neyeb city of Kuchani was built around the forest with tree tamers brought in to guide and move the trees in various directions. It always seemed as if the city had sprouted within the forest overnight rather than being the product of centuries of cultivation and careful planning.

The oak and maple forest spiraled around a series of hills. The temple had been built into the largest hill, shored up and supported with towers and walls to provide far stronger protection. As they entered the forest it became harder to see, until they emerged into a massive clearing. Trees that started to grow in this place were removed, and the grass only went as high as the knees.

Ordinarily, there was a steady hum of life, no matter the time. The Neyeb who lived here tended to be friendly and open, often speaking in passing with travelers of all sorts, but it was more like a ghost town than a central city. Few torches burned in the broad windows. No one rested in the gardens or on the flat-topped roofs of the clay and stone homes. No one was about at all. Not even the tree tamers or the lamp tenders. Only the attendants at the open gate to the temple, and they did not stop them.

Really, it was not going to be until they reached the main hall of the Tue-Rah that it would be even a potential issue.

They dismounted the terror birds. Killoth gave them the command to leave at dawn, which would arrive in less than an hour. He then fed each one something red and moist that smelled bloody.

Rhea grimaced, turned her face away, and hurried down the stone path with Tiehro. He always insisted that as long as you acted as if you had somewhere important to be, most people wouldn't stop you. These guards did not appear to be Neyeb. They were too tall and broad-shouldered and a little too uncertain in their gaze. Probably Awdawms or Shivennans who weren't sure what proper protocol was in a situation like this.

Indecision that benefited her now.

They hurried into the temple and down the corridors until they reached the Hall of Creation, which led to the Chamber of the Tue-Rah. While the Tue-Rah could access any location in the worlds, it had multiple immersion points where it was strong enough and clear enough to be accessed and commanded by sentients. This place here in the temple was where it was at its strongest and clearest in all the world.

Enormous fluted pillars stood staggered down the hall, carved from polished red-brown stone. Hammered braziers with scented coals stood at intervals beneath woven reed paintings and relief carvings that depicted various moments throughout the history of the world. In the daylight, sunlight streamed through the broad and tall windows and made the colors all the more vibrant. Here with only the light from the torches and coals, the gem-tone paints were deeper, sultrier, and the reeds some had been painted on glistened.

The darker and more disturbing depictions, such as the Coming of the Full Death, the Betrayal of Te, and others took on a far more ominous tone in the dim orange light. Especially one which depicted the Ki Valo Nakar standing on the other side of a marsh in a black forest beneath the moon, surrounded by corpses. In this depiction, it was impossible to tell that there was a Neyeb host at all. The skeletal face dominated the focus. It looked simply like some great monster intent upon cutting out souls. Its great glowing moon eyes seemed to follow her as she slipped along past the statues and various art forms. Even Tiehro glanced back over his shoulder at it.

As they neared the enormous white doors to the Tue-Rah, Tiehro lifted his hand. His fingers shook lightly.

There were only two guards in front of the door of the Tue-Rah, perfectly aligned with the massive starburst across the central split. Two Awdawms for certain this time. They carried more weapons than average. But when Tiehro's illusion struck them, they opened the doors to the chamber and hurried inside.

What had he shown them? Ever since Tiehro had started to show promise, he hadn't even attempted to make an illusion on her or Salanca. Yet now she understood why the sodiwa wanted him. He did it so effortlessly and without causing any harm despite his weariness.

Then those two guards moved away as if they had been called, responding to a summons as if it were real.

Rhea hurried with Killoth and Tiehro beyond those great doors and into the polished white stone chamber. The marble glistened, reflecting the low globed torches that were fastened in clusters of three along the walls at regular intervals. An intricate design of shapes and symbols sprawled out, carved across the walls and the floor. No windows marred the patterns. She had loved studying these patterns and imagining the light as it poured through those shapes and designs.

Their footsteps shuffled softly forward. Even at a run, it would be hard to cross this room swiftly. Their breaths echoed, heavier in the air than they should have been. The incense and scented coals masked most of the scents of travelers but not the empty chill that was so unnatural for this place.

At the very center of the enormous chamber stood a massive square platform with four broad-stepped staircases leading up, one on each side. The platform itself had been carved from a single piece of opalescent marble. On each corner of the platform stood a large circle which lay flush with the floor. A different geometric design was carved within each circle. From the center of the platform rose an ornate pedestal.

The great pearl pillars that reached out above them with three arms each practically glowed despite the low light, their mystical carvings all promising knowledge far beyond her comprehension.

Reaching the stairs, they quickened the pace. Each step was more than two-feet wide. The cold nipped through the bottoms of her slippers. Why were the stairs so much colder than the rest of the floor?

They moved to the top. No one was even here to watch at all. Or perhaps Tiehro had sent them all away?

The pedestal itself had similar symbols tightly carved into the opalescent frame. Hazy light radiated from the top of the pedestal, separate from the large crystalline structure that hung in the air above it. It glowed like a cross between a geode and a flame. So many times she had tried to sketch it or mimic the patterns she'd seen only to realize that she couldn't do it full justice. Even when she mirrored its design almost perfectly, it always felt as if something was lacking.

"You'll have to show it where to take us," Killoth said, stepping away from her.

"It was his bedroom. Hopefully no one is there," Rhea said. Certainly not a dead body. She adjusted her bag over her shoulder and set her hand on the hilt of her short sword.

"If someone is, our hornless friend will cast an illusion to let us escape, and I'll work my own particular skills," Killoth responded.

As bloodthirsty as she had felt, it no longer was so strong. Relief pressed through her at the thought that perhaps Killoth could handle it all. What she had to do was get them there.

"Remember, if you freeze, just get angry," Tiehro said, squeezing her shoulder, concern bright in his eyes. "Anger will push you out. It gets to your primal side. And if you have to get primal to survive, it's worth it."

"Sure, though being angry can make you stupid, and being stupid can get you killed, just like being afraid," Killoth remarked dryly. "Besides, we're going to be there with her. It isn't like she's going into this alone."

No. She wasn't alone at all.

She bowed her head, placing her hand on the pedestal. Her fingers pressed hard against the cold stone. "Please. Whatever is done, they need help. *Please*. Please let us go through."

As she closed her eyes, she drew the image of the room into her mind. It would be strange for Chicory—perhaps even dangerous—if this was where she appeared, but it was the one image that she could give the Tue-Rah that she knew was accurate.

So she focused on it with all her strength.

Please.

Some said the Tue-Rah was sentient. Not in the same way as people. But in its own manner. With reasoning of its own. Perhaps even a sense of humor.

For now, she just prayed that it could understand what she showed it, and that it wouldn't refuse.

But it probably would. And if it did, then they'd have to go and try to tell the authorities why they should speak with the Paras. It would be even harder to convince the Paras and the myriad of people in between. Why should they listen?

She didn't have a good reason why the Tue-Rah should let her through aside from the desire to help and the fact that this could not be proved. The fact that she liked Chicory as well? Would the Tue-Rah care about something like that?

The golden light flared out. Tiehro's hand tightened on her shoulder as Killoth edged closer.

They were going!

She clenched her eyelids shut as the pedestal disappeared from underneath her hands. The light was warm, comforting, soothing. But then she realized it was only the light she felt.

She tried to open her eyes, blinking in the brightness. It was just fading. Something solid formed beneath her feet. The air went cool, sharp, and scented with mushrooms and stone.

She stood in a hall with fragmented lines of glowing purple light. Killoth and Tiehro were nowhere to be seen. She turned slowly.

A dark stone passage with oil-soaked torches stretched on in both directions, no trace of either one. Oh, polph. Where were they?

Her spine prickled with awareness.

Someone was coming.

She darted behind an outcropping in the rock wall and crouched out of sight as she reached for her sword. Her mouth fell open. It was gone! Her sword was gone. This—this really was bad.

13

IN THE HALLS OF THE NAGA KING

R hea wedged herself down farther, pressing hard against the stone wall. Two warriors strode down the hall, each carrying a large bloody box. No. Not two warriors. Two warrior monsters.

She pulled her body in tighter, her mouth going dry and her heart racing faster. A minotaur with metal shoulder pads and a startlingly elaborate belt over brown trousers and a pale-yellow naga with a long scar from the corner of his left eye all the way down to his shoulders, beneath the dark-blue fabric of his flowing vest.

"Can't believe we're meeting again today," the minotaur growled.

"It makes no difference," the pale-yellow naga responded. "Last week. Today. Next week. Not gonna fix anything."

"Everyone knows what we need to do. Nobody wants to do it."

She clenched down tighter, holding her breath as if that would help her be invisible. They continued on down the passage, grumbling about all that was happening and the lack of effectiveness.

She peered out after them, her heart hammering. Why had the Tue-Rah done this to her? Her brother and friend not being here with her made this all the harder. And Chicory was nowhere in sight. Besides all that, it had taken her sword.

Wait.

She struck her hand to her breast band then cursed inwardly.

It had even taken her little blade for sharpening pencils. What was that about, Tue-Rah?

The ground trembled. Silt and debris sifted down, and the walls creaked and groaned. She cringed against the wall, clenching her eyelids shut. Oh.

The spasm of awareness had barely passed through her before the earthquake finished. The purple veins in the walls flushed brighter and deeper in coloration at turns, pulsing as if with breath. Doors had jarred open all the way down the hall as well. One opened into what looked like the study rooms in Dohahtee, simplistic and intended for focus. Two seemed to hold random goods in wooden boxes.

Wait.

What was that in the one down the end? Some shiny metal glinted in it.

She scurried forward, keeping close to the wall, her senses alert for any signs of attackers or newcomers. Almost to the very end of the hall before it split, one of the doors that had jarred open was a small armory with large wooden racks and staggered shelves. Only melee weapons. Most had been cleared out, leaving behind gaping spaces in a room without debris or cobwebs anywhere except in the corners.

The people who lived here had probably cleared it out when they battled the nagas.

The knot of emotion in her chest tightened.

No scent of blood or bile contaminated the air. If there had been a fight, it hadn't been here. Or they had failed so thoroughly that they were all captured. Maybe to be sacrificed? Chicory had said something about them wanting blood. Prisoners probably made good sacrifices.

She would need a weapon, though, and what was in here was certainly better than nothing.

What to choose, though? A dagger or knife of some sort seemed obvious, and there were four left on the simple dark-red shelves, all in sheaths. If it came down to it, she'd mostly be relying on what Killoth had said about how you put the pointed end in the other person, but if it required actual skills, she would be in trouble. Still, she should have one, right?

Killoth and Tiehro always carried knives. Most people did. She always kept her little blade on her person in case she needed to sharpen her pencils or cut reeds, but that was not one she ever wanted to use in a fight. Not that there was even a choice with the Tue-Rah being foolish enough to take that away from her.

She picked up a sheathed dagger that had a blade the length of her hand. The sheath itself was slim enough she could easily fasten it to her belt. That seemed the best choice. Somehow, it was much heavier than it looked.

For the actual fight, though—well, it wasn't as if she had much experience.

She turned slowly, her gaze drifting over the mace which was clearly going to be too heavy and the flail which was just as likely to wound her as opposed to her opponent. She stopped at the rack with one spear remaining in it.

Spears gave distance. That one also had a good pointed blade. And hadn't Tiehro said they were good for piercing hearts?

She picked it up carefully, taking care not to brush it against the spokes. The last thing she needed was to make some sound that got her caught.

Hmm.

She tested its heft, then frowned. The spear did not feel good in her hands. It had solid weight to it, more than she had expected. Instead of making her feel powerful, it made her feel clumsy, but at least it was long enough she wouldn't easily impale herself.

She shifted her weight and tested it again. Yeah. Much better than nothing. Still—she scanned the shelves to see if there was anything better. A spiked club then a similar hooked one as well as another flail. No. Not good choices.

This would do.

Unease spasmed through her, tightening in a painful coil in her belly. The thought of killing this naga king was becoming less and less comfortable by the second.

Didn't matter how she felt though.

This had to be done. And swiftly.

She peeked out the door once more, gripped the spear tighter, and slipped out.

Her gut told her she needed to follow those purple veins. Just a gut instinct, but it made sense. Besides, it gave her a simple track back to follow.

The mottling across the stone was almost beautiful. It fractured and thinned the farther back it went, but as she followed it, the lines grew thicker and stronger as if they were indeed markers showing the way. Some of the lines joined together into a glowing purple line that was thicker than two of her fingers put together.

The damp in the cavern intensified as she followed this path. Side passages cut away at different points, uneven and crooked roofed.

Footsteps sounded in one just ahead. She dropped down behind a barrel, clenching the spear in her fist.

A man with the lower body of a spider strode along, his pace uneven. He staggered a few steps, put his clawed hand to the wall, then pinched the bridge of his nose. With a shake of his head, he resumed moving forward.

Relief blossomed through her as she straightened. She might be clumsy, but at least she was up against people who weren't observant. That had to count for something. She'd been crouched down beside a barrel with a literal spear protruding, and that one hadn't seen her.

Was that right, though?

It didn't feel right.

Something was wrong. The tang in the air. It left an unpleasant coating in her mouth.

Her nerves spiked as she rounded the corner. More voices. Lots more voices. Protesting and humming, speaking about something she couldn't make out. Her nerves still buzzed, her muscles jittery.

She kept as close to the wall as she could as she crept forward. No more doors on either side of the hall now. And the passage itself was much more roughly hewn, as if carved in part by pickaxes rather than sculpted out by geo Shivennans or formed from a natural cavity in the earth. Even if her feet had made sounds on the uneven surface, they would have been masked by the increasing clamor of voices.

She crept along the stones that slanted upward. It grew more treacherous the higher she went, but it did hug the cavern wall and curl around.

Down below, a large assembly had gathered. At least a few hundred people. Monsters. Almost entirely monsters. Monsters of all shapes and sizes. Minotaurs, blood drinkers, men made of fire, golems, nagas, spider people, and beings

137

she didn't even know the names of. They all stood on this flat stone, arced in a half moon around a speaker.

One of the larger pillars of stone blocked him from sight. To the far right, a large tar spill covered up something. It looked like something with a white circle based on the edges. Even beneath the tarry darkness, it was glowing faintly, flickering as if struggling to breathe and moving between gold and white.

She crept farther down the ledge as it continued to press outward.

That voice...it sounded similar to Chicory's. Except no. She blinked. No. It wasn't. Just a trick of her mind because she missed him. It was larger, deeper, and heavier. Angrier too.

Adjusting her grip, she moved steadily forward. The great blue-green naga wore a rich indigo vest, open in the front and loose about his purple-belted waist. A dagger had been thrust, sheath and all, into that belt. Not that he needed it. The tiger-like stripes along his shoulders and arms spoke to great strength, his bare abdominals ridged and hard.

Then he turned his face in her direction as he stretched out his hand. "Is there no alternative?" he bellowed.

Oh! Oh, by all that was holy, he was wearing Chicory's face!

Her gut twisted. She covered her mouth as tears sprang to her eyes.

No.

What greater insult could there be? He was speaking with something like Chicory's voice and wearing his face, distorted though it was in this larger frame with teal skin and indigo stripes.

Chicory was a prisoner somewhere. She'd guessed that. He was just a prisoner and not dead. He couldn't be dead.

This had to be the naga king from her dreams. The one

who had reared up in front of the purple rift. Though there did not appear to be an actual rift here unless that was what the sea beyond the stones was: a mass of purple, indigo, lavender, and cerulean, dotted and streaked with shimmering silver. Far more beautiful than anything in the dreams. Something like steam rose from this sea, the same color as the fog, though it lost its color when it curled over the cliff and onto the stones.

Her gut clenched all the harder. This was the right place. Salanca's incantation had worked, and the answer had been presented. All she had to do was kill that naga king, find Chicory, and—well, if that hadn't solved it yet, the two of them could work it out. He had to know what was going on down here. And now that he would know she was real and not a dream, it would be far easier for them to talk.

But what if—no!

She pulled at the anger over all that had happened. Countless lives trapped in nightmares, tormented in unyielding slumber. And here was the cause.

The naga king drew to the left, nearing the ledge she crouched upon. "Is blood what this Rift requires? Is blood what you demand?"

She swallowed hard, staring down at the scene below. A knot of rage burned in her stomach.

The assembled crowd shouted, their roars rising to the cavernous ceiling. Archers stood on the edge of the rift along with spearmen and guards with swords.

She gripped the spear tighter. Never had she even wielded a bo staff before this day, let alone a spear or a sword. It no longer felt so possible.

But she would kill him.

She had to.

Actually kill him.

Take this spear.

Drive its point through his heart.

The jittery strength and tension in her body broke at the vividness of this thought.

She winced as she imagined the crunching of the bones and squirting of blood.

Tiehro was right. This—this wasn't going to be easy.

Especially not when that naga wore Chicory's face.

No.

No! She could do this.

Rhea straightened her shoulders, letting the anger bubble up. She pulled on all the anger that she'd ever felt and pushed away. The fact that this horrible illness had come in and destroyed what little time she had left with her family before they all went their separate ways. The fact that her family was going to leave her. The fact that she had fallen in love with what she thought was a dream and yet who turned out to actually be real and might now be dead.

The rage boiled up inside her as the bellows continued. If they wanted someone to die, she'd give it to them.

The naga king was almost within striking distance now. She could just lunge down at him, stab him through the chest, and then deal with all the rest.

Yes. That was clearly the best plan.

He slithered even closer.

Swallowing a scream, she lifted the spear and jumped.

14

IMAGINARY FRIENDS

Rhea launched herself off the ledge, aiming for the heart of the naga below.

Her stomach lurched up. The wind tore at her threaded brown trousers.

Elonumato save her, that hurt!

She yelped and nearly collapsed. Somehow, the spear twisted around. She jammed it into the stone butt first, gripping it as a support.

Dropping fifteen feet onto solid stone wasn't as easy as she'd thought. She nearly dropped the spear as she staggered, her legs aching as the force jarred through her entire body.

"You're going to die!" she shouted, struggling to straighten.

The naga king stared at her in shock, mouth agape, one clawed hand still lifted.

Shock rippled out amongst the crowd of monsters.

Good. That shock worked for her. She needed a minute.

Polph, her whole body ached!

And the stupid spear felt heavier now.

She wrenched the spear up and pointed it at his chest, the spearhead wavering. A spasm spiraled up her side.

Bowstrings zinged taut as the archers pointed their arrows at her.

Let them.

She could probably hit him faster than they could hit her. Presuming she could actually aim this thing. Why was spear-throwing feeling so much harder than she'd thought?

The naga king swung his hand toward the archers. "Stop!" he bellowed, his gaze fixed on her. "Everyone, out!"

Startled responses followed, spiking through the air with increased alarm.

She fell back a half step herself. What? Why was he saying such a thing?

"Your Majesty." A man of living flames stepped forward. Even his clothing appeared to be made of fire.

"Just go!" The naga's voice boomed as he gestured toward the door.

Rhea adjusted her grip, her breaths tight. Her whole arm trembled. She hurled the spear at him with all her strength.

It clattered on the stone floor, rolling a good seven feet away from him.

Polph! She wanted to scream, but she ran for the spear instead, half-expecting him to lunge for her.

He remained at the edge of the cliff, motioning for everyone to leave.

Stupid naga. What was he planning? What kind of idiot didn't pay attention to a full-grown adult grabbing a deadly weapon?

She kicked the spear and sent it rolling.

Oh, good grief!

Lunging down, she snagged it. Yes! She spun and prepared for her next attack. No more throwing this time.

The assembled monsters continued filing out of the room, some glancing back at her, others rumbling about what this was all about and the impropriety of the interruption.

"How did she even get in here?" one deep voice demanded.

"Is the portal working again?" a scratchy one asked.

"Hurry up!" the naga king bellowed. He turned to face her, his eyes white-rimmed.

She dropped her gaze at once to his chest, refusing to make eye contact. He wasn't going to get her that easily. Besides, those were going to be imitations of Chicory's eyes. Poor Chicory.

Rage flared within her as his image rose in her mind. How dare this monster wear his face! She clenched the spear tighter and moved to the side, putting a rocky pillar between her and the enormous naga. From this angle, it was far easier to assess him, and down here, well, he was huge! At least sixteen feet long with a fair bit of him hidden behind another rock, so it was hard to tell. Probably longer actually.

She ducked behind another pillar and braced herself. No more throwing. Only stabbing.

The heavy doors slammed shut, echoing through the great chamber. Now in the stillness, there was his breathing, her heartbeat, and an irregular hum that buzzed in her ears. Dripping water sounded off in the distance as well.

Thick scales slid across the stone floor.

Oh! She shuddered. That sound was horrifying. He was coming for her. Her palms sweat.

"We should talk." His deep voice echoed more in the cavernous chamber than before. "Salt-Sweet. Salt-Sweet, if you're real, please come out. You seem upset."

She gritted her teeth together. Seemed upset? And how dare he call her by that name!

She leaped out from behind the pillar. "Do not call me 'Salt-Sweet,' you pathetic predator!"

He was only a few feet away, and he instantly lifted his hands, palms facing her. "What do you want me to call you instead? It's the only name you gave me."

"My name is none of your concern. If you want me to spare you, tell me where Chicory is."

Not that she would spare him, but he seemed determined to trap her into thinking he was more harmless than he was. And if he gave her answers she could use, so be it.

"Salt-Sweet, I am Chicory." He gestured to himself.

"Liar!" She lunged at him, aiming for his chest.

He seized the spear before it even grazed his chest. His muscles tightened. "Salt-Sweet, listen to me. Maybe you didn't see me as I was—"

"Die!" She twisted around, dragging on the spear with all her strength. Her feet slid on the stone.

He held it fast, then pushed her away, sliding it out of her hands.

"No one uses this spear for combat. Did you raid the melee training armory? This is for very particular exercises." He tossed it up onto the ledge before looking back at her. The spear clattered as it settled easily in the cleft of the rocks above. "Salt-Sweet, look at me. Please. Don't you know me?"

She pulled the dagger from its sheath. "I know you're going to die because I'm going to kill you and set my family and Chicory free. All right, you big scaly monster?" She paused as she looked at the blade.

The dagger was dull!

What kind of armory had she been in? Who stocked dull daggers and over-weighted spears?

She jabbed it against his tail anyway.

"Hey!" He flinched, his tail tangling around her ankles and coiling up her legs as it spun her around.

Polph! She couldn't get free of that.

She started stabbing him faster, her hair whipping in front of her face. He cringed even though the blade didn't pierce.

"Stop that now!" he commanded, scowling.

His coils swept up around her faster now, gripping her tighter than manacles. The blunt dagger twisted free, caught in the slithering mass. She barely moved her arm out of the way.

"Let go!" she shrieked.

"You need to calm down before you hurt both of us," he said. "All I need is for you to listen."

Listening was for the dead. She swept her bag up, reached inside, and removed the vial of lemon juice. "If you want me to listen, let me go!"

"No, because you're just going to keep attacking. This seems to be rather shocking for you, Salt-Sweet, but—"

"I said don't call me that!" She twisted the lid off the vial of lemon juice and flung it in his eyes.

He yelped, then swore, his hands at once flying to his eyes.

Served him right. Monstrous sidewinding beast! She tried to wriggle free, but his coils remained tight around her. Too tight. They constricted as he shook his head and scrubbed at his eyes.

She pulled a nail file out of the bag next and started digging into his scales. "You will let me go, or I'll skin you alive!"

"Give me that!" He seized the bag out of her hands and then twisted the file out of her fist as well—but not before she stabbed him in the palm. "Salt-Sweet, I am Chicory."

Polph he was!

She started pounding on his coils as he brought her closer.

"Don't you dare disgrace his name. Get that name out of your mouth. I swear I'm going to kill you, you slimy, crooked-fanged asp spawn! Let go of me!"

IN NO WAY had Tengrii anticipated this turn to what had already started off as an alarming and challenging day. First, an assassination attempt and now?

Now, the gorgeous woman from his dreams was here to kill him too? How had this even happened?

If it weren't for the sparks of intense attraction flooding through him and the very real weight and pain of her body against him, he'd have guessed it was a dream. It was almost ludicrous enough to be precisely that.

She looked as she had the night before. Radiant. Practically glowing. But gone was the gentle companion who had whispered sweet words with gentle encouragement and gotten as close as she could. Instead, she glared at him with utter hatred and rage that seared her features.

But without doubt, this was her. He knew her voice as well as her form.

What he didn't know was how she had gotten in here.

She twisted and writhed as he tightened his length around her still further. Not that he could fully immobilize her with her arms free like that.

"You have to stop," he said sternly.

His scales could be sharp if someone moved against their grain, his strength hard to manage, and she looked alarmingly fragile despite how hard she fought.

"I will stop when you are dead."

This was—if she really thought he was dangerous, why

would she say that? It wouldn't even take that long to suffo-
cate her. All he had to do was tighten his coils when she
released her breath, and that would be it for her. She had to
hold her arms mostly up in the air to keep them out of his
coils while all the rest of her was bound. She couldn't even get
her head down to bite him. But still she sounded like she was
the one in charge of this situation.

"I do not want to hurt you," he said.

"Doesn't matter because I'm going to kill you. You hurt
people I love. You stole Chicory's face and his voice! I'll never
forgive you for that. If he's here, I'll find him. I'll find everyone
you've trapped, and I'm going to free them. Then I'm going to
make you suffer."

He set his jaw. Crespa, if she ever did get free and didn't
listen to sense, she might cause him serious problems.

He gripped her tighter. "Wait. Wait. You think I murdered
Chicory and stole his voice?"

"You are a naga. Of course you did."

"Salt-Sweet—"

"Do *not* call me that!"

He sighed, drawing his hand over his eyes. That was the
only name she had given, wasn't it? If another had been
offered, he couldn't remember it. Though he did remember
her insisting that she was not to be called 'Honey' or 'Sugar.'

"Well, I know not to call you Sweet alone. So what do I call
you instead?"

"You may call me Imminent Doom because that is what I
am to you."

This was not going well.

"All right. Fine. As you wish. But look at me." He paused as
she turned her head farther away. "Is there a reason you won't
look at me?"

"Everyone knows that nagas hypnotize their prey with

their eyes. I am not an idiot." She strained and twisted even farther away.

"I'm not a naga."

She almost looked at him, then scrunched her eyes shut. "You'll have to do better than that if you want to fool me. And if you have hidden Chicory, I will find him, and I will kill you. Actually, no matter what you do, I will be killing you. So you better kill me now because I will run you through or cut your throat or do whatever it takes."

It was hard to remember all that had happened within the dreams. He'd savored the moments and the feelings more than the actual words exchanged. In fact, he doubted he remembered even half of it. His dreams weren't the most clear, though some details had made it through. He massaged his temples. But she was certainly real, and pound for pound, she might be the angriest being he had ever encountered.

"Perhaps we could talk."

"Only if you die first."

He released a tight breath. She continued to writhe and struggle. She was close to bursting a vein. And if he squeezed her any tighter—she wasn't going to still any time soon.

"Fine." He took in the chamber around him, weighing his options.

He had to get her some place secure. Half his kingdom might want to kill her just because she was an outsider who had arrived without warning. The other half—well, it wasn't going to be good. Already, questions likely swirled about this strange woman if he knew his court and kingdom at all. All would know before night fell.

There was only one place to take her. Through one of the inner passages to his quarters. He could lock her in the study until he figured something else out. Crespa, it was just the other night he'd wished she was real and could be his wife.

Now, here she was, and he was going to have to bind and gag her. And not in a way she was going to like.

She continued to glare at his chest. Her brow was creased, and her eyes dark with rage. Something seemed off with them. She kicked about within his coils as well. "You loathsome venom-blooded toadstool, put me down!"

"It doesn't matter what you call me, but you're going to need to stop."

"Your mother was a sidewinder." Her nose scrunched. "And you smell like rotting mushrooms."

Hurtful. He resisted the urge to smell himself. It was probably the salve smeared into his shoulder from the morning's attack. Usually, it didn't take him so long to heal himself. But these days, everything took longer, and his former ally's blade had been coated with poison.

In his court's departure, someone had lost a blue sash. He picked it up, then tore it in half.

"I am not going to hurt you. I promise. I can explain everything if you just listen." He caught her wrists and then bound them. She continued to swear at him and tried to bite his hands. "Stop that!" he snapped, drawing his hands back before she could do any damage though her teeth still raked him. "Do I need to render you unconscious, woman?"

She spit on the stone floor and glared at him. "You taste bad. But you know what will taste worse?"

He pressed his lips. "What?"

"Death."

He really shouldn't have asked.

"I'm not going to kill you," he said.

"No! It's going to taste bad to you when I kill you." She scowled at him.

"If you cannot behave, I will have to tie you up. Can you be a reasonable person—"

She tried to bite his coils, but her teeth couldn't gain a grip. Her teeth clicked together with a sharp click, leaving his scales with an unpleasant though not painful sensation.

This time he swept in, gagged her, grabbed hold of her wrists, and tied them.

Her hazel eyes bugged with rage. She thrashed, kicking and pushing. One of his scales lifted enough to slice her arm twice.

Crespa. He tightened the bonds around her wrists and checked the wound. Not too deep fortunately. He then released her from his coils and picked her up. She still tried to flail, but he clasped her tight. Definitely not the way that this was supposed to go.

He hurried out through one of the side doors into the back passage.

Somehow, she got the gag free and spat it out. What followed was an utterly vicious tirade.

If anyone had any doubts about there being an intruder, they were now being treated to an echoing barrage of creative insults that proved she was an Awdawm with a penchant for name-calling and a hatred of anything remotely snake-like.

His guards and attendants started to appear in the hall, but he waved them off. Sometimes, he had to shout additional orders just to be heard over her infuriated deluge. The only mercy was that there weren't as many along the back passages as in the main ones where then everyone would be exposed to her tirades.

But still it felt like the slide of shame. Already, many of his people doubted his ability to control things, and now this exceptionally loud human was insulting him from the crown of his head to the tip of his tail with all sorts of bizarre suggestions and comparisons to other unpleasant creatures.

By all that lived and breathed, could she stop yelling at him? How did she have this sort of strength?

He reached the back outer door to his chambers, opened it, and continued to the inner door. Thank all that was good.

He navigated her into the smaller sitting room. "You're going to stay here, Salt-Sweet—"

"Don't you listen? Do not call me that, you pot-bellied liver-spotted lead muncher!"

"You're going to stay here until you calm down," he said louder this time.

He then adjusted the fabric on her wrists so she could get it off and flung her in. She struck the thick-cushioned settee and tipped back. Her slim booted feet kicked. He hesitated only half a breath to ensure she started to get up. Then he ducked back and slammed the ironwood door shut.

Her enraged screams followed him. "I'll destroy you for what you did to Chicory. To everyone! I will cut his face off your skull and feed you to the Rift!" Small direct pounds followed as if she thought she could beat her way out.

He pressed his hand to his forehead, blinking. Just how? And why? What sort of divine mockery was this? A miracle and a curse at once. The woman of his dreams he'd fantasized could be real actually was, and now she was here to murder him because he'd stolen his own face...crespa, what a horrid world.

15
FROM BAD TO WORSE

Tengrii swayed back and forth. The beating and shouting on the other side left no doubt about her feelings. She had to stop being so angry eventually, didn't she?

An insistent rap on the other door alerted him that his other responsibilities had come searching for him.

Elthko, his steward, and Yoto, his general, stood on the other side. Among his council, these were the two he relied upon most. The Rift and its toxic fog had changed both as well. Elthko had been broadened and distorted until he was trapped in the shape of a green-eyed dread howler with shaggy grey fur and heavy curled horns. Even his own family would not have known him if he had not been capable of speaking. Yoto had been straightened and lengthened to an abnormal height, his body seeming to be made of lava and flame. For now, he seemed more solid than usual, his expression masked in neutrality. Every time the Rift pulsed, the flame form became stronger for longer, almost breaking apart his limbs as if the mold that kept his shape was disintegrating.

One day, his form would shatter, and all that would be left was flames. Similar things had happened to so many others.

For now though, both appeared in control of their faculties and aware. How much longer until that was no longer the case? How much longer before he, too, lost his mind or fell forever into this cursed form?

Elthko cocked his head, his eyes narrowing. "Do you have a guest or a prisoner?"

"A guest," Tengrii said.

Something shattered on the other side of the door. Probably the vase his mother had made. And after it had survived months of earthquakes too.

"A hostile guest," he corrected. "She is not to be harmed."

"One might wonder where she came from," Elthko said, "especially considering the status of the Tue-Rah."

"I wonder," Yoto said. "I wonder how anyone got through at all. That incantation was supposedly irreversible. Or so the Daars claimed."

"No spell is irreversible," Tengrii responded. The words rang hollow though. He used to believe that. Now, though, hope was in short supply in general.

"What plans do you have for her?" Elthko asked.

"She is a friend—"

Something crashed in the room. Wooden from the sound of it.

"Putrid maggot rot! May you be skinned alive and impaled on tiny forks until you've paid for every drop of blood you've shed and every ounce of suffering you've caused!"

"Does she know this?" Yoto asked.

"She's just a little confused about my identity." He gestured for them to step back then pulled the door shut. Her infuriated shouts vanished. "Let's tend to the business at hand."

His steward and general did not require further encouragement on this point. The kingdom was falling apart by the day. Everyone had retreated to the palace, at least those who lived or remained conscious. All the rest had died, fled, or fallen into relentless comas.

Not much could be done aside from maintaining what little they had and searching endlessly for a cure. Feeding the Rift more of their energy had staved off any further expansion, and the demands for the instigators to be fed to it had returned with renewed vigor.

He was running out of ways to stop it. The affected young ones were hidden in lower parts of the dungeon to avoid anyone even attempting to drag them up and throw them in the Rift in some vain attempt to appease it. It had nearly happened twice already.

The Grand Council meeting would be held the following day. Even though there was nothing grand about what remained. Twice a week they gathered, and the results were always the same. No one even dared hope any longer. At best, they hoped nothing in the meeting would turn violent or that the disputes would be postponed to another day.

Pathetic. That was what they were. Pathetic with no hope in sight.

And Salt-Sweet's arrival would only complicate things.

Even if the Tue-Rah was working, they couldn't let anyone else come to this place. Opening up any portal would worsen the spread, and it would also expose them. Neither Elthko nor Yoto mentioned it, but Salt-Sweet was never going to be able to leave. Especially not when she was screaming for blood like that.

Crespa. Crespa. Crespa.

There was already more than enough to focus on. Plans to make and delegate. Situations to oversee. The new dungeon being cut out of black rock. The infirmary with the growing number of beds as night after night their numbers of the conscious and sane shrank. None of it good. None of it pleasant.

That didn't mean it didn't require his attention now. So he did as he had for over the past weeks. He handled what he could, made what small steps were possible for their future, and then left it behind after the mind-numbing hours spent working and meeting. The whole time, he had fought not to think of Salt-Sweet and whether she was all right down there. Whether she needed water or food. Whether she had hurt herself beating on the door.

In days past, he had returned to his chambers with the solace and hope of encountering his beautiful dream friend and finding comfort with her. Now, he knew he was going to see her. Just—his stomach clenched. Who knew what state she would be in?

Perhaps she would be calmer now. More willing to listen.

As he reached the inner hall of his chambers, the door behind to the outside cavern firmly shut, he dared to hope. His hand hovered over the handle. Please. Please. More than ever, he needed her.

Salt-Sweet couldn't have known how much she meant to him. How she had given him strength to find each day. He'd never told her. At least he was fairly certain he hadn't. It had been enough for him to hide in that pleasantly hazy sanctuary, curled up as close to her as possible, listening to that soft voice of hers talk about nothing at all. A few bits and pieces tended to stick with him but never the whole, and that had seemed fine.

But had he known she was real, he would have committed every word to memory. Somehow, he had to find a way to make her understand and find a way to keep her safe in this place.

He unlocked the door, then pressed it open.

The shouts were weaker now. Hoarse as if she'd strained her voice.

"You let me out! I'll find Chicory, and then I'll skin you."

She was still going. The dreams had never conveyed this side of her.

Of course, the dreams had also shown him as he had been. With legs and feet and no tail at all.

He paused. Maybe. Maybe there was another way to get her to listen.

He slipped to his wardrobe and removed a pair of boots. Then, using his tail, he shut the chamber door loud enough for her to hear. She went silent. He slid his hands into the boots and leaned over the ground, making the best approximation of footsteps as he got closer to the door.

More silence followed. She was listening.

Moving up next to the door, he tried to make his voice sound smaller and higher. Shifting wasn't really possible for him any longer. At least not at any grand scale, but something so small as this? It could work for a short time without putting him in too much danger. Even so, his throat itched with the constriction.

"Salt-Sweet, I know you're in there. Can you tell me what's going on?"

"Chicory?" Relief sounded in her voice. "Chicory, is that really you? Are you all right?" She stopped abruptly as if suspicious. "How do I know it's you and not someone pretending to be you?"

"Yes. It's really me. It's going to be all right."

"Are you going to get me out?"

"As soon as I find a way. But we need to talk while I do. We don't have much time."

What to say next? How could he convince her?

He set the boots down and scratched the top of his head. It wasn't as if he could just turn back into what he had been. Somehow, they were going to have to get over this hurdle of his naga-esque appearance.

"You're just going to have to trust me, Salt-Sweet. And you know me. You do."

A rustling sounded on the other side of the door. Something shifted and thudded a little. Her footsteps were almost too light to hear. "What did they do to you, Chicory? Are you hurt? Where were you?" Her voice was farther back in the room.

What was she doing? Uncomfortable suspicion rose within him. Maybe he didn't know her as well as he thought, but she didn't seem like the sort who was just going to acquiesce and go along with things. This was too easy. What even was in the back of the room that she might be able to use?

He placed his hand against the door. "It's all very complicated, Salt-Sweet. I had no idea you planned to come."

"How could I not when you were under attack?"

"I've been under attack quite a lot lately. Did you actually see or hear what happened? How did you know?"

"I heard a lot. I know that your kingdom was overrun by nagas, and they have done something that resulted in the fog or whatever it is you call it. And that it is trapping all of the psychic races into comas. Comas where they suffer."

He bowed his head. Crespa, yes, she had mentioned that in the dreams. But that, too, he had brushed aside as his own fears whispering louder. That meant that they truly had not contained this. This toxic fog was spilling out into the other worlds and bringing about grave harm. Elonumato help him.

157

"I'm so sorry, Salt-Sweet. Your friends, they have been harmed by it?"

"Yes. Almost to death." A strangled sob followed. "Oh, Chicory, I'm so glad you're all right. We'll get out of here, and then we can stop it. You'll help me stop it, won't you?"

"I want nothing more than to stop this plague or curse or whatever it is. I swear that to you, Salt-Sweet. I will do all that I can. The people here are getting desperate too. Those of us who remain, at least. The assassination attempt this morning was one of my counselors and scholars. We need to talk about why this has happened. It may be hard to hear."

Something scraped beneath the doorway. Oh, crespa. The little flash of the mirror was probably just enough. Had she pulled that off his wall? How had she managed that in the little time she had?

Before he could even pull away, an angry screech pierced his ears. "You liar! You horrible, horrible liar. May your bones be turned to mush and your heart to rot and—"

"Salt-Sweet, it really is me. I know you're confused. So am I. But I can explain."

"What is there to explain? You were protecting that rift and the attacks that come from it."

"No, I am not. I swear that I am not. And I'm not actually a naga."

"You look like a naga. You sound like my friend because you stole his voice like a naga. And his face, you repulsive slimy pustule! You slither like a naga. You talk like a naga because you're full of lies—"

"Where did you get all this knowledge about nagas? They're mythical!" He rested his hands on the top of his head. Myths and stories that had haunted his nightmares for years as a child. "Nagas aren't real."

"Really? Says the naga."

Crespa, she bit those words out like they had actual venom.

He tilted his head back as he leaned against the door. "This isn't my true form. It is a curse. A disease. It changed some of us into what we fear, and to others—it made them so many things. There isn't time for all that. But I swear to you I am Chicory..." It felt wrong to not call her something. "Salty."

"Salty?" she spluttered. "I will pry the fangs out of your skull and cut you with them."

"Fine then. Tell me what I should actually call you if these names are so offensive."

"You can call me—"

"If you make it a threat, I won't call you that. But you know my voice. You do. You know me. And I am sorry that I am such a disappointment to you and so repugnant. In dreams, I am who I was. I've been fighting to make my way back. But it's been almost as impossible as waking the sleepers."

A heavy pause followed. Her voice sounded closer to the door. As if she might be directly at the seam. "If you aren't a naga, what are you?"

"I'm—" He lifted his arm, then dropped it to his side. What did it even matter? "I might as well just be human. You can consider me an Awdawm."

"Consider you an Awdawm," she muttered on the other side, her voice moving back. "As if I don't know what my own people look like, you trolling liar. You are distinctly not. Now, if you want me to listen to anything you have to say, what did you do with Chicory? I want to talk with Chicory. The real one!"

"I am he."

Silence followed.

"Stop saying that." Her voice had gone ragged, even

hoarser now than before. "I know that you've done something horrible to him. Did you kill him, you monster? You won't fool me. Just because you have magic that lets you take his voice and face doesn't mean I can be fooled. I came here to save him and my family. You can't stop me! You won't keep him from me!"

Her words at once pierced and comforted him. It was a torment. She had come here for him?

He placed his hand on the door. If only she could understand.

"Chicory isn't dead. I promise you that."

"Then what did you do to him? Why did you stab him? Why did you steal his face?"

Was there a lie he could whisper that might reach her? Some way to wrap the truth up so that she could accept it or at least be still enough to hear him? Really truly hear him?

Besides, he didn't have much time. He needed to get this resolved so that he could return to the matter of the Rift. But he couldn't pull himself away. The thought that she hated him and wanted to kill him—it devoured his focus.

That she should be real was a miracle. That she should hate him and not understand who he was? That was a curse.

He pressed his hand against the wall, tugging at his hair as he fought through the possibilities.

They had spoken. And often. When he slept. But not always. Sometimes, he had slept, and she wasn't there. She had never found him in the space of his mind when he had been awake, so perhaps she had been sleeping as well. Their dream conversations had all been real.

But...he halted. It could go poorly for him, but it wasn't as if there was much he could do to make this worse. He just needed to make her sleep. If she slept and then he slept, they could talk the way they once had.

Sleep had been difficult to find. He'd burned the sleeping mushrooms and soft-leafed herbs to find his own rest. They were harmless but effective. He removed them from the drawer, placed them in the bowl, and set them alight. Carefully, he directed the thick curls of smoke under the door.

"What are you doing?" she exclaimed. "Are you drugging me?"

Yes. He pulled one of the sitting cushions over and placed it next to the door. "It's going to be all right, Salt-Sweet. I promise. I'll find a way to make it all right. You'll see."

He breathed it in as well. As he had been using this combination for weeks now, it would not keep him under as long. But it would be long enough...at least, he hoped it would.

16

DREAMS

The woodsy pleasant scent filled her nostrils. Rhea shouted out her alarm before the room started to swirl. The naga's voice boomed in her ears, distorting into strange sounds that had no meaning. Fuzzy dots spread over her vision as she dropped to her knees, then hit the cushions. The turquoise fabric pushed against her cheek as she tried to push herself up.

No. No, she wasn't going to sleep.

What—what was going to happen to her if she did?

Everything blinked into darkness.

A pleasant fog descended over her. Warmth as well as bliss.

Oh.

What had happened?

She breathed out.

What had she been doing?

The tightness in her chest loosened, though a rawness permeated her throat as if she had been screaming. Light blossomed around her. She sat on the edge of Chicory's bed, one knee drawn to her chest. Whatever she had been bothered about, it had been important.

She was wearing the same clothes—the loose brown trousers with the open stitching up the sides and her soft butter-yellow tunic. That felt right. Even if she was barefoot. She shouldn't have been barefoot. And there was a bag...she should have had a bag too, the one she carried her drawings in when making deliveries to Dohahtee.

"Salt-Sweet!" a familiar voice exclaimed from behind her.

She turned. Her heart leaped.

Chicory!

He crossed over to her, running around the bed rather than remaining on it. Before she could even say his name, he swept her into his arms.

Gasping, she grabbed hold of him. He felt real. She almost burst into tears as she held him close. His heart beat against hers. She'd been looking for him. Yes, that was part of her alarm. Something had been wrong. Yes! The last time she had been here, someone had wanted to kill him. Images flashed back into her mind, too distorted to recognize.

"You're all right? You're safe?"

"Yes." He buried his face in her hair. "Oh, Salt-Sweet."

His voice sent shivers through her body. Her fingers curled against the back of his neck, tangling in his hair.

"I was so worried about you," she whispered. "I was trying to find you. I saw him stab you. That naga." She pulled back enough to see his shoulder. There wasn't a wound there. Not anymore. Just a dark mark where the blade might have pierced. Something like a scar.

"That was one of my council members," he said, his arms dropping to her waist. "He disagreed with how I was handling matters. Not an invading force though he would have killed me if he could. But, Salt-Sweet, please." He tilted his head, his beautiful eyes rich with emotion. He pressed his thumb beneath her chin. "I need you to listen to me."

"I'm listening. I'm actually around where you were. I'm in some kind of underground dungeon or something. If you tell me where you are, I'll break out and come find you."

A smile pulled up on the corner of his mouth. "I can't believe you found a way. I would never have asked it of you. This place is far too dangerous. But not because of nagas."

She laughed sharply, shaking her head. "Have you seen what all is here? There's one wearing your face. He had a whole horde of monsters with him. He's got me locked up in this place. Are you in the dungeons?"

A muscle jumped in his jaw. "I need to say something to you that is going to be hard for you to hear, but I need you to keep an open mind." He clasped her hands between his. They were strong, calloused and scarred along the pads of his fingers. "First, tell me, what is your name?"

She tilted her head. Her body tightened. "You said it wasn't safe to share our real names in dreams."

"I didn't know if you were real before. Now I do. My name is Tengrii. What's yours?"

For days, she had wanted to know his name. Wondered about it and the significance it held. Her gut clenched though. She bit the inside of her lip. Why was he suddenly so willing? If names held power, how was her being real suddenly the resolution to the issue?

She stepped back from him. "What do you need me to keep an open mind about?"

"What should I call you?"

"Impatient." She kept her hand up and tugged free. "Something has gone wrong. Something's gone very wrong. I may just be an artist and a human, but I'm not an idiot."

"Fine. Don't tell me your name. We can have that conversation when we're both awake, all right?" He lifted his hands as well, his brow creasing. "I know you're here, Salt-Sweet. I know exactly where you're at."

"You do?" She raised an eyebrow.

"And I know—I know you came to rescue me."

She nodded slowly, crossing her arms. What was going on? He didn't sound right. Was she seeing him? Really seeing him? Was this really him? How would she even know?

Other things had happened too. What were they?

She squinted at him. "I did. What's wrong with you? Where are you then?" Her gaze dropped to the mark on his shoulder. The naga king had had one there too. It was much more like that than what a spear impalement would look like. "What are you really?"

"I am..." His expression contorted, his voice halting. His face flushed to a green-blue shade.

"What are you really!" she demanded. "Show me what you really look like!"

"This—I don't know why this is happening," he cried out.

Distress distorted his features. But it was worse than that. He changed—changed into what he really was. His skin turned blue-green, his body broadened and lengthened, his hair grew longer, and his trousers and legs turned into a long tail that almost reached the other end of the room. Sharp scales formed on his shoulders, bristling with the emotion. He held up his hands.

"No!" he shouted. His voice deepened and slowed. "No, Salt-Sweet. This—" He gestured toward his body, his claws glinting in the low light. "This isn't who I am. It changed my form but not me."

Her awareness returned. Memories. The smoke. The drugs.

Monster!

She jerked even farther away, seizing a pillow. "You tried to fool me. Again! What have you done with him? This is low even for a snake! Why are you tormenting me? Get away!" She hurled the pillow at him.

"I don't know how to convince you." He lifted his hand to shield his face. The pillow glanced off him harmlessly. "It's me. I am Tengrii! Your Chicory!"

"Get away from me. I never want to see you again!" She jumped up onto the bed and grabbed another pillow. "You're a monster!" She slammed him in the head with it as he started to reach for her. "You killed him, and you're killing my family! How dare you even exist!"

She flung another pillow at him and leaped away. The floor vanished, and she found herself spinning into darkness. A ragged sob strangled her. How was she supposed to get out of this place? How could she make any of this right when she couldn't kill even one wretched naga!

TENGRII JOLTED AWAKE. His gut ached with hollow pain. Oh. That had been such a bad choice.

His head ached. What time even was it? He pressed himself up from the cushion, one hand on the cold stone. The water clock on the far corner of the room indicated it was within the early morning hours.

Time had passed so much faster within the dream.

Another day already. Crespa. He held his head for a moment. The dull pounding showed no signs of fading any time soon.

She'd probably be unconscious for another four or five hours at least. The first time he had taken the herbal compound, it had left him sleeping nearly ten hours without stirring. But that gave him a bit of time to try—in some small way—to make matters right.

Opening the door to the little study, he found her collapsed on one of the cushions, snoring. The entire room was in shambles, the bookshelves taken apart, the furniture upended, the drawers turned out. Everything except the books. Those had all been stacked neatly in the corner.

He righted the settee, grounded it back into place so that it wouldn't move with the earthquakes, and set the cushions in place. Then, he picked her up and laid her on it. After checking to ensure that the purple and blue woven blanket had no glass or pottery shards in it, he swept it over her, tucking her in. His hands lingered on her shoulders.

She really was beautiful. Her honey-brown hair curled around her shoulders, tangled around the layered dark leather necklace. She was so much more than he had ever expected. Even with her brow still creased as if she were caught in a nightmare. Perhaps she was. Perhaps she dreamed about him even now. Who he had turned out to be. Who she feared he was. Who he feared he was.

He started to press a strand of her hair back from her cheek, then stopped, seeing his own claws. He recoiled, his shoulders tightening.

No wonder she wanted to kill him. And she hadn't seen him at his truly worst yet.

His eyelids slid shut. The Rift would open and pulse more of that toxic nightmare fuel out. And nothing would work—they had nothing. He pressed his hand to his forehead. How much worse could it get?

Salt-Sweet was here now. Salt-Sweet was an Awdawm. Awdawms weren't affected, but they were vulnerable. Especially when people like him went mad.

His gut twisted. He'd avoided it thus far. Clung to his sanity even as that horrifying energy flooded through him and filled his mind with all the worst of his fears and terrors. He'd fought back the worst of this form as well. Struggled to reclaim his humanity. It wasn't a certainty that permanent madness would come.

But if—no. He released a deep breath. He would not let these torments claim his thoughts. Everything had a solution.

They would find something. Somehow. He'd find a safe place for her before then. And some way to explain this.

A soft rap sounded on the outer door. He didn't go to it at once. He knew the sound. They were bringing his breakfast.

Not that he had much of an appetite.

He went to the door after a few minutes and retrieved the tray. Word had gotten around. There were two full servings for breakfast. He would need to thank Dulce again. Almost losing her form had not kept her from maintaining some sense of compassion and striving to create normalcy. Today's breakfast was salted fish with mushroom bread and fresh water.

As he brought the trays in, another idea occurred to him.

Salt-Sweet had told him about breakfasts. How sometimes, after a frightening night or bad dreams, her brother Chickadee or her sister Tapir would make smiley faces on the breakfast meal.

He didn't have fruit to make smiles. Just toasted mushroom bread and salted fish. So he took the knife and cut a smiling face in each slice of the bread. Not the most appealing, perhaps. But something.

Something had to reach her.

The thought of her not knowing him—no—she would. Eventually. There had to be some way. Had to be.

After losing every other member of his family and almost

every friend, he couldn't—wouldn't lose the one person who had made his life bearable.

But maybe he wouldn't drug her again.

He set the small octagonal table back up and placed the breakfast offering on it. He then swept up the shards of pottery and righted a few other pieces within the room. Still, she rested. It wasn't all set to rights, but there was no more time for anything else. His council needed him.

Leaning down over her, he brushed his lips over her forehead. "Please, know who I am when you wake, Salt-Sweet," he whispered. "I don't know how to explain this. It is as much a nightmare for me as for you. But I am still the friend you knew just as you are mine."

A tear leaked from each eye and rolled down his cheeks.

Please, Salt-Sweet. Please.

17

SET UP

The warmth did not leave Rhea as she stirred.

No.

It didn't smell quite right though. Certainly not like home.

Something soft tickled her chin.

Slowly, she opened her eyes. An unfamiliar stone ceiling greeted her. And a large soft blanket had been wrapped around her, her feet snugly tucked in. This was the little room the naga king had trapped her in.

Had he cleaned this place up and tucked her in?

She had unfastened and turned over every bit of furniture in this room she could and even disassembled the shelves. But there they were, all put back together. Even the little mirror had been hung up on the wall again. And the octagonal table had its drawers once more. On it sat a tray with—toast.

With smiley faces.

Her stomach knotted. Emotion choked her.

Carefully, she picked up the plate, staring down at the mangled bread. One of the two smiles was rather distorted, seeming far more like a grimace. Could the naga have over-heard that from her dream talk with Chicory?

The myths hadn't mentioned that exactly. Nagas could wear the face. Use the voice. Mimic to a degree. They might know some things from an intensive interrogation. But why would Chicory have told a naga about breakfast? Why would a naga have even wanted that information?

A small smile tugged at her mouth. She'd told Chicory about this more than once. He'd joked that one day perhaps she'd do the same for him because he dreaded mornings so much. She understood that. It was hard to get up when you knew that the day would close out with something as horrible as the psychic attacks and the torment of your family. But that didn't stop the day from starting.

Could it be?

Her stomach continued to twist. The dream trickled back into her mind. The utter sorrow in his eyes. The way that the transformation had torn through him. Similar to when Vawtrians shifted but slower and more violent, distorting him as if he fought it with every breath.

But she'd seen that naga stab Chicory in his bed. And there had been the naga defending the strange rift. They were the same, weren't they?

She pushed the table away. Her head hurt.

Standing, she combed her fingers through her hair. There had to be an answer.

The mythology books hadn't addressed this. What were the limits of naga magic?

She turned back toward the toast. If she trusted her gut, then there was no way that a naga king would worry about finding out such a small detail. But if her gut was right about that, then—

Footsteps sounded outside the door.

She froze.

The lock turned, then the door scraped open.

Instead of the naga king in all his imposing glory, a hooded figure stood there, a bronze-tipped spear with a wooden shaft in hand. "You were sent to us in our time of need," the hooded figure said, their voice rasping and so quiet she had to strain to hear. "Come and fulfill the destiny for which you were sent." They offered her the spear. "Our world needs you."

"Who are you?" She remained where she was, not entirely certain she trusted this newcomer. This seemed a little too convenient.

"Someone who has people trapped and in danger. Just like you. This curse has gone on too long. It must be ended. Now hurry." They shook the spear as if she should just accept this. "You must be swift. The Rift will pulse again tomorrow, and we may not be able to withstand it."

She frowned. Between the gloved hand and the sleeve, she glimpsed something of what might have been an arm though it seemed largely translucent. Almost like ice. The way this stranger spoke about the rift though made it seem like an actual location. As if that was in fact its real name.

"Do you know Chicory? I came here to find him too." She stepped closer.

"I know no one of that name," the hooded figure said. "But there are many—hundreds now—who are captured, held captive in dungeons. This naga king seeks to expand those rather than do what little is needed to stop our torment. Handle the naga king, and we will happily aid you in finding your Chicory."

"And this naga king—"

"Tengrii," they said softly, the name practically a growl.

Her chest tightened. He'd given that name in the dream

this last time. That wasn't the name that Chicory had called his attacker though. So why the change? Perhaps to fool her? To make her believe he was her beloved Chicory? How cruel was he! And he had seemed so sincere. If she had not known how treacherous nagas were, she would have believed him.

"Tengrii is the naga king. And he is—"

"He is evil," the hooded figure whispered, offering her the spear once more. "He would let us all die rather than pay the price to close the Rift. He does not suffer as we do, but all of the worlds will die because of him, including your beloved."

"What price does the Rift require?" she asked. The spear's shaft was far easier to grip, its weight much more manageable than the last one. It actually did feel good. "What does the Rift want?"

"My companions and I will see to that. You deal with the naga king."

"And then my family and Chicory will be safe?"

"Everyone will be safe once he is dealt with. You are the answer to our prayers and the end to this curse. Just do your part. You will find him in the council chambers here." The figure sketched out a map on the stone wall with chalk. "This is the way you should take."

Rhea committed it to memory. "Do I need to watch for guards?"

"Stay low. Don't draw attention to yourself. If you take these passages, you won't be seen. There aren't enough of us any longer to maintain fully effective watches. We are nothing compared to what we once were. Tengrii and those who follow him desire only our destruction in the maw of the Rift.

"Another attack will drive him into this room. Be there waiting for him. Strike fast and true. All of the worlds are counting on you. We will see to the rest."

She adjusted her grip on the spear. It fit easily in her hand,

and it even had marks that made it easier to position her fingers. What was on the blade, though? It glistened.

"What's on it?" she asked.

When she looked up, the hooded figure had disappeared.

Her heart beat faster. There was her answer. Both what she should do and whether she could trust him. She'd been given a weapon and a way. Her family now needed her to do this.

She glanced back at the wall. She'd come to this place to kill the naga king. That was what she would do.

As she stepped out of the room, she glanced back once more at the toast, dull brown and cut with jagged smiles next to the salted fish.

Her stomach tightened.

It was nothing. Perhaps Chicory had mentioned it in his sleep. Perhaps there was naga magic that allowed them to see such things. There was some other explanation. For now, she had a chance to do what she had come to do, and she needed to do it fast.

Tengrii sat at the head of the stone council table. The day's meeting had already dragged on for three hours, and the end was nowhere in sight. Mostly because they had no other answers. He would have rather stayed with Salt-Sweet, even in her current condition.

Raimu stood at the far end, his face knotted with emotion. "We have exhausted all other options. We can pour no more of our energy into the Rift. It no longer does anything. Bring out all involved with opening the Rift. Let us see if giving them to it works."

"No," Tengrii growled. "Not while I rule. Blood sacrifices and sentient sacrifices alike have no place here!"

"But what are we to do?"

"We keep searching. There is another answer."

"What if there isn't?" Jaiku, one of the few remaining original nobles and founders, demanded. He had been turned into some spider creature though his face and most of his upper body remained the same. He gestured with four limbs toward the wall as if the Rift was just on the other side. "It expands every third day. The energy it puts out is greater and greater. We have done everything we can to reverse it. Now we know that it is not isolated to our world. It is spreading and contaminating the others. Almost all our psychics have died or been trapped in comas. And look at us!"

Tengrii did. Not that he had to. He had watched the impacts of this curse multiply over these past days.

Some could not even bear to be in one another's presence any longer. Jaiku's wife and Todric had turned almost entirely to stone and could scarcely move. The next few phases were likely to trap them in those forms forever, suffocating them or starving them, depending on how strong the pulse from the Rift was. Yoto's and Dulce's forms had weakened so much they could no longer risk being near one another. None of the elementalists could risk being near one another for long in case temperature surges weakened their bodies more and led them to disintegrate. Elthko fought more and more to maintain his sanity during the Rift's pulsing as all the trapped shifters did. Jaiku likely struggled just as much though he refused to admit it.

Not to mention all those who broke, the ones who lost their minds when the Rift wasn't pulsing and gave in to their bestial forms, becoming the very worst of what they feared.

Two days ago, young Seyn was killed in such an attack. How many had already died?

His claws raked across the table as he clenched his fist. These were good people. All of them. Good people driven mad. Their voices droned in his ears.

"Gao," he said, addressing the last of the scientists and physicians still capable of appearing at the council sessions. "Is there nothing else?"

"We have been able to trap even more of the substance from the Rift. When bottled, it retains its potency rather than diminishing." The once slender woman had been transformed into some tentacled abomination with six eyes and over a dozen limbs. The cobalt sash she wore around her middle was the only garment of clothing she had been able to manage. "But further exposure to it only worsens symptoms and in some cases induces madness faster."

That wasn't new. They'd been doing that for over a week.

"And what else have you discovered with it?"

"Nothing," she responded softly.

He picked up his goblet of wine and took a long drink. The bitter liquid filled his mouth. It was little more than vinegar, and it did nothing aside soothe the dryness in his throat.

"We cannot close the Rift with our energy or shared blood. We cannot free any additional resources," Jaiku said, "unless you want to throw our new visitor into the Rift and see what happens."

"No one is to be thrown into the Rift," he growled. His claws clenched so tight against his palm they sliced his flesh. "How much clearer can I make that?"

Angry murmurs broke out from more than half the table. The respect afforded to a king had all but vanished, and it would only get worse in the coming days.

"Silence," Yoto snarled. The flames over his body intensified.

Those near him drew back. More than once, he had set things on fire. Even a chair that was simply close to him.

The heat in the room rose as he moved back against the wall and raised his voice. "We gain nothing through fighting amongst ourselves."

"But we are running out of time. How much longer can we endure through this?"

More voices rose in agreement.

Not again.

His throat tightened, and his tongue thickened.

Crespa, these fools!

Over the past weeks, these assassination attempts had become more frequent. It was the fourth time someone had tried to poison him. He even had the antidote for this poison in his sash.

He struck his fist against the table and gestured for Elthko to take over. Elthko's shaggy eyebrows lifted, the glowing in his green eyes intensifying, but he nodded.

Yes. It had happened again.

Tengrii grabbed the waterskin and then slithered to the door at the end of the room.

Yoto struck his fist against the wall. "All will continue with their assigned tasks. There is nothing left to discuss. We do not sacrifice the young adventurers or the new guest, nor will we discuss it further."

Elthko would affirm that in quieter and more detailed terms, but the message would remain the same.

Tengrii pressed the door open. Perhaps he should thank his would-be assassin for this. It had cut the meeting short by a couple hours and saved him the time and frustration it usually brought. The only price was a headache, dry mouth, disorientation, and a limited risk. What a bargain.

As soon as he was secure in the hall, he took the antidote and washed it down with several mouthfuls of water. There had been a time when assassination attempts were a matter of great concern. Back when all this was relatively new.

He almost laughed as he stared into the darkness of the passage before him. Oh, for those days. The days before the Tue-Rah's formation began and the Rift opened. He closed his eyes. His parents would be ashamed to see the fate that had befallen this kingdom. All of its beautiful levels and layers, all condensed. Most of the other structures abandoned. Cut off from the outside world in all directions. The embodiment of connection trapped beneath a miserable oozing substance that expanded. Insanity that threatened everything. And tremors through the earth itself.

And now, poor Salt-Sweet had come to join him in this miserable fate.

It was almost fitting. He had let his thoughts drift sometimes to the possibilities of a life with her. Wondered if it was the transformative nature of these attacks that had altered him enough that he had actually joined with a dream woman or a sign he could never be with anyone. It was hard to tell.

Yet here she was, and all he could offer her was fear and oncoming death in a dark cavernous world.

A small laugh rose within him. She hadn't come to join him. She'd come to rescue him and also to kill him. By all that was holy, how had this ever happened? It was as much an abomination as what had happened to all the rest of his people. Not one of them—not even among the worst— deserved it either.

Soft footsteps caught his attention. A distinct but odd scent as well. He turned.

His heart leaped, then dropped.

There she was.

Carrying another spear.

That acrid scent came from the spearhead. Someone had poisoned it. Had she just found that on her own? Did she understand what it was? What he was? Did she know she had as much risk of killing herself with it as him, the poison on that blade was that deadly?

He lifted his hand slowly. "You do not understand—"

"I understand enough," she said tightly. But her face was pale and her body taut.

If he knew anything about her, she did not actually want to do this. Something had changed within her. She wasn't as sure as she had been before. But whatever transformation had started, it wasn't enough.

"They told me what you are doing here, and I have seen what you've done to my family. To so many people. So I am here to kill you, Tengrii Naga King. Even if it takes my own life as well."

18

CONFRONTED

The spear stopped feeling quite so good, even though she wasn't sure why or how. After all, it was actually intended for battle, and something had been smeared along the blade that suggested it had been made toxic in some way. This was what she needed.

All she had to do was drive this spear through his heart. And if it was poisoned, it wouldn't even take that much. The sharp tip would pierce beneath his scales.

So why did it feel so wrong?

She made her way down the passage. As the hooded figure had told her, this section was all but abandoned. There was no one in sight. Not even footsteps. Whatever sounds of life existed in this place sounded far away, the great emptiness far stronger and interrupted only by dripping water and the occasional groaning of rocks.

Rounding the corner, she glimpsed the naga king's tail before him. Stark turquoise against the dark rocks. He stood, hand over his eyes and waterskin in the other hand. The color had faded in his face and neck, his breathing more ragged.

This didn't look like a terrifying warrior. Weariness hung on him, dragging his head down. Grief, too, perhaps?

She stepped out farther, gripping the spear tighter.

If she hadn't read all she had about nagas and if it hadn't been for the hooded figure, she would have asked him what was wrong. Probably even asked if he would like tea. If she didn't, Tiehro would. But the lore—it hadn't said anything about them faking tears as a way to gain sympathy. And even if they had, why would he be waiting in this place?

He turned then, facing her as he dropped his hand. Emotion flashed in his eyes. Surprise. Hope. Sorrow. His brow creased.

Her breath shortened, and she averted her gaze. Those eyes were familiar. He'd come so close to mastering them. If she looked deeper, she'd see how they were different from Chicory's but also risk being hypnotized.

His scales clicked lightly over the stone. "You do not understand—"

Her heart clenched. She forced her own breath out, steadying herself. "I understand enough. They told me what you are doing here, and I have seen what you've done to my family. To so many people. So I am here to kill you, Tengrii Naga King. Even if it takes my own life as well."

It might even be easier if it took her life. And if it ended this?

She swallowed hard. A sick feeling spread within her stomach. Where was all the rage and steel she'd felt yesterday? She adjusted her grip on the spear and watched him while avoiding his eyes.

He shook his head. "I will not harm you."

"That makes this easy then."

It didn't.

She lifted her chin. Her hands shook. "I mean it though. I will kill you."

He shrugged. "Do it then."

"You want me to kill you now?"

"I want you to get it over with if you think that this is the only way."

She lunged at him. He coiled back, moving out of her range easily. He could have struck her, but he didn't.

She drew the spear back, her knuckles whitening around the wooden shaft. This was necessary. She had to do this. He was the one keeping the Rift open. He was the reason so many were dying.

Except—was he?

That hooded figure had told her this. And the dream connection had shown the naga. But was this the naga that had stabbed Chicory? Was it a coincidence he had a marking in the same place on his shoulder where the attacking naga had stabbed him? And that he knew about toast with smiles? And Chicory had called out that naga's name. It wasn't Tengrii. It was— "If you are Chicory, then you were attacked in your bed. Who was it who attacked you?" She started to pace out, forming a circle.

"Steltro. A friend and council member driven mad." He matched her movements, arms still spread. The space between them remained steady. "Fear and hopelessness have struck my people hard. It has destroyed much of what we were."

"So he tried to kill you? Why?"

"Because I will not let them sacrifice anyone into the Rift. And that is the only thing that anyone here can think to do to stop this horror from continuing."

She stabbed at him. He pulled back once more. The blade struck the stones. It jarred in her hands.

He wasn't calling for help. Even if he didn't want to kill her, why wasn't he doing something except dodging her attacks?

She pulled back, gritting her teeth. The sick feeling in her stomach intensified. She wanted to throw up. "If I have to kill you, I will kill you," she said tightly. "I will kill you to save my family and everyone else. Because—because you are a monster."

"This has been a torment for all of us. I am only trapped in this shape because it is what I fear. So will you kill me? Really?" He brushed the back of his knuckle against his cheek as he lifted his shoulders.

She froze, her gaze fastened on his hand. Chicory was the only person she'd ever known to tap his cheek like that when he was concerned or troubled. She lowered the spear.

Tengrii lunged forward. He grabbed the spearhead and placed it just above his heart, the other hand clasping the back of her head. "If you think I am such a monster, then go ahead and strike me down. My heart is pierced and broken because you do not know me. And if you cannot see me through all this, then—" He shook his head. "You were my comfort in dark nights and long solitude, Salt-Sweet. The one I thought who understood my heart. If you do not—if you cannot see me—then run me through. It would be kinder. And who knows? Perhaps in some unforeseen way, it will end this curse, though I cannot imagine how."

He sounded so much like Chicory, and the way he'd touched his face just then... What kind of naga would have known to mimic that?

She dared to glance up. Her heart raced faster.

Those eyes.

They were...

Her breath caught in her throat. His eyes were larger now,

but they were unmistakable. It wasn't hypnosis that rooted her in place. It was recognition. Somehow, it all settled into place.

She tried to say his name, but tears filled her eyes. Emotion knotted in her throat. How? How was this possible? "You?"

"Are you going to kill me, Salt-Sweet?" he whispered. His fingers caressed the back of her head, tangling lightly in her hair.

She met his gaze. Her heart melted, heat pooling in her core. Drawing the spear back, she continued to stare. It was him. Not with a stolen face or forged voice. Really truly him.

"No," she whispered.

He leaned closer, the length of his fingers pressing against her scalp. "I am glad."

She swallowed hard. "But..." Her mouth went dry. "I came here—I came here to save my family. And you. I don't understand what's going on. I don't know what to do. If you are Chicory—are you the cause of all this? If I saw you—"

"I did not cause this. I am simply trying to find a way to stop it before it destroys everyone. I had no idea that it had actually spilled out into the other worlds, but I do not know what else to do." His gaze searched her face. A small smile pulled at his full lips. "But I didn't know you were real before yesterday. Now, anything feels possible."

What were they going to do, though? This solved nothing.

His tongue moistened his lips, his hand not moving from the back of her head. "I can't blame you for being afraid of me in this shape. The truth is that I have been fighting to reclaim my true form this entire time," he said. "I used to be significantly more monstrous. At best, all I can do is modify it."

She scanned him up and down as best she could from this angle. That could easily be true. When it came right down to it, he wasn't entirely terrifying as he might have been, even if she was afraid of snakes and nagas. Especially not when he smiled. There was a warmth in those eyes. They'd been a weakness for her from the start.

"So you were...scarier?"

"Big cowl. Heavier brow. Huge fangs. Shoulder scale spikes. Vertical pupils." He twitched his broad shoulders, gaze still fixed on her. The heat intensified between them. Aside from the claws, his hand felt like a man's against the nape of her neck.

"So are you—does that mean you're a shapeshifter?"

He smiled. "You know, you have asked me many questions, and I have tolerated them. I'm even happy to answer most of them. But I have some of my own, Salt-Sweet."

"Fair enough." She released a tight breath. "What do you want to know?"

"Why did you come here?"

"I told you—"

"Yes, but when you attacked me, you weren't shouting about Salanca or Tiehro or all of the psychic races. You were shouting something else."

Her cheeks heated, probably turning scarlet as well. Traitors. She tossed the spear aside and set her hands on her waist though she did not move away from him. "Well, it didn't look like you were wearing their faces."

"You leaped from a ledge that was almost fifteen feet off the ground and tried to stab me through the heart with a weighted training spear, demanding I return Chicory to you."

"It sounds like you have your own theories about why I did what I did. So why don't you enlighten me, Chicory."

She steeled her expression before looking back into his face. So much of him had changed, but those eyes hadn't. Not just their deep-green with black and hints of gold and indigo. But that quiet contemplation that took in everything.

He pulled back though when she called him Chicory. His smile broadened. "That's the first time you've called me that since you came here."

"Is there a reason I shouldn't?"

"Does this mean I can call you Salt-Sweet again?"

She tried to roll her eyes and huff at him. But it turned into a little *mmmph* sound as she muttered, "Fine."

"You are much saltier than I thought you would be." He was still smiling. As if she hadn't just tried to run him through with a spear. His thumb stroked near her ear.

"You didn't think I was real."

"True. But I should have known. I have never been especially creative. It is unimaginable that I could have created someone so perfect as you."

"Perfect," she scoffed, dropping her gaze again. She had never felt so embarrassed in all her life. But that wasn't all she was feeling. It was complicated now. "Again. Tried to kill you. Failed horribly. Screamed in your face. Your definition of perfect is bad."

"Well, had you only jumped ten feet off the ledge, you would have a point. I refuse to have anything to do with a woman who can't handle *at least* a fifteen-foot drop. But in truth, I admire your intensity and your passion. And those nights when we spoke, even when it was about nothing, you helped me keep from breaking."

She swallowed hard. He'd helped her too, even when they talked about nothing. He'd brought her so much comfort.

"I—it was hard. I was so scared, but you were always the bright point. I knew that if I could get to the point when I could rest, I could see you. More importantly, hear you."

And she'd hoped—hoped so much that he was real.

Prayed for him to be real. Hoped against hope. Now—she glanced up again.

It was him...and yet not. So much larger than he had been in the dreams and somewhat alien.

"You like my voice?" he asked.

He had a voice that made her heart race and her imagination spiral. It was even better to hear him now in person, even if she did feel like an utter fool.

"It's nice." She tried to shrug.

If he would just let her go, this would be a little easier, but if anything, he'd drawn her closer. Unless it was her imagination. Was it?

"I like yours," he continued, "even if you are threatening to kill me. In these final days, I have wished to hear it more." A muscle jumped in his jaw, a strange hungry look pooling in his dark-green eyes. "Will you tell me your name?"

"Oh. Now that we aren't in a dream?" She tried to smirk, but her pulse had quickened even more. "Are you sure it's safe?"

"For names? Yes." He started to lift his hand as if to put it on her waist then pressed his claws to his own chest. "Let me start. As I said in the dream, I am Tengrii though you may call me Chicory if you like."

"And I'm Rhea. Salt-Sweet is still fine." She ducked her chin to her chest, shaking her head and pulling free. Oh, what was going on with her mind. She was—what was this?

He held his hand out to her.

What—what did he want her to do? She frowned, then slowly held hers out as well. Did he want to shake it?

He slid his under hers and caught hold of her fingers, then brought them to his lips. "I am happy to know your name, Rhea Salt-Sweet. And I am honored to have such a dedicated and beautiful rescuer here to save me."

Was he flirting with her? She couldn't even draw her hand back. Her skin prickled at his touch, discomfort merging with intrigue as his scales rubbed along her skin.

"You don't get many rescuers here, I assume."

"You're the first. Also the most beautiful."

"Careful," she said. "I might think you're in love with me." She tried to laugh, but the sound died in her throat. Was he?

He simply stared at her. "Oh, Salt-Sweet. It is far too late for me to worry about that." His gaze dropped to her lips. "It could be because this world here is likely to end and there is quite probably nothing more that we can do. Or it might be because you have been my comfort and my heart for weeks on end."

She flinched when he started to stroke her cheek, his claw scraping her skin.

He drew back as well.

"I'm sorry—" she started, but he lifted his hand.

"No. Do not apologize. I would be repulsed as well." He smiled at her, the expression warm though the sadness remained in his eyes. "So long as you remain my friend, I do not ask for more than that."

"Of course you're my friend." She bit the inside of her lip, unable to look at him anymore.

That didn't feel right or good. It hadn't even been intentional. Just—claws against her skin frightened her. His overall size. The snake-like elements in general. It was hard to go from seeing the naga as her enemy to suddenly realizing this was the friend she'd been searching for all along. Friend? That was what they'd both said just now, though he had suggested he felt more. Was that a light joke to ease the tension? Her feelings weren't. And she had been—she had been falling...

"I came here to save you. I wouldn't do that for just anyone. You're—you're..." The words died on her lips.

Would she have come just for him?

He picked up the spear and then set it upright in the cleft of the rock. "It's a good thing you didn't stab me with this. Otherwise, you probably would have killed me. Where did you get this venom?"

"It was—the person who broke me out. They gave it to me."

"You didn't break out on your own?" He frowned.

"No. Someone in dark robes broke me out and gave this to me. That's who said I needed to kill you to stop this curse."

Tengrii frowned, then raised an eyebrow as he looked behind her. "Elthko, what did you find?"

Rhea turned, then jumped. A large creature with glowing green eyes and arms that nearly touched the floor stood behind her. She hadn't even heard whoever that was approach. Those enormous paws made no sound on the stone. How long had he been there?

"There was another attack on the guarded ones," Elthko responded, "and someone raided the poison stores. It has been handled for now. Larkin was involved this time. She has been imprisoned despite her connections. Is this your guest? She seems calmer."

Tengrii smiled a little as he gestured toward her. She lifted her hand in greeting.

"Yes," Tengrii said. "This is Rhea. My friend. I am going to show her what remains of this place if all has been settled in the council meeting and this latest attack."

19

PALACE TRANSFORMED

Tengrii frowned as Elthko departed. How long had he been there? And why had he come that way rather than through the door Tengrii himself had used? That was odd. Then again, what wasn't these days?

He returned his focus to her. She was still staring after Elthko. "So someone in a hooded robe gave you the spear and sent you to kill me?"

"To this exact place. They said that you were the reason that this was happening. That you are not letting them fix it. But—" She bit her lower lip, her brow creasing. "You sound like this is ordinary?"

"As hope has waned, assassination attempts of various types have become quite common, unfortunately. My people are desperate, not cruel. But desperation can lead to such horrible things." He gestured toward the passage ahead and then clasped his hands behind his back. "Would you like to see this place?"

She nodded slowly as she took a step forward. "Yes." Her

gaze dropped at once to where his feet would be as if to assess how he was going to—well—walk more or less.

He moved forward easily, contracting the muscles that rolled and propelled him forward. It always created something of a swaying movement from one side to the next. His tail hissed and slid across the stone floor behind him. The coarser stone made this movement even simpler, but he felt more aware of it now than ever with her watching him.

"You'll have to be careful here," he said evenly. "We have not had guests in—ever, actually. At least, not in my lifetime. And the coming of the Tue-Rah is a source of great concern."

"Why? The Tue-Rah can access any point in time or reality. It's always here."

"Yes, but it isn't always available for us or others to access. That is the part that causes concern." He ducked his head to avoid striking one of the lower points of the ceiling as they moved out into a larger passage. He gestured to the right. "The Tue-Rah isn't what causes problems. It's other people. And right now, everyone is on edge."

"So they may hurt me?"

"Perhaps, though I'd like to say that it would not be for personal reasons. They are—there are simply those who are desperate for any solution, and so, as the time has passed and our situation becomes more dire, they are more willing to consider means that are far more barbaric and utterly unfounded."

"Like killing newcomers." She did not sound as alarmed as he might have guessed.

"Newcomers, instigators, people with the wrong birthmark." He sighed.

This wasn't who they were. But who they were becoming was terrifying indeed. Not that he blamed them either. Death was terrifying to contemplate. Madness even more so. And erasure perhaps even worse.

"I understand the temptation. Especially when it comes to saving oneself," he said, "but what good is it for a man to survive and yet lose all that made his life worth living? To violate or deny what is good and instead embrace cruelty and destruction? I have never had to lead my people in war or combat against anything except fear. And yet that fear has almost undone us and threatens to turn us into monsters in more ways than just our appearances. I have more say in what happens than most, but so long as I can, I will not compromise on those points. Other matters, such as opening up the palace to take in everyone who wishes to come, are far simpler."

She tilted her head as she smoothed her hair back over her other shoulder, revealing the smooth elegant lines of her neck. Her brow tweaked a little more as she contemplated his words. "I can't say I know what I'd do in the same situation," she said, "but I think I agree. It's frightening to think of how fast those compromises take us somewhere bad. It's kind that you brought everyone into the palace though. Almost like you are all one big family."

He almost laughed at that. She meant it kindly, he was certain. "It was the only way to keep the sleepers alive and the mad ones from killing themselves and others in their attacks."

It would have been nice if they had been more like a family. As it was, the distance he felt between himself and his people had grown over the past months.

"We do not spend much time together," he said. "All wish to be with their true families as much as they can, especially when a night like this one comes."

That was why she had been such a comfort to him— because he was always alone.

"A night like this one?" She rubbed her bare arm as she glanced back at him, her gaze moving from his face to his tail to his claws.

"Every third night, the Rift opens and pulses, and the fog comes to torment us." His wrists and waist ached already. These were the longest nights.

"On the other side, where I'm from, it comes every night."

"That would be hard to manage."

And it was their fault that her people suffered. One false comfort had been that the Rift's torment was contained to this place.

They stopped at the edge of the carved balcony. Though the light did not carry far, they could see houses carved from stone. Buildings stacked one on top of another. Evidence of a whole city that had once burned bright and hummed with life.

Back in his parents' days, this place had been alight with life, bustling with excitement and plans. Quiet plans to expand and develop. To plant fungal gardens. To explore more of the surface lands. To lay out paths to the most beautiful caverns that had the perfect resonance for song. Perhaps his own youth had clouded his memory and made it warmer than it was, but it at least had been nothing like this. The chill of the darkness bit into his soul.

"There were so many of us here," he said softly, his hand resting on the stone wall. "And now it is as if only the dead and those near to death remain."

"So this—we've been in the palace? This whole time? All of this?" She turned back to face him.

"The Rift opened in one of the chambers just beyond the palace in what was once a courtyard. Not that you can tell any longer. Those with strong enough skills helped to form walls to protect us—such as we could. We've cut off some segments and shored up others."

It was not much. Not nearly so much as he wanted to show her. Especially as she was an artist. There was no beauty left in this place. Only sorrow, shadows, and suffering. Had she come in the time before the Rift, she would have seen such wonders. Even the rocks themselves had been richer with life. The fungi sprouted with more colors. The surface skies had blossomed with rippling colors and majestic fogs with stars that exploded with life. And when spring came, the trees blossomed with trailing ivies and subtle pink flowers.

Just as he had once been handsome and impressive in many respects but now was monstrous, his kingdom had suffered a similar fate. All that he could impress her upon was its horror.

THIS PLACE WAS unlike any she had ever seen. Dohahtee's underground infirmary had made her uneasy in its clinical precision, though she had understood its purpose. This palace —despite all the trials and horrors its people had faced—it had a regality to it.

Whoever had sculpted this palace had done so with great care, creating contrast in the textures and a seamless balance. Almost a rhythm. Polished marble, textured granite. Alternating lines and strips of stone that created a subtle sensation of movement. Even the way that the veining of the marble itself had been chosen in such a way that it resembled something. Water rushing over a stream or perhaps low clouds over a mountain?

Artists had worked here, crafting and sculpting works of

art in places most might never see. Even in the low light, it caught her breath. From block to block on the floor, the swirls and veins had been joined and seamed. They were the sort where you could almost envision pictures forming: otters playing in a river, trees heavy with fruit, baskets brimming with olives, dancers swirling in grand clothing. As the floor and walls carried on, it became clear that the designers had created large whorling loops that increased that sensation of movement.

The passages they had been in had to be newer. There was something rawer about the stone, an urgency in the cutting and shaping that wasn't present here. She trailed her fingers lightly over the wall, taking in the distinctions of textures.

He was watching her.

She pulled her hand back to her chest. Heat flashed through her. "Should I not touch?"

"No. You may touch whatever you like." He smiled a little.

"Your home is beautiful, you know," she said.

"It isn't what it once was, but it is kind of you to say." He gestured to the arched top of the ceiling. Jagged sections at regular intervals suggested something had been removed. They stood out like great scars. "You should have seen the sculptures. Winged messengers, chimeras, gryphons, manticores, and so much more."

"What happened to them?"

"The earthquakes. Those that weren't destroyed we removed to save. One day, perhaps, we can restore them to their rightful place. If that time should ever come."

Footsteps jarred the silence as a strange figure appeared around the corner. Though his upper body was that of a man, his lower body was a spider. Three red eyes emblazoned his forehead as well as two regular brown ones. He wore flowing garments that likely had been his ordinary garb when he was a human like her, but now it hung and sagged and twisted in odd shapes around his unusual form, the embroidered designs snagging on the raised scales of his arms.

"What is this? Are you wasting time then?" the man demanded, his gaze moving from her to Tengrii. She drew back, hugging herself tight. "Our world is falling apart, and you are—"

Tengrii straightened, lifting up so that he was even taller than this person. "I am showing an intelligent woman what remains of our kingdom in case she sees something that we have not. It is possible she has knowledge we do not yet possess, Jaiku. Regardless, she should see this place if she so desires. If other matters require my attention immediately, I will provide it."

Her cheeks warmed, and she loosened her arms around herself. Jaiku did not appear to be particularly impressed, but the note of pride in Tengrii's voice—the confidence he felt in her—well—she wasn't certain it was fully warranted, but it meant something that he would speak for her in that way.

"If there is any way that I can help, I will," she said.

"Yes, though I doubt that leaping off stone ledges will be high on the list of useful things you can do," Jaiku said.

"Do not test my patience, Jaiku," Tengrii growled, his voice becoming startlingly low and guttural. "She is my guest. Now go. I am master of my time. Not you."

Jaiku bowed his head, but his expression did not change. He backed away.

"Our structure has become significantly less formal than what it used to be," Tengrii said to her once Jaiku disappeared. "But most do better at remembering respect than that. He was one of the original founders though, so he often feels that he is free to speak more freely."

"And he's afraid?"

He nodded.

"Is it possible to go aboveground? Perhaps that's made some of this worse. In Dohahtee, the infirmaries were underground as well just because there were so many and to make it easier to care for them. But it made most everyone uneasy. Maybe that's doing something here?"

"The upperworld is far too harsh to easily sustain structures," he said. "We used to go up more frequently for hunting and gathering as well as some limited cultivation and farming. But over the past months, it has been too dangerous. The storms have become more constant, and then a collapse trapped the most secure exit. The air remains clean for now. And we have more than enough food. Starvation won't be a problem before other issues." He sighed, moving forward once more. "If I had had to guess what would likely have been the problem that befell my people, it would have been loss of food sources or clean water. Yet that isn't even a concern."

As they rounded the next corner, a staircase cut down to the one side and up on the other. The steps were broad and flat, their edges smoothed down. Delicate ridges and grips had been cut in an interlocking diamond-like pattern. She placed her hand on the railing to make her way down. Tengrii took the stairs far easier than she had anticipated. Not that she thought he'd fall on his face. But he really did move with such grace.

"I'm glad you were able to save those sculptures," she said. Her steps here echoed up and down the chamber. "Even without them though, this place has its own beauty to it."

The way that smile pulled at the side of his mouth made her heart skip. As if proof that somehow her observation soothed him.

Warm golden torchlight poured out into the hall ahead. Great double doors opened up. The ceilings here were far higher, almost three times as high actually. More life and movement bustled through here than anywhere else. Footsteps echoed out from within. Someone called for fresh sheets, and another promised they were on their way. Not panicked voices. Calm voices. This had to be one of the infirmaries, but when Tengrii guided her inside, she paused.

Yes and no.

It was actually a grand library, the walls filled with books of all kinds. But instead of benches and couches and places to sit, there were beds. Beds of all types, all with bodies on them. Each one covered with white sheets. The bookshelves themselves had been boarded up, and the beds appeared to be fastened to the floor. Many of the books were pressed against the boards though some shelves appeared to be entirely bare. Only the skeleton of a chandelier hung above.

Most likely, he saw this place as being stripped of its beauty and turned into something far more functional, yet there didn't seem to be the same level of regret about this place.

"Do they need help?" She shivered in the cool of the room. "I don't have formal training, but—"

"Not unless you can wake them," a gurgling yet feminine voice said.

Rhea nearly recoiled as she saw the squid woman standing a few feet away at a desk bolted into the floor. Padded boxes sat beside her with bottles of a purple gaseous vapor inside.

Tengrii extended his hand toward her. "This is Gao. She is one of our lead physicians and heading up the task force on finding a cure as well as one of the founders."

Gao rolled her lidless eyes. "For whatever that's worth." She seemed to use two dark-pink tentacles like hands more than the rest though she did use the others for balancing.

"Those of us who can manage are managing. It would take more time to train you than it would be worth. But the offer is appreciated. Try not to cause more trouble. That's the best way to help."

Rhea shivered as she hugged herself all the tighter.

Several humans hurried about. They did not have carts like the Unatos. The air smelled like mushrooms, cotton, fire, and some pungent tea. Their steps, though not as confident, had the air of people on a mission. A weary mission without end.

As it was in Dohahtee, so it was in Serroth, only less organized.

"There are more rooms like this?" she asked.

"Every room on the first three floors of the palace is like this," Tengrii said softly. "The dungeons are where we keep those who..."

She turned toward him. "Who what?"

"The ones who lose their minds," Gao said. She shut the book she'd been marking in with a sharp clipped movement. It thudded on the wood. "Those of us like this?" She gestured to herself. "It isn't enough of an indignity to become what we fear. We also lose our minds. Some of us. Some worse than others. When the pulse happens, we go mad regardless. But for some, there's a further breaking, and it never ends. It is indignity on top of indignity."

"Birkii will be freed," Tengrii said, his voice soft but firm. "He is not lost. He is not dead."

Gao stared down at the book, biting her tongue. "It would be easier for him if he was. Easier—" A tear rolled down her cheek before she wiped it away clumsily. "Well, no time for that."

"Honored Scholar." A human woman darted up, her face pale and her muscles tight. "It's back."

"What?" Gao leaned forward.

"It's back." The woman shuddered. "It's taking another."

Tengrii stiffened as well. His arm moved toward Rhea as if to shield her.

"What? What's back?" Rhea asked.

What other nightmares existed in this place? Rhea looked in the direction the woman had come from. The double doors to the library had been left open, and through it, she could glimpse another hall and another large room.

"An ancient being that walks between all the worlds," Tengrii responded. "The Ki. It comes to take the souls of those in the comas."

"The Ki Valo Nakar?"

"Perhaps?" Tengrii raised an eyebrow. "I've never heard of it by that name, but it is an antlered creature with glowing white eyes and enormous claws. It comes and takes the souls of a few at a time. We have no way to fight it."

Gao shook her head. "Stay away from it. No one can best it. There are other tasks that require our attention. Pray it does not take too many." She pressed the book open once more. "It's come early today. At this rate, well..." She glanced back at Tengrii. "We'll keep searching until the end, bitter though it may be."

"Until the end," Tengrii repeated.

The sleepers here reminded Rhea of the ones in Dohahtee and throughout, but if the impacts of the Rift were different for the others, perhaps it was different for them too.

"Do you have any mindreaders here?" she asked. "Anyone who might be able to reach them?"

"No. All our psychics—they passed at the beginning. There was nothing we could do to save them. Every single one of them. Kailto was the last. He held on as long as he could. Impressed what knowledge he gathered in those tablets." He gestured to another box that seemed to be padded and sealed. "In case anyone came who wanted to experience it or could read what he put there."

Gao placed one tentacle over the box and hugged it closer, a mistiness coming over her eyes. "They were very brave. Kailto especially so." She lifted her gaze back to Rhea. "If you want to help, there are two things you can do. You are an Awdawm. Assuming something else doesn't kill you down here, you are fairly likely to survive this. So learn our stories. Learn our names. Don't let us be forgotten. Whether you find your way back to your home or remain here. Even if you are the last to breathe in this place. Remember us. Remember those who have fallen in this place. Because time is cruel, and we are being erased."

"I can do that," she said. Tears stung her eyes. "Yes. I can— I'll do my best with that."

"And the second thing is take care of that one." Gao gestured toward Tengrii. "Tonight, he has to be chained up. Just like me—"

"Gao—" Tengrii started, his expression darkening.

Gao raised her tentacle and shook her head firmly. "No. She offered to help. It may be humiliating, but it will save us time. And yours takes the longest. Especially with your current quarters being so far removed. Yadeta and Gomal are tired. Assuming you're keeping her with you and not putting her in the dungeon." She gave him a knowing look. "No, let the guest help if she wishes. It will allow her to keep her sanity longer."

Rhea brushed her fingers over Tengrii's arm. Though he did not pull away, he did start, his gaze dropping to hers at once. "I want to help," she said.

The creases in his brow deepened, but then he nodded.

Soft footsteps padded behind them. "Your Majesty," a breathless voice called out.

She turned with Tengrii, startled to see what appeared to be a young squirrel man. He'd been so afraid of squirrels he turned into one? Though his teeth were indeed alarming. Blood stained his loose tunic and dark trousers.

"What?" Tengrii frowned. "Speak."

"Two more have broken. They need your help. Beyond the Well of Forgetting."

Gao rested her tentacle on the top of her head, swearing under her breath. "Leave the Awdawm here then. I'll look after her. We both know it wouldn't be safe for her down there."

Tengrii looked back to Rhea. "I will return."

"It's fine. I'll be fine here. Stay—stay safe." She hugged herself. Was she really saying that? She almost laughed at how ludicrous it was. But it convinced him, and he left with the squirrel man.

A heaviness fell over the large room with his absence. Gao watched her. Her skin prickled with discomfort. The silence was too much.

"He seems like a good man," Rhea said.

"One of the very best," Gao responded. "Perhaps too idealistic for a time and place such as this but a good man nonetheless. He does not deserve what has come to this place any more than the rest of us, but it may yet rob him of what he values most."

"You think it will kill him?"

Gao chuckled darkly. "Oh, death is not what he fears. It isn't what most of us fear in truth. It is separation. Isolation. Madness and loss. Death is only a part of it. Knowing that, after all these years, nothing that we did mattered. That, though we have fought for months on end, there was just such loss. And all because the world went mad."

It was horrible. And she couldn't stop that. But perhaps—an idea sprang into her mind.

"Do you have pen and ink and paper to spare?" Rhea asked, fidgeting.

"Of that we have more than enough," Gao said.

"I will listen to the stories and do my best to remember, but I can also—I can try to draw portraits of those who have passed or been changed. You can describe them or tell me about them."

Gao pressed her thin lips together, then nodded. "Yes, that would be a help." She pulled a cracked chair over and motioned to her. "Sit. Listen and draw. We will do this between the tasks."

20
UNDONE

The last thing Tengrii wanted to hear was that two more were broken. He hurried away with Mouru. Mouru struggled to keep up.

"Where did it happen?" Tengrii asked.

"Dungeon G. Right at the entrance. It's Iban and Dalgo."

Crespa. Iban had been trapped in wolf-man form with uneven arms and claws so jagged he often cut himself. And Dalgo had turned into an acid biter. They might just kill everyone themselves if they didn't destroy one another.

"We've got them trapped, but with Dalgo producing that venom, it won't last long," Mouru continued.

No. It wouldn't.

Tengrii quickened his pace. Reaching the stairs, he practically slid down them, not even thrusting his arm out to slow his pace against the wall. Even from this distance, bellows and shrieks rose from the dungeon. Metal groaned and clattered.

As he neared the barred doors, the guard opened it, then returned to attention. Tengrii seized a trident from the armory locker and then continued down the slick stone path. They'd had to cut these extra dungeons out as quickly as possible to house those who went mad before they could harm anyone else.

The dank cold air swept up around him, carrying with it the scents of blood, bile, adrenaline, and sweat as well as the horrid bite of Dalgo's acid. The torches flickered, shadows stretching and creeping along the wall.

An unearthly screech tore through the air. He grimaced internally. Dalgo. Mouru flinched and hung back as Tengrii continued to the final door.

Elthko stood at the reinforced door with three guards. The last barrier before Dungeon G. "They're not exactly working together, but they tried to attack in unison," he said. His green eyes narrowed. "Sometimes, they recognize the door and attack it. Other times, they attack the walls. Either way, they will escape, and Dalgo, at least, cannot be permitted to continue like this. No matter where we put him, he will get out."

The aged blacksmith turning into an acid biter had certainly been a heavy blow to their community. He was well-loved, one of the softer-spoken founders. With the Rift's pulse, he had lost the use of his hands. Now that he had lost his mind, he was more dangerous than almost anyone in this dungeon.

Through the cut points in the door, Tengrii glimpsed Dalgo biting at the rocks and bars. His face no longer bore any resemblance to the man he used to be. His eyes had vanished into deep layers of skin, and his jaws had become thick and square, oversized with heavy tusks. His hands were more like hooves, sharpened and sturdy but useless for most tasks a human would usually attempt. With some focus on his shift-ing, he had been able to bring back his sight as well as hands and fingers. But, from the looks of him now, that had been lost too.

Iban, the young tailor, was almost as unrecognizable, rocking back and forth in some deformed wolf-man form. The jagged claws that protruded from his fingernails dragged along the uneven stone floor. His head moved back and forth, his reddened eyes blinking as he twitched.

"Do we know what happened?" Tengrii asked. "What caused this? We are hours away from the Rift's pulse. Are there any additional clues or symptoms this time?"

Elthko shook his head, his gaze sliding back to him. His vertical pupils narrowed. "What caused it is what has caused everything else. There is no choice this time, Your Majesty. They must be put down." He indicated one of the guards who held a shortbow. "We have arrows and poison. It will be swift."

"You brought me here to grant their execution?"

"Your orders," Elthko responded quietly. "None are to be harmed if possible. But in this case because of what he has become, those who go to restrain them will face even greater risk. Perhaps even death. There are too many breaks already. And if this increase in breaks is the next phase of the Rift's pulse and the fog itself, then this gets much worse for us in the coming cycles. Dalgo broke Iban out accidentally and chewed his way through to here."

The three guards listened, grips on their weapons tight.

"No," Tengrii said. "Dalgo was a good man. He would not do this willingly. We restrain him, and then we bind his jaws. We'll determine the rest from there. This may not be possible to accomplish without inflicting some injury, but some injury is better than certain death. If you are all afraid, I will enter. Open the door on my mark. Then close it fast behind me."

He gripped the trident tighter as they prepared.

Inside, Iban continued to stare at the wall while Dalgo attacked a stalactite.

Once both looked away, he nodded toward the guard. He pushed the door open, and Tengrii shot inside. The entrance into Dungeon G had been carved out of the stone and designed to have plenty of room above and to the side with the choke point at the door. Combat was the one thing he had been especially proficient in before the Rift had come. No one could best him in the tournaments. Not even his own father. His particular skill set had centered around speed, strength, and silence.

These two didn't even realize what was coming for them or how much worse it could be.

He caught Iban in the chest with his tail, knocking him back against the wall. The wolf-man's claws tore into his scales as Iban uttered a strangled howl. Hot pain seared through Tengrii's tail and up his spine, but he struck Iban again and flattened him before he turned on Dalgo.

Dalgo spun about from the stalactite. His great jaws snapped and slavered. The acidic spittle struck the stones and hissed into the air.

Tengrii recoiled, a guttural snarl escaping him. He swiped the trident forward and clipped Dalgo in the chest. Dalgo launched backward and then scrambled to the side. His jaws snapped. Iban threw his head back and howled.

This time, Tengrii flung the wolf-man up against the wall beside the dungeon door. He struck the stone with a heavy crack.

The door snapped open as two of the guards raced in and pounced. They bound Iban's arms and wrists with manacles and put a muzzle over his ragged jaws. Iban tried to howl, but it was little more than a whimper. Two of the guards dragged him away while the third manned the door. Elthko looked on cautiously.

Tengrii bolted to the side as Dalgo charged him. The great hooves clopped heavily on the stone.

"You're still in there, Dalgo," he said, more for his own benefit than Dalgo's. "You aren't really gone. I know you aren't. You're going to find a way back, and you're going to find a way to do what you love again. You and Iban and all the rest. No one is lost here."

Dalgo snarled. He staggered, then charged again. A few drops of acid struck Tengrii on his side. He slid out of the way and struck Dalgo again, but then Tengrii scrubbed at his side, fighting to stop the acid from burrowing deeper. He channeled his healing directly into those spots, even as the acid became like knives in his flesh.

It would be easier to let him die. To order the guard just to shoot him. There was no trace of humanity left in his expression or in his voice.

Rage pooled in Tengrii's belly and burned through his muscles. No. No! Dalgo had to be in there. Just as Iban had to be. Just as every other one of his people had to be in there. It was just a matter of holding on. Just like he had to hold on when the madness took him!

Tengrii struck around and used his tail to bludgeon Dalgo in the side of the head. The blacksmith staggered.

Tengrii shot around on the other side and struck him again. More acid struck Tengrii's arm, slicing into him like a blade. He struck the blacksmith yet again, rendering him unconscious. Dalgo collapsed, his head lolling.

"Bind his jaws and his arms fast," Tengrii ordered.

The guards sprang in at once, following his orders.

Tengrii shuddered as he forced his arm to heal. The flesh stitched itself up, the scales regrowing, but it all moved slower and more painfully than when he had been at his weakest before the Rift opened. A few drops of blood spilled onto his vest but disappeared into the dark fabric, leaving little more than dark dots. It wasn't nearly as bad as it might have been.

Elthko approached. He shook his head, his over-long fingers clasped over his arms. "Your Majesty, ...we are—I do not know what we can even try. This is unbearable. This cannot continue. They may have been our peers and even friends at one time, but those people are gone. It is one thing when they can be saved and preserved with little risk, but at points like this, though you performed admirably, you must concede that it is dangerous, even for you. Look at the burns. You've managed to stop them from going deeper?"

"Yes." Tengrii didn't add that they pierced more than before. That he had struggled to cut them off before they sliced into even deeper muscle. But Elthko probably guessed that already.

"We cannot save everyone. Not even among those of us who have turned. To allow this to continue is cruel."

"We have lost enough," Tengrii responded, his voice sharpening. The weight of it all pressed harder on him. "These men and women did not ask for this. They should not be treated as animals."

"It is what they have become. It is what we will all become. And who can even imagine the torment they endure while in this state? It would be kinder to let them die. If it happened to me, I would ask you to let me pass rather than to endure under these conditions."

"And if we find a cure for this—if we discover—"

"It will be a tragedy, but you know as well as I—" He broke off, drawing his arm over his eyes. He then gripped Tengrii's arm and guided him away. "We need to talk."

"There is nothing to talk about," Tengrii said sharply,

pulling free. "The order stands. We do not kill our own people so long as there remains a choice. For now, there are many choices. We have survived here for hundreds of years and never had a single war or violent uprising. And yet now within the course of six months, we are a fraction of what we were and destroying one another. No! This does not continue. We may all fade into nothingness. We may all perish in this godforsaken place, but we will die as people. As sentients. Not animals."

"You need to know something," Elthko started. "About how we came to be in this place."

"Do I not know it?" Tengrii scowled. His claws dug into his arm. He tore his gaze away and focused on intensifying the healing.

Sighing, Elthko turned his face away. "I need to prepare. Tomorrow, after you have eaten and settled your initial tasks, meet me at the cave-in. You were planning to visit the guarded ones tomorrow as usual?" When Tengrii nodded, he continued. "Good. Find me after you see them. And when you are there, really look at them and what they have endured. Think of what all of us have endured this night and the price of continuing on this way. Do not bring the human with you."

"Why not?" He frowned.

"Because you may decide this is something you don't want her to know, and that is your decision to make." Elthko cleared his throat, then strode away.

Tengrii watched him go, still gripping his wounded arm. He frowned. That was both cryptic and unnerving. Regardless, there were still too many tasks that required his attention for him to focus on that long.

21

NOT ALONE

I t took hours longer to sort out the confinement and restraint methods for these tormented members of Tengrii's kingdom. Then others needed him. More requests. More fears. Another member broken and in need of subduing. General Yoto had to subdue three others, though they were of a much milder nature.

And always, time marched onward, drawing them closer and closer to night and the coming of that dreaded hour. When all was finished as much as it could be, he returned to the library to get Rhea.

He hated that she was going to be present for this third night. Third nights were among the worst, unless one broke before then. Mercifully, that hadn't happened to him.

She had to stay somewhere. So long as he was chained and she remained safely in the study, she would be all right.

Really, aside from his maddened roars, it was the safest place for someone like her. He'd never broken free from those chains despite his enhanced strength. One small comfort in a bleak sea of despair.

But, crespa, he didn't want her to see him that way anymore than he wanted to be a monster.

Softer happier voices reached his ears as he neared the library. What was that? How was that possible? People talking in louder voices. Almost...almost happy. He blinked. What were they talking about?

He slipped inside silently.

Rhea sat on the stone floor, papers scattered around her and her tongue sticking out from the corner of her mouth. Several individuals gathered around her, their voices overlapping so much he could scarcely tell one word from another. She seemed able to understand though.

Her one hand supported the plank with the paper while she hunched over it, her other hand moving with a life all its own. Dark lines of varying thickness formed beneath the movement.

Gao stood at her desk, two sketches tucked beneath one tentacle as she called out observations. "Margo always dried those mushrooms to make those pretty little crowns. Does anyone else remember those? Crushed up some amethyst to give them a little sparkle."

He tilted his head, recognizing the faces on the sketches. Gao's beloved. It seemed like forever since he had seen Birkii in his old form. He'd almost forgotten how gentle a person Birkii had been. Somehow, without ever seeing him, Rhea had captured his essence in a simple stylized drawing. That prominent hooked nose and gentle pondering eyes and scruffled hair that barely reached above his ears and a mouth that was always quirked a little to the right. Kailto, Gao's adopted brother, was likewise impeccably realized. Seemingly no-nonsense and serious as stone but with just the slightest glimmer in his half-shaded eyes.

Other sketches sat around the room like memories from

the past. Faces of those long gone or long transformed. Her drawings were not so much beautiful as they were expressive. As if she somehow could see through the morass of words and tumbled memories to capture the heart of her subject.

How different it was here, even among those who were dying. Unlike in the dungeons, here there was—hope? Was it hope?

What was this hope even for?

Did she have some magic of her own? Some special trace of the old Awdawm powers before they had been taken? Or was it simply that showing the way they and their loved ones as they once were gave hope that in time they could return to what once was?

He watched a few moments longer, arms folded over his chest. This was almost like another world. A world lit up with soft golden light and eager speakers, ink sketchings placed around the room. The sleepers beneath the sheets no longer seemed like corpses. The attendants bustled about, talking between one another and reminiscing, some with tears and others laughing, many with both.

She drew a flourish on the page and presented it to Len. "Is that right?"

Len's lips trembled as she took it in hand. "Incredible."

"Good. I'm glad. She seems very striking." Then, Rhea glanced back at him as if she had sensed him watching her. Her eyes met his.

His heart skipped faster.

Look away.

It wasn't good to stare at her.

But he couldn't break that gaze. Not even as electric sparks and nervous energy cycled through him, making him straighten his shoulders. Crespa, she was a vision.

Then she smiled, and he felt like he had been pierced. She

tilted her head, her hair swinging over her shoulder as her gaze softened.

He straightened, clearing his throat. "The hour is late. We all must make our preparations."

None argued with him. They simply gathered their items or returned to their tasks.

Rhea didn't question him either. She flicked her hair back, then stacked the pages and wiped off her ink-stained hands. A half beat of hesitation followed as she glanced up at him once more before crossing over. "I guess I'm going with you."

He gestured toward the hall. "This way."

She fell in step beside him, that partial smile on her face and her hand hooked over one of the loops on her trousers. She moved with the stance of a friend and an equal, and his heart warmed further. His orders didn't have to mean anything to her. She only did as he asked because he was her friend.

There always had to be a measure of distance between him and his people, especially after his parents' deaths. The only ones who really challenged that from time to time were the founders who had survived, but they were not particularly close with him. He had consigned himself to stoic celibacy after realizing he was incompatible with any who might have been his mate. And that had not been such a dreadful thing. It meant he could focus, and it had reduced entanglements.

Then those children had tried to access the Tue-Rah on the same night the Daars attempted to stop it from opening at all. After that, the Rift had torn through.

Day by day, night by night, his kingdom had shrunk or fallen apart. Despair had been his constant companion.

Then she had appeared, and it had become bearable again.

He glanced down at her once more. She seemed to be trying to pretend she wasn't paying attention to him. But it was clear she was watching him through her periphery. Probably because he was so monstrous.

Though...it had seemed that before—once she knew who he was—some of that revulsion had faded. Until he had touched her and she had seen his claws. Then she'd flinched.

That memory burned through him.

How could he blame her though? He'd nearly torn his own scales off when he'd seen what he'd become. It was why the only mirror left was the one in that little study he never used and only kept because it had belonged to his mother.

But Rhea was wondrous. She'd come to this place with nothing but the clothes on her back to save him and her family. He'd known she was strong and brave from their pillow talk. But he'd never have guessed her capable of this.

A deep pang of longing pulsed through him.

How vividly he recalled the night he'd woken from dreaming of her and wished she could be real. It was the first time he had ever longed for a—

No. He released a slow breath. He wasn't even going to think about having a veskaro—a beloved—a mate. He was a monster. Physically, at the moment. But it would get so much worse. She cared about him as a friend. That was enough. If more developed, it would be because she wanted him. Because she gave him some sign that he was not utterly terrifying.

And it was good to be beside someone who understood at least part of him and didn't need him to be the figurehead and icon of strength for the kingdom.

Her being here was not good for her, but a selfish part of him was grateful that she was. There were many things he needed. A good friend was one of them.

"Was everything all right?"

"Hmm?" He shook his head, startled at her voice. It had

215

felt for a moment as if she had spoken right into his thoughts. That was odd.

"I was just wondering if you were able to fix what was broken." She had her arms wrapped around herself again, but her posture seemed looser. "It sounded important."

"It was." He touched one of the burns beneath his arm. It had mostly healed. The scales had grown back over it. But deep within, the flesh remained tender and bruised. "And, for now, it has been tended."

How long until it became a bigger problem, though? What if Elthko was right? What did the steward want to speak with him about? That whole conversation had been strange in and of itself. He couldn't guess what it would be about.

He cleared his throat, realizing that the silence was becoming awkward. "You were drawing the faces of family and friends for anyone?"

"Yes."

"How do you capture their personalities so well? It was as if you glimpsed their souls."

Her gait faltered as she looked up at him, her cheeks flushing brighter. "Oh...well..." She chewed on her lip, then quickened her pace to catch up to him and explain her process.

He tried to listen as much as he could. The words glazed over him, though he appreciated the sound of her voice and the intensity of her passion. With each passage they crossed, his dread grew though. This fondness she showed him was certain to fade when she saw what he became this night. But what choice was there but to keep going? He had to protect her. From himself as much as anyone.

He took her to his chambers using the back passages. Not that they were likely to run into anyone. Even Jaiku would be preparing for the torment that this night would bring. Gao's suggestion that Rhea be the one to help him made sense, though it grated on him. He didn't like having to receive help from anyone. Especially when he was so vulnerable.

These third nights always left him spent, nearly wasted with exhaustion and terror. They stretched on endlessly, showing no signs of breaking until they simply stopped. And after tonight, she wouldn't look at him the same. She'd likely recoil even further.

He paused, realizing she had asked him something. About how the Awdawms were doing.

Yes. He raked his hand over his scalp, clearing his throat. "We have some Awdawms who have survived. They are what is keeping this place from falling apart completely. But the burden of this place weighs heavily upon them."

She nodded, her brow furrowed with contemplation. "The Unatos and Awdawms on the other side are carrying most of the tasks as well. Everyone does what they can. But it is a lot. A few are immune. The Vawtrians and Shivennans are not affected though, so there are more who can help. Are there none here?"

Hearing those names, the names of what they had once been, stung a little.

He simply shook his head. "It has not worked that way here. For those of us affected as I am, the opening of the Rift and the pulse turns us into the nightmares we fear and robs us of our sanity. It is why—it is why we look as we do. It is why I am in this form."

And why he hoped that it was indeed a reversible curse and not simply an incurable illness.

As they reached the last hall before his chambers, he continued. "When the Rift opens and the pulse starts, you must stay away from me," he said somberly. "As much as I care for you, I will not be in my right mind. We have learned

the hard way that we all must be bound with chains or else..."
He released a slow breath, blocking those memories from
rising. "Many died in the early days before we knew what to
do. The first nights were a bloodbath. So swear to me, no
matter what you hear. No matter what you see. Do not come
near me. I have lost so much, but to think of losing you...I
cannot. You are my dearest friend."

And so much more than that.

So very much more.

But that did not need to be said.

She halted beneath one of the scars where a statue had
been removed, hugging herself. "So this will happen tonight."

"Yes."

"This was what Gao was talking about." She hugged
herself a little tighter. "What you said happens on the third
night."

"I'm not asking you to stay with me. You shouldn't actually. I don't..."

He closed his eyes. Visions of Dalgo and Iban flailing and
attacking in the cell struck his mind. How alien they had been.
How unlike themselves. The thought of her seeing him in a
similar state filled him with shame. Even if the state was only
temporary.

They had reached his chambers. He pressed the door to
the inner hall open and allowed her in. She slid by so close she
practically touched him.

"I don't want you to see me that way," he said. "I don't
want to be a monster, Salt-Sweet. You can go into the other
room. Cover your ears. Wait until morning. Then release me.
Or wait until the servants bring breakfast and ask one of them
to do it."

Turning, she faced him, hands still tucked under her arms.
"Listen. Setting aside all of the points where I was trying to

kill you because I didn't understand who you were, I know you aren't a monster. And nothing will make me believe that you are. All right?" She tapped his cheek, forcing a smile. "Come on. I'm trying to be funny."

"You aren't especially good at it right now." But he smiled nonetheless. Even now she could make his heart lighter. "Please understand, though I do not intend to be, I will be terrifying tonight, Salt-Sweet. I will be a monster in every respect, no matter what I want."

"Good thing I'm not easily scared." She set her jaw and flicked her eyebrows up as if daring him to deny this.

"You are very brave. I don't deserve a friend like you."

He closed the door behind them.

22

THE THIRD NIGHT

Tengrii led her back into the same room he'd carried her into kicking and screaming just yesterday.

For the first time, she noticed the bed at the other end of the room. These were his private quarters, and yet they seemed very small and—well, lacking when one compared them to the lavishness of the library or the other rooms she had glimpsed. The kingdom wasn't impoverished. The palace wasn't small. But these chambers—well, this room was perhaps twice the size of her tree home. The study he had poked her in had been about that size, and there were three more doors that might lead to other rooms of similar size. All in all, it was quite modest considering who he was.

"Your quarters are rather far away from all the rest of your people," she said. "Do you just prefer solitude?"

"It was one of the lesser guest bedrooms," he said. "All rooms on the first three floors were converted into infirmaries. And I had an exceptionally large bed with room for far more. There was no reason for me to remain in there when so many were in dire need."

That explained why the turquoise bed seemed to be too short and too small for him despite being a double. He'd have to sleep coiled up in this one to keep his length from falling off the edge even with all the pillows removed. Yet she couldn't help but note that all those pillows had been placed on there anyway.

"You gave up your own quarters? That was kind of you."

"It was the only decent thing I could do. And then the transformations happened. It suddenly became even less important." He removed the dagger from his sash and placed it in one of the cupboards. Then he gestured toward the green door on the far end of the room. "This is where I sleep on the third nights."

His broad shoulders nearly filled the doorway. He moved beyond the frame and into the small room.

She halted at the threshold. This room was not like the main room or the little study. Instead of having even some furniture bolted down, it was nothing except chains and manacles over a thin mat. They reminded her of the ropes she had fastened in the wall for Tiehro and Salanca but far thicker and heavier.

He stretched out on the mat and began snapping metal clamps over his tail. He had to adjust his tail into coils so that all of it fit in the room, but at each point, he pinched it down to the ground. Then he laid back and placed his wrists against the ones on the floor.

Those snapped into place automatically.

She rested her palm on the wooden frame. There was no comfort in this room at all. Not even a single torch. The only light illuminating it came from the torch fastened just beyond the door. Had she stumbled upon it earlier, she would have assumed it was for torture. Monstrous didn't describe him, but it described this room.

"How do you get free?" she asked softly.

"In the morning, someone unchains me." He winced as he adjusted his left wrist. "You should go. Stay away until the screaming stops. Close the door behind you."

She rubbed her arm slowly, remembering what she had seen her brother and sister endure. There wasn't even a torch or lamp in this place. No sign of anything bioluminous either. "You're here? Alone? In the dark?"

He nodded.

"Are you afraid?"

He remained silent, his eyes shaded. Then he nodded once more. "Sometimes so much so it feels as if my heart will stop." He halted, then shook his head, his brow creasing. "No. Don't. You can't stay in here. When this happens, Salt-Sweet, I am the monster you fear me to be. If I got free, I would not know you. I would crush you or bite you or worse."

"Have you ever gotten free?" She gestured toward the chains and manacles. The stone looked a little worn in some places, but even from this distance, she could tell the bolts were deeply fastened and secured.

"No. But you'll still see." He turned his face away, his breaths tight. "Just close the door. I will call you when it is safe. Or you can come find me at breakfast."

No. What could be worse than being trapped alone in a place like this?

She picked up a cushion from the other room and dragged it in along with an oil lamp. "I heard the nightmares of my brother and sister for weeks on end. I sat with them and sang them songs to soothe their dreams. Maybe I can do the same for you."

"I won't be able to hear you."

"Maybe not. But I can try. And you will not be alone."

"At least get the spear then," he said tightly. "In the wardrobe, there is a spare. When it happens—"

She sat beside him, out of reach of his hands manacled to the floor. Leaning in, she pressed her palm to his chest. His heart fluttered faster beneath her hand. "Chicory, I'm here. I'm safe. And you're safe. I'm not going to leave you. All that matters is to get through tonight. Then we handle the rest."

We. It was so natural to say.

A muscle jumped in his jaw. "I am sorry for what you will see."

"It's all right."

"If something goes wrong— very wrong—and I try to constrict you, go limp. Prey always tightens and then tries to lunge away from the mouth. It is what makes the most sense. You'll have the best chance of escaping if you move to the side and toward me, but you'll have to be quick because I will bite you, and the venom will kill you instantly. You go limp, then in the split second before I tighten, you lunge out. If you can move fast enough." He turned his head and lifted his jaw. "Do you see the line just above my throat?"

She slid close enough to see, then nodded. It was very thin. "Yes."

"The scales are weakest there. There's another spot under my arms. If you need to stab me, they are the most likely places to work."

"Of course *now* you tell me how to kill you."

"Go get the spear."

She clicked her tongue at him. "I'm not going to kill you, Chicory." She frowned slightly. "Do you have a preference for what I call you?"

"No. As long as I know you are calling me, that is all that matters to me." He pressed his lips into a tight line and turned his gaze up toward the ceiling.

"How much longer before it strikes?" she asked.

"Maybe minutes. Perhaps another hour. We always bind ourselves down early. And most of the doors lock and seal each night at sundown, thanks to Loteb."

She gestured back over her shoulder. "This one too?"

"No. That's an inner door. They didn't have time to prepare those. Only doors to bedrooms. Infirmaries. Dungeons. Cells. Rooms that may have someone who has gone mad."

"So I can leave it open?"

"Whatever you prefer."

"Let's leave it open. Things seem scarier in the dark." She remained beside him. "So..."

"So..." He tested the bonds over his wrists. The metal did not give even slightly. "There will be an earthquake before the Rift pulses. Stronger than the other tremor."

"Then we have some time." She plucked at one of the threads on the side of her trousers. "Is there anything else I can do?"

"No," he said. "This is already more than enough. And if you need to leave, then leave. I won't hold it against you."

"I'm not going anywhere." She placed her hand where his knee might have been, then drew her fingers back almost at once. Was that too much? She shouldn't be touching him like that. "It'll be—"

The ground shook. Everything swayed. Silt dropped down from above.

She closed her eyes. It was about to begin.

A stream of purple fog, intense with color, pierced the wall. It coiled over him, then shot down into his face. Far faster than any she had ever seen. She'd barely released a breath when the entire palace erupted in screeches and bellows of terror. It froze her. Heat prickled over her skin, adrenaline surging through her veins. Then she looked at him and bolted back against the wall.

Polph, he wasn't joking!

It wasn't like the nightmares she'd seen the others endure. Whatever horror it was, it seemed to be playing out in front of his waking eyes, drawing out primal terror and distorting his very being.

Even more, it changed him. His face was unrecognizable. His teeth elongated into razor sharp needles with great silver fangs in place of his incisors and extra rows deeper in his mouth, all curved back. His tongue became long and forked, far more like a serpent's. Jagged scales and spikes jutted out from his shoulders, grinding down against the stone and slicing into the mat like blades. A massive cowl flared out from his head and along his neck, similar to a king cobra's with vibrant colors. His claws had likewise grown longer and more curved, glistening like blades. His scales had gone lighter and brighter. And his eyes—oh those gorgeous gentle eyes! They'd become dimmer and harsher, pointed with rage and fear and hooded by sharp pointed scaly eyebrows.

He twisted and roared.

How was this even possible?

As he'd said, there was no recognition when he looked at her. Not even acknowledgment that he saw her. He struggled and fought, ripping back and forth, fighting to gain any sort of traction. But the bonds held him fast.

At this point, he was only hurting himself. His poor wrists and tail had to be massively bruised with the amount of force he exerted trying to get free.

She edged closer, holding up her hands. "It's all right, Chicory. It's safe. You're safe. I'm here with you. And it's safe."

His bellow hitched, and his eyes rolled forward. They blazed brilliant green now, no longer so dim, but the pupils were now vertical slits rather than circles. He bared his teeth at her like some cornered animal. The fangs arched out, but he couldn't get any closer.

She placed her hand on his chest, her own terror pounding stronger within her. He didn't even look like Chicory now, but he was. This was Chicory Tengrii. And he felt scared and alone.

"It's going to be all right," she said, louder than before. "You don't have to be all right now, and you don't have to feel like this is good, Chicory. I know you're scared. I would be too. I can't even imagine what you're seeing. But listen to me." The words failed her. "It's going to be all right. You are going to get through this."

The words died in her throat.

All she could think of was the lullaby she sometimes sang to Tiehro and Salanca.

So she sang.

He howled and bellowed and rattled the chains. Bits of rock and debris flew from the stone where the metal had been fastened, but they held tight.

She sometimes held her ears. Other times she pressed one ear to her shoulder and put her hand over his chest. His heart thundered beneath her fingertips, and his voice covered hers. Sometimes it was so loud, she couldn't even hear her own attempts to sing.

The minutes stretched into hours. Two more times, the strange fog shot in and attacked his face, so much more violent than what she'd seen previously. And slowly, his voice hoarsened, and the snarls lessened. She sang louder and talked to him, practically shouting at points herself.

At last, panting, he fell silent. Sweat rolled down his face, mixing with what might have been tears.

He blinked slowly, struggling to smile. "I—this is usually the point when I find you, waiting for me. In the dreams."

"Has it passed, Chicory?"

"Should have." He nodded, gulping in great breaths. His teeth returned to normal. The jagged scales on his shoulders vanished. His scales turned a deeper shade of teal.

She brought in the wash basin and a cloth. Gently, she wiped his forehead. "Do you want me to unchain you?"

"No." His breaths remained heavy. "I don't—they don't come for me until the morning. We can wait until then."

"Isn't that just because there are too many people to get to you quickly? Gao suggested I take care of you through this."

She continued to wipe the sweat away. His muscles pulsed and trembled. Even so, a deeper calm appeared to have descended over him. His breaths were easing.

"Perhaps," he said, a slight frown creasing his forehead. "But I've never been unchained before morning on the third night."

"Has it ever returned after you broke free?"

"No."

"Well, you need to rest. I don't think the night is even half over."

"It isn't. We still have another six hours. For whatever that is worth."

She rinsed the cloth in the basin and then wrung it out. "I suppose this is why sometimes in the dreams you weren't really able to talk." She shook her head. "I thought you were just tired. I suppose you were, but for a different reason."

He managed a weak laugh. "Yes. It was you—always you that gave me the courage to return. Even when I couldn't remember it all. I don't know how I would have endured without you."

"I suppose that means you should go to sleep now."

He smiled a little, his brow tweaking up. "I don't think you can sleep though."

Her pulse certainly raced. The terrifying sight of him hadn't left her enough for her to calm down. "Probably not right away, but it's fine. I'll get some rest soon."

"I just don't want to be apart from you." His fingers fumbled a little against the metal.

She pressed the rag once more to his chiseled jawline and then down his neck. "I'll be here. Where else would I go?" Heat flashed through her when she realized he'd noticed her lingering touch. "You sweat a lot for a snake man."

"I'm not actually a reptile, Salt-Sweet," he said with a dry smile. "I'm a man with a snake tail and scales. And occasionally some other features."

"Yeah?"

"Even if I was a naga, it wouldn't mean—" He broke off, then shrugged. "If you are not afraid of me, the key is in the top drawer of the dresser nearest the door. Or you can continue stroking me with the wet cloth."

"I was not stroking you. I was helping you." The heat intensified in her face as she pulled back even farther.

"Hmm." He shaded his eyes as he studied her. "I appreciate your help. And you are welcome to continue."

"I'll get the key." She turned her back on him.

He smirked at her when she returned. She avoided giving him the satisfaction of a reaction as she unfastened first his left wrist, then his right. Then she moved onto the manacles that had pinned his tail down in multiple places. As hard as that metal had pressed into him and as much as he had struggled, he had to be fairly bruised. But she couldn't see more due to the formation and color of his scales. If he had waited until night passed, he would have been in exceptional pain.

He winced a little as he unfolded his coils. Reaching down,

he rubbed along the points that had been twisted. Then he rolled his shoulders back. His spine cracked.

Half snake or not, the man was built. Polph.

She turned and hurried out into the main room, hoping he hadn't noticed her checking him out. "I'm going to make us some tea," she announced.

23

TEA AND REST

Had she been admiring his body?

Surely not.

Tengrii hesitated, the intense pain radiating throughout his body no longer occupying his mind so much. She had been staring at him in a particular way. Then she'd rushed out as soon as he looked at her. He certainly didn't mind studying her body, although that might make her uncomfortable.

Probably shouldn't dwell on it.

The torment of the Rift's pulse usually left him weary in soul and body. But this time, he fought to push back the weariness. Salt-Sweet didn't want to rest. Likely couldn't yet. And he would not miss a single moment with her.

As he rubbed new life back into his wrists, he sat up. Usually, he had to remain here for hours longer. It was a pleasant relief to be free so much earlier. Too bad he couldn't kiss her for that kindness.

He eased out into the main room and then pulled the door shut.

She stood on the other side, cheeks flushed and arms folded over her chest. "I just realized there is no kitchen in here, and your door is now locked. So I don't think I can make you tea."

"Ah." He held up one finger and managed to smile.

Already, the humiliation and unease were fading. She was adorable. He wanted to wrap his arms around her and hold her tight. She looked so embarrassed, her cheeks all flushed as she fidgeted. Even her nose had gone pinkish.

"You might not be able to, but I can. Hot water is one thing we do have in abundance in this place. It's part of what keeps us from freezing as well during some months." Leaning to the side, he cracked his back and rolled his shoulders. "At least until the earthquakes ruin it. But for now, it has survived. They designed it to be flexible at least, so there is that."

She stepped away from the wall, her arms still tight around herself. "You had brilliant architects."

"Everyone here is brilliant in one way or another." He opened the cupboard and removed one of the large pitchers that had been secured. Everything in this place was secured or padded to keep anything more from being destroyed in the tremors. "The earthquakes were among the easiest elements to sort until recently. And they've never been too intense. At least not compared to what they could be."

He then pressed open the stone covering over the spigot and let the boiling water pour out.

"Why until recently?"

"The elementalists are affected by this too. They are becoming more and more...like their base element. No balance. No harmony. It happens at different rates. The geos are turning to stone. Several are trapped. Jaiku's wife, Oidra, has not been able to move for nearly a week."

And she likely only had weeks left, though her husband

saw to her care and would do all he could to keep her going. Elonumato help them, they had to find a solution soon.

"And there's no cure for that either?"

"None we have found. Except ending this...however that happens." He scoffed. "In time, they fall apart. No matter what their element is."

"The man who looked like fire," she whispered. "When you sent everyone away, he didn't want to go. He was protective of you."

"General Yoto. The last of my generals actually. A good man. One of the best I've ever known."

He placed the pitcher onto the table and then removed one of the boxes of dried tea leaves. He had not drunk this for months. Perhaps years. It was a blend his mother had created from what she considered to be the best flora of Serroth that was fit for steeping. The startlingly fresh scent of juniper and lemon brightened the room at once.

"I know you came here because you were trying to end the curse, so I will guess that you do not know how to end it on your own. But, tell me what it is like over there in your world. Maybe there is something."

"Well, it isn't all underground," she said with a smile.

He chuckled, then listened attentively as she continued. He could have listened to her talk about anything for hours. Especially in that thoughtful way she took on when she was trying to ensure she remembered everything or the passionate way she spoke about drawing. She fidgeted with the leather ties of her necklace and shifted her weight back and forth, but at least she didn't flinch when he moved near her.

The story she wove about the other side with all these worlds and so many millions suffering weighed on him. It was all so similar, most especially in the fact that they had no answers. And they were running out of time as well. Someone had to figure something out though. Surely someone would.

The conversation faded as he poured the tea into two thick mugs. The fragrant liquid resembled a deep amethyst. He placed her mug on the table beside her. Heat did not affect him nearly so much in this state, and he couldn't tell if the mug itself was too hot for her to hold.

"I am sorry that it is so in your worlds as well. I do not think we will come to a solution this night. It may be easier for rest to come if we discuss something else."

"What do you want to talk about?" She picked up the mug.

Were her cheeks still rosy? It had seemed at points that she had been watching in a way that suggested more than mild interest. But it could have been his imagination.

"Whatever you would like to talk about."

She leaned forward then, resting her elbows on her knees. "All right. Why nagas? What scared you so much about them?"

"Have you seen them?" he asked, leaning back on his tail. Sometimes, he looped it to make it easier for resting while having conversations and to keep it from being trod on. For now, he coiled and looped just enough to support himself and let himself relax as he healed from the bindings.

He gestured to himself, steaming mug of tea in hand. "Nagas are terrifying." He shook his head. "It was a combination of things, I suppose. When I was a child, I fell into a snake pit. Some massive gathering of snakes of all types. Nothing too venomous, mercifully. But I couldn't get out. They made it impossible. And the idea of snakes in general combined with the thought of people who were half human and half snake, well, it did not take long for the nightmares to form. There was this rock formation that looked something like a naga. I could see it from my bedroom window. I always thought it was coming to strangle me as I slept."

"Hmmm. I'm assuming it didn't." She gave him a small, almost coy smile, one brow arching.

Was she flirting with him?

He narrowed his eyes at her. "Actually it did. It strangled me one night, and I was reborn as a naga."

"Ah. Well, that makes far more sense." Giggling, she inhaled the steam.

"Rhea." He turned the mug in his own hands. The heat seeped into his palms. "There is something I need to ask you."

"What's that?"

"What do you need?"

Her brow tweaked up. "I'm sorry?"

"What do you need to be happy that can be provided? From what I understand, you spent so much time caring for your family during this tragedy. Night after night. And now here you are in my kingdom. You stepped into the role of portrait sketcher within a matter of hours once you determined assassin was not a role you wanted. And then you spent this night with me. Not simply ensuring that I was bound but that I also had a friend to see me through. All of that takes its price. So what do you need?"

"I—I don't even know how to answer that." She straightened her back against the wall, her gaze fixed on the mug. "I—no one has ever asked me that. What about you? It's not like I'm a leader. You are."

He shrugged. "The hot waters on my back. Recalling points when I was loved and secure. Resting and talking with you. Before the storms and the crushing at the entrance, I also enjoyed walks—slithers now, I suppose." A muscle in his mouth twitched. "But there are still passages that are calm and still during the best of times. When there is time, I like to pass it there."

"Those all sound lovely."

"What about you?"

She bit her tongue, smiling. "I don't—I actually don't know. I suppose it used to be drawing for my own amusement. Then it became what I did to earn money. And walking, too, when it was peaceful in the forest, but then I didn't want to go too far away. Hot baths haven't been a thing for a long while. Takes too much time. Taking my cup of tea and sitting on the edge of the porch though and watching the sun rise through the branches. That was always good. The birds would sometimes come and sit and sing. I'd let my legs dangle off the edge of the platform, and the breeze would blow through my hair."

"Finding a way to be outside is not especially likely for now. We haven't been able to reach the surface levels for nearly four months. But please, consider what you need and tell me so that I can ensure you get it."

"There are other more important things to worry about right now."

"The unimportant eventually becomes important. At least in some cases."

"I just don't see that it's the most important thing right now. Like fashion." She lifted her mug in his direction as if this somehow made her point.

"I don't understand." He frowned.

"You don't worry about the clothes you're wearing beyond a belt and a vest. Anyone else, and I'd be saying you're naked. But I understand that you have simply adapted to this situation."

"I'm not naked," he responded, raising an eyebrow. "I am fully clothed."

She mirrored his expression, incredulousness shining in her face. "You're shirtless and pantless, sir. I have eyes."

"Shirtless, I'll grant you. But I am wearing a variant of pants. Trousers on snake buttocks look ridiculous."

She turned her face away, seemingly choking on a laugh. "I did not hear you say what I think I heard you say. *What?*"

He grinned. Her laughter delighted him. "You think they wouldn't? I'm surprised you didn't notice. All that poring over naga lore, and you paid no attention to their fashion? Or are the books in your library that lacking?"

"I..." Her mouth screwed up as she contemplated this. "Well, I guess some of the fashion choices meant they'd have to attach them to the scales."

"Good guess."

He lifted the dark-purple sash to reveal a thin strip of fabric that ran beneath it. It was nearly the exact same shade as his scales. It formed a panel that ran down his lower torso and beyond the groin region before it fastened along multiple scales with a series of hooks. It had been awkward to learn how to dress as a naga, but going without it had been worse. Anything more elaborate had simply been too uncomfortable or unworkable.

"Doesn't that hurt?"

He hurt almost constantly since the transformation. This was little more than an occasional discomfort. "Not unless someone tries to rip it off. But no one has ever tried. It's also part of the reason for keeping it the same shade as the belly scales." He adjusted the sash once more. "It just looked strange otherwise. Even tubal clothing rides up when you try to move, and only putting it over a section looked ridiculous."

She covered her mouth to hide her smile.

He cocked his head, pulling a more dour expression.

"What? Are you trying to determine whether I'm clothed or naked at the moment?"

Rather humiliating that she would assume he was just going without pants. But her amusement soothed that initial sting.

"Just...it's rather—I don't know, it's just interesting to think about you worried about fashion after all these horrible things that had happened. You took the time to figure out what would work and what would let you keep some dignity. I know that it destroys my points about a time and place, but...I suppose it's better that way."

"Yes, well, apparently not much," he muttered, narrowing his eyes at her. He took another sip of his tea.

"You look good in them though."

"For a naga."

"No. Just good." She picked at a loose thread. "Do you think that this—do you think this means that there are nagas and minotaurs and spider people on the other worlds out there?"

He scoffed. "Who can say? It would not surprise me. They haunted my dreams enough to be real. But here on this world, it is only us."

"You're certain of that?"

"The world was empty when our parents and grandparents came. No one was supposed to be here at all."

"Oh? So...how did you all find out? And how did you know for sure there wasn't anyone else?"

"We had mindreaders with us. A couple. They searched and searched. Sent out calls. Nothing at all."

"Still, the world is a very large place, isn't it?"

"It would be an interesting surprise if there was anyone else out there."

In some respects, it would also be an answered prayer and granted wish.

"Can I ask you this then?...Are you a Vawtrian?"

He hated that question. Hated it perhaps more than anything in his life. But it was fair. How could she not wonder?

"I suppose you could call me a Vawtrian," he said slowly, aware of her gaze upon him, "and I was skilled. I would have been what is known as a Melspa Vawtrian. Water-based forms were some of my best. My people here, we do not consider ourselves such. We are separate. Whatever we had in common, it vanished after the Rift opened. I used to be a shifter, but I don't know what I am any longer. Or what I will become. I've been trapped me in this shape. At best, I can adapt and fine tune it, but I am terrified that this is what I will be for the rest of my days."

It had changed so much about him. He actually did like some sugar now. Honey was delicious whereas before it had been vile. And if he understood what had happened, he had locked with Rhea perhaps even before they met. And that meant—he pushed the thought aside.

No.

Now was not the time to think about that. He did want her sexually. That was true. But—no, maybe the alterations meant he had been able to sexually awaken without bonding to her. But what did that mean? How could he even determine it?

She gestured toward him. "Whatever this plague curse is, it hasn't done this to the Vawtrians on the other side."

"Perhaps because they aren't directly exposed to it. It did not happen all at once here either. It took a few weeks. Then— it happened all at once."

"And the...nightmares only happen once every three nights? Was it always that way for you?"

He nodded. "All but the Awdawms suffer it. And they suffer in their own way, I suppose."

"It's been getting worse with time too. As if it is getting stronger?"

"Hmm, hmm."

He rested his palm against the back of his head and tapped his finger against his skull to soothe the itch that had formed. More and more were breaking too. Shifters who lost their minds and became so exceptionally violent they started trying to kill anyone they encountered. Dozens of cells in the dungeon had been filled with these members.

She set her mug down. "You're very different from the Vawtrians I have met."

"Our cultures and our worlds have grown apart," he said.

For one thing, those on other worlds were also actually capable of being shifters. This plague had denied him the essence of what made him a shifter and certainly what would have bound him to others of his race had he ever wanted to know them. It had altered everything about him and trapped him in a form that originally terrified him and now most of the time simply annoyed him. What it had done to those of other races was just as bad, if not worse.

"I don't know how many years it has been on your side," he said, "but for us, it has been about a thousand since the camp came here. Perhaps longer. I have never left this world, nor did I actually wish to until recently. I was happy here with caring for this place and watching it transform. Now, though..." As he trailed off, he noted that she had tried to stifle a yawn. "We should get what rest we can. Let's make up a bed for you in the study."

She offered no objections to this, and it didn't take long to make her a comfortable nest-like bed with blankets and pillows. He provided whatever else he could and showed her where the washroom was in case she wanted to use it, then left, shutting the door behind him.

It was strange to have so much time left on a third night. If he hadn't passed out by this time, he would have been willing away the agony in his wrists and the cramps in his tail. The dream connection with Rhea had been a lifesaver in more ways than one.

He made his own preparations and then curled up in the bed. Though the bed was large enough for two, he had to layer and then drape his tail over the headboards and in a specific alignment to fit all of himself on it. If he coiled around something, that made him fit, but the movement and position only made him feel more alien and uncomfortable. At least it gave one good use for his socks. He always put one on the tip of his tail to keep it from getting cold at night as it was too difficult to keep the blankets high enough, and waking up with a cold tail was somehow worse than cold feet.

He fell asleep almost immediately. Once more, he found himself in that room he'd shared so many nights with her. She appeared in the bed beside him seconds later.

Oh, his heart.

Was he a naga or a man now? All he could see was that sweet smile. He didn't want to tear his gaze away for even a second. He'd appeared as the man most likely. That form had been attractive. She had been drawn to it.

"Does it hurt you? You being in the naga form in the waking world?" She was all the way on the far side of the bed, but she laid her head upon the pillow.

"You mean what I was supposed to be? What I used to be?" He smiled a little. If only she knew just how much it hurt. How much it masked everything else. "In this place, I do not hurt. But my altered form—the naga form—it is not pleasant. Not even when I make the alterations. I don't like it. In any sense. I understand why it repulses you."

"You don't repulse me," she started. Then she dropped her gaze. "It just..." She picked at her fingernails.

"What I am, what I look like when we aren't in this place? Of course it repulses you. It is monstrous. I am a monster, even though I do not wish to be."

She shook her head, then pressed her hands over her eyes. "I just...yes, it's strange. And it's not the easiest to accept. But please know, I thought that the naga devoured you or killed you. Definitely that it invaded your kingdom. And I'm—you aren't repulsive. You're—unlike anyone I have ever known. And you certainly are not a monster. I am so sorry if I hurt you."

He laughed wryly. "I hate the form," he said. "You said nothing to me that I would not have said of myself."

She continued to stare at him, brow creased in thin lines. "It doesn't change who you are inside. What happens when you go mad, that's something separate. Yes, you are dangerous then, but you have taken steps to protect yourself and others. And there's got to be a cure for this. I know there has to be. Despite that, I do see you, and you are no monster."

He glanced down at his arm again, relieved to still see the warm tanned flesh of his human form. What would he give to be able to return to his true state of rest? What cost would be too high? He hated the sight of his blue-green scales.

"It's funny." Her honey-brown hair spilled out over the pillow as her eyes searched his face. "This connection feels like it's getting stronger. I can actually feel the sheets like I did the last time. I think we're both probably going to remember more of what has happened."

"One can hope." He stretched out as well but kept his hand at his side.

More than anything, he wanted to reach out. To curl his fingers along her cheek and then tangle them in her hair. To draw her close and press his lips to the curve of her neck and make his way up to her lips before seizing and devouring her.

But friendship?

That was what he could have.

Was that enough?

Enough to soothe his soul and calm his mind?

No.

Enough for him to find contentment somehow?

Yes. Because it was what she wanted.

To be here in her presence, so close to touching her and yet so far away—it burned and stung and ached all at once, more than the curse that wracked his body and trapped him in this shape.

But he would not pull back from it. Not ever.

There was love in her eyes.

Perhaps not the romantic kind. But a kind of love. More love than anyone had looked upon him with for years and years.

For most of their connection, they had not been able to make contact. She had been close, and he had loosely been aware of her heat. But there had been no actual contact. That other night, right before his former comrade tried to kill him, it had been more. Now, it somehow felt like they were closer still. As if he might be able to put a hand to her shoulder and slide it down to her breast.

Could he make love to her in this place of dreams and thought? Could he vestov her and bring her pleasure while seeking his own?

Probably not.

They said that dreams could never allow for what had not been experienced in its equivalent in the waking world. Not unless one was especially powerful. He certainly wasn't. And it didn't seem like Rhea was either. Even if she did seem to be expanding their connection. But she certainly wasn't interested.

So he kept his hand at his side and contented himself with her presence. Her scent did not reach him. Nor did much of her heat. But that smile—it was there. So beautiful, curving over her mouth as she watched him and told him about the different teas her family enjoyed at different times of the year.

He told her then about his own. His father had always loved tea more than his mother. So much so that they had often teased him about it. But his mother had become quite skilled at preparing distinct blends. Many were intended for healing or nourishment of some kind, but some were simply for pleasure.

All meaningless talk. All unimportant and yet the sort he would not miss for all the world. Soon it stilled between them to a gentle comfortable silence. All the worlds might be falling apart. The danger might still be at hand. But here, in this little place, for now, it was safe. Just the two of them.

And if he could have that for the rest of his life—then yes, yes. He would take that. Or for however long he could have this.

24

THE ONES TO BE SACRIFICED

Rhea woke more rested than she expected. The dream connection was clearer this time as well. It didn't haze or muddy at all. Her heart beat faster as she remembered the way he'd looked at her. How tempted she had been to edge closer. Just in the dream, of course. It wouldn't have been wrong to do that? Would it?

She rubbed her forehead as she sat up. The makeshift bed had been one of the most comfortable she had ever slept in. The purple and blue woven blanket that he'd wrapped around her shoulders was soft enough she could drift off in it again if she remained in bed a few seconds longer.

No time for that though.

Her feet bare, she padded to the door and slipped it open.

Tengrii still slept in his bed. He filled it up almost entirely, one bare arm steepled over his face. And—was that a black sock on the tip of his tail? It protruded from the blanket with only the smallest of gaps between the tail and the coverlet. Another few blankets covered the rest of his looped length.

She covered her mouth, smiling. Taking care not to wake

him, she slipped into the washroom. The hot water was a joy, though it did swiftly become a little too hot. She scrubbed her hair clean, washed her body, and found herself feeling a thousand times better. Even if she did have to put on her old clothes. As she finished combing out her hair, she left the room.

Tengrii had roused by that time and changed into a clean purple vest with more red than blue undertones, making his dark-blue hair stand out all the more. He stood in front of the wardrobe, hand on the door.

"You probably need fresh clothing. I should have offered earlier." Before she could answer, he opened it. The warm pleasant smell of lavender, amber, and some woodsy scent she couldn't place wafted out. "You are welcome to wear any of these if you like."

He removed a couple tunics and laid them out on the bed. They were all quite lovely, cut from shiny silk or fine cotton.

"That's thoughtful of you," she said, stepping forward.

She almost started to ask why he didn't wear them, then stopped. Obviously, he had grown much larger. Not just based on the dreams but based on the size of his biceps alone, he would burst this shirt if he tried to wear it. Not that the vest-only style didn't work for him. He filled that vest out and made it look better for the wearing. He had been one of the most handsome men she had ever seen when they had first encountered one another in the dreams. His tanned skin had no scale-marks, and though the stripes existed on his cheeks, shoulders, and biceps, they did not seem so intense. More importantly, he had legs. Real legs. Strong muscular legs with powerful calves and essentially ordinary ankles and feet. No signs of snakes about him at all.

But was he that much different now? How much of it mattered? His mind and his personality were clearly the same.

His appearance was really quite similar in most respects, those indigo stripes now even more striking and his face just as kind, if not rather broader and squarer. What he battled did not change his essence.

"Are you certain you don't mind?" she asked, brushing her fingers over the exquisite fabric.

"Someone might as well get use out of them. I'd be pleased if it was you," he said. But apparently the fashion choices concerned him because he tapped the back of his knuckle against his cheek, pulled out two more tunics, and then selected another one to present to her. "This might suit you better."

It was a deep burgundy tunic without sleeves, covered in slightly darker but shining embroidery that formed elaborate fern-like patterns.

"What makes this one so special?" She took it in hand, smiling as she imagined what he must have looked like wearing it. This was a good color for him, both now and in his former shape.

"It was one of my favorites," he admitted. "The fabric softens when it gets warmer. And the color suits you. If you want this for a belt, it might work." He offered her a broad band of colorful fabric that tapered at both ends.

"Back in a moment." She took it, shyness stealing over her as she slipped into the washroom to change. The sleeveless tunic actually did fit her well though it gaped beneath the arms and exposed her breast band if she put her arms over her head. Still, the fabric was light and warm at once, and it felt good against her skin. She kept her own trousers, even though the tunic was long enough to wear as a short dress. The trousers made her feel more confident, the psychic stones still in her pocket, a reassuring reminder of what she was here for even if they weren't likely to work aside from screeching

Killoth's name out into all of space. The bright turquoise, warm cream, and rich black of the sash he'd given her for a belt contrasted beautifully against one another as well as against the burgundy.

As she emerged from the washroom, she made a flourish. "I think it works."

She only expected him to agree or maybe tease her a little bit. But the great smile that appeared on his face made her heart somersault.

"You are exceptional," he breathed.

She tried to shrug it off, though suddenly, she couldn't hold eye contact long. She rubbed her fingers along the thin seam of the tunic. "Not really. Just put on some clean clothes. Anyone can do that."

"They can't make it look like you though." His gaze lingered on her body, that hungry expression more vivid than ever. A question danced in his eyes.

She swallowed hard.

They called each other friend, both within the dreams and without before she'd understood the naga situation, what she had felt had certainly been sexual attraction. And what she felt now—what was it? Could she be sexually attracted to someone like him? Was he human enough in the right ways? Were they compatible?

It was strange to even think about. Sexual relationships hadn't been part of her life, though she had hoped to one day find someone she could love that way. He'd said she was repulsed by him. That wasn't entirely true, nor was it fully wrong.

It was...complicated.

Yes, the snake aspects unnerved her. The way his tail twitched and moved like a third limb. The claws on his fingers could easily tear into her, though he had demonstrated nothing but tenderness. Except for last night when in the throes of the fog, but even then, he had taken great steps to protect her, even so far as being willing to stay in that room all alone.

She chewed on the inside of her lip. What was it Killoth had said? Love didn't take time to be real but to determine whether it was safe. In truth, then this wasn't a question of whether she was falling for Tengrii but what she would do with those feelings.

Tengrii slid closer, his breaths slow and controlled. "I do not want to push you or make you feel uncomfortable," he said softly.

She glanced up just enough to confirm he was looking at her still. Polph. He was. Oh, those eyes could undo her. Her breaths quickened. "I know you wouldn't."

If she reached out, she could easily place both hands on his chest. But she stayed still, arms at her sides, fidgeting with her clothes and tugging at her brown leather wristband.

He placed his hand against the wall as he stared down at her. "And I don't want you to feel as if you have to do this or that you must even consider it. But in the interests of clarity, I have to ask." He paused, closing his eyes. "Rhea, do you—"

A soft knocking interrupted them.

He pulled back sharply, his breath hissing through his teeth. "Already?"

The knocking sounded again, more insistent this time. He dropped his arm to his side and moved over toward it.

Rhea released a heavy breath, not certain whether she was relieved or disappointed he hadn't been able to ask the question.

Tengrii greeted whoever was at the door, then returned with a large tray and easily enough food for two people. He placed the tray on the table on the other side of the room. "Dulce sent us breakfast. You should eat."

"What were you going to ask me?" She hugged herself, her fingers digging into the soft burgundy fabric as she drew closer.

Tengrii put the plates on the table, his gaze fixed on them. His claws scratched the black stone plates. "I have matters that require my attention today. I need to visit the ones that half my kingdom wish to sacrifice. Do you wish to meet them?"

She chewed the inside of her lip. That hadn't been what he was going to ask her. But how could she blame him for changing his mind?

"All right." She forced a smile. "Though I doubt I'll want to sacrifice them after I meet them."

"No one should want to." He paused, then dipped his head, the ghost of a smile on his lips. "Another joke. Yes. I'm certain you will not want to sacrifice them. This is breakfast. You really should eat."

"Did you want to talk about something else?" she asked, her breaths tight.

"It's the only thing that is important for now," he responded. He frowned at the food, then moved away. "I'm afraid I have no appetite. Please don't let that deter you. I'll be ready to leave when I finish in the washroom. If you want to see more of this place and the ones whom we are protecting, then be prepared to leave at the same time. This day will hold much."

Yes, it would.

She picked at the food, her own appetite gone. Without sitting, she picked at the food while he bathed.

How quickly things changed. Again.

Perhaps it was good he hadn't asked her that question. What would she have been able to say?

He'd confirmed he was a Vawtrian. More or less. There was nothing wrong about a Vawtrian and an Awdawm like her becoming intimate, though it was a lifelong commitment. Vawtrians never vestoved casually. They didn't participate in any sexually intimate activities casually. They couldn't. Biologically, they took only one mate, and all of their sexual energy and focus was devoted to that one person.

Yet some part of her hesitated.

She didn't have a solid answer even when he returned, freshly washed, hair neat and feathers smoothed. It was time to leave. He didn't even take a bite of the grey porridge before they left. She walked alongside him in silence, her thoughts occupying too much of her mind for her to feel uneasy or embarrassed about the silence. There were so many more important things to be considering than whether she wanted to have sex with or get involved with a shapeshifter who looked like a naga. And they were friends. Good friends. Had been for weeks—actually months now.

He wouldn't hurt her. Not intentionally. But those claws and the sheer strength in his coils. And who even knew what equipment he was working with. There really wasn't a delicate way to ask that. It wasn't even any of her business if she wasn't interested in him. It wasn't as if she had ever asked Tiehro or Killoth about their genitals.

Was there some subtle way to bring it up?

It was so easy to visualize going further with him. To imagine the pads of his fingers pressing down her spine and pushing her against him. And the claws weren't so bad if lightly raked through her hair or over her skin. His mouth near her ear and her neck. Just imagining it sent her heat rising.

It didn't help that he smelled divine. Spicy and earthy,

amber and incense with bakhoor. She closed her eyes. For so many reasons, it would be so simple, so easy to just collapse against him and surrender.

She halted. Of course, she was also assuming. Assuming that he had locked with her. But he hadn't said as much. Only that he wasn't a good Vawtrian. Most Vawtrians went nearly mad with need when the locking bound them to their mate and awakened sexual desire.

Had the fog changed him to such a degree that even the locking and sex was different?

Or was it possible she had misread the situation and the way he looked at her?

Yes. Of course it was! She'd gotten many things wrong in the past. Though what he was thinking or feeling? What was the alternative?

"Is everything all right?" he asked, eyebrow slightly raised.

"Yes. I just—why are these people kept so far away?"

He almost seemed relieved by the question. With a shrug of his sculpted shoulders, he gestured down the long dark passage. "We have to keep them all the way down here so that no one tries to throw them in the Rift. At the start, no one would have suggested such a thing seriously. But people do strange things when they are desperate. Things that would shame them in the future if they ever live long enough to consider it."

They passed through five sets of doors, each one reinforced. Only two had actual guards, the last one having two. They bowed and pulled the door open as soon as Tengrii arrived.

"They are doing well, Your Majesty," one of the guards said, her grip on the gate tightening. "All things considered. Their parents are with them as well."

Rhea blinked as she peered into the large cell. These were

the ones his people wanted to sacrifice? They were mostly kids. Teenagers perhaps with a few adults. It was hard to say their ages because they, too, appeared to be monsters. Just small youthful monsters. They stared at her with wide eyes, some wrapped in blankets, others simply sitting on the floor. The adults drew the younger ones closer.

"Hello, young ones," Tengrii said, a heavier note in his voice despite his smile.

They greeted him with quiet politeness, but none approached.

"Someone tried to get through before nightfall," one of the girls with a large blue blanket wrapped around her shoulders said. She appeared to be one of the older ones, two smaller ones beside her. "It sounded like they might make it, but General Yoto caught them. He came back to tell us we were safe."

"He doesn't look like he feels so good," said one child.

"How much longer before we can take them home?" one of the adults, a woman who now resembled some sort of bird-human hybrid, asked. Feathers sprouted irregularly from her arms as she clasped two of the young ones close. "Is there any word at all?" Her gaze darted toward Rhea. "Is this the newcomer they mentioned?"

"We are still working on solutions." He gestured then to Rhea. "Yes. This is Rhea."

Rhea lifted her hand in greeting.

She took in the large cell. Efforts had been made to ensure it was at least somewhat cozy and habitable. Blankets and pillows on each of the beds. Books stacked up against the walls. Clay with wooden tools. A few games involving markers and chips as well as something which she guessed was similar to besreds and dragons. A few other boxes also sat at the far side of the room. Bars and handles fastened into the ceiling

252

and along the walls allowed for something of an obstacle course. But for all that, it was still a prison cell.

He moved about and spoke with each one in turn.

A pale-green naga girl with long fangs and soft round eyes tugged on her tunic. "Is this happening where you are too?"

"Something like this. My people are working on a solution as well," she said, forcing herself not to pull away. This girl's features were far more snake-like, perhaps because she was a much younger shifter who did not yet have Tengrii's skills to adapt the shape.

"We didn't mean to cause so much trouble," an older youth said from behind a pillar. "It seems like it's getting worse. We just—we heard that more people want to finish what the Daars started."

"The Daars?" She glanced up as Tengrii approached.

He placed his hand on the girl's shoulder. "A small faction. When the Tue-Rah's formation point appeared, it created alarm throughout the entirety of the kingdom. Some wanted to flee. Others to petition. And some decided it should be settled with violence. We do not want to be disturbed here. They attempted to seal the Tue-Rah in place and keep it from forming its access point at the same time that these young ones made their own attempt."

"To seal it?" Rhea asked, surprised.

"No." The girl shook her head. She stared at the ground. "We wanted to see if we could slip through and visit one of the other worlds and then get back. It was supposed to work both ways. The Daars had already started doing—something."

"What did they do exactly? Was it something from the Forbidden Arts?"

The others had gathered around as well.

"No one knows what it was," said one of the adults, a minotaur with dark-red fur. "The children didn't know enough to recognize it. But from what we can tell, the Daars were in the middle of some sort of process. A ritual of some sort."

Tengrii brushed the back of his knuckle against his cheek.

"We tried to slip through," the smaller minotaur child said. His ears twitched. "And then—then everything changed." He ducked his head.

"It was bright," said another small voice, "and it was like the air was tearing open."

"Part of the ground fell out," said a child who looked more like a terror bird than a human. "The whole ground just fell away. And two of the Daars fell in."

Three of the children started crying.

One of the women, possibly their mother, guided them aside. "Shush now," she whispered.

Another of the women looked to Rhea. "It has been so difficult for them," she said softly. "They do their best, but even here, they suffer."

"Not for much longer, I hope," Tengrii said, his voice unusually heavy. "We will have news soon. Thank you for your time."

As they bid them goodbye, Rhea found her mind twisting and turning over this new information. There was an answer here. This was what the Paras and the others on her side needed to know. As she thrust her hand into her pocket, her fingers struck the psychic stones. Hope cut through her, then faded as Tengrii guided her out.

The psychic stones could be taught to hold another message. Tiehro and Salanca had shown her how to do that, and Killoth had taught her some tricks as well. The problem was that she had no way of getting the stones to Killoth or anyone who might be able to receive the message.

"Are you all right?" Tengrii asked as they continued down the passage.

"I'm thinking about what has happened. On my side, the big problem has been they could never understand what caused this. But this—can you tell me anything more about it?" She stopped, taking hold of his arm. "Can you show me where the Tue-Rah was trying to emerge please?"

His gaze dropped to her hand, his brow drawing up. Then he nodded slowly. "Yes, I think I have enough time for that."

25

EMERGENCE

Rhea's mind worked faster as Tengrii guided her through the maze of passages. It felt as if she was on the verge of a powerful discovery, and she pored over the thoughts and concepts, trying to organize them.

By the time they reached the ragged passage and uneven stone cavern where she'd first accosted Tengrii, a rough picture had formed in her mind.

"So, if I am following this correctly, the Rift is an interaction between the two events? What the children did and then the Daars?" Rhea asked.

Tengrii slowed his pace to match hers. "Yes, as best we understand it."

"Why do some of your people think those children need to be sacrificed to the Rift? It can't just be because it's the only thing left."

A muscle in his jaw jumped. "What the Daars did involved killing one of their own members. We found his body when we came to investigate. He had been drained of his blood. The children, mercifully, did not see him in the darkness, but the theory is that they were unable to complete the ritual. And that because the children interrupted, they or others who may have been chosen, could perhaps be used to complete the ritual and protect us. It is a monstrous thing. But we have found no reason to believe that that is the case other than the dead body."

"And none of the Daars survived so you could interrogate them?"

He shook his head. "They all perished before we could learn anything, and then the slick formed." He gestured forward as they entered the chamber.

It seemed much larger now that there was no one else in here. The ledge she had climbed along wound around the left side and then jutted out. Over on the right, another more jagged ledge appeared at intervals. The sea of purple and blue gas at the edge of the cliff moved in slow-sifting patterns. Soft light rose from it, and a low fog clung to its surface.

They stopped at the edge of the cliff near the large black spill of what looked like tar. It was too large for her to jump across completely, though she suspected Tengrii wouldn't find it a challenge.

"When some first suggested through rumor and intrigue that the young ones should be sacrificed because they had interfered and the Rift now wanted them, most everyone was horrified." Tengrii crossed his arms as he stared down at the slick. "I still do not know who started those rumors. They were smart to keep themselves quiet. Larkin, the one who broke you free, eventually came to agree with that opinion as have some others. I never would have thought it possible. For some, it seems like the only option left. If we could give them an alternative, they might stop the demand entirely. But..." He tapped the back of his knuckle to his cheek.

She halted, realizing the source of his uncertainty. He

actually didn't know that sacrificing the children wouldn't work. "You think it might be real?"

He glanced around, then lowered his voice. "I am no practitioner of magic, no matter what my form looks like or myths says. But what has come from this Rift has forced all of us to endure what we fear most in one way or another. If the Daars did something evil, then it would take evil to complete it. In which case—we are doomed." His gaze drifted out across the purple sea of light and mist. "The psychics will either die by the Ki or from fright or starvation. The elementalists will disintegrate. The shifters will go feral and destroy themselves. And the humans—we just have to pray that they can find a way out or else nothing will remain at all. For many of my people, completing the ritual and finishing the sacrifices is all that is left."

"The only thing left that you can see. The Tue-Rah—you said that it was starting to form here. This world is preparing to join with the other worlds and cease to be separated?"

"In theory, yes. But ever since that slick formed over it, it hasn't grown much though the spill itself does."

"It hasn't grown in a way that you can see, but what if that is part of what's making the Rift worse? The pressure from the Tue-Rah's formation will keep intensifying. It will break through. You can't stop the Tue-Rah forever. It's a force of nature. It's like holding back an ever-increasing wall of water. And the formation of a new point is a huge deal."

"And what is your point?"

"We need help from people who can figure this out. They might have a chance if they can see where this is actually coming from. It'll at least help them eliminate a lot of other probabilities."

"Half my kingdom is likely to rebel if I suggest such a

thing," he responded. "There could be a complete revolt. They are terrified of being dragged from their homes."

"But why?"

"Because we aren't supposed to be on this world at all." He bowed his head, frustrated.

She halted, frowning. "Then how did you get here?"

"That doesn't matter. What does is that allowing the Tue-Rah to continue forming is dangerous," he continued. "It poses a great risk to your worlds as well. Yes, this plague or curse or whatever it is has reached where you live. It is hurting your people, but it is not as bad there as it is here. If we open that gateway, it may spill over even more."

She crouched near the dark substance. It shone like oil, but its thickness was more like tar. She picked up a rock and then pressed it against the substance. When she pulled it free, a little dark residue remained. It reminded her of the sealing gum used in some of the pipes, only stronger, thicker, and apparently self-replicating. There were hints of something glowing beneath at points, but the spill appeared to be just large enough to cover it almost completely.

"And you said it's expanding?"

"Yes. Every time the earth quakes, it seems to move as well. Sometimes the lines down there expand and almost break free. Or at least they used to. As matters worsened, it became unsafe for anyone to remain here driving those points."

She scowled. It actually reminded her of the substance that they put in broken pottery as well. She'd worked with something like this before, and while it was hard to get out, it was easy to break once hardened.

"So it's filling in those lines."

"Yes."

There was something odd about this.

She peered down from the ledge. Up here, the spill seemed far more intentional in its placement and perhaps marked its growth if the ridges in the spill were actual indicators. But it also showed even more stress upon the rocky floor. The mosaic marble tiles had been almost entirely upended, indicating significant strain and stress throughout the entire cavern floor. If this continued, it was likely to break off completely into the chasm. That force might be enough to destroy the entire cavern. Perhaps the whole kingdom. And the multiple tremors certainly didn't make that easier.

How much longer could it endure?

"I don't think we have to remove all of it," she said. "Perhaps we just have to remove it enough to let the Tue-Rah continue its formation. In the temples, there are designs and patterns cut into the stone. It's hard to tell in the chamber itself when the Tue-Rah fills it because the light goes everywhere, but it looks as if it moves out while following the pattern. And all of the designs are connected. Maybe it's like water flowing through channels. You don't have to clear all of it away at first. Just enough at the points where it will then be able to flow. What have you done to try to remove it?"

"No one has tried to remove it. We don't want the Tue-Rah opening here."

She folded her arms. "What happened exactly that makes you think the Paras' first response will be to take you away from here?"

He scoffed, then shook his head. "It doesn't matter. We won't be opening it."

"So you would all rather remain here and die—"

"We will pursue other options."

"Excluding sacrifice."

"Of course," he snapped. His brow furrowed as he glared

at her. "We are not animals, no matter what we may look like."

"I'm not suggesting that you are. But something does have to change. There is nothing left. Uncovering the Tue-Rah and allowing it to form while opening you up to receiving more aid may actually help solve this problem. They may be able to come in and understand what needs to be done." She sat down on the edge of the ledge, frowning. "But there's something else, isn't there? You didn't say the Daars were evil. You said they had a reason. And no one here wants the Tue-Rah to work even if it could save your lives and you had to leave."

"Can you accept that it would be dangerous for us to allow the Tue-Rah to connect our world? Not just for us but for everyone."

She pressed her hands into the stone. "I don't understand. You all could die in this place. I thought you were desperate for another solution."

"There will be another solution. We just have to find it."

"What if the solution is letting the Tue-Rah do what it is supposed to? What if its formation is exactly what is needed? I think that we need others to help with this. We don't have enough people here. Or enough skills. If this ship is sinking, then shouldn't we call for help wherever we can find it? The only reason that most of those who have fallen are still living in the other worlds is because we have come together. Our communities are working together to save one another. You have tried to do the same here, but we have to open one to the other." She rubbed her arm. "If it hadn't been for the Dohahtee community and a friend there, my sister would probably be dead. My brother, too, would be in bad condition. Perhaps dead."

He dragged his hand over his eyes, then shook his head. "Salt-Sweet..." He shook his head. "Rhea, we were never supposed to be in this place. We came through a tear ourselves. It opened up on Uodri, and someone was doing an experiment. Some fungal spores got through the tear between the worlds, and it started to spread."

She'd heard of these tears or rips before. Points where the fabric between the other worlds and realms was so thin it could be passed by anyone. She climbed down from the ledge.

"It was known as the Blight," Tengrii continued. "It was this black crumbling mold that formed over everything. It attacked the stones and the flora. It spread so quickly, but it could be stopped through channeling our energy into the affected areas. Vawtrian energy. So my parents called for help among their kin and community. It was a secret they all swore to keep. We built camps initially. Complications developed because, of course, we brought more spores and seeds and all manner of things in with us and took more out. But we started to make progress. Somehow. The worlds balanced. They adapted. And it was as if we had our own private world that we could access at any point with all its wonders. The Blight was nearly under control." He dropped his gaze to the slick as he shook his head. "Eventually, though my father concluded that as the leader of our village, we could not continue in this way. Yes, we had stopped it almost entirely. But as soon as it was dealt with, we needed to alert the Paras to have the proper individuals come and investigate the matter. Those who might be considered guilty would be hidden.

"Some decided that there should be one last night of celebration in this wild world, untamed and unknown to any but us. And everyone in our village came. Even those who had sworn to keep the secret but never set foot across the tear. And at last, even my father relented. For some reason, that night, the tear mended itself and sealed everyone on the other side. Our entire village was here. And with that energy surge, the

Blight reformed and renewed." He dragged his hand across the back of his head as he stared off toward the Rift. "Much has changed over the years. Most everyone who lives here now was born after those events, but we all know the stories. And the risks. What we did all those years ago was wrong. Those spores should never have been introduced to this world, and we are fortunate that it was not far worse. We have all sworn to care for this world, and we have lived in such a way to avoid creating more harm as best we can. But unless there was a way to warn those on the other side of what they may find here, restoring the Tue-Rah may unleash only misery and more suffering and more death."

"Why would everyone want to come over here? How did you have enough supplies to survive?" She chewed on the inside of her lip. That sounded odd. Not as if he was lying to her. It just didn't settle with her.

He shrugged. "I asked my mother why it was we would risk contaminating this world with a celebration if our purpose was to protect it, and she said they had taken precautions. It was just that they loved it so much, and everyone wanted to say goodbye."

"What was it called? The fungal spores?"

"Pulka spores."

That was odd too. How had his parents or anyone even known that the Blight came from those spores?

"I didn't think that that could just happen accidentally. I thought someone had to bring it over. Or take it back. Like intentionally. It's not like when these rifts happen you can just see straight into the other world."

He shrugged. "I do not know all the answers for it, but I hope that you can see why this must be let go. In addition to all of this, my people are afraid of what will happen. And we are—we share very little in common, especially now, with the races we originally came from. It has been over a thousand years, and yet they would not know us. They would not accept us."

She frowned, tilting her head as she studied him. All the other questions faded away. "How can you be so certain they would not accept you? You don't know them either."

He scoffed. "My parents brought books to read on this side and kept them in the camp. I have learned quite a lot about my father's people and my mother's people. We are not the same at all. And now, more than ever, I—we—all of us here—are disgraces to our source."

"You are one of the finest men I have ever known," she said sternly, moving back to meet his gaze. "Tengrii, I don't know what you've read—"

"Salt-Sweet." He grasped her hand in his. His claws raked her skin lightly as he pressed hers between his. "All that is irrelevant. The camp, the celebration, everything, because of one very important question. Would you really risk all the worlds to save us? We were never supposed to be here, and we have impacted this world. Who is to say that we would not unleash worse? In truth, I would say that that is not only possible but far more likely. And those who came before me believed the same."

She bit her tongue. Fair. That was fair. Still... "So what you're saying is that you would need to know that there was a way to protect against that? That you are willing to die—that you are willing to let your people die—rather than risk sending out worse? Even if it costs countless others because there is no cure?"

"We will keep searching for the cure or the way to break this curse. Whatever it is. We will search for it with every last breath and every last scrap of sanity we have. But we will not condemn others to a worse fate to save our own skins. What we might unleash here? That could be far worse than us perishing here and being forgotten. I hope you can understand that. If there is one thing I know beyond any doubt, it is that the Blight is a terrifying thing. It adapts and changes, and it could utterly destroy all these other worlds as well."

She nodded slowly. Yes, she actually did. And it also meant she would never be able to return home either.

Setting her hands on her hips, she drew in a deep breath. "All right then. So what I am hearing you say is that if you did know that the other worlds—the Paras—the leaders—all of them—if they were able to prepare for this, then you would be all right with it? If they know how to handle pulka spores and whatever might come from it, then that would change things."

"If that could be done, yes, though my people would not be glad of that change. The matter of our removal, if it came to that, would cause problems, but at least they would live long enough to face it. Our Neyeb were never able to reach those on the other worlds. But it doesn't matter. No matter how powerful your friends on the other side are, there is no way to reach them and no way to give them that knowledge. So we will have to do what we can to resolve the matter here on this side and pray that if Elonumato hears those of us in this place so far from all the rest, that He will bring healing, because we of Serroth will not be the harbingers of death to all the rest of creation." He glanced at the door, then shook his head. " Come. I have other matters that require my attention. Time is passing too swiftly."

26

REVELATIONS

Tengrii took her back to the library at her request, then went in search of Elthko. He found the steward near the back entrance of the palace where there had once been a beautiful marble dais with a fountain. The earthquakes had cracked it early on, and they had channeled the rivers off elsewhere, the repairs to this particular location not nearly so important as the others. Eventually, a massive cave-in had blocked off the external access still further, making this point in the palace nearly useless.

Elthko had lit one torch on the leaning pillar, and he stood with his back to Tengrii, staring into the great cracked fountain. A cool draft from lower within the mountain rose, making the flames on the torch dance and scattering the shadows along the coarse wall.

"Do you remember playing in the fountain when you were a child, Your Majesty?"

"Yes. Though I was not aware that my memory was at issue."

He drew closer, cautious. After so many failed assassination attempts, he didn't like to be too exposed. The dark grey stones could hide so much, and the passages to his right and left twisted and coiled into darkness.

"Margo was the one who asked that we put it here. The design was taken from her childhood home. Before she was taken. She so wanted us to have koi. Your mother tried to find an equivalent, but the best she could do was to form these mossy balls that loosely resembled fish."

Margo had been like an aunt to him. A low pang struck him as he recalled her. How long since she had passed? It felt as if it was a lifetime ago.

"I do remember that." He smiled sadly. "And my mother would take me here to tell me the stories of how we came to be in this world and of our charge and the Blight."

Elthko kept his long arms clasped behind his back, his voice sadder now. "Yes. I respected both your parents very much. They were noble individuals, and they never forgot the larger purpose which they served. In truth, their leadership and compassion are the reason any of us survived. And I know that they would have rather you never heard this, but...there is no other choice."

"Heard what?" His gaze shifted to the great pile of rubble in the cave-in. The air was colder here, but their voices did not echo. It smelled sharper and clearer as well.

"Our kingdom started off as a village, and our village started off in a camp. A horrible camp. We were with many, many others. It was run by a man who had many names but whom we generally referred to as Caoxius. He had a Machat prophet known as The Tiger. He had horrible visions of a coming future that was so cruel and vicious that none would survive. All the worlds would be laid bare. Unless we learned to defend ourselves. Unless we became proactive." He bowed his head. "That camp was an abomination. They tortured us.

Experimented on us. Cut us to pieces and left us alone only long enough for us to heal so they could do it again. If he found any Vawtrian had locked, he would intentionally put their veskaro or veskare in grave peril to force them to complete the experiments or enter the rifts he formed. There was no escape."

Tengrii leaned closer. He had never heard anything remotely like this.

Elthko's voice shuddered. "Your parents found one another in that camp, though they tried to hide it. You might not have known this, but it was a dangerous match. Your mother was an Unato blight tamer. For a Vawtrian who hasn't mastered all those venoms and poisons, that is a grave risk. But your father did not care. They made one another stronger from the very beginning. And that strength and cunning is what led to them arranging the great escape.

"Because of them, we were able to break free. It was a harrowing and violent escape, and the journey that followed was almost as hard. But when we finally reached civilization again, no one fully believed us. Something horrible had happened to us. That everyone agreed upon. We showed obvious signs of trauma, abuse, experimentation, and worse. But no one believed that there was a Caoxius or a Machat prophet named The Tiger who had spoken what he had, nor that there were these entities or monsters that were coming to devour all that lived upon the worlds.

"It was useless. After all, justice requires evidence. There was never enough evidence to prove what all had happened. Only we truly understood. So we banded together and traveled to a remote place. We tried to build new lives for ourselves. But the fear never left." The muscles in his jaw and neck twitched. "When things like that are done to you? You can't forget. You don't. The knowledge that one day Caoxius could return. Or even worse, what he and The Tiger foretold would come true, and the monstrosities that they sought to battle would come for us as well as everyone else. It was too much. We knew we had to get somewhere safer." He turned then to face Tengrii, his eyes sharper. "Then fortune blessed us. Gao returned from hunting and told us that she had seen a caravan with some of Caoxius's guards and attendants among the members. Neither Caoxius nor The Tiger were present. These individuals were simply traveling. But we caught them. And that's when we decided to protect ourselves."

Tengrii straightened. The grim note that had entered Elthko's voice unsettled him. "What did you do?"

"We captured them. All of them. And we used them to create an opening through the dimensions. A painful passage into a Separated World, ripped right into the fabric of our reality and made stable by draining their life forces. Not a blood portal precisely. It was stronger than that. More stable but slower to build. Dangerous if not properly navigated. But we had all been forced to endure this before. Now we did it of our own will and for our own benefit." He shook his head. "None of you who came after us have ever really questioned us, and that perhaps makes this all the more painful. You were all willing to accept that our whole village passed through an unintentional opening into another world just so we could celebrate one more time. And that we just so happened to have exactly what we needed." He lifted his hands. "A miracle, I suppose. And all of you did seem to love it."

Tengrii's stomach tightened. Nausea welled within him. His parents, the founders, everyone who had come before him, they had used murder to gain access to this place.

"So it was all a lie?" He blinked. "I've seen the Blight. I saw what happened when—"

"You saw what you were told was the Blight. The Blight

was an invention to ensure that when the Tue-Rah formation came—because we all knew one day it would—it would ensure that there would be a good reason to keep everyone here. How could we open up portals to other worlds when this threat—this Blight exists within our own?" He lifted his shoulders. "It was effective. Everyone who needed to fear it feared it. Your mother cultivated the pulka spores in her medical work, trying to find a cure for some of the side effects of the experiments and to perhaps reverse it as well. But they are not actually dangerous. It was an accident that she ever even called them that. It's far easier to convince people of something dangerous when it's a name they don't recognize."

Tengrii closed his eyes. The world was spinning. "Why are you telling me this?" he demanded.

"Because we cannot allow the Tue-Rah to form here if we are to remain in this place. We cannot be on any of the inhabited worlds. The threat has not changed. It could come at any point, and we would have no way of knowing. No way of defending ourselves. The Daars did not act with our permission. The remaining founders all intended to speak with you, but the Daars did not want to wait. And one thing led to another. The children interfering—" Elthko shuddered, his eyes shutting as well. Thin lines of green light escaped beneath his eyelids. "They interrupted the ritual before the Daars could finish it, and they became bound to it. The Rift does require their blood. It must be done, Your Majesty. There is no other way to stop it. But if you spoke with those children and their parents, you know that already they suffer."

"So you—you did know about this? You knew what they were doing?" he demanded.

Elthko tilted his head. "It must be completed in a particular way, Your Majesty. I do not pretend this is not difficult. Survival is. We have searched for every possible alternative.

None of us want this. But what other choice do we have? We have exhausted every alternative that would reverse all of this, cure the illnesses, and take us back to what we were while also keeping us safe."

He froze. "It would turn us back into what we were?"

"Jaiku believes so. So did Birkii, though he fought the idea as much as you. Raimu as well at first. Gao is uncertain. I—I do not know, but even if all it stops is the pulsing and keeps it from getting worse, that would be enough. This formation will ensure that the Tue-Rah is removed from our world and unable to continue developing."

"*This* is monstrous." His lips curled with disgust.

Even if it did turn them back to their old selves, it was horrifying to contemplate. And yet it connected to a far deeper fear. What if this was the solution?

"Yes. But so is allowing this to continue. Seven Daars intended to sacrifice themselves so that we would be saved. It was noble and good despite being forbidden. It was the children's own inability to follow rule and law which put them in that situation. None of us would have chosen this. They cannot be substituted either. If that were the case, we could ask for volunteers. It has to be them. Consider now how many have died in these past months. How many more will perish if this continues. Even if the Tue-Rah forms and the outsiders come here, what guarantee is there that we will be restored? Will they help us heal? Is that even possible? Will they let us stay? Probably not. And if they knew the truth of how we came to be in this place, they would surely imprison us."

Tengrii stared at him, struggling to find the words. The old steward spoke with both sadness and calm, as if he truly had weighed all the options and concluded this was the only possible solution. As if he wasn't actually suggesting throwing children into a glowing mass of energy to die.

"You will need to decide soon. The ritual can only be completed on certain days. It needs to be started on the morning of the third day and completed before the third night. We can prepare a substance that will dull their fear and allow them to enter a state of bliss. The ritual does not require their terror. They don't even have to know that it is happening."

"This—" His mouth had gone dry. He brushed the back of his knuckle against his cheek. "I would never have thought you capable of this."

"No. But I am. It was your parents who came up with the initial plan to use Caoxius's attendants for the lifeblood of the ritual. If they were here, they would make the same choice at this point. As our leader, you must look to the greater good of your people and make the hard choices. If we do not complete this ritual, there are no guarantees. We will all fade and perish, and what good will any of this have accomplished? Let the young ones fulfill the ritual's requirements. We will mourn them and honor their memory, and we will bless their names for their sacrifice. And one other thing."

What could there possibly be? He braced himself for even worse.

"You have found your veskaro."

He stiffened. "Are you threatening her?" he demanded, bristling.

"No." Elthko actually chuckled, a faint smile pulling up beneath his thick mass of hair. "I am reminding you that you have someone for whom you should want to live. And someone to protect. If the ritual is not completed, I do not think that the earthquakes will cease. They are getting worse. Eventually, this whole place will come down. And even if by some miracle the humans do manage to escape, they will not survive long. The surface of this world is harsh. Especially for

272

them. She is a beautiful and idealistic soul. Much like you. Make the hard choice and protect her so that you may both share in the good that this life has to offer. She does not have to know about this. In fact, I would recommend against it. She will not understand."

"And if I refuse, will there be more assassination attempts?"

Elthko tilted his head. "Are you suggesting I have been behind those?"

"Have you?" he demanded.

"I should not be surprised you need to ask that after what has been revealed, but no." He huffed a small laugh, his voice softening. "I have no designs on your life, Your Majesty. Nor, would I add, do any of the other remaining founders. We are trying to save you and, by extension, your beloved. It is the younger and more desperate members of your kingdom who have tried to take your life. They are impulsive, terrified, ineffective, and ignorant, lashing out only because they don't know what else to do. Further proof that this cannot continue because, mark my words, Your Majesty, if anyone attempts to perform the ritual and fails or destroys those young ones without completing the ritual properly, then it is over for us as well. There are no longer any substitutions. The young ones must be guarded with great care until we are ready." He glanced over his shoulder at the path leading back into the palace. "There is another matter that needs my attention. But consider this proposition, Your Majesty. The council will convene again, and if there is not some other viable solution that will resolve all of these concerns, then this is the course that we must take."

27

DANGEROUS MEETINGS

Though Gao greeted Rhea gruffly, it was clear that the scholar was pleased to see her. Rhea took her place by the cracked seat, choosing to sit on the floor once again as she had in her own home. Then she resumed sketching.

Gao glanced at her from the desk. "Some of the servants overheard you. You were talking with the king about finding a way to connect us to the other worlds. You have such faith in them that you think the benefits outweigh the dangers? Have they done better in caring for the fallen? Are they closer to finding a cure on your side? Or preventing the threats that we might pose?"

Rhea picked up a small stack of paper and tested the quill. It was hard to find the words. "I don't know how close they are. Only that they have been working toward it very hard. They're fighting to save all those in comas. But some..."

She dropped her gaze, recalling the Ki Valo Nakar once more. Her stomach dropped. Those horrible moon-like eyes. The skeletal face over the man's. The way it had called out that man's soul. How many others had it claimed? What of Salanca? Did she still fight? Had Tiehro fallen? Was Killoth still immune? Those questions gnawed at her.

"Some have still been lost," Rhea said. "More will be. If there was a way to warn them of the threat, then that might make this simpler. I just think that there is a greater chance of finding the solution if we all work together. Everyone wants this to end."

"That much is true," Gao muttered, returning to the book, "but even if we could assume that the Tue-Rah finishes its formation in enough time to allow us to connect to the other worlds, there is no guarantee that what it brings will not be worse in its own way. Or that we have enough time left to find the cure."

No. But with so many millions already at risk, could it really get that much worse? Perhaps she was being selfish. It was her family in jeopardy. But there were so many others as well. Half the races of the worlds were in this state, and who was to say it wouldn't spread on its own?

She refilled the ink pot. A little bit splattered over her fingers and the back of her hand.

Tengrii was not onboard with the decision, though, and he was not likely to change his mind unless she could find some way to confirm that the other worlds were prepared for them. She did have the psychic stones, but for a message this complicated, she needed to pass it through somehow. And she had to ensure it reached Killoth.

She bit her tongue. The introduction of Serroth to the rest of the worlds was going to be more challenging as Separated Worlds were not to be inhabited before they were opened. Surely something like this had happened before? Especially with the Tue-Rah. It was all so complicated, far beyond her comprehension, and utterly terrifying. But she couldn't shake the feeling that there was an answer.

"Are you doing more drawings today, newcomer?" a soft voice asked.

She lifted her head. One of the younger attendants stood near her. Probably Awdawm like her.

"Yes. Who do you want me to sketch?"

It was quieter today. Everyone was worn from the events of the previous night, and who could blame them? It was hard to endure under something so relentless. She still found it easy, though, to listen and bring their descriptions to life with her quill and ink.

It should have been a comforting way to pass the time. At points, it grew chaotic as the residents who could speak clustered about and gave their interpretations and thoughts. But she sorted through them and drew face after face. Gao brought her additional paper and ink. She had those pictures of her husband and brother still on the desk where she worked.

Two of the younger Awdawms came to sit with her, asking questions about how she managed it. This wasn't their skill set, they insisted. Their drawings looked like bad circles and rough sticks. So she tried to show them how to improve their skills and pointed out strengths in each.

More people joined as well. They didn't only want to talk with her. Some took the drawings and showed them to friends and family members. There were tears and smiles and sobs and laughter.

Around what was likely midday, Tengrii joined them, more resigned and contemplative, his brow heavy and his manner quiet. He insisted it was simply fatigue.

Dulce, an air elemental who looked as if she were made

entirely of glass, brought them food—more salted fish with a fungus salad and something like dried plums.

Rhea found her own appetite wanting. Not because the food tasted bad but because of the weight of this place. It crushed her. No wonder all the psychics had collapsed beneath it and fallen into comas. She set her plate aside.

"I'm going to get some more paper and prepare for the afternoon," she said, standing.

Tengrii nodded, looking up at her at last, his gaze still heavy. "You'll still remain here then?"

"Unless it's a bother?" She glanced toward Gao.

"It's not a bother," Gao interjected. "She stays out of the way, and it's nice to have reasons to talk beyond death, suffering, and dying. Don't worry. I'll protect her."

Tengrii smiled. "Thank you." He released a low breath as he picked up one of the pages, then shook his head. "Rhea, your sketches have brought more comfort to my people than anything in the past four months. So yes, if you wish to remain here, you can."

Her cheeks heated from the compliment. It was perhaps one of the kindest things anyone had ever said about her art. She turned so that he wouldn't see and crossed over to the box with the paper. It was of a thicker texture and heavier quality than what she used on the other side, but she liked its weight and grain. She took her time, though, separating out precisely what she thought she needed.

A faint scent similar to ash and smoke struck her nostrils. She glanced to the right.

General Yoto, the man of living fire, stood in the doorway, away from the wood and paper. His gaze was fixed on Dulce, who was fussing over some of the younger attendants and insisting that they eat. Then, when Dulce lifted her gaze to the door, her voice grew silent, her expression both sad and warm. Lifting her long, thin hand, she pressed a kiss upon her fingers and then blew it to him.

He mirrored the gesture, then stepped away, a mournful weight in his stride though he carried himself tall and straight. The red-orange glow of his presence faded beyond the doorway.

Rhea's heart ached at the sight. Polph, the sadness and suffering that these poor people went through. She could practically feel the pining for one another. She returned her focus to the box of paper. Fixing any of this felt impossible.

"He comes to see me every day," Dulce said, suddenly standing right at her elbow.

Rhea started, almost dropping the pages. "What?"

The tall woman barely had any coloration at all. Even her hair was translucent. She still offered a smile as she lifted her arm stiffly toward the doorway. "My husband. We have not been able to share a bed or even be in the same room for months now. But we find what ways we can."

"Yet you are cooking? Around hot temperatures? Doesn't that hurt?" She stared at the woman in shock.

Dulce kept her arms folded, her manner far more at ease than Rhea would have guessed coming from someone who looked as if a single stumble could shatter her. "I have help. But more importantly, the temperature is constant. For now. It's the flares that make our being together almost impossible. Mine as well as his. I chill him if I am too close, and that sets him to burn hotter. It is almost funny, I suppose. We fell in love with one another decades ago in part because of how different we are from the other, and now those differences have been fashioned into such a state they may kill us."

That sounded excruciating. "I'm—I'm sorry."

Dulce shrugged, then dipped her head, her voice dropping to no more than a whisper. "Two of my aides heard you speaking with the king about uncovering the Tue-Rah's formation and allowing us to join the other worlds. Do you think they could heal us?"

"I've never seen anything like what you are going through, but there are so many places of healing. They might have something. Just—we have to find a way to let the other worlds know of the risks so they can prepare."

Dulce nodded again, her manner now tighter. "Then I pray we find a way. I would rather open the gates to other worlds than kill the small ones and their families. Even if it means we would all be imprisoned for coming to this place and held accountable for the deaths that came about because of this travesty. At least then—" She shook her head, then glanced around as if afraid others might hear. "If there is anything you need to make this happen, tell me. But do not let anyone know."

"Do you think your husband will support Tengrii if—"

"My husband is loyal to the king and his family. No matter what he decides, he will follow his orders. But in this case, yes, he would want to support the decision as well. Neither of us has long. We would rather take the chance of imprisonment to the alternatives." She stepped away, her manner brisk. She at once called out to one of the grey-clad attendants and asked him why he had not eaten more of his fish.

Rhea hugged the paper gently to her chest, careful not to bend it. Elonumato help them, they truly needed answers. And fast. But where could they get them?

Slowly, she returned to her seat. Tengrii had remained there, resting back on his tail as if it were a chair. His expression softened as soon as he saw her.

Her mouth went dry, and her heart beat faster.

"You have excellent paper here." She held up the pages to demonstrate her point. "I worked with a much flimsier kind back in my home. It bent and creased far too easily. And the grain of this paper is just so much easier to work with. It has a character all its own."

He nodded, though it was obvious he didn't fully grasp why this was a positive point rather than a neutral one. "Well, I'm glad you like it."

"Have you drawn him?" Gao asked, tilting her head as she indicated Tengrii. "He's always been a beauty. Even when he was a young one. Took after both his parents and got the best of both."

Tengrii shook his head at her, his brow creasing. "None of that."

"Does not make it less true," Gao said, cutting her eyes at him. "Besides, artists draw what intrigues them."

Had she not been so busy with all her commissions, she probably would have spent hours and hours sketching Tengrii from the dreams. Even now, he would make an incredible subject. His eyes alone captivated her.

She tapped her finger against the quill, examining its point. Then she picked up the board and the drawing she had been working on before she went to get the paper. "There is never any lack of intriguing subjects to draw."

He peered over her shoulder at her current sketch of the library turned infirmary with Gao at the desk. He chuckled softly, his mouth so close to her neck it almost made her shiver. "You know exactly how to capture the intrigue."

Prickles of pleasure rose through her. His voice soothed her mind and stirred something within her.

She cleared her throat, finding it hard to look at him. "They're just ink sketches. A little sloppier and looser than what I'd generally like."

"No. It's perfect. All these sketches you've done are perfect." He smiled down at her, his incredible eyes warm and comforting and filled with—was it longing? Or was he just aware that his days were ending and he wanted someone to spend them with? Either way, she couldn't blame him.

She almost wished he would put his arm around her. Maybe she should touch him. But where? Was it appropriate?

"This is a very intriguing place," she said softly.

It was.

And he was so close still, his breath caressing her shoulder. She barely hid another shudder. Her own breath tightened. When he drew back, she missed his heat.

The midday meal passed swiftly after that. Then Tengrii left with promises to return once he had tended to his duties. She glanced up in time to see his powerful back as he disappeared beyond the threshold, lengthy tail moving along behind.

She continued on her sketches, taking additional requests and making drawings of loved ones and former appearances. As she worked, she contemplated the options available to them. If she could find a way to use the psychic stones and get that message to Killoth, he would handle the rest. She was certain of it.

But how?

She froze, the quill nearly falling from between her fingertips. There was one thing that no one had considered. For good reason too. Now, though, it seemed so obvious.

Her heart raced faster as she chewed on the inside of her lip and hatched a section of shadows in the drawing of an old woman with tightly curled hair wrapped in a colorful sash.

If the Ki and the Ki Valo Nakar were the same entities, then maybe...maybe they had more help than they realized. The Ki Valo Nakar moved freely between all the worlds. Wherever there were sentients, it was possible for it to travel, and it was of the Neyeb. Or so the myths said. And she had no reason to doubt that. Especially not here.

All she needed was a break.

Somehow, it happened. A minor miracle in itself. She wasn't even sure how. She had just passed the sketch to the old man with great tusks and watery eyes, then blinked, realizing everyone else was handling other tasks. The last traces of the midday meal had been cleared away. Only the faintest hint of fish lingered in the air, mostly obscured by the heavy scent of peace incense.

Gao continued to work at the desk, a couple of her tentacles twitching and flopping. They thudded against the wooden frame and stone braces. She picked up one of the vials from the box beside her and studied it.

Rubbing her arms, Rhea crossed over to her. "Is that just the fog?"

"Hmm, hmm." Gao chewed on her thin lip. "We're still trying to understand it. The one thing we do know is that if you hit a shifter with this, she goes out of her mind. The larger the dose, the stronger the effect, so obviously, we don't want to do that."

"Obviously. Did you say that the Ki Valo Nakar comes every day?"

"The Ki? More or less."

"Could you tell me where it is likely to be today?"

"You want to see it?" When Rhea nodded, Gao shrugged. "It shows up most often near the patients who have been comatose the longest. Today that would be in the resonance chamber." She indicated a room on the map. It didn't appear to be too far away. "But be careful. The Ki is not fond of interruptions. Not that it's ever killed anyone like you to my knowledge." She squinted at her. "What do you want with it, anyway? More drawings?"

"I need to ask it some questions."

Gao cocked her head, her purple-pink skin flushing brighter and turning almost violet at the top of her peaked head. "Well, I hope you get helpful answers as opposed to killed. I'll let the attendants there know you are coming."

"One more thing." She held up her finger. "May I take a vial of the fog to it?"

"Why?"

"I want to ask it if it knows what it is or what can cure it."

Gao's skin flushed even brighter. She almost laughed, then shook her head. "Fine. A small one. Do not break it. Go straight there. I need to get these boxes and the rest of the samples into a safer place anyway." She pointed at her with her quill. "And I want to hear what the Ki has to say about it."

"Yes. Of course. I'll be sure to tell you."

This wasn't nearly as dangerous as it sounded. The Ki Valo Nakar didn't kill unless it was provoked. Assuming that this was the Ki Valo Nakar and not something else entirely.

She picked up one of the smaller vials and slipped it into her pocket. It was securely corked, and the glass was thick and solid. "Thanks. And if something goes wrong, I'm not expecting anyone to rescue me."

She took one more look at the map and then hurried down the hall. With the map committed to her memory, she found it easy to locate the resonance chamber. The two attendants on duty there lifted their hands in greeting to her, but they carried on with their tasks, one feeding broth to a patient while the other tucked the blanket in around another.

She took in the entirety of the room, searching for the uncanny entity. The resonance chamber had an enormous domed ceiling that had been polished until it practically glowed. The natural veining in the rocks looked to have been the base of the design, and someone had found a way to draw those veins out into delicate designs and whorls and intersecting shapes until it reached the center where it became a grand depiction of various events. Men and women streaming through a tear, crawling on their hands and knees to pass through. The cutting away of what was likely the Blight. Some sort of dancing and celebrating. All had been accomplished with only the natural tones of the rocks.

The walls likewise were smooth. They captured the light and made it brighter, but the heaviness of the air and the way every footstep echoed made it eerie. Her own breaths seemed loud. That should have made it easy to spot or at least hear.

She halted.

There.

Not by sound. It moved with utter silence. It almost blended into the shadows entirely.

But there it was.

The Ki Valo Nakar.

It stood over a motionless body on the far side of the room, clawed hands extended as the soul shimmered and formed within the chest. The darkness around it shimmered while shadows danced on the polished stone walls, the dramatic curves accentuating and distorting them at once.

She reached the bed on the other side of it, then cleared her throat. "Hello."

It turned abruptly, almost as if shocked to be addressed. The Neyeb host beneath the garb and antlers and brilliant moon eyes was not especially large. Easily two inches shorter than she. And yet the Ki Valo Nakar seemed to loom over her. Perhaps a trick of her mind. Perhaps the shadows. Perhaps both states were true at once.

The attendants froze as well. They backed away, moving to the opposite side of the room.

The Ki Valo Nakar stared at her now with inexpressive

curiosity, a silent demand in the air for her to speak if she was going to take away its precious time.

"I know this is unusual." She moistened her lips. "And I do not mean for this to be in any way offensive, but I need your help—"

It started to turn away.

"You are of the Neyeb! You require a Neyeb host. At this rate, there will be none left! They're all dying. They will all die if we don't find a cure except maybe one or two. And who knows if they can last through this? It keeps changing. We've all seen that. So, even though you don't normally intervene, you have to this time. Because what happens to you then? Who is to say that you can continue to protect your host from this? What happens if he falls too? The myths say that you'll be condemned to wander the worlds until the end of time itself when your hosts are gone if you are not released. And clearly your host did not choose to release you. Helping me is the only way you can survive more than a few years with a host."

It halted, straightening. Slowly, it turned back to her. Those eyes sliced into her. Energy bristled off it as if she had angered it somehow.

She nodded, speaking faster. "Right. See this does affect you." She steadied herself as it moved closer. "I know you're doing what you must. Nothing personal in any of this. I understand. But see, we might have a way to fix this. No one here will agree to it because of the risk to the other worlds. Because they are afraid it may unleash far worse and far greater diseases and curses."

She reached into her pocket and removed one of the psychic stones. "In Dohahtee, there is a Neyeb named Killoth. If you give this to him, he'll get the message, and then he can tell the right people. They can make preparations."

Its eyes narrowed as it studied her. Then it spread its arms and gestured toward her and tapped its ear.

"How will I know the answer?" she guessed.

It nodded slowly.

"Perhaps you could bring it to me?"

It stared at her long and hard.

She lifted her shoulders, wincing. "I'm sorry to trouble you, but I don't know what else to do. But this benefits you too, right?"

It shook its head, sighed heavily, then held out its long bony hand.

"All right. Just a minute. I didn't—didn't prepare these first. I wanted to make sure you'd agree before I wasted them."

It shook its head at her again but kept its hand out.

The longer the message, the harder it was to replace. Her palms sweat as she pulled the psychic stones out. Killoth had only done a basic telepathic imprint on it and bound it to himself. She couldn't really erase that fully, which meant that he was going to get an earful of his own name and Salanca's screamed at him from the start, but this was workable.

She placed the psychic stone against her mouth and began whispering and imprinting every scrap of relevant information she could on it, praying it was enough. She'd done it many times before. It would probably be faint compared to someone more skilled, but Killoth was strong enough he could translate.

Stepping closer, she placed the psychic stone in the center of the Ki Valo Nakar's hand. "And one more thing." She pulled the vial out as well and placed it next to the stone. "Maybe they can test it. It's darker and thicker here, so maybe it's different from what reaches the other worlds. Unless you want to tell me something about it?"

It pulled its head back at a sharp angle, one eyebrow

dramatically cocked now as if to ask whether she was serious. Then it vanished, its great glowing white eyes disappearing last.

She fell back, gasping. Had it worked? Maybe?

"What was that about?" one of the attendants exclaimed.

She staggered away, almost giddy with hope and excitement. It was better than nothing. Much better than nothing.

She hurried back to the library. Her mind spun over what had happened with hope—intoxicating hope.

"Were you successful?" Gao asked when she returned.

Rhea nearly collapsed onto the crate and leaned against the wall. She wiped the sweat off her forehead. "I don't know. Maybe. I need to think about it."

"You did what you could." Gao's voice sounded...almost kind. "What did it have to say about the vial?"

Rhea almost told her what had happened, then stopped. A stab of unease passed through her gut. She couldn't put her finger on why. "It disappeared with it. It never said a word."

"Well, it was a long shot at best, though certainly bold. I suppose the worst that can happen to it is that it traps the Ki in a coma as well. I wouldn't be sorry to see that antlered bastard go down after all the terror it has brought here." Gao continued scratching out notes as she referred back to a series of pages. "When the shift ends in the next twenty minutes, you'll likely have more guests eager for sketches. You're up to it?"

"Yes. I'll probably need more black ink." She nudged the practically empty ink pot with her boot.

"Storeroom is just over there." Gao gestured toward a dark door without looking up. "Box labeled ink and wrapped in cloth. Maybe drink some water while you're up. You're looking pale."

Probably so. Her heart was racing so fast she was a little dizzy.

Crossing to the storeroom, she opened the door. Like most of the other rooms in this place, it was well-ordered, and everything was fastened or sealed or added to avoid breakage. It smelled like cedar, pine, charcoal, and cotton, and the air was several degrees cooler in here yet also somehow dryer than in other parts of the cave. It stretched on beyond her line of sight, the light from the doorway not enough to illuminate the entire room. The box with the ink was clearly labeled and on the first shelf with a strap holding it to the wall.

She opened the wooden lid. Inside, nestled among cloth and something similar to straw, were several large containers full of ink. She reached for one when footsteps sounded behind her. She started to turn. Something struck her on the back of her head. Her knees struck the stone floor. Everything went black.

28

TO THE RIFT

Tengrii pored over the reports, resting his jaw on his hand. Rhea's words and Elthko's confession gnawed at him.

Was he willing to let everyone here die? And all of this toxic fog that pulsed and flowed out of the Rift—they hadn't protected the other worlds from it after all.

But the cost.

The sheer cost of it all.

If only he could go back.

The choice had been easy. The Tue-Rah's formation had brought about so much alarm when it had initially started because of the lies about the Blight and the fact that they should not be here. Then the Tue-Rah had ceased to be an option.

He closed his eyes. These new reports Elthko had set aside for him proved how little time they had left. They were finally at a point where food was going to start growing scarce. These reports predicted dire results in the coming weeks. Yet at the rate that the Rift pulsed and the intensity with which it seized them, did they even have weeks left?

Seven more shifters had broken as well. And they hadn't come out of the madness. They raged and raved within their cells. A total of 152 now. Elonumato help them. That didn't even count the ones who had died from their maddened ravings.

But if this was a curse that was in flux because the ritual had not been completed—then all these lives were just being wasted. Eventually, the children would have to be sacrificed.

Yoto appeared at the door, hand to the stone frame. "Sir, there's been another incident."

"Another?" He lifted his head wearily. "What kind?"

"An attempted attack on the guarded ones. We weren't able to take any prisoners this time," he said. "They are getting more brazen in their attacks."

And the number of those loyal to him was waning.

"Find extra warriors and put them on duty there."

"We'll have to pull them from—"

"Just do it," he said quietly.

"With permission, sir," Yoto said, standing just in front of the wooden door frame. The fire that burned through him was not nearly so strong, but his frame looked thinner.

Tengrii nodded, indicating for him to continue.

"We do not have much longer. We will need to condense again. At the current rates, we will not be able to protect the guarded ones or the families and keep the broken ones contained. That is to say nothing about continuing to care for all those who are incapacitated. And..." He drew himself up taller, his voice firming as he spoke. "The strongest of the elementalists can survive perhaps three more third nights."

He nodded slowly. "There are hard choices ahead. We will need to discuss this further tomorrow."

He flinched as a pressure along the edge of his mind intruded. His vision doubled. Ah. What—what was that?

RHEA BLINKED SLOWLY, once more in the small room she and Tengrii had spent so much time talking in. The dream room.

She rubbed her head, her nerves shrieking at her. Grey fog obscured most of it, a haziness as well. It was as if she couldn't fully bring it into focus. And Tengrii was nowhere to be seen.

A dull pain vibrated through her head. Slowly, it came back to her. She had gone into the storeroom to get some ink. Someone had attacked her. But why? Was she still there? Was Tengrii here as well?

His voice seemed to come from a great distance. Yet it was clear despite the softness. "Rhea? Is that—what are you doing?"

She straightened and turned around the room. "I don't know what's going on. I was in the library. Went to get some ink. Then..." She chewed on the inside of her lip. "Something hit me! I'm unconscious."

How were they even talking right now? The bond between them really had to be getting stronger if it wasn't requiring both of them to be asleep. How long would it continue to strengthen?

"Stay calm. Wake up if you can. I'm coming for you."

She swayed on her feet, then staggered against the bed, grasping for anything to support herself.

How did you wake up in a place like this? The room was a construct. What was it Tiehro had said about breaking out of a thought-projection or a dream? Oh, that had been a long time ago.

The walls. Yes. Walls always had a weak point in a setting. She needed to look for places where there weren't as many details. In this foggy haze, that was tougher. Nothing quite wanted to come into focus. But there—there was a place that had no texture at all.

Lunging at it, she started beating on the wall. It dented but didn't fall. "Let me out!"

The darkness pushed back against her.

Good! She'd found the weak spot. Closing her eyes, she put her hands out and then rammed it with all her strength.

The wall collapsed. She sailed headfirst into the darkness.

Tengrii bolted up. "Someone has taken Rhea."

Yoto's eyes widened. He then stepped back and shouted for the guards to come.

Tengrii already raced toward the door and shot out into the hall. She had been in the library. Gao must have seen something.

His whole world was falling apart, but whatever evil worked its will within his home, he would not let it take her!

With a jolt, Rhea lurched awake. Someone was carrying her over their shoulder. She bounced with the movement. Someone who had long legs and big hooves. Rather bullish, maybe?

And where were they? A stone passage. Not especially insightful. She squinted, the world bouncing uncomfortably.

There was a large jagged tear in the wall roughly in the shape of an uneven triangle.

Someone else was trotting alongside them. They had bird legs.

"Hey! She woke up," Bird Legs whispered sharply.

The bull carrying her stopped short and swung her around. She punched him in the small of the back as she started to shout, but a sharp force struck her again.

The hazy room returned, even dimmer this time. She was laying on the bed this time.

Oh, that was going to hurt when she woke up. The dull ache across the back of her neck already throbbed.

"Tengrii!" she called out, cupping her hands around her mouth.

"Rhea?"

"There are two of them. One looks like he may be a bull, and the other has bird legs. I don't know where I'm at. They're taking me somewhere fast. We just passed a point where there was a statue that had been removed or something that had happened to make a jagged uneven triangle."

He huffed as if frustrated. "What did the doors look like?"

"The doors?" She frowned.

"Were they painted or plain or metal or wood?"

Hm. She closed her eyes, trying to remember. They had passed in such a blur. "Darker than the stone."

"That helps. What else?"

"More blue than red."

"Good. What else?"

"Um..." She pressed her hand to her forehead. "They were both wearing the same robes as the person who let me out of the room the other day. The one who told me to kill you."

He swore on the other side, his voice muddling and dimming.

"Tengrii? Are you there? Can you still hear me?"

"I hear you, Rhea. I can hear you. It's going to be fine. Don't fight them. They'd rather keep you alive if possible, but they can make this work if you're freshly dead. Do not provoke them. They think they can make the ritual work."

"I don't care for the sound of that." She shuddered, hugging herself.

"I'm on my way. I know where they're taking you. You're going to be all right."

Yes, but she didn't want to stay unconscious.

Her nerves tightened as her stomach twisted. What else could she do from in here? She could talk with Tengrii, but that was only useful to a point.

She returned to that spot on the wall. It had disappeared.

Figured. It probably was going to be harder to get out this time, especially depending on where they hit her. She rubbed the back of her neck as if that might soothe it somehow.

So fighting directly was off the table. Putting up a struggle as well. She'd find the next weak point in this unconscious state. Then she'd make her choice.

TENGRII PULLED up as she told him about the doors. Crespa, no, they were going to sacrifice her to the Rift! These had to be the young ones that Elthko had been talking about.

Spinning around, he indicated the opposite direction. "Go! They're taking her to the Rift," he bellowed.

Yoto and the four guards followed along, racing as fast as they could. There were multiple ways into the Rift, but they all joined together in that one chamber. And they could only be going there for one purpose.

Down side passages and along the shortcuts, he raced as fast as he could. The smooth polished stone and precisely laid marble floor soon turned to the coarse harsher cuts of the freshly hewn passage. They passed the storerooms and armories, then burst out into the hall that led to what had once been the courtyard but had since become the Rift's Chamber.

There!

The doors had been left open, one still vibrating as if it had just struck the wall.

Faster now!

He charged in. The air turned sharp, biting in his throat. The low light from the Rift had intensified, the fog spilling out over the stones like froth, turning to silver and grey as it moved beyond the sea.

The two robed figures had nearly reached the edge. They had her by the arms and the legs.

"Stop!" Tengrii bellowed.

The two glanced back at him, then swung her out, even as he and the guards charged forward.

They let go.

No!

His heart nearly stopped. Everything slowed. He could see her sliding through the air even as he leaped forward. He wasn't going to make it to her. He needed one more leap to cross to her.

"Rhea!"

She flailed to life, her hazel eyes flying open. Her limbs stiffened, and she clawed at the air, seizing onto a stalactite. Her clipped fingernails and ink-stained fingers dug into the thick grooves and grated against the stone as she tried to drag herself up. Her knees gripped. She clung there blearily, struggling to climb up and shaking her head as she hung above the purple sea.

Yoto and the guards attacked the two figures, dragging them back and away.

Tengrii stretched out beneath her, arms spread. "It's all right. I'm almost there."

She slid farther down the stalactite. Her muscles knotted and tightened visibly as she tried to hold on. Then, she slipped. Her eyes widened.

He swept beneath her just in time, seizing her to his chest and holding her there for one terrifying moment.

The sea of the Rift below churned, the pale fog puffing up and spreading on the low wind that stirred this place.

"Hi," she said, panting.

"Hi?" He almost laughed as he pulled them back to the relative safety of the ledge. "Are you all right?"

She released another fast breath and nodded. "Sure. Great. A little breathless. Bit of a headache."

He clasped her close, his chin on the top of her head. She was safe. She had survived. It was all right. They hadn't succeeded.

Yoto and the guards had corralled the two robed figures and unhooded them. Carob and Rona, new recruits to the watchmen before the Rift had come.

"This can't continue!" Carob shouted, his breath huffing as his hooves struck against the stone. "We have no time. The Rift must be satisfied, or we will all die! We need to give it what it wants."

Rofa hung his head sullenly, only shaking it. Despair and rage were equally present on his avian features. "They don't care," he muttered. "They don't believe it."

"We're running out of time," Carob said, louder this time. He balked as the guards pushed him forward. "We are running out of time, and soon we will all die!"

"Take them away," Tengrii ordered. "I'll deal with them later."

He gritted his teeth. Why had they picked Rhea? Was it just because she was someone they didn't know and thus easier to sacrifice? Was it because she had been trying to convince him to allow the Tue-Rah's formation to continue? He had to protect her from this.

Yoto gestured toward the door. "You heard him. Take them out."

The guards hustled both prisoners away, Yoto behind them. The heavy door swung shut behind them.

Within moments, they were alone. Again. And he was still holding her, her legs draped over one of his arms with his other supporting her and his hand supporting her head. She remained curled against him as well.

"You need to stop dropping in or falling from such heights." He smiled as he stared down into her eyes. "This is getting rather dangerous."

He grew more serious as he studied her. She was a little pale, and the start of a decent knot had formed on her head near one of his fingers. But she looked fairly good.

"Are you sure you're all right?"

She nodded and placed her hand on his chest, just over the vest, her finger pressed to the seam. "A little sore and disoriented. You're still holding me."

"I suppose I am."

He moved away from the edge. His scales gripped the stone easily and allowed him to move with steady enough ease that he didn't rock her uncomfortably. He hoped she wouldn't ask him to put her down.

Everything was falling apart around him, but holding her made him feel as if somehow something was going a little right. As if he could do anything, endure anything so long as she was with him. Had she been sent to him because he had to make this awful choice?

"How did you do it?" he asked.

"Do what?" She continued to press her fingers along the seam of his vest as if she were searching for something.

"Contact me. I wasn't asleep this time. I was working."

Her shoulder twitched. "I don't actually know. I just called for you, and you heard me. I think the bond is getting stronger between us. The drink that Killoth gave me. He said that it would enhance the connection if it was real. And—well, I don't want to alarm you, Tengrii, but I think it is."

He pressed his forehead to hers, bittersweet relief and awareness flooding him. If that connection hadn't worked, he would never have known. They would have thrown her in, and then...

He held her tighter.

She winced. "Careful."

He started to apologize.

She stopped him. "No, no, it's all right. You aren't the one who struck me." She moistened her lips, then met his gaze. "Tengrii." His name seemed a little harder for her to say now.

He tilted his head as his gaze drifted from her eyes to her lips back to her eyes. "Rhea?"

"This morning—" she started.

A low grumbling growl sounded from the earth as the ground began to shake. Bits of stone and sand trickled down. Everything bobbed and groaned. The sea bubbled and frothed, and the Rift above it sparked for a moment.

He needed to get away from here. The fog stopped being toxic within an hour of spilling out of the Rift itself. The purple fog that now gathered in this low sea was simply unpleasantly scented. But new fog breaking free?

No.

He swept them away from the edge of the cliff and the jagged natural formations.

"The earthquakes are getting worse as well," he said, his tone dark. His brow furrowed as he shook his head. "Come on. Let's get you somewhere safe. We can talk tonight."

29
ONLY ONE BED

Rhea's head stopped hurting much sooner than she had anticipated. Tengrii showered her with attention, hovering over her and insisting on examining the back of her head and fixing her tea as well as a poultice and an herbal bath.

She stayed in the bath far longer than usual, mulling over the events of the past hours. The Ki Valo Nakar and its reluctant assistance. Dulce and her plea to find a solution. The two men who had tried to sacrifice her to the Rift. The bond between her and Tengrii being strong enough that she could reach him while he was conscious and she was not.

Trailing her fingers through the water, she shook her head. Life was strange and getting stranger by the day.

And there was still that unasked question.

Did she know the answer herself?

The bits of herbs drifted through the water, fragrant and green, filling her nostrils and lungs and easing her muscles. The salts had long dissolved. It had to be getting late, perhaps even late enough that the doors had locked, which meant that it was just her and Tengrii until the morning.

She slipped out of the water and toweled off. He'd left a robe in here for her as well so that her clothes could be washed. A large fluffy pale-blue one that was likely his. The long sleeves stretched out farther than her arms, and the hem was all the way down to her ankles. Like the sleeveless tunic, it was some of the softest fabric she had ever felt.

As she stepped out from the washroom, she found Tengrii arranging plates on the table. Another stew with a red sauce, steamed fish, stewed onions, a fried mushroom bread, and a sort of pressed fruit and nut cake.

"You need to eat this time," he said as he poured fresh water into their glasses. "Even if it isn't much. Just —something."

"I can eat." Her stomach did not grumble or growl with expectation, but she sat at the table anyway. He used his tail as a chair once more, taking the position across from her. "Thank you for the robe. And for looking after me."

"I should have listened to my initial instincts on the matter," he muttered, the back of his knuckle pressed to his cheek. "I should never have left you alone. I thought that it was safe enough, especially after seeing how everyone was respond-ing. But I was wrong. I should never have left you alone."

"Would that really have solved it?" she asked, breaking off a piece of the fried bread and dipping it in the stew. "It isn't as if you have plenty of people available for the task. And I wanted to go to the library infirmary." She rubbed the back of her head again ruefully. It was the second blow that had hurt the most, but already the knot had diminished significantly. "They seemed very determined. I think they would have found a way to make that happen."

"General Yoto said that they found Gao. She had been struck as well. She's fine. Resting at the moment, I'd assume. No one saw anything though. The two that did this were able to strike at a point where they would not be as likely to be seen."

With as much that had to be done and everyone as tired as they were, there was a lot that wouldn't be seen in this place.

She took a bite of the bread. The savory earthy flavors filled her mouth with pleasant heat. "They sounded scared."

"They are." He stared down at his plate. Steam wafted up from the bowl and the fish. "Also, Gao and some others said that you challenged the Ki?"

"Challenged?" Covering her mouth, she laughed, then swallowed the bite of stew. "No. I just asked it for help."

He frowned. "Why would you risk speaking to it? It takes souls."

"Yes, supposedly if they want to go, if the myths are to be believed. Though I'm not sure how anyone could ever know that." She sipped the water, then shrugged. "I guess it's one of those things we have to trust. But it can and does move back and forth between the worlds without having to rely on the Tue-Rah's access points."

"And you wanted to know if it would find the cure or stop the Rift?"

"I asked it to take a message back to a friend. There may be a way to allow the formation of the Tue-Rah to continue and the other worlds not be put at risk. Or at least, not at too much risk."

"And it agreed?" He stared at her, eyes wide. "It listened to you?"

"I think so. I reminded it how our interests are actually aligned. This is going to kill off almost all of the Neyeb. It might not care about the other races, but it has to have a

Neyeb host. Otherwise..." She shrugged and tore off another piece of bread. "Dying doesn't sound nearly as bad as wandering formless throughout the worlds until the end of time. And after it delivers the message, it will bring me the response. Then I guess we'll see."

He leaned back on his tail, his hand dropping to the table. "I never thought of speaking with the Ki."

"If this works, will you be willing to allow the Tue-Rah's formation to continue? To strip away that slick and let it keep growing?"

His brow furrowed. He brushed the back of his knuckle against his cheek twice.

Something obviously disturbed him in this.

She tilted her head as she studied him. "Tengrii?"

He forced a smile. "I'm sorry. I was thinking. Let's see what the Ki does. If it can bring us a solution. If—it can." He shook his head, then resumed eating the stew, taking slow bites.

The conversation dwindled between them. Something weighed heavily on him. Occasionally, she noted that his hand trembled. When she tried to ask though, he brushed it aside.

"We should sleep early tonight," he said. "It was a trying day for you, and tomorrow will hold many problems."

She agreed. It wasn't as if they weren't going to see one another in their dreams. And she was tired. Her body ached a little from the ordeal as well.

He let her borrow one of his long tunics for a night shirt. And then, all too soon—she was back in the study.

Alone.

The nest of a bed beckoned her to come and sleep. It would be warm and pleasant. Soon she'd be with Tengrii in the form he used to have. He'd probably be more at ease then. They might laugh a little or just talk about the day or lapse into peaceful calm and let the hours pass in the contentedness of knowing the other was near.

Except—she paused as a thought struck her.

She pushed the covers off, picked up the cushions and blankets, crossed to the door, and opened it gently. He started up in his own bed, bare-chested and loose-haired. It didn't look as if he had been asleep or even near it. Only two of the lamps continued to burn, their lights now so low that the whole room was cast in dim golden light.

"Is everything all right?" he asked.

"I just didn't want to sleep in a room alone," she said, pulling the cushion behind her. "Do you mind?"

"No. You can do whatever you like." He dropped his arm as he stared at her. "As long as you rest well, you're welcome wherever you want to be."

She dipped her head in thanks. Then, taking great care, she arranged the cushions to form a comfortable bed. Without being scrunched up on the couch, these cushions were actually fairly large. She set it next to the other cushions on the floor to ensure it was large enough. In case she rolled around, of course.

Still on his side, he watched her, head propped up on his hand. "This is better then?" His arched eyebrow suggested he wasn't convinced.

"Yes." She crawled beneath the blankets. "I'm not used to sleeping in a room by myself. And if someone tries to attack me, well, this room is—safer."

It wasn't, but she wasn't good at lying either.

He nodded slowly. "I suppose so." He lowered his head to the pillow, still watching her. "If you need anything else, tell me."

She huffed a response as she burrowed deeper under the covers. Her heart was racing so fast, it was as if she had been out for a run. She released a slow controlled breath as she stared up at the ceiling.

Everything went still within the room except for the one timepiece that counted out the seconds with a steady *nok nok nok.*

The bed creaked.

She glanced over. He was on his back now, staring up at the ceiling, arms folded behind his head. His pulse thrummed in a vein along his throat. He, too, seemed to be trying to slow his breathing. The covers rustled slightly as his tail twitched.

So what next? It wasn't like she could just ask him what it was he had wanted to say this morning or whether he had locked with her. And, while it had seemed like a good idea to come out here, she no longer knew the best path. Go hop on the bed with him and tell him she was cold? Ask him if he was interested in more than friendship? Propose that they have a relationship talk about what they were going to do when this whole situation was resolved?

Polph! Why did this conversational gap suddenly feel insurmountable? It wouldn't even take all that much!

The mattress creaked again, then something slid over the silk. Her breath caught in her throat as she twisted around.

He stood near the oil lamp. "It's too bright," he said softly. "Will it bother you if I make it darker?"

"No. Not at all. Was the light keeping you awake?"

"It's just easier to sleep in the dark."

She nodded, the pillow pressed to her cheek. "Will you have any trouble lighting the lamps in the morning?"

"No. I can see decently enough in the dark. I just know you can't."

She smiled a little. "So you thought I might come out here?"

That was a little presumptuous.

"For the washroom." He blew out one of the lamps, then lowered the wick of the remaining one. The light was so low now that most of the room was in shadows.

She forced her eyes shut. Relaxed. That was what she needed to be. Yet her whole body had gone tight as canvas stretched on a wooden frame.

The cushions on the other side of her shifted slightly. She started, her arm shooting out in front of her as she looked up.

Tengrii sat at the edge of the makeshift bed, one hand pressed into the turquoise cushion. "It might be even safer if we were in the same bed."

"Hmmm." She nodded as she met his gaze. "I mean, you are the one who got stabbed in your own bed. How did he get in if the doors were locked?"

"I slept late. I was occupied in a rather vivid dream. It seemed for a moment to be real, and I didn't want to let it go." Even in the dim light, she saw that slow smile of his spread over his full lips.

Her insides melted. "Well, if you want to sleep here, there's more than enough room."

"Especially since you put out so many cushions." He eased onto the bed, staying almost on the edge. He laid his pillow down as well.

"I sometimes roll in my sleep," she offered quietly. She then closed her eyes again. "Good night."

"Good night." He lifted the blankets and slid under.

The pressure of the cushion changed, and his heat reached her even from all that distance. Her skin tingled as if he had just caressed her. Energy surged through her veins. It took almost all her willpower to keep her eyes shut. Maybe the bath had been so restful it was as if she had fallen asleep and now her body resented the idea of sleeping period.

Her mind played back the images of the day, focusing on

the moment when she'd startled out of the unconscious state, realized she was falling, and grabbed onto that stalactite. Then, that dreadful moment when her hands had slipped, but he had caught her.

He was the one who had heard her when she had called for help, and he was the one who had caught her when she had fallen. His arms wrapped around her had made her feel more secure than she ever had, perhaps in her life.

And that need in his eyes—something roused within her just as she remembered it. Her fingers curled against her collarbone. She shivered.

"Are you cold?"

That low voice of his made her shiver even more.

"I'm just—I'm thinking. That's all."

He shifted on the mattress. His heat intensified. "About?"

Her nerves tingled. What could she say? She wriggled a little, trying to find a more comfortable place on the cushion. How close was he really? She resisted the urge to stretch out her hand and brush her fingers over the heat of his arm or chest.

He was only sleeping near her to keep her safe.

A laugh rose within her. She bit it back. Yes. Even with him closer, the void between them felt insurmountable. She shivered again.

"Are you sure you aren't cold?"

"I'm—" She shrugged then. "It doesn't matter...maybe."

He moved closer. The heat coming from him was almost enough to take her breath away. She stiffened at once, his arm banding over her waist like a protective shield and his hard body behind her.

"Is this acceptable?"

"It makes no difference to me," she said as calmly as she could. She even twitched her shoulder as if it helped prove the point. "If you are comfortable there, then you can maintain this position. Or move away...Or get closer."

Was he smiling? Somehow, it felt as if he was smiling.

He nudged a little closer. "I do like this," he said softly. "You feel pleasant."

She tried to scoff, but her mouth was dry. "You too," she whispered.

His arm tightened around her, pulling her back more firmly against his firm body and warming her in more ways than one. But that didn't change the actual reality of what was going on here or what he was. No matter how good he felt. No matter how her skin prickled with delight as he scooted even closer still so that her buttocks were practically pressed up against his groin.

Wait.

Nope.

Not practically anymore.

She turned her face down into the pillow.

The ache inside her intensified.

She fought the urge to push back against him. He was at least a naga look-a-like. And he was cursed or something. Was it appropriate for her to be having feelings about him? Feelings of any romantic or sexual sort at all?

"If this makes you uncomfortable," he said, his breath caressing her shoulder and neck. "Just tell me."

She resisted the urge to shudder once more. Oh, by the Eight Races, he felt good against her. She bit her lip and fought the aching itch that formed within her.

"Rhea," he said softly.

Damn him. Another shiver coursed through her.

She dug her feet into the thick cushion and away from him. "Yes?" she asked as sweetly as she could manage.

"No matter what happens, I will find a way to keep you

safe. I know it isn't the same as your home, and I am sorry you can't go back."

She twisted around. Then realized that that put her in an even more intimate position. She closed her eyes. "It's not your fault, and I'm not your responsibility, Tengrii. I appreciate this. I appreciate all that you have done to keep me safe. I truly do, but you can't really—"

His nose brushed against her cheek. He ducked his head farther. "You are in my kingdom. I intend for you to leave this place as safely as you entered it. And with all intact as much as I can. Not simply because you are a guest."

No. She was really more of an invader. A would-be assassin.

A small smile tugged at the corners of her mouth. "We're going to find a solution, Tengrii. There is a way out of this." She settled back against him, resting on her side.

"Yes." He did not sound so certain. He laid his head down as well, his breath now stirring her hair and caressing her neck. "I used to wish I could hold you in those dreams."

She bit her lip. She'd had the same wish. So many times.

A low ragged sigh escaped him. "I am so sorry, Rhea. If I were different, I know—I used to hope that the fog and all that comes from the Rift was a curse rather than a disease. Because curses can be broken. Somehow. They can be reversed. Though perhaps not if they aren't completed. I don't know. I used to think that the Blight was proof we could handle anything that was the equivalent of a disease. That we fought it and beat it. But this—this fog—it's—" He fell silent for several breaths. "It is destroying people the way I thought the Blight destroyed plants and biomes. Even if we stop it— even if we find the answer—it may just mean that we have to move on from that point. And—" he sighed. "There are men and women and children trapped in comas and struggling to even survive, and I am—" He dipped his head forward, his nose brushing her shoulder. "It doesn't matter. What will be will be. After we find the answers, we will just have to pick up the pieces and hope there are enough left to rebuild."

She placed her hand over his. "There are answers. It will work out."

"I wish there was a way I could spare you all this and send you back to your home."

"Even if you could, I'm not safer anywhere else. This fog will continue to spread." She stroked her hand over his a little more firmly now. "I came here to find a way to save my family. And you. I can't do anything to help Salanca back home. Or Tiehro. But we're going to find a way. There has to be a solution."

He chuckled, but the tone was sadder. "What if the only solutions are horrible, Salt-Sweet?"

"Then we'll adapt. We'll find a way to make it work. Plans and solutions have to be changed sometimes. I mean, look at me." She shrugged, trying to sound more playful in the hopes of making him smile. "My first plan was to kill the naga king, which apparently is you. And—I'm not really the kind of person who makes secondary plans. I sketch in ink. But because of you, I've made an exception and found another solution."

"I am still rather awed by one element in particular," he said. His hand moved to her stomach. "You came to save me."

She scoffed, but inwardly, she clenched, aware of his fingers and the light pressure from his claws. "You would have done the same for me."

"What existed between us before this, it was more than friendship, wasn't it? Even if we could not touch."

She found herself nodding, still staring at the wall across from them.

"It isn't supposed to work this way," he said softly. "The discomfort from this continued form has been such, I did not realize it fully until it was done."

"Didn't realize what until it was done?"

He pressed his face against her neck, drawing her tighter against him. "I don't expect you to love me or to want me. Especially not when I am—like this. And that's all right for you to feel that way. I am a monster, whether I want to be or not. This may never change. You gave me such joy and comfort, and I will always love you, Rhea. No matter what happens."

She twisted around then to face him, flipping to her other side. "Tengrii—" Her breath caught in her throat as she pressed her hand to his cheek.

Polph, maybe he hadn't actually asked her, but she did need to tell him. Somehow, it was excruciatingly clear.

"Tengrii, I fell in love with you even though I didn't mean to and even though I was afraid you weren't real. This has been the strangest relationship of my entire life. And you— looking like this—yes, it's a little unnerving. But it's still you. I know you wanted to ask me something this morning, and I think I know what it was. You wanted to know if I could love you like this. I already do. You say that I was your joy and comfort. You were the same for me. Maybe that's why Salanca's incantation worked. Killoth said that it would take something extra to reach someone on a Separated or a Cutoff World, but we found each other. What if it was because..."

"Because you are my veskaro? My most beloved among all the worlds?" He hugged her closer. "That still doesn't mean that you have to accept me when I am so—so monstrous. No matter how much I want you, it doesn't change that." His tail flicked around her feet, teasing between her ankles. "But if I unnerve you too much for us to—" He stiffened against her,

311

his gaze no longer fixed on her. "What are you doing here, entity?" he demanded.

She twisted around, then gasped. The Ki Valo Nakar stood in front of the lamp, glowering at them. But in its clawed hand, it held a polished grey psychic stone.

30
QUESTIONS

Rhea bolted up. "You have a message already? You found Killoth?"

The Ki Valo Nakar narrowed its eyes at her, then motioned for her to move away from Tengrii. The long black cloak rustled with the movement.

"I'm his veskaro," she said, knowing she was probably blushing. She smoothed the tunic down so that it covered her thighs better. "There's nothing wrong—"

It tilted its head and then held out its palm with the psychic stone on it. The disapproval was hard not to grasp.

"Thank you for handling the message," she said.

It dropped the stone into her hand, then stepped back.

"*Bunny!*" The psychic message blasted into her mind with Killoth's ecstatic voice filling her ears. "*They can. All good. Allow formation to continue. Pulka spores not issue. Vial good. Curing psychics more likely. Stay on your side. Aid will come. Reaching Sal too. Chickadee fine. We'll be waiting. As long as it takes.*"

She burst into laughter, hugging the stone and then setting it aside as the message started to repeat. "Thank you!"

The Ki Valo Nakar had already vanished.

"What is it?" Tengrii asked, coming alongside her. "And why did it care whether I was touching you?"

She shrugged. "It worked though. Pulka spores aren't a problem. They want us to let the formation of the Tue-Rah continue. We're to stay on our side. And when it's connected, they will come through. They're going to help us. They think they can find a cure for the comas too!"

She closed her eyes, tears of happiness leaking down her cheeks. Salanca was all right. Killoth was getting to her. And Tiehro. Thank Elonumato. Good news and more good news!

"All right," he said. His shoulders dropped. "Salt-Sweet—"

"Does this mean we can move forward with the plan?" she asked. "We can strip the oil or tar or whatever it is off the Tue-Rah. We can get help!"

"Tomorrow, we will present this to the council. This is very good news. It changes quite a lot." He lightly tugged a strand of her hair as if he was weighing something. That heaviness still had not vanished.

"Chicory?" She tilted her head. "You still look sad. What's wrong?"

He stared at the rug, then lifted his gaze back to hers. "There is no easy way to ask this. Do you want to be intimate with me, Salt-Sweet?"

"Yes. No, I just—" She found herself laughing. Oh, this wasn't right. She covered her mouth, wishing she could take that back. She'd just made it awkward. Was this why he'd seemed so troubled? "I'm sorry. I just have questions now."

"Oh? Questions? Such as?"

Somehow, her response had seemed to set him at ease as well. He traced a line down her shoulder, smiling as she shivered. His confidence seemed to have returned, and the tension both eased and intensified between them.

"Such as..." She tried to bite back a laugh as she covered her eyes. "Are you a reptile or a mammal?"

His eyebrow flicked upward. "Mammal."

"Don't say that like it's obvious." She shook her head at him, giving him a playful scowl. "It isn't as if you'd stop being handsome just because you were reptilian."

His expression grew even more pleased when she said he was handsome.

She stumbled a little more over the words. "And you do have scales, though I do remember you saying you weren't a reptile before, so maybe that's a little moot."

"Some mammals have scales."

"Oh? Like?"

"Me." He stuck his tongue out at her. "But if I were guessing what your actual question is, you want to know about something in particular. Something you can't see."

"Possibly."

"My lungs are broader and more expansive than human lungs and much more efficient than snake lungs."

"Oh. Good. Yes, that is precisely what I was wondering about. Do you...have a gallbladder?" She folded her arms. He was standing so close now that, if she wanted, she could have touched him just by taking one step closer.

"Maybe. I haven't checked. But I have kidneys in the proper formation."

"Great. Glad to hear it. That's been at the top of my mind since we met."

He wobbled his hand back and forth. "Blood vessels are not entirely structured the same. I may have twice as many arteries as you. Maybe not."

"Riveting."

Why did he have to look like he was enjoying this conversation so much? And more and more by the minute?

"Liver works the same too. Probably better than yours, actually. I can't become intoxicated, which is tedious in this place. I envy those of my people who can." He tilted his head. "Would you like me to go over everything you can't see and compare it to yours or a general human?"

"Why not?" She twitched her shoulder at him. "Tell me everything."

"Everything? Hmm." He stroked his chin. "Well, if you aren't asking about anything in particular, I would tell you that my stomach acid is probably stronger than yours, and the average human's is really more on par with that of a snake."

"Really? That's just absolutely delightful."

He nodded. "If you had something you really wanted to ask about, it might be good to ask. Because I am a terrible guesser. And humans have over seventy different organs and things that might be considered organs or the like."

"I think you know exactly what I'm asking about."

He sighed dramatically. "Well, perhaps. It is an awkward question to ask. But it is one of the first things I realized about nagas and serpents when I turned into one."

She narrowed her eyes at him. Was he really going to go there? No. He was teasing her. And enjoying it way too much despite the somberness of his earlier mood. It was hard to hold back her own smile.

"What's that?" she asked.

"Something to do with the legs," he said. "People think snakes don't have legs, but some do."

"You mean lizards," she said with wry amusement.

"No. No, they're still snakes. But they have vestigial legs. Tiny little leg bones that are collapsed down near the tail and under the skin and scales. But you know what's especially fascinating?"

"I can't even begin to guess."

"Snakes don't have hip bones. Nagas do." He nudged his hip against hers as if to make that point.

"Uh-huh." Heat flared through her. She couldn't stop smiling. "I noticed that."

He tilted his head. "That was what you were asking about, wasn't it?"

"I think you're the one making jokes now," she responded, "which, given where we were just a few minutes ago, is all the more remarkable."

He huffed a small laugh. "Once again, you make my life better in every respect. For you, I would do anything. And, for what it's worth, I'm not reptilian anywhere it would matter."

"Have you really already locked with me?"

He nodded slowly. "I wasn't certain at first. This form is so uncomfortable that it masks many signals. And the nature of this fog has changed things with that as well."

"How did you figure it out?"

He smirked at her. "There were cues. Some less subtle than others." He then took her hand in his. "You understand though...this—" He gestured to himself. "This may be permanent. Especially if we go through with this plan of allowing the Tue-Rah to finish forming. The locking didn't allow me to change back to what I was."

"Even if you don't change back, it'll be all right," she said gently. "I love you and accept you for who you are, Tengrii. Maybe some things take a little time, but you—I love you." She placed her hand on his chest just above his heart. "You are the *man* I love."

He pulled her closer then, his hand working along her

lower back. With his other, he stroked her cheek. "So this means you have thought about *it*?"

"Yes." She tilted her head and pressed her body against his. "Have you?"

"It's all I want to think about." He leaned in closer, his hand trailing down her neck to her shoulder. "I want you so much, Salt-Sweet. I want to make you mine. To keep you. To hold you. To know you in every possible way." His teeth scraped the side of her neck and then to the shell of her ear. "And even if I didn't turn out to be who you thought I was and even if your main reason for coming was for your family, I am grateful you came to my rescue."

She shivered, keeping her body taut against his. "I would have come to rescue you even if it was only you," she whispered. "And knowing what I know now, I would have come to find you all the sooner."

"I am grateful for that." He pressed his forehead to hers. "I am grateful for that even more than I am grateful that you have poor aim."

She started to duck her head, laughing again. But he caught hold of the back of her neck and guided her gaze back to his. That gaze of his pinned her and turned her molten. His other hand slid down her back, pressing her body into his, his own hard as stone against her. His breaths rumbled deeper.

She parted her lips, wanting to say something, but she could think of nothing, nothing except that this moment was exquisite. As if everything had been decided, settled, and resolved. And here she was, right at the start, knowing it would be good and simply ready to surrender to the bliss.

He nudged her face with his, his lips brushing over hers. She held her breath as he came back, teasing at her lower lip. A moan escaped her lips.

That sound seemed to undo him. He grabbed hold of her

and thrust forward, his mouth claiming hers. That incredible scent of amber, jasmine, incense, and bakhoor filled her lungs, and he tasted even better. He took her breath away, and she flung herself closer, trying to hold onto him as he lifted her into his arms. His mouth moved to her throat, then to her shoulder, his teeth scraping harder over her sensitive skin.

She cried out, the heat rising within her as she arched against him.

He pulled back just enough to look at her, his eyes wide with desire. Then they hooded. He threw her onto the bed.

She'd barely put her arms out to catch herself before he pounced. For a moment, she sat there, staring up at him as he towered over her.

"Do you want me, Rhea?" he demanded, his voice low. "As I am? Even if we only have a few days to live?"

She let her gaze travel up his body from the sharp V's of his tapered waist to the ridged muscles of his abdomen up to his powerfully sculpted shoulders and thick yet elegant neck and then to his sharp-cut jaw and, at last, to those incredible eyes. By everything that was good, holy, pure, and lovely, she'd been lost the moment she'd looked into them.

"I do. As you are and even if you change. For the rest of my life, no matter how long that is." She rose up on her knees but did not touch him. She mirrored the light sway of his body. "And do you want me, Tengrii?"

"Now. Always. As you are. However you may change. For as long as I live and beyond that if I may." He moved closer, only a breath away now.

If she stirred even a little, she would touch him. The heat emanating from his body stroked the length of her body. His broad chest rose and fell.

Another exceptional moment. She committed the sight to memory, biting the inside of her lip. She was definitely going

JESSICA M BUTLER

to have to draw this, but were they just going to stand here staring at one another until—

He lunged forward, tackling her to the sheets.

She gasped, then laughed. "Well—" she started.

He thrust his lips over hers. Corralling her with his arms, he chased her with his mouth. She made a small attempt to push up against him, but then she collapsed and settled for thrusting her fingers in his hair and down his back. His strength or weight alone could have pinned her. Both combined left no chance.

His tail coiled around her ankle, flicking up her calf and up her thigh, searching her.

She arched and ground up against him, her entire body alight. He played the nerves along the side of her neck as well as down between her breasts as expertly as if he had always known them. The anticipation built within her. Each time she tried to reach down to touch him, though, he pushed her hands away and nuzzled her.

"Patience," he growled in her ear, his chest against hers and his hands pinning her wrists to the bed.

"What kind of man are you to do this?" she demanded with mock rage. "Are you torturing me?"

"Yes, and proving I am a man and not just a male."

"I am harboring no doubts." She set her jaw as she glared at him affectionately. "But women don't just like to have a man grind on them. And besides, I can do things too."

He rubbed the tip of his nose against hers and laughed softly. "I'm sure you can." He kissed her again, his tongue pressing between her lips.

Oh. The way he kissed her made her see stars. And with him holding her arms down, she could only answer with her own lips and tongue and teeth. All that remained between them was the thin fabric of her tunic and his belt and front piece, and it was driving her insane.

Those blissful kisses continued as he worked himself against her body, making her ache and long for so much more. He was hungry for her but also a relentless tease. He'd almost driven her out of her mind already, and there was no end in sight. Her hips bucked as he continued to play the curve of her neck and her ears and pressed between her legs but never entered her despite the heat and his bulge making it apparent that he was more than prepared. Instead, he nudged her entrance and tested her with his tail as he kissed her. Taking care not to cut her with his claws, he pulled the tunic up over her head.

She trailed her hand down his abdomen, sticking her tongue out at him as she swiped at his groin. Her fingers barely grazed him before he caught her hands again.

"I get to look," he said.

"And I don't?"

"You will."

He claimed her mouth again. Then moving back, in a single swift motion, he removed his sash and frontpiece and tossed them aside, allowing himself to spring free. Her eyes widened. As flat as he had seemed, she would never have guessed he could have been hiding that much in all dimensions.

But he left her no time to contemplate anything beyond the size and how human he was aside from his coloration as he pressed between her legs.

She gasped, startled but not in pain.

His hands splayed into the mattress, his claws cutting into the silk. "You tell me if it's too much," he said, almost breathless.

"Keep going." She rubbed her hands along his chest and

down his abdomen to the muscles leading to his groin. "Do you plan to make me beg?"

"Not that I would mind," he said with a grin. "But no. Just —I don't want to hurt you."

"I'm good."

"Good."

He held his hands with care along her sides, the prickling glances of his claws that never did more than lightly tickle.

All at once, he thrust himself deeper and swept his arms beneath her. Lifting her up, he kept himself sheathed within her and then straightened.

"Oh, hey," she said, her arms dropping to his shoulders. She tightened around him, intensifying the pleasure in some degrees and yet heightening her awareness. This wasn't a position she'd heard or fantasized about. "What're you doing?"

He coiled his tail around her again, the loops looser this time but enough to support her. All his scales had gone almost perfectly flush except for a minor ridging that made it feel as if he was stroking her all over at once. Her skin tingled, her feet bracing against his loops. She moaned as the intensity of the sensation built within her and around her.

This was—actually, this was better. He left her enough room to maneuver, and she rolled her hips and rocked against him, matching his rhythm. Sometimes, he moved his tail up in a long loop along her back or swiped it up between her legs. Other times, he rocked her closer to him.

Oh.

She let her eyes slide shut. Yes. This was him. More than she had hoped. Better than she had dreamed. Her friend in darkness. Her companion through trials. Her most beloved among all the worlds.

He clasped her face between his palms and kissed her

again, demanding her attention, holding her tight. He swallowed up her moan and then growled against her when she started to tip her head back.

The rhythm between them intensified. The tension within her built and built, delicious and agonizing at once. It grew with each stroke, with each press. She tightened, her breaths faster. Pleasure pounded through her, her pulse thundering.

There was nothing but him. Nothing but heat, scales, muscles, and coils. All building and pushing and grinding and drawing until—until she went wild.

Her body spasmed. She rose and fell, screaming and digging her fingers into his shoulders, his neck, and his scalp. They tangled in his hair as he dragged her closer and then erupted in his own release.

That intense spiraling twisting pleasure shot out between them. For a moment, it seemed as if it would last forever.

Forever and ever, beyond all the boundaries of this world and beyond.

He collapsed against her, then kissed a line from her shoulders up her neck to her lips. "I love you, Salt-Sweet," he whispered. "More than anything. More than life. You were worth every moment of waiting and pining and fearing it would not be."

She laughed breathlessly and twined her arms around his neck once more. "You are the most wonderful man I have ever known."

He dropped onto the bed, resting on his back as he drew her up into his arms as his coils loosely wrapped around her. "You've made me the happiest man, Salt-Sweet."

She thought about teasing him again, but her eyelids became too heavy. Her fingers curled against his chest as she relished his heat and the comfort of his scent. "I...love—"

Once more, she found herself in the bedroom, the same

one she had met him in so many times. He lay in the bed, waiting for her. Not as the man she had first seen but as he was now. His face lit up when he saw her.

That blissful delight vibrated through her even now. She climbed onto the bed and practically collapsed against him.

"You," she murmured, finishing her previous thought.

He rubbed his chin over the top of her head, a happy hum vibrating from him. He coiled around her again and then pulled the blanket up over them. He fit perfectly in the bed now. And she fit perfectly against him.

31

THE COUNCIL

Rhea still rested in his arms when Tengrii woke, his tail coiled around them both. For the first time in months, he had remained fully covered by the blankets. Warmth engulfed him.

How blessed was he? How lucky?

He tilted his head to better see her, still luxuriating in the blissful release of last night. Only days ago, he had considered himself cursed beyond reason. Yet now—was there anyone better off than he?

She was perfection. All luscious curves, soft breasts, and so distinct from him. Exactly what he needed. Precisely what he wanted.

A pit formed in his stomach. Should he tell her what Elthko had confided in him? Was there any way to avoid it?

He pressed his chin to the top of her head and held her a little closer.

It would be all right. She had accepted him as he was. Loved him as he had been and how he was now. She said he was a good man.

He wanted to be one. More than anything.

A good man would not allow children to be sacrificed when there were other ways.

There had to be another way.

Yesterday, he had not believed there was a way to be the man Rhea needed. Nor had he thought it possible that he could ever feel this happiness. It had never occurred to him that the Ki might be anything other than a lurking threat that winnowed away his people while they lay trapped in comas. Truly, he had never even considered the possibility that he might become trapped in a naga form or lock with a woman and barely even realize it had happened because the start occurred through dreams.

Really, the past year had been full of examples he had never even considered possible. Situations and realizations he had never even thought to contemplate. The reality of his parents and their decisions as well as how they came to be in this place—he turned his face down as he tried to block those thoughts.

No. He wouldn't dwell on them.

There was good in the world. There was good curled up in his arms, snoring softly with her slightly upturned nose pressed against his chest. Beautiful. Brave. Tenacious. He almost laughed. Quite literally the woman of his dreams.

He kissed the top of her head and then her fingers. She stirred slightly, groaned, then pushed her hand into his face, and fell back into a deeper sleep.

"Rhea," he said gently, cupping his fingers beneath her chin and tilting her face toward his.

She grumbled at him and tried to push away. "Why?"

"I need to talk with you."

She cracked one eyelid blearily. "Good thing you're charming," she mumbled. Yawning, she pressed her hand to his chest, then shook her head. "What?" She sat up, still naked.

He pulled the blankets higher over them so he wouldn't be distracted. "If there was the possibility that I could be returned to my former state and all of these effects that we have seen from the Rift could be undone except for the deaths, do you think I should take it?"

She rubbed her eyes, then looked at him, suddenly seeming far more awake. "Why does it sound like there's a 'but' in there? What's the cost?"

He managed a faint smile. She really was sharp.

Choosing his words carefully, he told her what Elthko had said. About the camp. His parents. The tear. The deaths. The ritual. The Rift. The young ones. Everything.

Her eyes widened. Her posture stiffened. But she remained silent until he finished. "What are you going to do?" she asked, meeting his gaze with quiet intensity.

"Despite everything, I truly believe they—my council— my people—they aren't bad people. They are just desperate and afraid. Not simply for their own lives but for the continuation of this kingdom. For what was endured. If we can give them an alternative that addresses all their concerns, then they will take that route. I am certain of it."

"The very best minds will be working on that cure."

"But the cure is only for the coma," he said, motioning toward her.

He stopped as he glimpsed his own claws. Already, they curved and gleamed, noticeably longer than when he had fallen asleep. If he and the others remained stuck in these forms—perhaps the pain would leave once the Rift was sealed. Perhaps they could heal faster. But if this had become all of their states of rest—he would never look like a man again. And he was far better off than some of his people. This did not affect them all equally.

She wrapped her fingers over his hand. "They may be able to find a way to help with your forms as well, but that will take time. There are so many healing resources. The Sands of Efil, the suphrite springs, and so much more."

"Will those work even if this is a curse?" He studied her face.

Her brow creased, then she shook her head. "I don't know. This is so far beyond my knowledge, but the cure for those in the comas is good, isn't it?"

"Yes. It just might not be enough." He kissed her fingertips. "I also intend to hold myself responsible in the eyes of whatever authorities come for whatever misdeeds may be laid against my people."

She frowned. "Multiple murders? Torture? Invasion of a Separated World? Practice of the Forbidden Arts?"

"I don't know what the penalties will be, but I am the leader of this place. It is one thing more that I can do to protect my people. And if that is the ultimate cost for our being reunited with the other worlds and to stop this suffering—then it's a very good price."

A long silence followed as she stared down at his hand in hers. She closed her eyes. Tears leaked down her cheeks. "You're a good man, Tengrii. I will stand by you no matter what they do to you."

The knock at the door announced the coming of breakfast. Though he was not hungry, he brought it in. Porridge, mushroom bread, and fish.

Rhea cut smiley faces in the toast, one piece tearing so that it looked more like a grimace. He managed to laugh, and she brought her chair to sit directly beside him rather than across from him. With the blanket wrapped around her body, she tucked her foot in his tail and played with his tail tip as if it were his foot while they talked. But when it came to discussing how to present his decision to the council, she grew somber and still.

Nothing settled quite right. He felt more ill at ease than he had on his first day of addressing the council or after dueling his father. But as in both cases, he simply had to do it.

Once they finished eating, both prepared for the meeting. Rhea gave him an almost shy smile as she slipped into the washroom. He nearly went after her, his fingers stretched toward her, but he stopped himself.

No.

Not now.

If he went in there after her, no matter how good his intentions, they'd wind up vestoving. And not briefly or swiftly.

The pulse of intense desire urged him to ignore that bit of common sense. What did it matter?

It mattered a lot. After this was resolved, he and she could curl up and indulge in all manner of pleasure and satisfaction. And oh—oh—that would be wondrous. But not now.

He washed and neatened his hair while she cleaned and dressed, then adjusted his vest once more. It was immaculate, lacking wrinkles, holes, or snagged threads. As he waited for her, he filed down his nails.

These days, there wasn't much for him to do for his appearance. He did not care for how limited his options had become. Such an irony that before this transformation, he had loved shoes and boots, in particular. Especially the ones that laced high and had intricate designs worked up their sides.

If he ever found a way back to his true form, how he would delight in choosing clothing and footwear once again. Thank all that was good that he wasn't actually cold-blooded, or else wandering around in nothing but vests and sashes would have been particularly uncomfortable in caves like this.

If things did improve enough, he would delight in getting her clothing as well.

As if she heard him, she stepped out from the washroom, fully dressed and refreshed. "All ready," she announced.

His breath sharpened. How could she be so beautiful in something so simple?

He had no cosmetics to offer her. Nor any dresses or gowns nor skirts, aside from the few tunics and shirts long enough to serve in that fashion. But she had already put her cleaned clothing back on, the brown trousers with the open side stitching and the butter-yellow tunic that clung gently to her curves. Her matching arm and wrist band as well as the brown layered necklace brought it all together. It also was precisely what she had worn when she arrived, and especially with the jewelry, it emphasized that she was not from their world.

Perhaps for the best. She was not one of them, though she belonged to him and he to her. There would soon be many who did not belong coming to this place. Her soft smile and gentle eyes might also remind them that not all from different places were a threat.

His stomach tightened at the thought, but he brushed the unease away. If these other worlds and leaders could end these nightmares, it would be better than the alternative.

"Well?" She tilted her head. "I'm starting to get a little worried."

He broke into a smile. "You are beautiful as always, Salt-Sweet." He placed his hands on her waist and kissed her forehead. "Are you ready?"

"Yes. As long as I am with you, I can face anything."

He felt the same.

Together they went to the council room. The long room had been recently tended, the lamps filled and the floor swept. But the cold had not faded from it any more than the scent of cloves and mushrooms. Half the council had already arrived, sitting silently at the table.

He stepped away from Rhea just long enough to speak with Yoto and Elthko briefly, telling the highlights of what he intended to discuss. Yoto reacted with somber acceptance, his manner almost suggesting he hoped that this course would be their path.

Elthko's eyes widened briefly. "You surprise me, Your Majesty. Time has become even more pressing. Councilor Raimu broke last night and had to be restrained. Even if the matter of the disease is set aside—"

"We will discuss it in full with the Council, but yes. I am certain. This is a better alternative than sacrificing the young ones. Out of respect for you and your counsel, I wanted to ensure you were aware before I made my announcement. I am counting on your support."

"You have it," Yoto responded.

"Understood, Your Majesty." Elthko twisted his head, his manner more hesitant and his posture stiff. He moved away and took his seat near the head of the table.

Yoto pushed his chair to the side, closer to Tengrii. Then he left and returned with another. His flames were well under control. The sealed stone showed no burn marks and only the faintest scent of smoke. But the general did look even thinner today as did Orje and Muna, air and water elementalists respectively. Muna sat especially still, her hands in her lap and not touching the table at all.

This had to work.

He turned his gaze to Rhea, who remained in the back, and gestured for her to come closer. Her eyes widened briefly when he gestured to the chair beside him. Almost hesitantly, she stepped closer. He brushed the back of his hand over her arm as she sat, relishing the touch even as he moved to his own position.

All stared at him now, far tenser than before. Gao fidgeted in her chair. Only Jaiku stared at him openly with an expression that suggested he better be quick. The rumors of Rhea challenging the Ki to aid them had probably spread as far and as fast as the knowledge that she had nearly been killed.

"As this is a matter that requires immediate attention, we will dispense with formalities. Rhea, the Awdawm from beyond, asked the Ki to help us, and it did. A message was carried through to the leaders of the worlds beyond. Rhea, please inform them."

Rhea stood. The shyness lasted only a moment longer as she brushed her fingertips on the stone table in his direction. Then she turned her gaze on the members of his council and began her explanation.

It was hard not to smile. If he could listen to anyone all day, it was her. She had told him before how helpless she felt. How ineffective. Yet here she stood near the head of this stone table, at his side, offering hope and a plan. Her voice had taken on a firm quality, stronger and slower than usual.

Confident.

It suited her.

He kept his expression schooled in neutrality though, observing his council members. They, too, were remaining neutral in expression.

"The Ki Valo Nakar—I mean the Ki—brought back a message. They are willing to accept us. They want us to remove the substance that prevents the formation. And then the Tue-Rah will connect us. After that, we are to wait, and they will come to our aid. By working together, we will find a cure for this." She glanced toward him, then sat as he rose.

"We will not pursue anything further with the ritual or the Rift," he said. "I realize that there are concerns about how this will be handled when we are reunited with the other worlds, whether there will be judgment. I am willing to take full responsibility for all the actions of any here so long as we move forward with this course. For whatever happened in the past, if they wish to hold us accountable, I will take full responsibility."

"Is there a cure then for us?" Muna asked, her brow furrowed. "They are working on a cure, but is it only for the psychics?"

"They do not have any who have reacted as we shifters and elementals have," Tengrii responded. "But once these gates are opened, they will be able to assist us. They have many healing skills and options that are not available to us here."

"And they are working on it," Rhea interjected. She curled her hand in her lap. "They will find something. Now that they have a more direct sample—"

Jaiku struck his fist on the table. "What guarantees do we have that they are truly here to help us? And how do we know they are not going to force us to leave this place? For all its flaws and weaknesses, this is our home."

"That can be handled later. Killoth said nothing of that."

"That does not make it safe," Jaiku responded. He gestured toward Tengrii. "Will you let this off-world woman poison you against our interests? We must remain secret."

"We are no longer secret," Tengrii said. "At a minimum, we can presume that the Tue-Rah is fighting to complete its formation. If that is the case, it is contributing to the earthquakes, and it is quite possibly contributing to the pulses the Rift emits."

"No longer secret because of her." Emeka pointed one hooked claw in her direction.

"No." Tengrii placed his hand on the table. His own claws dug into the stone. "The Tue-Rah is what has exposed us. These Paras—they know the Tue-Rah. They study it, and they know we are here. They may even know when it is that we left. An entire village disappeared with our forebears. That would not happen without drawing some notice. We thought we could escape detection. That we could do enough. But that is no longer the case. Regardless of what the consequences are, at least we have a better chance of living."

"Do we?" Jaiku demanded. "What is the penalty for entering a Separated World? Is it death? Is it enslavement? How do we know?"

Rhea's eyes widened, her cheeks flushing with color. "I can't imagine that it would be."

"But you do not know," Jaiku said, jabbing his finger toward her. "Were you a leader or a council member in your world? Were you a part of any assembly?"

She shook her head. "I was—"

"No." Jaiku slashed his hand through the air. His grey-blue eyes shone bright, his grey needle-like teeth bared. "What knowledge could you possibly have, you foolish—"

Tengrii lifted his hand. "Do not insult or speak down to my veskaro."

Jaiku shook his head. "Apologies." He bit the word out. He bowed his head, his breaths tight. "The Rift requires the young ones. It is barbaric. It is vile. But it is fact. We have all danced around this for far too long."

"What is fact is that we will not make sacrifices to the Rift," Tengrii growled.

Disgust twisted in him despite all his attempts to be understanding. He could no longer argue that it would not resolve it. The reality was that it likely would. But he would not be a leader who participated in such a heinous act.

"We cannot allow what has happened to us turn us into actual monsters," he said.

"It is not monstrous to want to live," Emeka responded. "But there is no time, and there is no guarantee that these other worlds can truly help us. We have less than nine days before all here are likely dead. If this is a curse, then the curse must be satisfied. Otherwise, there will be no end to this until we are all dead."

Yoto had his fist balled up on the table. The flames burned with intermittent strength along his forearm. "We do not murder our children," he said.

"So you would rather murder your wife and everyone else with your inaction," Emeka responded.

Jaiku growled as he gestured toward Emeka. "Precisely this."

"It will not work," Yoto snarled, standing. His chair rocked back.

"It will. And if it doesn't, we can move on to something else. Those children are dead regardless. We all are. Let them at least die for the good of this kingdom."

"Silence!" Tengrii shouted, rearing up on his tail. "I am your king. You will all do as I say. The children will not be cast into the Rift. Not them. Not any others. We do not know what these other worlders will be like. But they are willing to help. We knew that the day when our world would be joined to theirs was coming. And it is now here. As I have said, I will take the blame for whatever was done even if it was before my time. But that means that we must take this course." He eyed them all, the anger sharpening his words. He placed his hand on the table. "No." His claws grated across the stone. "Regardless of what the consequences are, at least we have a better chance of living like the people we claim to be rather than becoming monsters who destroy children and innocents!"

"Allowing the Tue-Rah to continue its formation is more dangerous," Elthko said. "We do not know what they will bring here, nor do we know what they will do with us."

He leaned back in the heavy stone chair, startled. Elthko did not go against him publicly.

The steward's claws trembled slightly as he shook his head. "It pains me to disagree with you, Your Majesty. But we cannot rejoin the other worlds. It is too dangerous, and it would put all here in far greater risk than simply enduring and searching for an alternative. Even if we do not sacrifice the young ones into the Rift, it would be better for us to continue as we have and suffer the consequences. We can put it to a vote."

"This is not a democracy." Tengrii braced his hands as he leaned forward, scanning the assembled council members. Rage gave more bite to his words than usual, but it was precious little compared to what he felt. "These long years, I have listened to your counsel and considered your words. Especially in these past weeks and months. But this is my order. We strip away the substance that covers the Tue-Rah and allow the formation to continue. We join with the other worlds, and we consider what our next steps shall be from there. That is all!"

Something struck him against the back of his head. He slumped forward.

32
TRAPPED

Tengrii's head throbbed and pulsed. Why was he back in that hazy-walled dream room with Rhea beside him?

"Hey." He placed his hand on her shoulder. She was almost as warm as if she was really there.

Her head turned up a little, and she smiled at him from the silk pillow.

"Did something hit me again?" she asked. She drew herself into a seated position and looked around.

He sat up slowly as well. There was an odd haziness about their shared space this time. His words distorted in his ears as if he wasn't fully there.

As he worked back over the past events, his gut twisted. "I don't think the council accepted the proposition."

He probably shouldn't have been so surprised.

She rubbed the back of her head, giving him a rueful expression. "I think that's safe to say." She shuddered. "I feel stiff. Like I can't really move but want to."

"We need to wake up."

"Look for the weak points in the walls. Places where it doesn't look quite right. Then beat it in." She slid off the bed, moving far stiffer as well. "In this case, violence is the answer."

He moved off the bed as well and maneuvered to the wall. The coloration was distorted here, flatter and duller. He pressed upon it.

A muscle twitched. Not in his body here. Elsewhere. As if his actual body was far away and he could still somehow feel it.

What a strange sensation.

He pressed harder.

Rhea grunted and attacked another point farther away. "You have to go after it with all your strength," she said. "Sometimes it's big, sometimes it's small. But once you break through, you wake up."

He nodded grimly, lifted his fist, and struck the surface. It resounded dully as if something had muffled it. But a spark of awareness flooded him.

This was it.

He beat on it harder and faster. The air itself caved beneath his fists, and the heavy thuds intensified. Then— darkness swept over him.

He blinked, finding himself now in a new place. His blurred vision took an extra moment to clear. The aching pain of his entire body dragged him all the way back into consciousness.

He groaned. The council had certainly made their feelings about his decision clear.

He lay on the stone mosaic floor. Neither his arms nor his tail moved. Even if he hadn't been bound, he was so stiff he wouldn't have struggled.

Rhea lay on the ground near him, also bound but at the

ankles and wrists. She remained unconscious but breathing. Her mouth twitched.

Steam wafted into the humid air above a large stone pool. What were they doing in here? This was one of the smaller bath houses, an old one that had been set aside for refurbishing or storage, depending on what they decided to do with it. Storage, it looked like. Boxes had been padded and stacked throughout the room. They filled two of the smaller vats. It looked as if the only one that still had water in it was the natural one that lay directly beneath the stone channel of the hot stream and drained off into another, keeping the water at a steady level.

Why hadn't the council put them in the dungeon? And they'd only bound him with ropes.

He grunted and swore as he realized that despite being no more than ropes, they were still effective at holding him in place for now. He'd break out eventually. But that was just further confirmation that keeping him confined even for a full day wasn't the purpose. They only needed to keep him here long enough.

The intent wasn't to hurt or to kill but simply to keep him out of the way long enough that they could complete the ritual. It had to be started on the morning of the third day.

What time was it now?

No timepiece was present to tell him what the hour was.

Had the oil lamps in this place remained tended? If he knew that, he could take a guess at the time they'd been in here based on how much oil was used. Except—well, he didn't know when the last time was the lamps were tended or whether they had been lit before this.

He strained at his wrists further, continuing to slide them back and forth as he flared his scales. Not much movement was possible. But he'd get it.

Rhea woke blearily, lifting her head. "Good night that hurts," she winced. She strained around to look at him. "What are they going to do with us?"

"Leave us here until they finish the ritual," he said darkly.

Who knew what would happen then? They couldn't think he would accept this. Perhaps they had no delusions of that, only of ensuring that their people were safe. He sawed at the ropes.

"I can feel one of the ends of the rope," she said, her face contorting as she rocked back. "If I could just get ahold of it, I think I could get myself untied."

"Here."

He angled himself around. They'd bound him well, but they'd left nearly a foot or two of his tail tip out. That might be just enough. He rocked closer, then stretched his tail tip. The folds they had forced his body into prevented him from uncurling farther. Already, they ached and pulsed with inten-sifying discomfort. But this—this would work.

"I'm going to need to move you. Hold still." Carefully, he wrapped his tail around her ankles and turned her around so that her back faced him.

Her fingers flexed, moving against the ropes. She could almost reach one of the loops and the end. He pulled her closer and then slid his tail around the end of the rope.

"Just a moment. Can you feel the rope now?" he asked.

"Yes." Her voice hitched. "I can't pull the strand any higher."

His tail did the rest, then brought the strand back to her.

Together, they maneuvered the rope. His tail didn't have quite the full dexterity of hands and fingers, but it was better than nothing. And the more he loosened the key points of the bindings and guided the rope end into her hands, the faster she undid them.

The ropes fell free. She sat up and untied her ankles at once. "How long do we have before they sacrifice those kids?"

"A few hours," he responded. He continued to grind his scales against the ropes until she crossed over to him and unfastened them. Puffs of dust rose from the rope as it thudded to the ground. "Maybe several. It depends on the time."

"Too bad we're underground in a place where it's almost impossible to tell," she huffed.

She untied the last of the large knots over his coils.

Bursting free, he shook himself loose. He lunged for the door, his movement returning awkwardly. The tall ironwood door, sealed and treated, stood on the other side of the room, adorned with delicate carvings along the long metal strike plates and flanked by the tall archways and pillars that masked other pipes within the room.

He seized the handle. It refused to turn. It didn't even rattle when he shook it. Nightfall. He set his shoulder to the door and shoved just in case.

It did not budge.

If it was night, then that meant there was another door just beyond this one that had the same locks. Loteb had considered this and a few other chambers worthy of such focus. That was probably why they had been put in here as well. Far from all the rest of the others and perhaps those who remained loyal to him.

Crespa.

They had to find a way out.

Rhea was already investigating the storeroom closet near the pool.

Nothing would be in there. Those storerooms didn't even have ventilation shafts. And the ventilation shafts here would be far too small for either of them to get through.

He scratched the back of his head, his gaze falling to the water pipes. Most of them would be too small as well. But those natural forming ones over and around the pool might hold the answer.

He shot over to the deep stone pool and peered into it. Disappointment flared through him. He might manage to get his arm through it.

He turned then to the one the water flowed through. It was the broadest and the most irregular. If they could get through any of them, it was going to be that one.

He jumped over the edge of the pool. The hot waters engulfed him. He swam a few strokes to cross to the other side and then examined the grate.

This might work. The hot springs themselves were even higher than this. He remembered visiting those chambers just a couple years ago. Though the passage was narrow in some places and had possibly been damaged in the earthquakes, they could theoretically pick a path from the water's source back to the palace.

"Does that water ever get hotter?" she asked, returning from the storeroom.

"Not until you get closer to the source. Even then, it's manageable."

He unfastened the grate and cast it aside. The hot water rushed and gurgled over him, not nearly so soothing now as it usually was.

He peered up into the steamy darkness. Though his eyes allowed him to see decently enough in the dark, he couldn't see much in this place. It was nothing but a narrowing passage. He thrust his arm in and caught a solid handhold, then pulled himself up.

The water pressed against him, bubbling and frothing at his intrusion. Still, he hauled himself up, fighting for every handhold and using his tail to brace and propel himself upward.

The heat filled his nostrils with its distinctive steamy scent. It splashed in his face and got in his eyes. The rocks scraped the top of his head and pulled at his hair. With each new handhold, the passage narrowed uncomfortably. It scraped his shoulders and his back.

Grunting, he struggled to thrust his way higher. The water intensified, splashing in his face and surging up his nose. The rocks refused to budge, his shoulders too broad. If he pushed any farther, he'd be stuck. He struck the rocks. They thudded and gouged his hand, but they did not give.

At last, he dropped back, growling. He landed in the deep pool with a splash. Shaking his head, he dried his eyes. That wasn't going to work. Even if he had managed to get at least thirty feet up the shaft, there had been no exit in sight. The hot springs were probably another hundred or two hundred feet beyond that.

Rhea had moved over to a stack of boxes on the other side of the room. "I thought maybe they put something in storage we can use. The first two boxes were just samples of rocks and soil." She crouched down and pulled a lid off one of the boxes. "Oh."

"What?" Wiping more water from his eyes, he lifted up on his tail to better see, then swore. It was a whole vat of fog samples, each one glistening purple. Why did Gao have so many saved? "What are those doing in here?"

"I don't know." She placed the lid back on. "There were a bunch in the library too. Gao said she needed to get them moved out to a safe place. That she had too many." After she fastened the lid, she pulled another box over. She laughed darkly. "You'll never guess what's in here."

"More samples?" he growled.

"More samples. Frankly, I'm shocked anyone had enough vials for all of this."

"Yoto's sister is a glassmaker. She's exceptionally skilled." He checked another of the natural aqueducts. Too small for either of them. Rhea wouldn't even be able to fit a leg in there.

"And apparently can make lots of vials." Rhea slid the lid back over the box. "I guess I'll keep checking these." She glanced back at him, then gestured toward his arm. "Your shoulder's bleeding."

He swiped his hand up over his bicep to his shoulder cap. It stung now. He hadn't even felt that.

He took in the rest of the chamber once more. No windows. The one door was thoroughly locked. And the air shafts and water pipes were too small. If he had had his shifting skills, he could have transformed into something strong enough to dig through stone.

She pushed away another box, sighing. "I think this all might be samples of different sorts."

The ground and walls trembled. He tilted his head back, water dripping from his hair and rolling down his scales. The rocks groaned. Everything shook. He grabbed Rhea, pulling her to him and then beneath one of the reinforced stone archways. She gasped and curled against him, her cheek to his chest.

The shaking continued. Larger chunks of stone fell this time, breaking free from the ceiling. The sculpted and etched artwork within the domed ceiling cracked.

Her eyes widened as she pointed up. "No!"

Up above on the far side of the room, a large chunk of rock separated. It dropped straight down and smashed through two of the boxes.

Low curls of purple fog leaked out. They didn't turn silver or grey.

His blood froze as he gripped her closer. No!

No, not that!

"Oh, polph," she whispered.

A great knot of terror formed in his throat. The purple strands of fog coiled up, moving in his direction.

"Rhea, you have to get away from me." He shoved back from her and then lunged for the staircase. The ironwood banister thudded under his weight as he struck at it and beat the spindles free.

Seizing up what looked like the sharpest one, he tested it against himself. Already, the adrenaline had caused his scales to thicken and tighten, the primal terror surging through him.

Not nearly sharp enough.

He swore again.

Rhea ran into the small closet. "I'll barricade the door."

"I'll find you in there in seconds! I can smell you."

"I can't hide in the vats! You'll find me there too." She bolted back out, then turned around as if searching for something.

Where to send her? He bolted back as the fog continued to move in his direction. The enormous chamber felt as if it had shrunk, no longer nearly large enough. And there was no way to restrain him.

Realization flooded him.

"That pipe," he shouted, pointing toward the hot water vent. "Get up that pipe. You'll have to find a way to hold on up there."

It would be difficult, but at least she would be alive. As long as she could hold fast and not let the powerful waters push her free.

Her mouth fell open, then she became grim. Nodding, she pointed at one of the fallen spindles. "Toss me that. If I have to hang on in there, I'll need help."

Yes. Good.

He hurled it toward her, then jerked away as the fog continued to spiral toward him. It thickened and grew in strength and coloration as if combining forces with all the rest of the fog.

"Go now!"

She scooped the spindle up and jumped into the pool. For a breath, she disappeared beneath the waters. Then she sprang up, paddling as fast as she could toward the stone pipe at the far end.

He tore his vest off and wrapped it around his face as he kept backing away. The fog's curls intensified, all of it honing in on him. She could get up in that pipe, but every minute—every second—counted. He only had a few left. What could he do?

He backed toward the farthest point in the room, his breaths coming faster.

The farthest point in the room. The archways!

He bolted to the end of the room and then scaled the wall. The archways covered the entirety of the room, hiding additional pipes for transporting hot water. Maybe he'd fall. Maybe he'd break an arm or part of his spine. But that would be better.

The fog spiraled up after him.

Rhea struggled to pull herself up into the pipe. The water splashed in her face and nearly knocked her back. She held the spindle fast.

"Faster, Rhea!" he bellowed. He covered his face with his vest again.

She spluttered and shook her head, then jammed the spindle in and hauled herself up. Already, she was soaked and shaking.

A nauseatingly familiar bitter pungent scent filled his nostrils even through the vest.

No! It was happening too fast.

He barely glanced down before the fog was upon him. It coiled up and surrounded him, trapping him in its acrid fumes.

He could still see her through the purple fog and heavy mist. She still hadn't gotten in. Her bare feet slipped on the slick stones.

No. Faster, Salt-Sweet, faster!

His muscles twitched. Agonizing pain seared through him, shooting up through his veins. It attacked his consciousness. Black dots formed along his vision, spreading like mold.

It was happening. Now. His nightmare. His terror.

He forced himself to turn away so that he wouldn't see her when the horror took over. He braced himself against the stone, praying as his consciousness faded.

33
MONSTER

Climbing up a steep stone pipe of hot water had never been something Rhea had planned on doing. It certainly wasn't something she was prepared to do. She struggled to catch her breath as much as to find purchase.

Her hands and arms shook, her fear increasing.

She knew what was coming. But even if she hadn't, Tengrii's terrified bellows would have scared her still more. And he wasn't afraid for himself. He was afraid for her. That made it even worse.

She got a solid hold on one of the stones and then shoved up. This time, her elbow caught in an indentation in the rock. For a moment, she swung there. Her muscles burned as she gathered her strength and then struggled up and pulled herself all the way into the pipe.

The hot waters surged around her and poured down past her. Awkward, she held her position and then lifted the spindle. She had to get higher. Otherwise, all he had to do was peek in, and he'd be able to grab her.

She forced her way up, struggling to keep her grip. The passage soon started to narrow. The water grew stronger the higher she pressed.

A blood-curdling roar followed.

She froze.

It had happened.

She ducked her face almost into the water. Her beloved was not in his right mind. She could practically see him now.

The low guttural roars continued. They sounded high off the ground. Loud, snarling growls echoed back and forth.

Something crashed.

Stone shattered.

The hot water rushed all around her, her lungs filling with steam. The spindle gave her something to hold on to, or else she'd already be struggling.

The hissing continued for three more breaths.

All went silent except the rush of the water.

Her heartbeat hammered in her ears.

How long would this madness last?

It had been a couple hours before. Maybe three. But that had been the fog on its own. What had been in the vials? Was it stronger or weaker? How long could she stay up here?

She imagined what he looked like now, all sharp scales and maddened eyes. Based on the sound, it was even worse than before.

She bit the inside of her lip. He'd told her not to go into the storeroom closet, that he would find her. Did that mean he was hunting? And if he was hunting, what senses was he using? Could he hear her breathing?

Snakes hunted via scent. He'd said he could smell her if she went into the storeroom closet.

She adjusted her grip on the spindle. Why had it gone so quiet? He hadn't gone quiet during the nightmares.

She glanced down at the opening.

Her heart clenched. Oh, polph!

Tengrii, fully transformed, peered up at her from the base of the pipe. His eyes now glowed brilliant green, shadowed and narrowed by thick horned scales. Long sharp teeth filled his mouth, and a cobra-like cowl framed his head. Jagged scales had formed on his shoulder caps, each one like a blade.

Her nerves prickled with fire.

It was going to be all right. This was only temporary. She just wouldn't move. Movement triggered snakes, right? He hadn't even seemed to notice her on the last third night, so fine, he could watch all he wanted—oh.

Oh no.

He arched up into the pipe, water streaming past him. His long forked tongue snaked out, scenting the air.

Polph!

She peered back up into the utter blackness of the stone shaft above her. Hot water continued to pour down. She reached up and sought out a handhold. It didn't matter how dark it was up there. She had to get as high as she could.

Another louder hiss followed. Closer this time.

She forced her way up faster, choking on her terror and the steaming water. Her left hand slipped. She jammed her foot into a pocket of stone, then looked down.

All the light had been blocked out of the passage. But his eyes glowed, swaying up closer. Narrow vertical pupils, burning with rage. Monstrous. Worse than any of the sketches or paintings in the lore books.

She struggled to climb faster, her head scraping against the top of the passage. He had gotten pinched earlier. He had to stop at some point.

The water surged harder and faster, getting hotter as well. She had to twist her head to keep from putting her face all the way in the water. The stone scraped along her shoulders and her back, and it pinched at her sides.

His hissing snarls grew louder, then angrier.

The stones jarred.

She cringed, unable to move any higher. Her muscles burned and ached, her arms and legs starting to shake.

Another rage-filled bellow followed. Something swatted at the water just beneath her. A swift sliding sound followed.

Inching around just enough, she squinted through the water past her face.

Oh, thank goodness.

He was dropping back down, the line of light appearing once more at the bottom of the pipe. His eyes had turned away from her.

She gasped, dropping her head back. A sob rose in her throat as her pulse thundered.

Oh, thank goodness. He'd given up. Another sob followed. She couldn't even put her head down to cry, or she would drown, but it was all right. She was going to be all right. And he would get through this. They'd both get through this, and then they'd save the children, stop the ritual, and—

Something struck the water near her.

She glanced down.

Something smaller was angling up toward her. His tail? She barely recognized it before it wrapped tight around her ankle and ripped her down.

She balled up, shielding her face with her hands. The rocks scraped her back and side as her belly curled. Stinging pain erupted over her entire body.

Then she splashed down into the pool.

She flailed away from him, thrashing in the water. Surfacing, she gulped in a desperate breath and seized the stone edge of the pool.

His tail tightened around her ankle and ripped her down once more. The bubbling waters swallowed her up as her grip broke. She kicked and flailed, driving her other heel into him.

His coil relaxed, and she broke free.

Shooting forward, she reached the edge. She flung her arm over the side of the pool, and dragged herself out.

He struck at the side of the pool, narrowly missing her and striking his mouth on the stone wall. Snarling, he pulled back and spat out a mouthful of blood onto the floor. He then rose out of the water.

She gaped as she clambered backward. Long curved fangs protruded from his mouth and dripped with venom.

"Tengrii," she said, pleading. "Tengrii, you're in there. I know you are. Tengrii, can you hear me?" She struggled to her feet, her bruised body protesting and her movements clumsy. "Chicory! It's me! You know me. You can fight this!"

He moved out of the pool, sloshing great quantities of the steaming water out with him. His lips curled as he snarled.

No recognition. No compassion. No pity.

He bared his teeth at her. His eyes flashed over her body like lightning, not with desire or knowledge of anything about her.

Only rage.

Her heart rioted. She held up one hand as she groped for something—anything to fight him off.

He lunged with a roar.

Screaming, she dropped and rolled. A loop of his tail collided with her, then another swept over her and tried to pin her.

Shoving back, she stumbled away. He lashed out in front of her. Part of his tail snagged around her leg.

"Tengrii, no!"

The world spun as his coils snapped her up. Disoriented,

she struggled to push away and kick free. But the more she fought, the more he wrapped around her. He appeared in front of her, jaws agape and fangs bared again as if preparing to bite her.

She froze.

Those fangs. If he bit her—she remembered what he'd told her.

There was one chance yet to reach him. No way was she fast enough. But could stop him from biting her and get a few seconds more.

She drew in a deep breath and went limp, dropping against his coils. He tightened around her at once, but he drew back his fangs as he sniffed her.

The pressure intensified.

She blacked out.

"Tengrii," she cried out, finding herself now in some strange dark place. She was half-suspended, her feet kicking.

Tengrii materialized in his old naga form, appearing slightly lower than she. Staggering, he blinked, then looked at her. Confusion filled his face.

"Rhea..." He lurched toward her. "Rhea, what—" He shook his head, then reached for her hands. He blinked again, seemingly struggling to focus.

"You got exposed, Tengrii. It's the fog—it's made you insane. It's changed you."

Where were the walls? The room? How did you get out of a place like this? Why wasn't the rest of it forming?

"What? No!" His eyes widened, becoming white-rimmed. "No. No! Where are you? Are you safe?"

She managed a weak laugh, then broke into a ragged sob. The room wasn't going to form. This was it. Oh, Elonumato, not like this. Please, not like this. It was too late. There weren't even walls here to press against. No way to escape. These were her last seconds.

"I need you to know that I love you, Tengrii. I love you, and I know this isn't your fault. You're a good man."

"No, I have to wake up. I have to—I have to wake up. This is my body, and I am master of it!" He tore at his hair, then lashed out at the darkness. His fists struck only air. "Let me out! Whatever it takes, let me out! Don't let me kill her. Stop!"

She collapsed on the floor, aware of a great pressure along her ribs and chest. Couldn't move. Couldn't—couldn't breathe. Her pulse slowed. Stopped.

"You aren't a monster."

Tengrii scooped her up in his arms, sobbing. "Rhea, I'm sorry. Salt-Sweet, I'm so sorry. Just breathe. I'll wake up. I'll find a way. Don't die. Please."

She struggled to press her lips to his. Tears rolled down her cheeks.

She couldn't even feel his lips against hers. Only pressure. Unending and relentless pressure all around her body. The darkness swept in around her. It swallowed him until even his beautiful tear-filled eyes vanished.

34
BELOVED

Tengrii held Rhea close, scarcely able to breathe around the grief. This couldn't happen. He wouldn't let it. Never. No. It would not be real.

The thundering of his own heart and the chaotic screeching outside his mind reached a fever pitch.

There was time. He just had to wake up. Somehow!

Her body started to fade.

No. No!

This was his veskaro. If anything could rouse him, it had to be this. She was his one and only. His most beloved among all the worlds. He would not be the instrument of her destruction. He tried to will life into her. Perhaps he could pour his strength and life force into her, and she would—

Her body was going cold, evaporating in his arms. She was dying. Dying! He clutched her tighter, but she slid through his arms and floated to the floor like a thin scrap of silk.

In seconds, she would be gone.

He flung himself back against the walls of his mind. The

shrieking thunder intensified, deafening him. Terror burst through him. Tendrils and serpents and coils of darkness swept up over him, trying to drive him back. He flailed into the darkness. The breath left his lungs.

Everything vanished into that suffocating inky sea. It stretched on without end as he flailed through it.

Then—the world blinked back into focus. She was with him. He felt her, her clothes soaked and her pulse gone. She was slumped toward him but wrapped numbingly tight within his coils.

He uncoiled at once and swept her up. She went limp, nearly falling to the ground. Water dripped from her hair.

No, this could not be so. This could not be!

He tried to channel his healing energy into her, but the golden healing light only sputtered. There wasn't enough.

What kind of shifter was he even? He could barely heal himself, let alone shift. Now, he couldn't share that with his mate? He focused again and poured what little remained into her body. Please, wake up!

He laid her down, checking for her pulse.

She uttered a strangled gasp, her eyelids fluttering open. She slumped back against the ground with a ragged choke.

"Rhea?" He leaned over her, his hand pressed to her jaw. Her pulse was steadying. Mottled bruises covered her arms and likely her torso and legs in thick red-purple bands. "Salt-Sweet, I'm so sorry."

She licked her lips, her eyes half-shaded as she struggled to focus on him. Lifting her hand weakly, she brushed her fingers to his cheek. "Chicory." A weak smile pulled at her lips. "I knew you could hear me."

He pressed his hand into the stone floor to keep from collapsing against her as a sob nearly tore through him. "Rhea—I—"

"I'm fine," she whispered. She caressed his cheek to his jawline. Softness shone in her beautiful hazel eyes.

How could she be looking at him this way? As if he hadn't just almost killed her.

A gentle smile pulled stronger at her lips. "You heard me."

"Barely." He bowed his head over hers, his breaths ragged.

Relief and shame fought within him. He lifted her back into his arms, savoring her breath against his shoulder as he inhaled her scent. These marks on her body, these broken blood vessels and rippled pain, all of it had been his doing. He had done this to her. To her, the one person he had never wanted to hurt or frighten.

"You heard me, though," she said, firmer this time. "You heard me, and you came back. That's what matters. This wasn't your fault. It was the farthest thing from it."

"You should not be comforting me." He pulled away, his voice taking on a gruffer tone. "You are the one who nearly died. Not me. Stay there."

He retrieved a mug from one of the stone cabinets and got her some water from one of the smaller pipes with cool water. It sloshed onto his hand. Great quantities of water soaked the stone floor now, making it slick. Steam still rose from the pool.

"Drink this."

She accepted the mug and sipped the water. Her chest still rose and fell too fast. "Are you all right?"

He tried to scoff but his breaths snagged in his throat. "I almost killed you, Salt-Sweet."

"*Almost* is the operant word."

He studied her, not certain she wasn't just putting on a bold face for his benefit. Those bruises on her arms alone made him cringe. How much worse was it beneath her clothing?

"Catch your breath and drink that water. We're going to get out of here, and then we'll get the rest of this handled."

Somehow, he would make this up to her. For now, he could scarcely bear to look at her.

RHEA RUBBED her arms in between sipping the water. Her fingers and toes still prickled and tingled as the circulation gradually returned to normal, and her heartbeat grudgingly slowed to its normal pace.

Tengrii had returned to his normal form—well, his previous naga form. The one she had grown used to seeing him in. Gone was the cowl and jagged shoulder scales and curved fangs. His claws were still larger and sharper than usual, but not nearly so bad. Most importantly of all, his eyes had returned to their previous shade and shape, the pupils once more circular. That alone made him seem far friendlier, even though right now it was obvious he was distraught.

He searched the room multiple times, sometimes glancing at her but focusing mostly on the door and the access points.

He tugged at his hair, then growled. "It can't be past the sleeping hours yet. We'll just have to listen for the lock to come undone."

"Do the others do that?" she asked. She stood shakily. Oh. She grimaced. Breathing still hurt, and standing made it worse. Her pulse thundered. "I've never heard it."

"It isn't a loud sound," he said. "It's subtle. Loteb never wanted it to disturb the children. And you should not be on your feet. Find a place and sit."

She drew in a deep breath and steadied herself on one of

the pillars. "We're going to be in here a few more hours?" She shivered. Despite the steam, it was getting cold. Her skin prickled.

"At least." He started to draw closer, then stopped. "Rhea, please rest."

"I will. I'm just thinking about where. Do you have anything like lamb root or lark leaf here?" She rubbed her wrist, flinching.

"For the pain and bruising? Yes, I'm sorry." He pressed his hand to his forehead, then returned to the cabinets. "No, we don't have that exactly. But—" He removed a few cannisters of ground roots and dried mushrooms. Scowling, he set them on the counter, then pulled out more. "I don't—I don't know —this maybe?" He held up a jar labeled "Aches and Pains." Inside appeared to be a mixture of salts and powdered flakes.

"Let's try it," she said.

He returned the grate to its place on the naturally formed hot water pipe and tested the handle to make sure that the grate could be shut so that the water could be turned off when the pool filled once more. Then he poured the salt in.

"There are seats carved into the stone on this end," he said, gesturing in its general direction.

He was hardly looking at her at all. It didn't take mindreading to guess what troubled him.

She caught hold of his arm. "Tengrii," she said softly. "I don't blame you for what happened. You know that, right?"

"You should," he whispered. Shame filled his voice. "I nearly killed you."

"That wasn't you who attacked me, all right? If you had had any say, I know it never would have happened. We both know that."

He swallowed hard.

She squeezed his arm, then stepped back. "I'm not afraid of you, Tengrii. But if you want to help me, you can join me in the water. I'm very tired after all, and I might slip and fall." She placed her hands on her waist, then winced. "I need to get out of these clothes if they have any chance of drying."

His brow creased as he studied her. "I wish I could heal you. I am a failure as a shifter—as a Vawtrian. What kind of shifter can't even heal his mate? What greater purpose is there for being able to channel the energy out than that?"

"Bruises aren't fatal. And my ribs aren't cracked. Or anything else for that matter. So you see, nothing for you to worry about." She patted him on his chest then trailed her fingers down the ridges of his abdomen. "I'm fine."

Her body throbbed as she stripped off her tunic and trousers, hung them over one of the empty vats, and then climbed gingerly into the pool. The hot water rose up to her neck as she made her way to one of the stone seats.

He still watched her, his expression mournful. He flinched each time she grimaced or twitched. Then he picked up her garments, carried them into the storeroom, and returned without any of his clothing either. Most of the feathers and beads had fallen from his hair as well, giving him a far sadder and more harried appearance. He pulled the storeroom door shut.

"The clothing will actually dry in there," he said.

Settling into the stone seat, she leaned back. The heat and salt already worked through her body. Hopefully by morning, she would be feeling much better. Otherwise, the only place she'd be going was into a pile of blankets.

She tilted her head as she noted him still standing there to the side, his brow furrowed. "Tengrii?"

He brushed the back of his knuckle over his cheek. "Look at what I did to you."

She had avoided looking at her body even when she had taken off her clothing, but she could imagine that it was a dreadful sight. It certainly felt horrid.

Lifting her chin, she met his gaze. "It wasn't your choice. You did everything you could to avoid it. I know this. You know this too. It was frightening, but now I would like my veskare to hold me. That would make it better."

He hesitated, his brow still creased.

"Hmmm." She set her lips in a tight line. Then she smiled, feigning more enthusiasm than she felt. "Well, if you're that worried, maybe you could examine me, and then maybe we could do a little more?" She lifted her arms over her head with a flourish, tried to shimmy, and then doubled over. "Oh, polph!"

"What's wrong? Did you hurt yourself more?" Tengrii rushed to the side of the pool.

"Hah." She grimaced, bracing her hands against her thighs, then sitting up. That would teach her to be dramatic and seductive. "Fine. All good. I was going to say that if you wanted to vestov, we could."

"You are greatly bruised."

"Just—just a little." She nodded tightly. "I'm fine though. Just, I shouldn't have tried to be so dramatic." She released a tight breath. "I had thought maybe vestoving would make us both feel better. But—maybe not. Unless you know a way for us to do that without me being moved or vibrated or jounced in any sort of way—"

He shook his head. "I have no idea how to vestov anyone without movement. I have never vestoved anyone before last night. Maybe it would be better to just rest tonight. You need to heal."

"You need to heal too."

"How can you even want to see me? I would not want to

361

see me." His voice moved behind her now. "Not if someone had done this to me." His hand settled on the ledge beside her. "Not if someone hurt me like this."

She reached back and clasped his wrist to keep him from pulling away. "I tried to kill you, Tengrii. I came at you twice with a spear, but you still looked at me after."

"You were trying to save me before you knew the monster I was. And you didn't actually hurt me."

"I think I hurt your feelings."

He laughed a little. His clawed fingers curled slightly over hers, then stopped. "It was understandable. What you thought of me was understandable."

"But I did hurt you. When I first came, you thought I would know you because I knew your heart." She threaded her fingers through his. "Well, I didn't then because—I just didn't expect—I thought the nagas stole your face and your voice. But you were right. I do actually know you. And I know you well enough now to be clear on the fact that that was not you who tried to kill me. You did everything you could to avoid it. Even going so far as to try to injure yourself. So yes, you're right. If you are like that again, I'll know to be cautious and to avoid you. But that isn't you. I know your heart, and your heart is good and kind."

"I never want to hurt you," he whispered in her ear.

She shivered, her body prickling with nervous energy and increasing desire. "Tengrii," she said, aware of him leaning closer. "We both know what led to this. Are you telling me that you are a greater threat to me now?"

The water rippled out as his tail slid in.

"If this happens again—" He pressed his claws lightly along her scalp.

She kept her gaze straight ahead, her skin prickling with

pleasure at his touch and even the light sharpness despite the aching throughout her body.

"We will handle it. Together." She lifted her shoulders, then dropped them. The soothing waters splashed her chin and cheek. "That's how we'll have to handle everything, you know? There are no guarantees. I could go mad myself."

He slid in the rest of the way. The waters rippled out all the way to the edge, lapping at the sides. As soon as he was immersed, she curled up beside him and rested her head on his chest.

He hesitated, then put his arms around her as gently as if he might break her with an errant touch. They rested in silence together awhile longer. The waters continued to rise higher as the steam coiled around them, the hot water and salts working their healing.

He smiled a little as he caressed her cheek with one claw. "When morning comes, we'll get out of this place. You can hide—"

"I'm not hiding," she responded. "I'm going to help you."

"I don't know how many of my people remain on my side. It could be only me."

"If it is only you, then I will fight by your side," she said solemnly. "And you will not be alone."

"Not for long. But if you die, then I will be." He gave her a dour glare, sounding a little more playful and a little more like himself. "It's all very poetic and beautiful, but you realize that I have seen you fight."

She stuck her tongue out at him, then rolled her eyes. "True enough, but there are other ways I may be helpful."

"Such as?"

"I don't know yet, but I'm going with you. Besides you'll need someone to help with breaking the Tue-Rah free."

"We're going to need more than the two of us to accomplish that," he murmured. "But we cross that bridge when we come to it."

"Yes. For now, we rest." She let her eyelids slide shut, relishing his presence and his warmth. With her hand pressed over his heart, she found it easy to drift to sleep and let the healing mend her body. "We will find a way. Together."

35

LOYALTY AND BREAKAGE

Tengrii could not sleep at all, but he was grateful when he realized Rhea had fallen asleep. Part of him remained shaken, unable to accept what he had almost done. She was so fragile in his arms right now, her bones as delicate as a bird's.

He ran his fingers through her hair, his claws tugging occasionally on tangles that he gently smoothed away. Her body had relaxed completely against his. As if she had no fear in the world so long as he held her.

He buried his face in the curve of her neck, breathing her in and willing back the deep emotions that surged higher and higher within him. Soon this would all be over.

Glancing toward the door, he shifted his weight. Morning had to be drawing near. He hadn't heard the lock click into place, so that confirmed his suspicion that it had happened either while he had been unconscious or while he had been maddened. With that being the case, morning had to be close.

She stirred, her hand pressing harder into his chest as she lifted her head. "It's—I fell asleep."

"You did," he said. It was adorable the way she blinked and rubbed at her eyes as if that would push the fatigue back. "How are you feeling?"

"Like I'm ready to finish this. I've been thinking about the spill over the Tue-Rah's formation."

"Oh?" He adjusted his arm to better support her as he studied her. "I thought you were sleeping."

"I suppose I can do both," she said with a soft smile. "Although I was sad you didn't join me."

"Hmmm. I will soon." He kissed her forehead. "What did you conclude?"

"You said that when it was cut away, it grew back after a little bit. That will make it challenging. But at the same time, we know the Tue-Rah is trying to form."

He nodded slowly, not certain where she was going with this. "Yes..."

"So if we take that and cut it out strategically, we can use the Tue-Rah's force to help break it free."

"How would you do that?" He frowned.

"It's all patterns and shapes." She traced her finger through the water, making a series of shapes. "Everything can be broken down into simpler shapes if you look hard enough, and the Tue-Rah has a design to it."

"So...we figure out what the design is..."

"We figure out what the design is and cut it away at those points, though I think I'll need something to paint with or mark the spill. It'll be too hard to tell even one or two people where to cut." She let her hand fall back beneath the waters as she peered up at him. "I don't know what that substance is for certain, but it reminds me of ulom gel. We use it for repairs. It's rather soft and sticky until you do something to harden it. But if you harden it in the wrong place, you can break it off and start again."

"How would one go about hardening it?"

"I'd test heating it or cooling it or pouring water on it. Maybe rapidly heating and cooling it. That'll break glass even if it has been treated."

He contemplated this. "General Yoto is surely on our side still."

"Dulce as well," she added. "They want nothing to do with the sacrifices."

"There may be a few other elementals who would be willing to help us."

"I hope so." She released a long sigh, her gaze turning to the door as well. "It's still locked?"

"For now. You're sure you're feeling all right?"

She pushed back a little farther. "I feel like I've been boiled. I probably need to get out and get dressed."

He wrapped his tail around her and lifted her out. The water splashed out onto the stones. Her body was still horribly mottled and bruised, though they had taken on a bluer cast as opposed to the livid red and vicious purple of several hours ago. A few even had a bit of a yellower tinge to them.

She pressed her hand to the side of the vat, drawing in a sharp breath.

"You're sure you're all right?" he asked.

"Yes. Just a little shaky." She offered a crooked smile, then made her way to the storeroom.

He hefted himself out of the water as well, taking care not to slosh out too much water. Some splashed out anyway. He had closed the grate that let the water in so that the salts would remain condensed within the pool. Sliding over to the far end, he flicked the grate back open. The waters surged out, mixing together with the old water and pushing it back up to the overflow line.

She returned, still shaky, their clothes in her hands. "Here." She offered him his vest, sash, and front piece. "Once we get into the old courtyard, I'll need to get up high to see the pattern currently present within the Tue-Rah. Then I can mark it. But that'll have to be after the children are rescued."

Tengrii contemplated this as he fastened the frontpiece. He fumbled with the thin strings before getting it straightened. "It depends on how many we can find to aid us. It would be better if we could handle it all at once. There are only four of the original founders. Yoto will not side with them. Orje is too weak to participate in anything involving physicality. Muna probably won't join either. The others likely will. As for the loyalty of their supporters—well, it is one thing to demand this. There would have been a mutiny had we just said we were joining this world back to the others, but now that it is actually coming down to this—it is a different thing to have to actually be involved in sacrificing children. We only suspected perhaps twenty or thirty were involved with pursuing the ritual. I pray it is not more than that, and I hope that the sacrificing of children will make it all the harder for all of them."

"How much time would a ritual like this take to get through? Before the killing part." She shivered, her skin prickling in goosebumps as she wriggled into her trousers.

He turned his gaze from her to give her privacy as he tied the sash on next. "I don't know. But I hope at least an hour. The Forbidden Arts aren't my area of expertise at all."

He wasn't even certain he understood their classification.

"I know that they involve suffering as part of their enactment," she said, "even if their end goal might not be terrible. But that certainly isn't the case here. I can't imagine it getting much worse than this."

The soft click of the lock releasing reached his ears.

He turned.

Morning.

Few sounds had ever been so welcome.

He pulled the vest on and slid then to the door. The knob rattled this time, the inner lock no longer deployed. But it would not budge.

"Is it time?" She hurried alongside him, straightening her tunic. Her movements were still stiff, but life filled her hazel eyes.

"May have to break the door down. If that's possible."

He set his shoulder to it and struck. It rattled but did not break. He attacked it again and again, struggled with the flush screws, and tried to pry it off. Nothing and nothing. The seconds ticked past. Rhea shivered and tried to help as she could.

Nothing worked.

Growling, he struck his hand to the door. It thudded heavily, but the wood was warm. So was the handle.

The scent of burning wood and metal reached him too. Smoke billowed under the door. He pulled back, putting his arm out to protect Rhea. Could it be—

The handle continued to heat. Then something snapped. The door swung open.

General Yoto stood on the other side, Tengrii's trident in one hand, his other hand gripping a fading fireball. The flames burned bright throughout his body, his eyes like embers. Over a dozen guards and another two dozen members of his kingdom stood behind him, all armed from an assortment of items from the armory as well as various odds and ends from what was likely the kitchen.

"Your Majesty," he said, bowing. "We don't have much time. But I gathered those who are willing to fight."

"Well done, my loyal friend." Tengrii gripped his shoulder.

"Dulce and Muna are with others, securing the door to the Rift. There weren't many present when we passed initially. Do we require anything else before the attack?"

"Yes," Rhea said, coming up alongside him. "We need paint. Do you know where we can get some that won't take much time?"

"On the way," General Yoto responded.

"Then let's go." Tengrii gestured toward the passage behind them.

General Yoto handed him his trident.

The weapon felt good within his hand. He motioned for Rhea to come as well. Then they all started down the hall.

An uncomfortable and heavy silence had descended upon the palace passages. Their heavy footsteps and breathing could not beat it back. With every second, Tengrii calculated the likelihood that the ritual was completed. How much time could it actually take? What would he do if it was done? How long would it take for Rhea to enact her plan and get the spill cleared off the Tue-Rah's formation? From there, how long for the Tue-Rah to finish forming?

Faster and faster, they went through the halls. A couple more guards and civilians joined them. They stopped at one storeroom to grab two large containers of white paint and a long-handled brush. Then back down the smooth halls until they reached the coarse stones of the freshly cut way to the old courtyard.

Dulce and several others waited for them at the doors that led to the Rift. The four guards who had been stationed there had been rendered unconscious and bound. This was going startlingly well. Elementals, humans, and shifters had all shown up for this final conflict.

Dulce stepped as close as she could to Yoto, stretching her hand out. He stretched his out as well, his forehead creasing with emotion as her eyes filled with something like tears.

"They are all inside," she said, her hand still out and in her husband's direction. "They have the young ones, and the door is locked."

"How many are with them?"

"Twenty-seven at least," General Yoto responded. "Most of the population does not know what is about to happen."

It was better that way. The more who were involved, the more risk there was of harm to them.

He gestured toward Rhea. "We think we know how to resolve this as swiftly as possible with minimal casualties," he said. "Here is what we do."

RHEA'S BODY was still stiff even after soaking most of the night in the pool with Tengrii, but the adrenaline that now coursed through her as well as the lives at stake gave her strength and stability. Besides, from the looks of it, these elementals were in far more pain than her. She prayed that this would work. These men and women were near death already.

General Yoto and another fire elemental stepped up to the doors. Dulce moved all the way to the back with Muna and the other elementals. Once the signal was given, the fire elementals shot flames from their hands into the locks.

Smoke rose as the metal heated, then started to melt through. Two humans appeared behind them with buckets of water. The locks melted, and the doors pushed inward with a heavy snap and thud. They charged through. The humans tossed the water on the molten metal to cool it, and then they cast the buckets aside.

Rhea sidestepped the steam, shielding her face. With the long-handled brush tucked under her arm and the vessels of paint in each hand, she hurried at once toward the ledge she'd climbed up on the first time. She tried to take in the chaos of the courtyard. Had they gotten there in time?

The Rift had appeared once more in the air as it had been when she first saw it in the dream state, a great livid tear floating above the sea of purple gases. No fog spewed from the opening, but the gaseous purple sea below churned.

The children lay at the edge of the cliff, seemingly asleep. Jaiku stood over one, a large curved knife in hand. Gao hung back, head bowed. Elthko stood beside her as if comforting her, his long shaggy arm around her shoulders. Guards and warriors surrounded them and the other council members, weapons at the ready. They braced as Tengrii, General Yoto, and most of the shifters charged toward them. As Tengrii and his warriors drew the aggression, Dulce and the humans raced for the children.

No one paid any attention to her up here. Why should they? They probably hadn't even seen her. And she had her own particular task.

She crouched down on the ledge and studied the spill below. From up here, she could see the design as it started to form. So similar to the one in the temple with all its stunning beauty.

At first glance, it always seemed too complicated. Interconnected lines and complex shapes. But as it was with all sketches and paintings, it could always be broken down into simple shapes with dominant lines and tapering paths.

She squinted, trying to block out everything else as she focused on this, on feeling the shapes and seeing the points where the thick dark crust had to be broken.

There. She spotted the center. It was a little lighter than all the rest, indicating the pulse of the light. In fact, it was moving just a little, wasn't it?

Yes!

The Tue-Rah was fighting to emerge.

As if in response, the ground vibrated, and the rocks groaned.

The earth elementals separated out from the fight below. They took up positions throughout the chamber, holding up their arms and pressing them to the walls. They poured their energy into the stones, shuddering as light sputtered and glowed within them. They'd hold this place together for as long as they could.

Shouts and bellows sounded from below as the fight continued.

"We are doing this for you, for us, for this entire kingdom. For all who suffered and who found the strength to make a new life in this place," Elthko shouted at Tengrii. "Do you think we have not had all of your best interests at heart?"

"Best interests or not, this cannot be permitted," Tengrii responded. "This is not who we are. We are *not* monsters."

"No, we are survivors!"

The earth shook even more. This time, more silt fell through, and a deep crack formed in the courtyard. The light from the Tue-Rah beneath the spill flared as if it strained to break free.

She traced out the design in the air. Yes. There it was. There it was!

It was so clear.

She telescoped out the handle of the brush farther, then opened the vessel of paint. The ground shook again. Digging her feet in, she grabbed the paint before it could spill over.

These earthquakes weren't going to make her task any easier. More dirt rained down. The clashing and clanking of swords on spears and knives against wood rose up.

A great split formed in the ceiling.

Down below, the dark substance seemed to bubble. Light flared at intervals. Pungent steam and acrid air hissed and vented up.

They were running out of time.

Another shake followed, cracking the courtyard floor itself. She stretched out flat on her stomach, her hands tight around the brush. She dipped it in the paint and then leaned out.

The brush was not nearly so unwieldy as the spear. The spear had been unpleasant. This—this was her weapon. She swept it down and marked the lines of the Tue-Rah's design, the marks of its powerful path and relentless energy. It was a force of nature. It could only be delayed. Never stopped. And she knew how to capture that representation with these lines.

She dipped the brush in the paint again and stretched out farther. The rocks scraped against her sore belly and her aching legs. More lines. More of the pattern emerging. The spill itself was almost as large as two of the feasting tables shoved together. It would be challenging to reach all of it from this angle. Maybe impossible.

Movement stirred on the rocks below her. She pulled back just in time as Jaiku shot up in front of her.

"What are you doing?" he demanded, hissing. "Why have you done this?"

"Because those children do not deserve to die and this is the only way that there is a chance for healing." She nearly struck her head. Lifting the brush, she held it defensively.

"None of us deserved what happened," he hissed, his eyes narrowing in on her.

"No, you didn't. You truly did not. Tengrii told me. I am so sorry. It was abominable. But these children—these babies—they have done nothing wrong. They were curious. They were in the wrong place at the wrong time like all of you when you were stolen. You didn't deserve it. You shouldn't have been asked to pay that. But you want to be remembered? What is the story that will be told, Jaiku? What will they say of the survivors of that camp? That they escaped and then murdered children and innocents?"

Jaiku lifted his hand to strike her, the sword gleaming in the low light. "That we did what we had to do."

Tengrii shot up between them, hissing as he wrapped around her. He then lashed out at Jaiku.

Jaiku dodged back, baring his grey teeth. He adjusted his grip on the sword and lunged forward.

A long pink tentacle shot up and seized Jaiku's sword hand, pulling him back before he could strike. "It is over," Gao shouted from the side of the wall. "We've lost. And I cannot do this. Not anymore. I could not look in Birkii's eyes if he were healed and say that this was the cost. Nor would Oidra support this. It is over, my friend. Don't make this cost more than it already has."

Jaiku relented, his shoulders dropping and the sword falling from his hand. It clattered to the stones below. All of the others had been subdued as well. "Stand down," he called out hoarsely as if there was anyone left still fighting.

"General Yoto," Tengrii commanded, glaring at Jaiku. "Take all those involved in this attempted sacrifice away. They will stand trial for what they have done when this is settled." He dropped his gaze then to Rhea, his expression softening at once. "Are you all right?" he asked, checking her over.

"Yes. I've almost sorted out the pattern. I just can't reach it to paint what's beyond this."

"I can help with that," he said.

"Oh? Oh!" She gasped as Tengrii lifted her up. He coiled himself around one of the boulders and leaned out, supporting her with strong arms and steady balance. "This will work."

She dipped the brush once more in the paint and stretched out herself. The thick white substance clung to the slick material below. Confident in Tengrii's strength, she marked the rest of the lines swiftly.

The pattern was beautiful, the design simple and elegant. The glowing light beneath guided her in several places, and in the others, she could see it as if it were already fully physically visible.

"Start breaking it apart along those lines," she called down.

Everyone who could gathered into the chamber and surrounded the spill. Gently, Tengrii set her back on the ledge and then returned to the spill itself, trident in hand.

Another rumbling growl sounded as the earth shook again. The Rift spasmed.

"Watch for the fog," Tengrii ordered. "If the Rift releases anything or if the fog crosses over and stays purple, give us warning."

Three of the Awdawms took up stances at the edge of the ledge.

She called down, pointing at the weakening points along the paint where the light needed to break through. Those who were made of fire turned it hot while the others turned it rapidly cool, and the Awdawms struck at it with pickaxes and hammers. The monstrous ones put their hands upon the hardening portions and channeled out gold light.

The earth trembled. Silt fell from the ceiling. Over the

purple shifting mass of energy, stalactites fell with loud crashes.

The few stone elementals who remained stood at intervals throughout the chamber, arms extended. As cracks formed in the ceiling and walls, they repaired them though their own bodies became stiffer. The water and air elementals poured their elements out on the tar as the fire elementals heated it. The shifters attacked and shattered the hardening spill and ripped out chunks along the painted lines.

Light shot up out of the cut-out lines. The sticky substance became solid in the center, cracked, and then shattered as a brilliant beam of light burst through. Bits of rubble and debris exploded out.

Some pulled back, shielding their faces. More and more light fractured out. The cavern shook.

Rhea dropped to her knees on the ledge. It was almost there. So close! But the earthquakes were getting stronger.

There wasn't going to be time to cut out all those lines. It felt as if there had to be one point where it would be enough for the Tue-Rah to break through and do the rest of the work. She scanned the slick surface, looking at the cracks and marbling.

"Tengrii," she shouted, pointing to the right. "There! That's where it's stuck."

He followed the line of her hand and the brush and sprang to it. He stabbed at that point and channeled sputtering energy through the trident's handle. For a moment, his trident shuddered. Then the knot shattered.

Brilliant golden light shot out, and an enormous crystal spiraled up from the earth, twisting up like a pillar of flames. Its light filled the entire courtyard.

Rhea turned her head, lifting her arm to shield her face.

The very air changed around her. It crackled and hissed as if something burned away.

The light then faded. Dozens and dozens of Vawtrian, Shivennan, and Unato warriors and physicians stood in the courtyard now as well as a Machat in elegant robes with a silver-blue breastplate.

One of the Paras had come.

36
New Arrivals

R hea remained crouched on the ledge, staring down in shock. White paint dripped onto her hand, cold and strong scented. One of the Paras had actually come. Which one was this? The Machat woman was a little taller than the average Machat but probably about a head shorter than Rhea. The natural striping on the Para's face and hands was more like reeds than ferns. Para Marnon, maybe?

Oh, how swiftly things had turned!

Dropping to her knees, she almost laughed at the sight of all those warriors in leather armor with swords, halberds, and other shining bladed weapons. If only they could have gotten here before this.

The Unatos all carried bags of supplies as well as weapons and thick bands with vials stripped to them. They moved at once to the earth elementals standing at the walls and to those who were collapsed or resting. Some of the new Shivennans moved to the elementals as well.

The Para stepped forward, flanked by four Vawtrian

warriors and four Shivennan warriors. "Who should I be addressing?" the Para asked.

Lowering his trident, Tengrii placed his hand on his chest and dipped his head forward. He did not move away from the fragmented tar-like spill where the Tue-Rah's emergence had formed. "I am Tengrii, ruler of this kingdom, such as it is."

"And I am Para Marnon. Correct me if I am wrong, but you are of the lost village of Muiris." She placed her hands on her polished staff. Light shimmered all around her.

Low gasps rippled out through all those assembled.

Tengrii raised an eyebrow. "You know of us?"

"Our records and some who yet live do," she said. "You disappeared before my time. But yes, you are remembered." She took in the chamber. "I see that there is much to be done. You are not entirely what we expected. But this is not beyond understanding. If your psychics here have not started to wake up, then take heart because we know how to wake them now." She lifted her arm toward him, her voice strong and warm. "Come. Talk with me about what has happened here and what is needed."

He bowed his head with respect, then motioned toward Rhea up on the ledge. "If you will allow me, this is—"

"Yes, the Awdawm who spoke with the Neyeb." The Para smiled, looking up at her as well. She cupped her hand at the side of her mouth. "Go to the hall, Awdawm. There are some people who are very eager to see you. You and your beloved will speak again soon, I think."

Rhea straightened. She dropped her gaze to Tengrii. He gave her a happy nod, a smile tugging at his mouth as if he understood.

Her heart raced faster, happiness and hope surging through her. Was it possible?

She clenched her fists to her chest and hurried down the ledge. The doors hung open at an awkward angle.

Unatos hurried about here too. A few Vawtrians as well, two carrying an elemental while one spoke softly asking if he needed water.

She stepped past the now-cooled metal and continued a few steps forward, looking from one side to the next.

"Rhea!"

She spun just in time to see Salanca. Gasping, Rhea covered her mouth. Tears welled up in her eyes. How? How did Salanca look so healthy, all things considered? Did it even matter? There was her sister, standing, breathing, laughing!

Almost sobbing, Rhea spread her arms wide as Salanca sprang to her. She was much thinner, her cheeks sallow. Heavy bags marked beneath her eyes. Maybe she wasn't as healthy as she'd thought at first glance, but the life and joy in her face could not be mistaken.

As she flung her arms around Rhea's neck, she cried out. "You're all right!"

Rhea gasped with pain, pulling back as her sister's arms clamped tight around her.

"What happened?" Tiehro appeared around the corner, wings bristling. He pushed Salanca back and grasped Rhea's arm himself as he stared down at her in horror. "Are you— what is this?"

"It was nothing. Just—there's been a lot. But I'm fine. I promise. Look at you! You're awake! And you're here! Both of you." She hugged them both, careful not to put too much pressure on her arms.

Salanca nodded, then broke into a hesitant smile as if not certain she believed Rhea. "Yes. I was almost lost, and then— then—" She shook her head, her voice thickening. "It was nothing but horrifying darkness and isolation and pain. I didn't think I could bear it. But at last someone broke through. It felt as if I was in there forever."

Tiehro smiled softly. The silver and white streaks in his hair had increased significantly, and a haggardness remained over his features despite his calm manner. "And she still doesn't know who it is. He has insisted on remaining a secret."

"No. Hotah won't tell me. Big bully that he is." Salanca smoothed her hair back, then smirked. "They were waking everyone up when I left. The cure is working, and it's working fast. They're already creating programs to help them with their recovery."

"Already?" Rhea paused, recalling that Tengrii had said that the fog came every third night whereas for them it had been every night. "How long was I gone?"

"About two weeks, I think." Tiehro rubbed his forehead. "The days have been blurring together. I'm just so glad you're all right."

"Yes!" Salanca gripped Rhea's hands between hers. "We have so much to catch up on. Let's walk." She turned toward Tiehro, beaming. "You want to see this place, don't you?"

"I'm happy to see this place or to stay here and talk. Just so long as we're together. For however long that lasts." He put his arms around both of them. He kept his arm so light over Rhea's shoulders it barely touched. "I can scarcely believe that it is over, but I don't think I will until we go for a full week without the nightmares."

"Did you fall into the coma at all?" Rhea asked.

They moved out of the way as four more Unato hurried down the hall. One carried a bowl full of flames and herbs while two others had large waterskins on their shoulders.

"No. Mercifully." Tiehro clasped his hands behind his back and released a sigh. His horns had grown a little more, suggesting that he had not shorn them down for a few days. "Though once or twice, I thought it would be so."

They walked down the hall, stepping to the side whenever necessary to avoid the physicians and attendants. Rhea mostly asked questions and listened, almost unable to believe that she was here with her brother and sister. Salanca refused to speak about what her nightmares held beyond what she had concluded about the one who had reached her. Tiehro, likewise, spoke of everything except the nightmares and Killoth, though that smile of his always grew a little softer and more contemplative when Salanca spoke of "the strange voice."

Rhea's thoughts turned to Tengrii often as well. What was the Para and all the rest saying to him? What would they learn? What would Salanca and Tiehro think of him when they met him? She'd loved Killoth as a brother early on. Her breaths tightened with excitement. How wonderful it would be when they could all gather together? Would they feel the same affection for Tengrii? Killoth would love Tengrii, but he had always been fond of Vawtrians.

The air was changing down here. Not that it had been bad before, but there had been a heaviness to it in these halls lately. An emptiness. Now, it bustled and hummed, rich with scents of fresh air, green medicine, pungent alcohol, bright herbs, and light flowers.

They passed one of the gathering rooms. The benches had been rearranged. Dulce sat on one near the door. A tall white-haired woman stood beside Dulce, her sturdy vibrant hand clasped Dulce's frail translucent one.

"Yes, both you and your husband are welcome," the Shivennan elemental said. She put her arm around her. "You'll be better faster than you became ill. I promise. This is similar to something my uncle endured. Now, deep breaths. Very deep breaths."

Perhaps it was Rhea's imagination but already Dulce looked to be regaining her strength as well as her coloration.

Farther in the room were additional Unato and Shivennan attendants and physicians. They examined the young ones who were supposed to be sacrificed as well as the elementals, shifters, and humans who had saved them. The library infirmary was probably even busier. Even better than the life was the hope that flourished now.

"It's hard to believe it all started here," Salanca said. "On this Separated World. I can't believe we were strong enough to make that connection here." She tilted her head, a coy glint in her eyes. "And Chicory was real all along? You are positively smitten. I understand better than before, I suppose."

"He is wonderful," Rhea responded. The heat that rose to her cheeks almost made her laugh. She could still blush about him. Oh, she hadn't realized how much she wanted this. To tell her brother and sister all about the man she loved and share the little details that made him him. "You're going to love him."

"I'm certain I will," Salanca said. "Although I hope that you haven't locked with him."

"Why?" Rhea frowned, surprised at this statement.

"It will be hard for you to leave if he has locked with you. Vawtrians get touchy about that sort of thing."

"I'm not going to leave," she said. "I'm staying here. With Tengrii." She dipped her head forward. "The one I called Chicory."

Salanca frowned then. "What?" Distress filled her voice.

"You're sure about that, Bunny?" Tiehro asked softly. "This is what you want?"

"Yes. I love him." She hugged herself, loosening her grip

when the bruises pulsed a protest. Once again, she felt as if she had missed something. As if both of them knew something she did not.

Salanca's scowl deepened. "You realize that this Rift means they're going to have to stitch up and seal off this world. That's what they've done when it has happened in other places. Is he planning to leave it?"

"I—I didn't actually know that that was what happens with something like this, and I haven't talked with Tengrii about it. But if he chooses to remain here, I will remain here with him."

It was strange to vocalize those words. But they had never felt truer. It hadn't occurred to her that after the Tue-Rah's formation was completed, this world would have to be isolated again. Was the Rift like a wound that required time?

"How can you leave us like that?" Salanca asked, shaking her head as if this was ridiculous. "This place is dangerous. You belong with us."

"No more than some of the other worlds," Rhea said. "And I would be with him."

"With Chicory," Tiehro said softly. "Is he everything you hoped he would be, Bunny?"

She nodded, then reached for both of their hands. "You will love him. He is absolutely wonderful. He is the sweetest kindest man, even if he has been cursed. They may be able to cure that now."

"But who knows how long it will be before this opens again? Rift wounds can take so long to heal! It could be years."

"I don't know anything about that," she said. "What I do know though is that I love him, and he has been good to me."

Mouru the squirrel man appeared around the corner. "His Majesty would like to see you and your family if you are ready."

"Yes. Yes, we are." She gestured toward him. "Come on. It's time you meet him. I think it'll be a lot easier then."

Mouru led them back to the council room. There was a chill about it, despite the fire burning in the braziers. The oil lamps were practically full of pale oil. The chairs all sat perfectly aligned around the stone table as if less than a day ago it had not been the site of betrayal.

Para Marnon stood with Tengrii in the back of the room, several guards from both sides present. General Yoto stood stoically to the side, barely acknowledging the Unato physician and the fire Shivennan who examined him.

As they approached, Tengrii turned. His face brightened as soon as he saw her. He stretched out his hand, the smile lighting up those gorgeous green eyes.

Salanca's eyes widened as she saw him. "You!"

Her voice echoed throughout the chamber. Everyone turned to look at her.

"What are you doing?" Rhea demanded.

Embarrassment flooded her. What was Salanca even talking about? How would she even know Tengrii?

Salanca continued to glare at Tengrii. "You're the one who did this to her!" She jabbed her finger at him. "He almost killed her. He is a monster! Someone arrest him!"

37

BROTHERS AND SISTERS

R hea wanted to disappear into the stone floor. Was this happening? The shock in Tengrii's face cut through her. The staring eyes of all the people from her side of the worlds.

She bolted in front of Salanca and held up her hands. "No, no, he isn't! He's done nothing wrong. This is Chicory—Tengrii. I love him, and he loves me. He's my veskare, and I'm his veskaro."

"I saw what he did. I saw him!" Salanca moved to the side, still glaring at Tengrii. "You nearly killed her. In the bath house. Just last night! You monster!"

Tengrii dropped his shoulders, nodding. "It was not my intention. But yes."

"He went mad from the fog! It wasn't his fault. He would never hurt me!"

"Except he did."

She lifted the edge of Rhea's tunic, revealing even worse bruises. Great black and purple bands that twisted over her entire body. Despite the special salt in the water helping her heal significantly faster, she still looked as if she had been badly beaten.

"Stop it!" Rhea struck her sister's hands back and pulled her shirt down again.

Shame filled Tengrii's face, his brow creased. His hand rose to his cheek to brush his knuckle there, then fell.

Several of the newcomers gasped. Even Para Marnon drew back slightly, her brown eyebrows drawing up. Tiehro stiffened beside Rhea as if he had been struck. General Yoto straightened, stepping away from those attending him, his eyes blazing as his fists clenched. Tengrii waved him back with a shake of his head.

"You shouldn't have been in my thoughts anyway," Rhea snapped. "How could you?"

Salanca's eyes widened. "I wasn't! It just leaped at me. It was resting at the forefront of your mind! How could I miss it? How could any mindreader miss it? And why would you hide this from us? If he did nothing wrong, why would you fear our knowing?"

"You should have seen then how heartbroken he was. How he fought with all his strength to keep it from happening." Rhea moved in front of her again.

"Yet it did," Salanca shouted. "And it was so swift! You are lucky to be alive, girl."

Para Marnon's gaze turned to Tengrii. Though her hand gripped the staff tighter, she kept her voice calm. "Perhaps it would be better for this conversation to continue in private."

Salanca bared her teeth, her chest rising and falling with rage. "Private or not, I will not rest until my concerns have been addressed. I demand that this is considered, and that my sister be removed from this place. He should have no claim on her. He does not get to keep her. She needs to be safe!"

Rhea shook her head at her. "You do not get to do this.

This is my life. You have your own that you are going to. Your upcoming marriage and your pursuits. Your *hobbies*."

"Yes, I do. But that doesn't mean I won't have time for you. Or that I'd be willing to abandon you in this place. How long will the Rift require that this world be separated again? Who will help you?" Salanca gestured toward Tiehro. "What do you have to say about all of this?"

"I would say that what needs to be said should be said in private," he responded, glancing about the room.

Rhea's cheeks burned with shame. Her heart ached at the thought of Tengrii being accused so publicly for something he had had no control over. The utter sorrow in his eyes shattered her. It all became a dull roar in her ears.

Para Marnon asked once again for privacy. Tiehro shepherded them out, gently taking hold of Rhea's arm as she stared back at Tengrii, shaking her head.

"He did nothing wrong!" she called out again.

Para Marnon held up her hand but looked to Tengrii, speaking to him in a swift but quiet voice.

Tiehro guided them to a small room away from the rest as the guards came to stand at the door as if to confirm this was an appropriate location. "I don't think that went particularly well."

Rhea glared at Salanca. "How could you do that?" she demanded.

"I have sent word to the one who reached me in my isolation. He says he knows an arbiter. He was actually with that arbiter, so he is on his way." Salanca pulled free and paced to the end of the room, her arms folded tight over her chest. She clasped her hand over her mouth, her face pale. "This is unconscionable. Unbelievable. I am so sorry for what happened to you, Rhea. He won't get away with it."

"Get away with what? It wasn't his fault," she said tightly. "He is a good man."

"A good man who turned into a psychopathic snakeman." Salanca spat the words out. "What's wrong with you? Why can't you see it?"

"That isn't going to happen again."

"Oh? You're certain? How do you know? You didn't think it could happen the first time. Just because someone loves you doesn't mean they won't hurt you." Salanca turned on Tiehro. "You agree with me, don't you?"

Tiehro offered a shrug, his lips pressed in a tight line as he stood in front of the door. "I agree about the concern. Not about the manner in which it was handled."

"You would have let that monster walk off with our sister?" Salanca demanded.

Tiehro narrowed his eyes at her, then shook his head. "I did not say that. What I will say is that Rhea's life choices are her life choices. After what has happened these past days, we are all at risk for things we never knew might come. We can't protect against them all. It does bother me that this happened to you, Rhea." He gestured toward her body, his brow tweaking tight. "I believe you when you say that you love him and that he loves you. I am happy that you both found each other. But if he did that once, who is to say it can't or won't happen again? Will this reoccur? How will you respond?"

"It was a curse or a plague or whatever it was that was coming out of the Rift," she responded. "And that is being dealt with right now. It had nothing to do with him or who he is."

"Are you siding with her?" Salanca asked. "Don't indulge her in this danger."

He held up his hands. "We are all going on dangerous paths of different sorts. Salanca, you test your own limits daily with knowledge and mindreading. I am to be a part of a sodiwa that specializes in illusions among the dangerous. And Rhea has decided to join with the king of a subterranean kingdom in a recently Separated World. The one thing that we all hold in common is that we believe that we are on the right course for us. The other thing that we share is the love we hold for one another, and our hopes and desires that all will be well. Yes?"

"I don't trust this Tengrii," Salanca announced. Her words grew sharper, her eyes almost wild.

"You don't actually know him!" Rhea exclaimed. "You got here, and you started judging him."

"I noticed he was a naga. Is he the one you came here to kill?"

"Yes. Then it turned out, he was the one I was looking for. It got mixed up in the dream state. Things change."

"Apparently they do." Salanca clenched her jaw. A muscle jumped in it. "You aren't in your right mind, Rhea. It's been warped. This man will destroy you, and you can't see it. Oh, Elonumato help you, you can't even see it!"

"Why wouldn't I be in my right mind?"

Tiehro held up his hands as he tried to step between them. "Yes. Things do change. Tapir, Bunny, please. We're all tired and worn. Bunny, I'm happy for you. And Salanca will be too as soon as she has time to sort through this. Just as you were both happy for me with my acceptance into the Red Claw Sodiwa, and just as we both were for Salanca when we learned of the nulaaming and the coming ceremony. I do not see any reason to think Rhea is not in her right mind."

Salanca shook her head, leaning against the wall, her expression downcast. "I will not rest until we get the arbiter here. The arbiter will see what's going on. He'll say we can take her back."

"I need some air."

Rhea ducked under Tiehro's arm and out the door. Tears stung her eyes as she hurried away. She made it almost to the end of the hall before someone called out, "Bunny!"

But it wasn't Salanca or Tiehro.

She turned.

Killoth?

She blinked. Why was she even surprised? Of course he was here. Why wouldn't he be?

Killoth leaped in front of her, arms spread wide and a big grin on his face. He tapped at her shoulders instead of grabbing hold of her as if he knew about the bruises. "It's going to be all right, Bunny."

She covered her eyes, sniffling. "She hates him."

Somehow, that even hadn't been a possibility she'd considered. Her family was supposed to love each other. Even as their family expanded.

He hugged her gently, his almond-scented hair swishing over her shoulder. "She doesn't hate him. She's just scared. That's all, Bunny. She's raw from all that has happened, but don't worry. It's going to work out."

She hugged him back. "I don't know how to fix this," she whispered.

"It's not up to you to fix it. There's really not that much you can do except what you already have done. They'll sort this. And I know the arbiter. He's a fair man."

"Can you talk to him about Tengrii?" Pulling back, she grasped his hands. "Tell him Tengrii is a good man and—"

"No. Listen, that's one thing I can't do in this. All right? Your Tengrii is a good man? Wonderful. But I can't meddle like that. It'd probably make my friend suspicious of him right from the start. And he certainly doesn't need that." He gripped her hands back, smiling. "He'll have lots of questions, but he understands the laws. He'll make sure there is justice. Besides, the matters on which he is supposed to consider the proper course are very limited. I'm sure he'll conclude you and Tengrii should be together. He might not want to admit it, but he's a romantic at heart."

"Why would she think that I had lost my mind for Chicory? She just—doesn't she know me better than that?" She ducked her head. It wasn't fair or right for her to even be bringing this up now to Killoth of all people. "I'm sorry. I know you—"

"Oh, shush." He grinned. "You think I don't know Salanca has a temper? I've seen her thoughts. She's worried about you. Wants to make sure you're safe. That's all. And she wasn't expecting to see a naga after everything else. You sort of left that part out when you told me what was going on."

She covered her mouth. Yes, that was right.

"I didn't think there was room with everything else I was sending you on the psychic stone."

He chuckled. "I almost spewed my tea when the Ki Valo Nakar showed up in my room in the middle of the night. It just stood there by the table until I noticed it. I am not ashamed to tell you that seeing the White-Eyed Death just standing there at the table corner like it was waiting for me to ask it to pass the lemons was something my heart did not need. The sound I made. Well, it woke Tiehro. And he made a similar sound. Exceptionally impressive specimens of our races, I must say."

That did make her giggle. She could practically see it happening.

Then the image flashed into her mind. Killoth screeching in a startlingly high-pitched voice and then Tiehro flailing and screaming in a similar manner while the Ki Valo Nakar looked on with perturbed annoyance, white eyes glowing and antlers glistening in the torchlight. Sometimes, Neyeb tossing memories into your mind was uncomfortable. Other times, the images conveyed things words could not.

"I don't know how you convinced it to do that, but it was quite insistent."

"It just occurred to me that that might be the only feasible way to get someone on the other side word of what was happening."

"Very clever indeed." He chucked her chin and winked. "You and your family will keep being clever, and we'll find a way to make all this work. Mark my words. When the formal celebration after the bonding is completed, you and Tiehro and Tengrii and whoever else you want will celebrate with Salanca and me."

"You know you might have another problem," she said. "You're still in the window where Salanca can say she chooses someone else."

"Hmmm. I have a rival, you think?" He gave her a coy smile.

"She seems to be falling head over heels for 'the one who reached her in her isolation.'"

"Yes, well, the only competition I could possibly have is myself. So long as she is happy, though, that is all that matters to me. And for what it's worth, I can tell how much you love this Tengrii. He seems a good fellow."

"He is one of the best."

"I know, and that's why it's all going to work out. I'm sure of it. Now, dry those tears. Naatos is with Tengrii now. He and Para Marnon will have their questions. The doctors will have their examination. We can just chat until you're ready to go back to your siblings. Maybe we ask if any of the Unatos have some suphrite and sand for those bruises. Get you all healed up. All right?"

38

THE ARBITER

At Para Marnon's request and Tengrii's agreement, two physicians examined him thoroughly, one focusing on his body and the other on his mind. They did not reveal their findings as they left the small stone room.

This was his kingdom, but he felt like a prisoner. All of these people from other worlds—people who were like them and yet so far removed—people who didn't go insane and nearly kill their beloved. He coiled himself so that he was tucked almost entirely in the back of the room.

There was one more person he needed to see. An arbiter. Rhea's sister had sent for him. Apparently, whoever had helped her had been so well connected that he had been able to convince this arbiter to come immediately.

He stared down at his claws and his coils. Were they going to take Rhea away from him? What would he say if he was in the arbiter's position?

Footsteps sounded beyond the door. Then it opened without a knock. A tall broad-shouldered man with black hair and sharp-blue eyes strode through. "You are Tengrii?"

He nodded.

The man wore an elaborate ear cuff. His father had had something similar that he kept hidden. A lithok. Vawtrians wore it to denote their strength, skill set, and type. Those markings on each of the bars meant something, but he did not know what.

"You are the arbiter?"

He gave a nod of assent. "I am Naatos."

"You may sit if you like." He gestured toward the single chair and the wooden table.

"I prefer standing in situations like this." Naatos looked him up and down, his expression masked. "This is your state of rest?"

He hesitated. "I can hardly shift at all. At most, I have been able to adapt some of my features to make them more in line with what I wish to be. But I have been unable to accomplish it on a large enough scale to return to what I was."

"I suspect your pilanars are ruptured. They're what allow you to change. And you have been in this form for so long that your body has adapted." His eyebrow lifted slightly. Then he nodded toward Tengrii. "Tell me what happened."

He did as asked. At intervals, the arbiter interrupted him with questions. About what he did as a shifter. About his relationship with Rhea. About how he had treated her. Mostly about whether he had used anything to alter her mind that was not part of her natural biology or his. Odd questions at some points. Others were more what he anticipated.

"So it was an external event," Naatos said. "An external event which you in any other circumstance had taken all necessary and effective measures to prevent."

"Yes."

"Were the Forbidden Arts involved in this at all?"

"What?" Tengrii tilted his head, frowning. "Do you mean

396

during the ritual? That was performed first by the Daars. Then by—"

Naatos shook his head, holding up his hand. "Something doesn't make sense. I was summoned here—abruptly, I might add—to determine whether a Vawtrian had wrongly locked with an Awdawm. The laws on this are relatively simple. The locking is sacred. You locked with her. This is not a situation in which an exception was required to justify alteration of her mind. Or is this about the fog? Is there reason to believe that this has compromised your veskaro's reasoning?"

"I do not think that there is."

"If someone has wasted my time," Naatos muttered, stepping back. He shook his head, then adjusted his grip on his spear. "I see nothing wrong with your conduct. The outburst that led to her near-death was unintentional. The source of future attacks would appear to be removed as well unless the physicians return with evidence that you are susceptible to additional ones for some other reason. This is simple. There have been no violations unless you are hiding something." He started for the door.

"Wait." Tengrii lifted his hand. "You are a Vawtrian, yes?"

"Yes, like you."

He flinched. "Am I actually, though?"

Naatos scowled as he angled toward him. "What else would you be?"

"I cannot shift. I cannot heal my veskaro hardly at all. The energy that I can channel out is weak. There may be other differences."

The scowl deepened, his eyes becoming harder. "You have been cut off from your people and denied the opportunities to learn to be one of us all your life. You have been crippled with a disease that has left your body far from what you wish it to be. But you are not less Vawtrian than I. What you have lost is precious. In time, you may find it again. Even if your pilanars are completely ruptured and you never shift again, all is not lost. You may find new ways to participate among us even as you retain this kingdom here. What does not change is that you were born a Vawtrian and you will die a Vawtrian. Illness and isolation only deprive you of the richness of the experience, not your right to it or to call yourself Vawtrian." He reached for the door handle. "Now there is one other who must answer my questions. For your part, consider what sort of leader you wish to be now that your kingdom has joined back with the rest of the worlds. Good day."

Tengrii watched him depart, startled at how comforted he felt. Yes. He had lost a great deal that was precious. He missed being able to shift. He did not want to be a monster or monstrous. But it did not sound as if the arbiter had found him guilty of anything. Did that mean Rhea could stay with him? That they weren't going to take her away?

If that were the case, then staying in this form was bearable. Everything was bearable if she survived and remained happily with him.

RHEA RETURNED to Tiehro and Salanca after she had spent awhile talking with Killoth, calming down, and seeing one of the Unato physicians who gave her healing sands and a suphrite salve to allow the bruises to finish healing rapidly. It soothed her muscles as well.

Salanca sat on the bench, her face in her hands, sobbing.

Tiehro stood next to her. "Then you need to tell them, Sal. We will all take the consequences. But if this is a possibility, it can't be ignored, and you can't get there sideways."

"Why are you crying?" Rhea set her hands on her hips. It wasn't going to work if she was trying to guilt her into agreeing to come back and abandon Tengrii. "And what do you need to tell who?"

"I'm so afraid," Salanca said. "If a man tries to kill you, you should be afraid of him. That is the right response. That is the valid response. And there's only one reason I can think of that you aren't."

Footsteps sounded behind her. Rhea turned in time to see a tall dark-haired man all in black arriving.

His brow was slightly drawn, his right hand gripping a black spear with white runes. "The veskaro is in here?"

Oh.

She recognized that voice. This was Killoth's Vawtrian friend, the one who got impatient when Killoth took too long gathering the drawings. He was the arbiter?

He looked her up and down, a sharpness in his gaze that made her feel as if she was being judged and automatically found wanting.

"That's me." She stepped farther back in the room, crossing her arms now. "He's a good—"

He held up his hand.

"You're a Vawtrian?" Salanca gaped at him, tears still glistening in her eyes.

He scowled. "Yes. I am Naatos."

She stood. "How can you possibly be expected to assess this situation fairly when he is one as well?"

The man's eyebrow arched sharply, his expression suggesting contempt. "I'm sorry?"

"Usually, arbiters are not—"

He gave a curt wave of his hand as if to dismiss her and turned to Rhea. "Has anything been done to your knowledge that altered your mind?"

"No." That wasn't the question Rhea had expected. "Tengrii has done nothing like that to me."

"He has used no love potions nor bonding implements?"

"None." She half-expected Salanca to point out that she didn't actually know what those items were. And that was fair. She just knew Tengrii hadn't used those on her.

"That's not the point. He nearly killed her!" Salanca moved between them. "Look!" She put her hand toward his head. "You see?"

Naatos flinched, blinking as if seeing something. Probably the actual memory that Salanca had pulled from Rhea.

Rhea balled her fists. How dare she!

Naatos stepped away from Salanca, glaring. "Do not do that again."

"Are you afraid it will keep you from doing what you have been charged to do?"

"No, because it does not change the nature of my decision. The laws of the Accord are clear in an instance like this. There is no justification for nullifying the bond or taking this woman away from her veskare. No reason for her to be taken from here. Especially if she does not want to go."

"Are you saying that because it's true or because you're a Vawtrian?" Salanca glared at him.

Rhea's mouth fell open. Had her sister really uttered those words?

Naatos blinked at her, his expression hard. "I did not hear you. But allow me to make this exceptionally clear. There was no wrongdoing on the part of the Vawtrian. He is diseased, but he has done nothing out of alignment with our laws."

"So your laws allow a shifter to nearly murder a human."

"The Accord only covers certain situations. That is what I am here to evaluate. Though I doubt you will have anything that will change my mind, tell me if you have any evidence of wrongdoing."

"She's not afraid of him. She should be afraid of him."

"I'm not afraid of him because I know his heart." Rhea stepped up to her sister, her arms wrapped tight around herself. "I—"

Naatos held up his hand again, sighing. "Salanca, I will address you now. Give me one fact specifically regarding the state of this woman's mind to convince me that wrongdoing occurred. Did he practice the Forbidden Arts?"

Salanca's jaw worked. "The Forbidden Arts were involved," she said tightly. "At the beginning."

Naatos's brow lifted. His expression darkened. "By his doing?"

Salanca's mouth pinched into a tight line. "No," she whispered. She then looked to Rhea. "I did it. It was how the connection was formed. It was the Roreheed Source." She gripped her elbow, staring down at the ground. "It was my idea, and we used it to make the connection. But it has altered her. She fell in love with him at the beginning. And that is my fault."

"You were practicing the Forbidden Arts?" His gaze hardened.

"I participated," Rhea said, putting her hand on her sister's shoulder. Angry as she was, Rhea couldn't let Salanca take the blame for this alone. Not when Rhea had participated in it.

Tiehro nodded and lifted his hand as well. "As did I."

Salanca gave them both something between an affectionate and annoyed glance. "I told them that it wasn't that until it was too late. Then they had no choice but to go along with me. It was my doing. And if my sister has fallen in love with a monster because of me—if she cannot see the risk to her because of this—"

Naatos tilted his head, his expression becoming even less amused. "Tengrii had nothing to do with the Forbidden Arts in either of these situations. He was as much a victim of them as anyone. The fact that through them he found his veskaro is to his fortune and not his fault."

"But it is mine. Have I blinded her?" Salanca demanded. Though fear shone in her eyes, she showed no signs of backing down. "Did I alter her mind and make her fall for him to the point that she cannot hear or see rationally?"

"What was used?" He set his arms akimbo as he listened, frowning.

Rhea's heart fell. What difference did that make? Was he going to find that their bond was not permitted? Was that a love spell? Or the equivalent? She didn't know nearly enough about magic or this sort of thing. And he sounded as if he was actually considering it.

Salanca listed off the components. With each one, Rhea wanted to sink farther and farther into the floor.

The arbiter shook his head slowly. "This is beyond my knowledge. It will require an investigation. Someone to examine the woman's mind to ensure—" He flinched, pulling back as if something had struck him in the ear. He held up a finger. "Just a moment." His eyes closed.

Rhea might have laughed if it weren't so serious. There was some Neyeb trying to talk to him right now. Probably Killoth. It was hard to get used to the way some Neyeb spoke with you in situations like this.

Wait. She lifted her head higher. Killoth had checked her!

Naatos sighed as he turned his gaze back to her. "You were examined by a Neyeb after the incident to assess the nature of the connection?"

"Yes." She nodded. "He was very thorough, and he tried to help me determine whether the connection was to someone real or a fiction. He couldn't tell, but he said nothing about me being forced to fall in love with him or anything even remotely like that."

Salanca plucked at her elbow, confusion in her face. Tiehro whispered something in her ear, but that only seemed to confuse her further as her frown deepened.

Naatos stepped back, sighing. The frustration in his expression intensified deeply. "I have been informed that this Roreheed Source is one of the lesser incantations in the Forbidden Arts. It is not capable of what any of you fear. The Awdawm's feelings are real."

Tiehro reached out and gripped her hand, smiling warmly. Rhea covered her mouth with relief, tears stinging the backs of her eyes. Salanca stared in shock.

"Thank you," Tiehro said. "What consequences can we expect from this confession though? We accept whatever is decided."

Naatos set his jaw. "Ordinarily, I would be required to report this. But with all that has transpired, not simply on this world but the others, it is possible that it does not have to be reported at all, especially if it's like was never to happen again."

"None of us will participate in any of the Forbidden Arts," Tiehro said. "You have my word on that."

"And mine," Rhea said.

Salanca dipped her head forward. "Mine as well."

"Simple enough." Naatos strode toward the door, not looking back as he continued. "I will inform the Para of the relevant facts. Return to the council room."

Rhea turned to face Salanca. "So that's what this is about?"

"I don't want to lose you," Salanca whispered. "You have been my sister for almost as long as I can remember. Always there. Always faithful. And I always knew that one day you would find someone. I just—I was reckless when I asked you to drink that potion. And when I saw what he did to you—" She reached down to touch her hand. "You aren't afraid of him?"

"At the start? Yes. Then I got to know him. Now? Not at all." She looked from Salanca to Tiehro, her heart swelling with emotion. She reached for both their hands and squeezed them tight. "I want both of you to get to know him as well as you can. I want you all to love each other. When we meet in the tea shop or at the festival in a year or so, I want all of us there. Whoever you are both with as well. I want it to be good."

"It may be longer than that," Tiehro said. "If the Para determines that this world must be separated again for a time to allow for its healing, we may not see you for many years. But if you are happy here with Tengrii and safe, then you have my blessing. For whatever that's worth. You're an adult. You can do what you like no matter what we think."

Rhea smiled. "Thank you."

Salanca nodded tearfully. "All right. I'm still not certain he isn't a threat. But—"

Movement stirred outside the room. One of the guards cleared her throat.

Swallowing hard, Rhea glanced out toward the hall. "I guess it's time."

39

COMPLETION

They returned to the council room. Tengrii waited there as well with General Yoto and Muna, the only remaining members of his council. His eyes brightened when he saw her.

Rhea lifted her hand in greeting, mouthed a kiss, and showed him her arms now free of bruises. Nothing would keep them apart. If the Para decided to dissolve their union, she would just run back to Tengrii. They couldn't keep her away. But it wasn't going to come to that. They would be allowed to stay together. And tonight she'd be curled up in his arms.

If she were a mindreader, she would have sent that thought straight to him. The concern so vivid in his face broke her heart. Not even the fact that she was healed was going to soothe him.

The door on the other side opened, and Naatos, Para Marnon, and several of her guards strode through.

Para Marnon went to the head of the room. Her crisp robes

swished with the movement, and her slippers moved nearly silently over the stone. "As all affected parties have been assembled, I decree that the bond between the Vawtrian and the Awdawm shall remain intact, honored, and given full force of law. The incident which led to the concern has been handled, and it is unlikely to occur again. By law, if the Awdawm calls for aid, her family may come to her defense and seek justice if she is harmed." She paused, frowning. "Yes?"

Salanca cleared her throat, leaned over, and pointed from Naatos to Tengrii. "You vouch for him."

Rhea stared at her sister, shocked again. What was she doing? This arbiter had already chosen to look the other way once. What more did she want?

Tiehro ducked his head as if he couldn't watch. Even his wings twitched.

"I have vouched that he has done nothing worthy of violating the locking and the bond he claims with his veskaro," Naatos responded coolly, the words calm but clipped.

"You vouch for him that he will not kill her or harm her," Salanca pressed.

He raised an eyebrow. "I have vouched for him that he has done no wrong in this situation. If there is something else you require, speak plainly instead of putting words in my mouth."

Salanca gestured toward Tengrii, her tone gentle but firm. "If you believe in his goodness, then will you swear that if there is need you will come to Rhea's defense? That you will strike down this...Vawtrian? Even kill him if you must. Even if he is a king."

"Whether he is a king or not makes no difference to me," Naatos responded.

Lifting her chin, Salanca turned to Para Marnon. "Please forgive me. I am not strong enough to defeat any Vawtrian in combat. Nor is our brother. Especially not when in a form such as that one's. So...if justice is to be served, then this one or one like him should pledge that protection. The one who reached me, he knows this arbiter. Arbiters can travel without obstruction. And as he has vouched for the Vawtrian, I think he should be the one to ensure that he keeps his word."

Para Marnon's mouth pinched. "You are asking the arbiter to serve as champion now?"

"Yes, and as this is a matter involving a king, it must be someone who will have the ability to arrive more swiftly than those of us who do not have such privileges."

Para Marnon gave a slow nod. "Certain details will have to be settled, but the basic premise is acceptable given the unusual nature of this situation. Naatos, you are hereby ordered to see to this Awdawm's safety in a limited capacity. In the event the King of Serroth harms her, it is your duty to defend her as if she is of your blood."

"I accept your orders, Liege Para," he said, his expression masked. "It shall be done. Do you require anything else of me?"

Para Marnon gave a nod of assent, then lifted her hand. "Thank you for your service, arbiter. No more is required of you. Now, onto other matters. Ordinarily, after a rift has been mended, it is considered best to isolate and enclose a world for its continued healing. In this case, based on what I have learned from the Tue-Rah and from all those present, there will be no separation. Contact will be minimal, and a council from Serroth shall be prepared. This council will be headed by Tengrii unless he chooses to delegate it. The council shall determine who may and may not enter and to ensure that the laws of this kingdom are respected. Exceptions will be made for the arbiter and for those who bring medical aid. Is this acceptable to you, King Tengrii?"

"It is acceptable," Tengrii said.

"Good. Then everything else will be as we have agreed, and we will manage the rest of the details later. I think, for now, that most likely what you need is calm and time alone. A pleasure to meet you all." Para Marnon bowed her head and then started for the door, followed by her guards as well as Naatos.

That was it?

Rhea looked around the room. "Is that all? Are we—" She stepped toward Tengrii. "We can be together?"

"Yes, child," Para Marnon said, pausing at the doorway. "If you wish to be."

Rhea cried out with delight and ran to Tengrii.

His face lit up as well. He swayed forward and then swept her up, spinning her in the air. She caught hold of his face and kissed him firmly on the lips. Her beloved Chicory. His hand tangled in her hair, his strong arms holding her close.

"I never want to let you go," he murmured, breathing her in.

"I was never going anywhere." She smiled up at him, kissed his jaw, and pushed away. "Now, awkward as this may be, I'd like you to meet my family."

With a flourish of her hand, she indicated her brother and sister at the end of the room. They were the only ones left now.

A wry smile plucked at Tiehro's mouth as he stepped forward. He extended his hand. "Perhaps a little late, but I am pleased to meet you."

"You are the only one in your family who has not tried to

kill me or threatened to do so," Tengrii said, gripping his hand in response.

"If you would like me to make a threat, I could come up with something."

"I am willing to pass on that," Tengrii said.

Salanca approached slower, her expression guarded.

Tengrii leaned down and took Salanca's hands in his. "I know you love your sister. She is a dear and precious woman. I never intended to harm her. That does not change the fact that I did. But you are a mindreader. You know how much I love her. How I would give my life to protect her. How I will do all in my power to ensure it never happens again."

She lifted her chin, her eyelids fluttering as if she fought back tears. "Yes. She is an Awdawm. She has no natural protections. No way to fight you off. So I will make sure she has ample psychic stones and resources to reach that Vawtrian arbiter. If you ever bruise her even a little, I will demand he come and inflict triple on you."

"If I ever did hurt her, I would want far worse done to me. I would deserve far worse."

Salanca smiled a little, her mouth quirking to the side. "She was right about one thing."

"Oh?" Tengrii asked as if uncertain whether this was good or bad.

Rhea cringed inwardly. What could her sister possibly say now?

"You have gorgeous eyes." She tugged her hands free and turned to Rhea. "I am sorry, Bunny. For everything. I want you to be happy. And if that is with him, then I will be. Unless he hurts you. In which case—"

"Yes, you'll see to it that something dreadful happens to him." Rhea shook her head.

"Yes, well, we can talk about threats and plans and all that later." Tiehro gestured toward the door. "But Sal needs rest, and I could do with a night without dreams."

"You are more than welcome to remain here if you like," Tengrii said. "The palace is your home as well."

Salanca opened her mouth to answer, but Tiehro pulled her back. "Thank you, but we will not impose on your hospitality further. It's got to be close to night. You two are—well—newlyweds. In between all this kingdom management and such, you'll probably want some time together." He smiled at Rhea. "I'm so happy for you, Rhea."

Salanca tugged free. "Yes." She gave him a light shove. "As long as he doesn't hurt you, we are very happy for you."

"Thank you," Rhea said.

"I give you both my word." Tengrii placed both his hands on Rhea's shoulders. "Rhea is the best and kindest soul I have ever known."

Heat rose within her. She reached up to touch his hand, aware he was careful not to press his claws too deeply into her skin.

His thumb stroked her sensitive skin as he continued. "I swear that I will always support her, love her, and encourage her in all ways for her best. There is no happiness for me in this life apart from her. She is under my protection, and I will only be glad so long as she is happy and fulfilled."

His arm banded around her waist as he drew her back against his hard body.

She tipped her head back and smiled up at him. Beautiful, perfect, wondrous, kind. She couldn't find any better words to describe him than that.

WHAT LITTLE REMAINED of the day passed swiftly with almost more help than he knew what to do with. Retreating to their bedroom could not come too soon though.

Rhea went up first a little before him. Otherwise, Tengrii would have carried her over that threshold and covered her with kisses.

But when he arrived, he found her already on the bed, sketching on a stack of pages with ink and quill. As soon as he entered, she peered up from her work, a great smile spreading over those infinitely kissable lips.

"Hello, handsome," she said.

"Hello, my love," he said, closing the door behind him. He slid up to the edge of the bed but stopped before slipping onto it. The ink might spill. "What are you doing?"

"Something I love and that refreshes me. Something that I need." She stuck the stopper in the ink pot. "You might recognize it?"

Tilting his head, he peered over her shoulder. Warm happiness spread within him. "You're drawing me?"

The pages on the bed showed his hands, his eyes, his scales, his face. All from her memory. All fairly accurate as well. With shading and highlights. Nothing depicting him as a monster. Simply showing him as he was now. Eyes soft. Hands gentle. As with the other sketches she had made, she had captured something that he would not have thought so easy to see or understand.

"I needed some time to myself and to draw. And this—this is what I wanted to draw. All those long days, I thought about drawing you, but I never had time. Now, well, I made some." Her gaze softened as she brushed her fingers over his shoulder up to his face. "I am sorry for what my sister said and how she accused you like that."

He nudged her with his nose, his arm around her shoulders as he eased onto the bed. "She loves you, and her point is true. I would never willingly harm you. But that doesn't mean that—something couldn't happen that would take my mind from me again." He hugged her close. "Whatever I can do to make your life better, I will take it."

She wrapped her arms around his neck, pressing against him, the quill still in her other hand. "You are not a monster."

He nodded slowly, then kissed her temple. "I will strive never to be one, but if ever you do wish to return to your family—"

She shook her head. "No. I know where my place is, and it is with you. Both Tiehro and Salanca have their own places and their own callings. This is mine. Here. Making a life with you. They can come to visit me, and I will go to visit them. We will all meet up at a little tea shop and talk about the wonders of the lives we've made for ourselves. And my stories will come from my time here with you."

He caressed her cheek, warmth flowing through him as well as happiness. So much happiness. It was hard to contain it all. Not just here and now but for what was yet to come.

The sleepers were waking, the broken were receiving treatment, all of the young ones were safe with their families, and the elementals were being strengthened. Yoto and Dulce held hands for a full five seconds before withdrawing. Concerns remained that the shifters might not be able to regain their shifting or full healing abilities. These new forms might wind up their permanent forms. And who knew whether they would then pass these on to their own children?

But if this was his life, he could accept it. They would have to determine what was to be done with the former council members and those who supported the sacrifice. Trials would be held. Challenging decisions made. Decisions that they were only now able to make because they were still alive. Alive and holding the possibility of a good and prosperous future.

The halls overflowed with physicians and attendants coming to help. Food had been sent through with the promise for more as well as help in removing the blockages from the cave-ins and repairing the weak points. Scholars wanted to come to learn their stories and commit them to the records. Before he had come up, General Yoto had informed him that Para Marnon had sent word of her vow to look into the matter of Caoxius and The Tiger.

But best of all, he had his veskaro. The love of his life. His most beloved among all the worlds.

He squeezed her gently to his chest. "Are you certain you want this?" He held his hand out before her, palm up, claws exposed. "That you want me? Like this? Even if there is never a cure for me?"

She brought his hand to her lips and kissed each one of his claws.

His eyelids slid shut. A shudder coursed through him as desire rose from his core. How much more beautiful could she be?

She set her quill and papers on the floor, then leaned back against him, stretching her arms up to play with his hair and his ears. "Yes."

He dropped his mouth near her ear. "Thank you, Salt-Sweet."

She tilted her head up, smiled at him, and then pushed up to kiss him. Her lips lingered against his as she whispered, "You're welcome, Chicory."

THE END

Read on for a note from the author plus a preview of *Slaying the Shadow Prince* by Helen Scheuerer—the next book in **Mortal Enemies to Monster Lovers**!

AUTHOR'S NOTE

Welcome to the TueRahVerse, dear traveler!

I hope that you enjoyed reading Tengrii and Rhea's story as much as I loved writing it.

This story is one that went through dramatic rewrites as I tried to figure these two characters out. I only knew a few things about Tengrii initially. For instance, I knew, he was descended from another character inspired from mythology, but that ceased to be relevant. Helpful, right?

Originally, I intended this story to be one dealing with prejudice and confronting biases with an actual naga race drawn more from our world's mythology rather than the new naga race that came about thanks to the permanent alterations from the Rift. I wanted to follow a more traditional enemies-to-lovers arc.

But neither Tengrii nor Rhea cooperated with that.

Tengrii, in particular, rebelled against his original concept. Despite intending to do a story involving an aggressive and cruel naga, it turned out Tengrii didn't have a cruel bone in his body. I found his strong moral center and determination to do what was right even in the face of literal nightmares to be compelling even as he was forced into grey situations. There was also a rather delightful twist on the typical naga casting, as oftentimes, they are cast as lawful evil to chaotic neutral. Tengrii turning out to be a lawful good character surprised and intrigued me. Though he was originally supposed to be a dominant arrogant beast of a man in need of humbling and confrontation, he turned out be someone far quieter, weighted down in the unending grind of leadership in an impossible situation that was steadily getting worse. Someone who had to deal with constant fear and under-standing the manner in which fear can change us.

Rhea was always a more chaotic character who showed up determined to take on the naga king, despite having no train-ing. That initial image of her going after him with a spear was one of the first I had of her as well as just the humor of someone deciding they wanted to complete an assassination with a spear (really not at all the ideal weapon for such a task). The only other things I knew about her to start was that she was Salanca's adopted sister and generally considered the less talented one. And that while the two had friction, they both did love one another dearly.

Tiehro showed up as a gentle surprise. I knew Salanca had an adopted brother, and he had a particular presence to him when he first slipped into the story. He's a soft soul with a rich story that has yet to be fully revealed. I was delighted to realize that he started his journey in this story.

Of course, as you might have noticed, a lot of my stories are interconnected. In fact, this one draws in multiple stories from the TueRahVerse. If you've read the Tue-Rah Chronicles, you've probably recognized a few of the secondary and minor characters. Killoth and Salanca are both Amelia's parents. Naatos, of course, is the primary love interest and villain in

Tue-Rah Chronicles (well, he might be relinquishing his crown as primary villain as the series continues). Tiehro will be returning in later stories along with Killoth.

As for Rhea and Tengrii, you'll have to let me know if you want to know more about them and what happens as they continue in Serroth. There are a lot of stories happening in the TueRahVerse, and I rely on my readers to know about which ones they most want to read.

I absolutely love hearing from readers, and I always try to respond. You can email me at jessicambutlerauthor@gmail.com or tag me on social media.

You can also visit my website for special bonuses at http://jmbutlerauthor.com/**slaying-the-naga-king-bonuses**/

Thank you again for all your support. Be sure to let me know if you want to see more of Rhea and Tengrii.

Much love to you and great joy in all your travels,

Jess

SLAYING THE
SHADOW PRINCE

PREVIEW

HELEN SCHEUERER

Drue Emmerson patrolled the northernmost point of the fallen kingdom of Naarva and looked into the festering darkness. As she gazed upon the looming clouds and the gathering night, she could scarcely contain her rage. Her homeland, the kingdom of gardens, had once been a place teeming with life and colour, its provinces lush, its gardens overflowing with vibrant blooms and its skies a soaring blue. But that was then.

Now, fear was the constant companion of all those who remained in Naarva, always begging the question: who would be next? The shadow wraiths had taken not only the kingdom's soul, but Drue's mother and brothers as well, leaving only her and her father behind.

She was one of many with such a tale.

The capital, Ciraun, along with the palace within its citadel, had been the first to fall. There had been no sign of the royal family in nearly a year; all the while their people lost their lives and loved ones, one way or another. An entire kingdom was scattered to the wind, with most now living underground or in rural strongholds across the broken lands, constantly on alert for the next attack. Drue's countrymen were still reported missing on a weekly basis and there were rumours of an increasing threat to what little remained of her beloved homeland.

'We shouldn't be out here,' said Coltan, her childhood friend, following her eyeline to the Broken Isles across the seas to the east, and then to the west where the Veil towered. Even from a distance it was a sight to behold: a wall of billowing mist that surrounded all the midrealms, a barrier of protection, so they'd been taught. A shield between the people and the creatures that lurked beyond. A shield that was fracturing.

'*You* shouldn't be here,' Drue snapped, his comment only reigniting her frustration.

'I didn't want you out here alone.'

'I wouldn't have been. If you hadn't messed with the patrol roster, I'd be here with Adrienne.' *And I wish I was,* her clipped words implied. She would choose the company of her best friend and the general of the guerrilla forces any day over the entitled demands of Coltan. What felt like a lifetime ago, Drue had made a mistake with him. They had known each other their whole lives, and thinking he understood the grief she was going through, she had sought comfort in his arms. She'd been paying for that mistake ever since.

'I was just looking out for you,' Coltan said, his mouth downturned.

But Drue didn't have the patience for hurt feelings of his own making. 'You were just sticking your nose in where it doesn't belong. Trying to claim what's not yours to claim.'

Coltan made a noise of disbelief.

Unclenching her jaw, Drue ignored him and scanned the burnished skies again. It was near dusk and she hadn't meant to stay out so late, but the latest less-than-detailed reports from this perimeter had bothered her. She had wanted to check for herself.

Drue was one of the best rangers to have risen from the fall of Naarva. She had shed her noblewoman's skin and shaped herself anew in the wake of all that death and destruction, spitting in the face of laws and tradition.

Her father had too, and as one of the few folk left who knew how to manage such things, he'd taken over the forge of Naarva and the crucial task of hammering the blades of the Warswords. For even amid the fall of a kingdom, the elite warriors of Thezmarr must have their weapons. They were the protectors of the midrealms, the only men capable of slaying a shadow wraith.

But Drue refused to believe they were Naarva's only hope, for they'd failed her people before. She had joined the guerrilla forces as a ranger, hoping one day she might discover the monsters' lair, that she might be the one to set the fucking thing ablaze and watch it burn. But, cloaked in dark magic, it had eluded her for a year.

Drue herself could practically smell a shadow wraith a mile off, and she had no shortage of rage to wield against them. Her hand drifted to the steel cuff at her wrist that she'd forged herself... An experiment that had become her obsession, the thing that filled her mind when the movement of constant travel ceased. She ran her fingertips over its dented surface. She was no master smith like her father, but the cuff wasn't for looking pretty. It sensed the power-hungry magic of the wraiths, warming against her skin when they were near. It was a glimmer of hope, on an otherwise bleak horizon, that there might just be a way to keep the monsters of the midrealms at bay.

'Drue?' Coltan's voice jolted her from her reverie. 'What's that?'

She followed his pointed finger to something in the clouds moving towards them, fast. Her eyes narrowed, her hand shifting to her cutlass, but pausing as the creature came into full view. A sigh of relief whistled between her teeth.

'It's just Terrence,' she replied, not taking her eyes off the wide expanse of those soaring wings closing in. She braced herself for her hawk's landing.

Sure enough, she had to dig her heels into the earth as a powerful gust of wind hit and the bird's talons gripped her shoulder, his substantial weight settling there. Drue found it comforting and reached up to stroke his feathers fondly.

Terrence gave her finger an affectionate nip with his beak before he cast his discerning yellow gaze upon Coltan with unmistakable disdain. Drue loved him for it, especially when it made Coltan yield a step back from her.

The hawk was an impeccable judge of character, to be sure.

'I really wish you wouldn't bring him everywhere,' Coltan muttered.

'Adrienne loves him.'

'Because Adrienne shares your sadistic sense of humour.'

'I have no idea what you're talking about.'

'Please,' Coltan scoffed, starting after her as she continued along the kingdom's perimeter. 'The two of you and that damn bird love ganging up on me.'

'We do no such thing.'

He fixed her with a lingering, longing stare. 'Am I so repulsive to you?' he asked, desperation ringing in his voice.

'I'm not having this conversation again.' Drue's fist clenched around the grip of her cutlass, her knuckles threatening to split. Terrence's claws tightened on her shoulder, as though he too couldn't stand Coltan's constant pestering.

'Drue, please... Just talk to me.'

'I *have* talked to you,' she snapped. 'I have told you time and time again that you have my friendship and nothing more. I have nothing else to give you. You are not entitled to or owed anything more, nor will this constant barrage of pressure from you result in what you want.'

'It truly meant nothing?' he asked.

'It was a night or two of comfort between friends,' Drue replied. 'I told you as much at the time and three dozen times since —'

In a rage, Coltan sent his shield flying. The steel disc clanged loudly as it struck a nearby boulder and bounced off, colliding with several smaller rocks before it rolled onto its face, the sound echoing across the expanse of an otherwise silent land.

Drue's heart had seized, not for fear of Coltan, but for what the rattling noise might draw out from the shadows. She waited a beat, then two, straining to hear anything that might indicate that he'd disturbed something in hiding...

Sensing nothing, she rounded on him. 'You fool,' she hissed, fury bubbling to the surface as she suppressed the urge to swing her blade. Not only was he an entitled, fragile man-child, but he was a fucking idiot as well.

'I didn't —'

She raised a hand to silence him, her scalp prickling.

Something in the air had changed. An unnatural stillness settled over the abandoned, sprawling citadel below.

And as if in answer, the steel cuff warmed against her skin and Terrence let out a sharp cry of warning.

Darkness blocked out the horizon.

Suddenly, the shadow wraiths were upon them.

Membranous wings flared, talons already carving through the air as wisps of onyx power whipped around them, disorientating, alluring.

'Fuck,' Drue shouted, drawing her cutlass and her sword.

Terrence launched himself into the air, and she had to bite back her shriek of fear for him. He was a mighty bird of prey. He could handle himself. Coltan, on the other hand...

'Draw your sword,' she snapped, finding her flint and striking flame to life along her blades.

While she was no Warsword and couldn't slay a shadow wraith to its bitter end, she could fight them off, and there was one thing they hated more than anything: fire.

With her back to Coltan, Drue braced herself for the first assault.

The monsters landed heavily, the earth trembling beneath their claw-like feet. There were seven of them – a bigger swarm than she was used to, but it mattered not, so long as her fire raged hot and her blades were sharp.

The wraiths advanced, their strange, sinewy frames dripping with cursed shadow, their skin almost leather-like, their eyes an eerie clouded blue.

They were not of this world – not anymore.

Magic lashed at her, but she sliced at it like she would a limb, severing it from its source with her fiery steel. She was from a family of blade wielders. Her brothers had trained her well, despite her skirts and jewels, and now... Now she was a force to be reckoned with all on her own.

One wraith screeched as she carved her cutlass across its wiry arm. The horrific smell of burnt hair singed her nostrils, for that was what these monsters reeked of as they shaped the darkness around them.

Behind her, Coltan shouted, but she couldn't turn her back on the wraith in front of her. The beast towered above her, its body elongated and horrific, eight feet tall, wielding its claws like a puppet master, manipulating the ribbons of power around it, its form taking a familiar shape. The monster's magic picked at the rotting trauma within her, shaping its curse of nightmares into those she had lost, manifesting warped versions of them before her.

'Mother,' Drue wheezed, hesitating just a second as she saw her – a crude imagining of the gentle woman who'd raised her, wrapped in shadow.

Drue lunged, the illusion shattering as she pierced the creature's leathery flesh with the tip of her sword.

But it was not enough. She needed to get herself and Coltan out of there. There was no way they could take on the entire swarm. She couldn't evade the lure of their horrors forever. Dodging another onslaught of lashing shadow, she rolled along the ground, slicing where she guessed the creature's heel tendon would be —

The answering scream confirmed it, black and red blood spurting from the wound.

Drue's hands were growing clammy around the grips of her weapons, but she didn't stop. She delivered an upward cut to another wraith's abdomen, hoping the flames caught alight across its flesh.

'Coltan!' she called, finding her companion further away than she'd realised and surrounded by wraiths.

'Go!' he shouted. 'Let me distract —'

She stopped listening. He was hardly one for heroics. Instead, Drue ducked and wove her way to him, delivering as much damage to the monsters as she could. All the while, her mind ticking through the options she had.

There weren't many.

She knew the top island of Naarva like the back of her hand, all the nooks and crannies, all the secret passageways the rebels and guerrilla forces had carved out under the noses of the wraiths. But those were no good to them when they were in the thick of a swarm, when Coltan insisted on fighting like a prized idiot. And over her dead body would she lead the monsters back to the citadel.

When she reached Coltan, she noted several lacerations and a scorch mark across his chest. He'd been hit hard... He was panting, raising his sword against an incoming swipe of claws. Drue blocked, swinging her cutlass at the exposed shoulder of another monster.

Above, Terrence shrieked, his wings beating furiously as he aimed his talons for the creatures' clouded blue eyes, clawing viciously, sending one of them stumbling and clutching at its face —

But they were outnumbered and outmatched. Two rangers of Naarva had no chance against seven shadow wraiths from beyond the Veil. Drue desperately scanned their surroundings, looking for anything that might hold them off a little longer, just to give her a second to think —

The thunderous sound of horse hooves vibrated beneath her boots.

Her gaze snapped up to see a pair of mighty warriors leaping from their stallions and into the heart of the fray. In the glowing light of the blazes, the palm-sized totems on their right arms gleamed: a design of two crossed swords with a third cutting down the middle, marking them with the highest honour Thezmarr could bestow.

These were no ordinary warriors. These were *Warswords* of the guild from across the sea.

Drue didn't question it, not then. Instead, she used their arrival and the wraiths' surprise to her advantage, slicing through legs and abdomens with as much force as she could muster, weakening the monsters so that the Warswords might pin them down to deliver swift justice. The warriors lit their swords aflame as well, the larger of the two wielding one in each hand as though the blades were an extension of himself. He moved with such precision and grace that Drue nearly stopped in her tracks to admire him.

The shriek of a wraith brought her out of her near-trance and spurred her into action. She parried and blocked, dodged and advanced, all the while inflicting as much pain and suffering as she could muster. These creatures were the reason her brothers were dead, her mother too, their screams echoing in her nightmares. These beasts of darkness had changed the fate of her entire kingdom and wrought despair upon the people of Naarva. Because of them, she and everyone else she knew on these shores lived a half-life, one cloaked in fear —

An ear-piercing scream set her teeth on edge, and she whirled around to see the Warswords working together to carve out the heart of not one but two wraiths. It was a horrific, brutal act, but when the black masses were cast aside, the monsters moved no more.

Drue allowed herself a moment to catch her breath, gasping in disbelief and awe as the Warswords took on another creature, moving as a single unit, as though they had done this countless times before.

Nearby, Coltan hauled himself to his feet and came to stand at her side, and Terrence landed on her shoulder with a quiet cry, but she didn't dare take her eyes off the wraiths. The Warswords' hands slayed two more, while the remaining three flung out their wings and launched themselves into the sky, leaving near-translucent ribbons of shadow in their wake as they fled.

The Warswords exchanged no words as they lit the carved hearts on fire, before stalking towards Drue and Coltan.

But something tightened in Drue's chest, for there were no more wraiths in sight, and yet... Her cuff was still hot against her wrist.

As the towering Warswords approached, she waited –

waited for the air to clear, for the remains of the dead creatures to drift into the wind... She watched as the smoke swept away the scent and ash of the monsters.

And still the heat against her skin lingered.

Still, the cuff sang to her.

Before she knew it, the larger warrior stood before her, a satisfied gleam shining in his hazel eyes. His dark hair was tied up in a knot. Olive skin peeked from beneath his black armour as he sheathed both his swords at his belt.

He offered a blood-stained hand. 'I'm Talemir Starling,' he said with a smile. 'And this is Wilder Hawthorne.'

Drue stared at him. He looked every bit the formidable warrior, every bit the handsome rogue his kind were reported to be: square jaw, corded with muscle...

But even though he smelt like an incoming storm after a drought, she didn't hesitate to thrust her blade to his throat.

For the cuff didn't lie.

And it told her that this man was a shadow wraith.

2
TALEMIR

With her cutlass to his throat, the beautiful young ranger actually *swung her sword at him*. Talemir leapt back in surprise, unsure how he'd managed to offend her so soon. Usually it took a good while for him to get a woman this riled up, but within moments he realised that the fury on her face was not born of a simple slight, but of a hurt so deep it raged white-hot.

He unsheathed his sword in an instant, a thrill surging through him at the new challenge, the pair of them moving so fast that his former apprentice still wore an expression of shock.

Steel met steel, ringing out across the empty lands as he blocked the woman's second strike. He didn't intend to attack, but merely —

Feathers and talons came out of nowhere with a blood-curdling screech, claws as sharp as daggers dragging down his face.

'What the fuck?' He tried to bat back what he realised was an enormous hawk.

'Away, Terrence. He's mine,' the woman commanded, and in a second the bird was gone and she was advancing once more. 'You're one of them,' she spat, whirling on her toes and delivering a surprisingly powerful thrust of her blade.

Her words sent instant dread coiling in his gut, and that strange cuff around her wrist seemed to hum as she pushed forward, but he deflected her attack easily. 'You mean a Warsword?' he asked with mock politeness, sidestepping another lunge. 'I thought that much was obvious.'

She parried, determination and hatred blazing in her ice-blue, kohl-lined gaze. 'A monster.' She feinted right and then struck, but with a downward cut, he knocked her blade aside.

'Talemir?' Wilder's voice sounded a few feet away, more curious than alarmed.

Talemir glanced over his attacker to see his protégé looking bored as he leant against a boulder, the tip of his sword poised at the Naarvian man's throat. 'I thought we were headed to Ciraun?'

'This won't take a minute. I've got it handled,' Talemir called back, returning his attention to the woman just in time for her to deliver a vicious slice to his bicep. Blood trickled, but he barely felt it.

'Do you?' she snarled, forcing him backward, drawing their fight away from the others. 'I know what you are.'

Plastering on his most charming grin, Talemir stepped out of striking range and sketched a bow. 'As I said, Talemir Star-ling, Warsword of Thezmarr, at your service, lady. Perhaps you've heard of me?' He winked. 'What should I call you, Wildfire?'

The word slipped from his lips before he'd even thought it, for that was what the woman was – a living flame, both in her violent actions and the streaks of red through her burnt-umber hair.

'Not that,' she said through gritted teeth, surging towards him again.

This time, their swords met close between their bodies.

'I have to call you something, Wildfire.'

She let out a cry of fury and attacked with renewed rage, her blades blurs of silver in the air before him. It was adorable, really, that she thought she could gain the upper hand against a Warsword. He certainly hadn't survived the Great Rite to be smote by a girl, however pretty, upon the ruins of Naarva. But she clearly sensed something within him, something that, until this point, no one else had... So he let her drive the fight backward, towards the rocky outcrop of the cliffs, so they were out of earshot. He let her hold her blade to his neck, just for a moment.

There was little space between them, and her body heaved with effort as she pressed her weapon to his throat again.

'You're a skilled fighter, I'll give you that,' he told her, utterly calm despite the trickle of blood he felt trailing down his skin. 'Though, you're breaking the laws of the midrealms by wielding that blade.'

Her lip curled into a snarl. 'Women of Naarva learnt long ago to abide by their own laws if they wanted to survive.'

'I can respect that,' Talemir replied. 'If they allowed women warriors at Thezmarr, you'd make a fine —'

'Enough,' she commanded. But her gaze had changed, as had her breathing. She pressed against him, her thigh forced between his, her eyes dipping to his mouth. 'Stop that,' she said.

He frowned. 'Stop what?'

'You're using your dark magic on me, bewitching me with shadows.'

A laugh escaped him. 'What?'

But she'd drawn his attention to it as well, to every part of them that touched. Her body was like a brand on his, awakening something that slumbered deep within.

'You're trying to seduce me into the darkness,' she breathed. 'I can feel it...'

He nearly snorted, but instead he leant in. 'Perhaps you just find me attractive. You wouldn't be the first.'

She blanched.

And that was the signal that whatever this was had gone on long enough. As much as he would have liked to continue rolling around in the dirt with her, he had his orders from the guild. He needed to find and kill the wayward son of the forge master: the man responsible for threatening all that Thezmarr stood for, its very culture and ethos, the protection of the midrealms. The strange buzzing at the woman's wrist told Talemir that the cuff was ample evidence of the man's meddling. There was no doubt it had been made with Naarvian steel.

In three quick manoeuvres, he had her disarmed, her dainty hands trapped in his, her back flush to his chest.

'You were toying with me,' she breathed.

'Only a little.'

'You're a monster...'

Whatever magic that cuff was imbued with – for it had to be the cuff – was powerful and alarmingly effective. There was no trace of doubt in her words. She clearly knew in her bones what he was, which unnerved him. Not even Wilder knew... But she had no proof. Here, he was all man, all warrior, and nothing more.

'I've been called worse,' he allowed. 'Do you yield?'

There was a lingering pause, and he tightened his grip. 'I know what you are, shadow wraith. I will carve out your heart before the end.'

Talemir gave a dark laugh. 'I'd like to see you try, Wildfire. Do you yield?' he asked again.

He felt her against every part of him, stirring something within, and he realised she smelt of lilacs and heather, of a home long forgotten.

'For now,' she said at last.

'Good.' He released her. 'Then you can take us to the forge.'

The woman stiffened. 'What do you want with the forge?'

'Warsword business. Best you don't interfere.'

He could practically hear her grinding her teeth, but the woman seemed to understand that he had her beat and slowly, her blue gaze still searing with rage, she sheathed her weapons. Seething in silence, she led them back down the crest of land to where Wilder waited with their horses, and the other man stood awkwardly, his complexion ashen from his encounter with both wraiths and Warswords. The giant hawk watched from a nearby rock as well, its yellow eyes utterly unnerving. Talemir glared at it, the scratches on his face already itching where the blood had dried.

Wilder handed him his reins. 'What was that about?' he asked under his breath.

'Oh, you know by now I have a tendency to cause extreme reactions in women...' Talemir grinned.

'That's usually after you bed them.'

'What can I say? Perhaps my powers of seduction are stronger in Naarva.'

Wilder snorted. 'She was trying to *kill* you.'

'Some of the best sex starts that way, my young apprentice.'

The younger warrior rolled his eyes in a long-suffering manner. 'I haven't been your apprentice in years. I'm a Warsword now.'

Talemir smirked. He loved baiting the young man. And now more than ever, after the fall of Naarva, after the fall of Wilder's brother, it was an extra joy to see him shed his shell of grief, even for a moment.

'You'll always be my apprentice,' he said, giving his fellow Warsword a gentle shove.

Wilder shook his head and mounted his horse. 'You get more insufferable by the day.'

'You wound me,' Talemir quipped. 'Aren't you forgetting something?'

'What?'

'Well, if we're to reach the forge in the next century, you'll have to make room in that saddle for one more...' Talemir nodded to the scowling Naarvian ranger.

'You can't be serious,' Wilder said, not keeping the disgust from his voice.

'Oh, deadly serious, apprentice. We both know the lady wants to be close to me.'

'I hope she sticks a knife in your back.'

'With a face like that, I might just let her.'

'Insufferable,' Wilder muttered, motioning for the male ranger to approach.

Talemir turned to find the woman closer than he'd realised. She was quiet on her feet. He'd give her that.

'Are you quite done with your dick-swinging?' she demanded, folding her arms over her chest.

He stepped back, presenting the stirrup to her. 'By all means, climb on.'

'You expect me to share a saddle with you? With a fucking shadow wraith?'

Talemir couldn't help but glance towards Wilder, checking that he hadn't heard. 'I don't know where you've got that idea, but I assure you —'

The woman closed the gap between them, her knuckles paling as she clenched her fists around her weapons. 'You may look like a man, but I know better. Don't insult me by saying otherwise.'

'Regardless of what you think, I bear you no ill will. My business is with the forge master. Once that's dealt with, you needn't see me again. But we have to get there first.'

'I can walk.'

'It'll take all night.'

'So be it,' she said, lifting her chin in defiance.

But no, that wasn't how this was going to go. In a single, effortless motion, Talemir enclosed his hands around her waist, the warmth of her skin seeping through her clothes into his palms, and he lifted her into the saddle.

Apparently, only shock stopped her from kicking him in the face, and before she could think better of it, he swung himself up behind her, settling her between his legs. Oh, he could feel the rage rolling off her in waves, but that didn't stop him from appreciating the brush of her soft hair, nor that intoxicating scent of lilac and heather.

A blur of movement to their left caught his eye as he urged his stallion onwards. That damn hawk was back, flying close enough to them that it felt like a warning. But he was a Warsword of Thezmarr. It would take more than some bird to ruffle him.

'What did you say its name was?' he asked the woman, his hands gripping the reins in front of her.

'Terrence,' she said.

'Terrence?' He baulked. 'What sort of name is that for a bird of prey?'

'A perfectly decent one,' she countered coldly.

'Right...' He watched the hawk fly ahead then, dipping in and out of sight. 'What does he eat?'

'Starlings,' she replied, deadpan.

He snorted. For that line alone, under different circumstances he would have courted her. But despite his jesting to Wilder, he was under no illusions about finding passion here. She offered nothing of the sort, or perhaps another form of it entirely – where the tip of her blade kissed the delicate skin of his throat.

As they rode south, Wilder and the other ranger looking equally uncomfortable sharing a saddle to their right, the woman spoke again.

'What are Warswords doing in Naarva?' There was no missing the hatred lacing her question.

'We're here by order of Thezmarr,' he told her.

'You're over a year late.'

He felt, rather than saw, Wilder's attention snap towards her, his rage palpable. 'We were here. We fought. We lost as you lost.'

'I doubt that, Warsword,' she taunted.

Talemir tensed as those words found their mark and Wilder twisted in the saddle, his usually handsome face contorted with unrestrained violence.

'What do you mean by that, ranger?' he bit out.

Talemir didn't blame him. In fact, the same rage simmered in his own veins. Wilder's older brother, Malik, who was also Talemir's dearest friend, had suffered greatly during the ultimate battle for Naarva. It had been he and Talemir who had fought at the centre of the horrific skirmish, and both had endured a fate crueller than death.

'Wilder,' Talemir barked, sensing that his young protégé was about to do or say something brash. And as much as he wished to throttle the woman for her thoughtless words, he knew better.

But she turned in the saddle, meeting his gaze, her own blue eyes intense with interest, as though she had just pieced a puzzle together. Her attention unnerved him and he pressed his stallion into a canter, so she was forced to face forward. The sooner he and Wilder spoke to the forge master and found his wayward son, the sooner they could leave the festering shithole of Naarva behind.

For it was festering. He had seen it before it had fallen – the kingdom of gardens, it was once called. Both the citadel and the university on the eastern island boasted the most extensive range of blooms the midrealms had to offer. Everything had crumbled after the shadow wraiths broke through the Veil, rendering it nothing more than an overgrown nightmare now. First, his own homeland, the kingdom of Delmira, had been taken... Naarva had followed years later.

He straightened in his saddle as the remains of the citadel came into view.

'You'll direct us to the forge?' he asked.

'If you insist,' she muttered.

'I'd happily enjoy your warm and welcoming company a little longer.'

'Then ride on, wraith. Perhaps the forge master has a special blade for your heart.'

He ignored this, ignored her as they approached the iron doors of the city.

He peered across at Wilder and gave him a subtle nod. For beyond those doors was their enemy: the man who had sabotaged the magical steel source. The consequences of his actions were dire – the weakening of Warsword blades and the consequent strengthening of the shadow wraiths. Talemir himself had sworn to kill the bastard...

Without further comment, the woman nodded to the

guards stationed above the gates and directed them through the eerily quiet citadel.

'Where is everyone?' Wilder asked, his brow furrowed.

'Underground,' the woman replied tersely. 'The citadel has been empty for a long time. It's no safer than out in the open. The only thing that operates above ground is the forge.'

Talemir shifted in the saddle, trying to ignore the press of her backside against him. Then, the woman was swinging down from the horse, catching him in the stomach with her boot. He let out a grunt of shock, rather than pain.

'Apologies,' she said, without an ounce of regret. 'You can leave your horses with Brax,' she told them, waving to a youngster who had appeared from the shell of a nearby building. 'It's not far from here.'

Talemir shook his head in disbelief as he dismounted. *This woman... She's something else.*

He stared in awe as that giant hawk soared towards her, landing on her shoulder, its yellow eyes flicking from one man to the next, full of suspicion. The Warswords followed her and her friend down several abandoned alleyways. All the while, Talemir's skin crawled as though he were being watched. No doubt they were. If the survivors of Naarva had sense enough to send rangers to scout the perimeters of their territory, then they'd have sense enough to have people on sentry duty. He'd have wagered that the woman leading them through the empty streets was a leader here. She certainly acted like it.

At last, they reached the forge. It was a simple building at the end of a laneway, but Talemir could hear the strike of a hammer ringing out from within. He knew all too well the calibre of the weapons crafted here, his hands drifting to the grips of his swords sheathed at his sides. Like all Warswords' blades, the iron had been mined from a Naarvian source said to have been created by the Furies themselves with a star shower. The steel forged from such a place was known to be the strongest in all the midrealms, was known to hold the power of the gods. The very same source that was now being threatened by some meddlesome fool.

The woman pushed open the door before them and strode inside, clearly familiar with the blacksmith and his family. 'Fendran!' she called loudly, scanning the somewhat cluttered space around them.

A giant hearth sat in the centre of the forge, with a bellows positioned right beside it. Numerous stands of smithing tools lined the walls, and several long benches, as well as a trough with water for cooling steel, took up the rest of the room. It was sweltering hot, and Talemir could already feel his under-shirt growing damp with sweat.

The hammer struck again and his attention cut to the far corner, where a middle-aged man stood tending to the blade of a dagger. Sparks flew as he hit the steel anew.

'What is it?' he near-shouted, not looking up, hammering away at the weapon. He was a muscular fellow, perhaps in his fiftieth year. His beard was scraggly and his face was lined with sweat and grime. He wore a thick leather apron and protective gloves.

'Warswords here to see you,' the woman called, leaning against a nearby bench and crossing her arms over her chest. She looked from the blacksmith to Talemir and Wilder, her gaze filled with disdain.

At last, the man named Fendran glanced up from his work, wiping his brow with the back of his glove, his eyes falling to the Warswords in his forge. Recognition flashed, and he approached them, huffing from the exertion.

'You're a long way from home,' he said by way of greeting.

He surveyed Talemir with particular reverence. 'Starling, isn't it?'

Talemir inclined his head.

'I saw you fight in the final battle of Naarva.' He turned to Wilder. 'And you – you could only be the brother of Malik the Shieldbreaker...'

'I am, sir,' Wilder replied stiffly.

But Fendran didn't seem to notice. Instead, he faced Talemir again. 'You have some reputation, even here, even after... everything. I saw the showdown between you and that wraith towards the end of the battle, after Malik was maimed.'

Talemir felt Wilder flinch beside him. Malik had been the best of them. He had not deserved the fate he'd met.

'We thought that wraith had you for a moment there,' Fendran continued, shaking his head as though he were reliving the horror now.

Talemir forced himself to remain stoic, even as the memories came rushing back. He let the panic wash over him as he recalled the wraith's talon-tipped fingers reaching for him, penetrating his chest, the pain searing every inch of his skin as the darkness called to him. Talemir kept his face neutral despite the wave of nausea that gripped him, although his knees buckled beneath him. For a moment, it was as though the change were upon him at the mere memory of it all. Nothing compared to that horror. Nothing compared to the feeling of shedding his humanity and the wraith form taking hold. To the way all the colour seeped from the world and he saw everything in black and white and grey. He'd been trying to find a cure for it ever since, entrusting his secret to one person alone in all of the midrealms: an alchemist called Farissa in Thezmarr.

He tasted iron on his tongue and realised that he'd bitten the inside of his cheek.

Fendran was staring at him expectantly.

Talemir recovered instantly. 'We are here to speak with your son,' he said firmly, leaving out the part about the kill order. 'He has been charged with treason for interfering with the Naarvian steel source. All Warsword blades are connected by its magical properties, and his meddling has left us vulnerable when trying to defend against the shadow wraiths.'

The woman made a noise in her throat, as if she somehow found this amusing. He shot her a warning glare. Ranger or not, this wasn't her concern.

Talemir met Fendran's confused gaze. 'By interfering with the source, your son has endangered us all. He needs to answer for his crimes.'

Fendran's brow furrowed, and he glanced across at the woman who stood picking her nails by the anvil.

'I don't understand,' he said at last. 'What's happened to the source?'

'That's what we're here to find out, but the effects have been felt in the blades of Warswords all over the midrealms. There will be consequences.'

'Who gave you this information? What exactly do you intend to do?'

'It doesn't matter who gave the information,' Talemir said, though he noted the male ranger's defensive change in stance. 'All that matters is that this is dealt with. We cannot have someone interfering with the steel at a time where the weapons of Warswords are all that stand between the midrealms and the shadow wraiths. Our blades have protected the people for centuries —'

'Where is the proof, then?' Fendran argued, pushing his

443

chest out in challenge, even though he had to crane his neck to meet Talemir's eyes. 'Proof that my... son is responsible?'

Talemir ground his teeth. The proof was wrapped around the young woman's wrist. He knew that for a fact, given that he could still feel the damn thing humming in his presence, but that was the problem. If he admitted he could sense the cuff, he was admitting to what he was: a monster. And though he could keep it at bay for now, on the darkest night of every month, there was no stopping it. He became a savage shadow wraith, enraptured by the darkness, by his own power. But that was neither here nor there. He had orders to follow.

'Sir, we just need to speak to your son,' Talemir pressed.

'Speak to him, eh?' Fendran said viciously. 'I have many sons. To which do you refer?'

Talemir exchanged a frustrated look with Wilder, who was growing restless beside him. His protégé wasn't known for his patience, especially after what had happened to Malik. Talemir could hardly blame him, nor could he blame the blacksmith for wanting to protect his child.

Talemir took a deep breath, almost choking on the metallic fumes. 'Your youngest. Drue Emmerson, sir. We need to speak to Drue.'

A grimace wrinkled the man's weathered face, and he pinched the bridge of his nose, as though he'd had this conversation many a time before.

To Talemir's surprise, Fendran turned to the woman, whose kohl-lined blue eyes glimmered with amusement, her fingers casually stroking the feathered chest of that great hawk.

'What's the meaning of this, Drue?' Fendran asked her.

Talemir baulked. *What did he call her?* Surely there was some mistake. She couldn't be —

But the beautiful, fiery woman turned to Talemir, triumph

444

gleaming in her gaze. 'Ah,' she said. 'It would seem I am the wayward son of the forge master...'

She didn't offer her hand, but she sketched a bow, similar to the one Talemir had mocked her with earlier.

'Drue Emmerson, at your service, Warsword.'

Continue Drue and Talemir's story in
Slaying the Shadow Prince.

COLLECT THE ENTIRE MORTAL ENEMIES TO MONSTER LOVERS SERIES!

Read these scorching hot romances in any order for monstrous romance, morally grey leads, and guaranteed happily-ever-afters!

Discover them at www.mortalenemiestomonsterlovers.com

GLOSSARY

Cities, Countries, People Groups (Non Primary Races), and Worlds

Chepi – a city ruled by Kumar Talutah

Ecekom - the primary world of the Vawtrians. Formerly the primary world of the Shivennans

Eiram - the name for Earth and primary world to the Awdawms and Neyeb (the world on which Rhea, Tengrii, and Salanca live before our known first historical records).

Dohahtee – a large city of Unato healers built around a mountain

Kuchani – one of the Neyeb primary cities and the city located around the Temple of Tiacha

Muiris – a village that escaped through a tear in the dimensions to populate Serroth

Serroth – a Separated World and the world on which Tengrii and his people live

Temple of Tiacha – the primary formation point for the Tue-Rah on Eiram located in Kuchani

GLOSSARY

Primary Races

Awdawms - the human race as we know it is generally referred to as the Awdawms, regardless of which world they are from

Bealorns - the beast talking and beast taming race

Machat - the prophet race

Neyeb - the mindreader race

Tiablos - the illusionist and telekinetic race

Shivennans - the elemental race. There are four types: geo (earth), pyro (fire), aero (air), and aqua (water)

Unatos - the healer race and poison power race

Vawtrians - the shapeshifter race

Foreign Words and General Concepts

Bealorns Nidawi – a community of Bealorns known for the training of predatory birds and speed runners

Besred – a large gorgonopsid-like creature that is able to seal its jaws and dissolve whatever it is with acid it pushes into its mouth

Central Races - the Central Races include the three races who were charged with the protection of the Tue-Rah because they stood by Elonumato during the Rebellion of Te. These races included the Vawtrians, Machat, and Neyeb.

Central Worlds - the Central Worlds include the three strongest Tue-Rahs that provide energy and sustenance to the other Tue-Rahs of the worlds. These worlds include Eiram, Ecekom, and Reltux

Crespa – a Vawtrian expression of shock and frustration

Cut-Off Worlds – a world that has been cut off from the Tue-Rah for a designated time either for healing of the bond or securing a situation

450

Eight Races – another term for the Primary Races who live on the known worlds

Elmis - darkened patches of skin on a Neyeb's wrists, ankles, lower back, forehead, and backs of knees that allow mind reading and extra sensory perceptions

Forbidden Arts – various arcane and magical practices that rely on suffering and pain from one or multiple persons to accomplish the intended goal

Kumar – an Unato leader

Locking - a bonding ritual whereby a Vawtrian awakens his or her sexual urges and connects to his or her spouse

Melspa Vawtrian - a Vawtrian who is particularly gifted in becoming any living creature that lives primarily in the water. Has added flexibility and endurance.

Nulaam - the state of someone who has been betrothed to a Neyeb in a formal evaluation ceremony conducted by the Council of Elders but is not yet married to that Neyeb because the waiting period has not yet passed

Para - rulers and overseers of the Tue-Rah. Their purpose is to protect the Para and those who tend, those selected from the Central Races to tend to the Tue-Rah and prevent its misuse.

Polph – an expression of shock and frustration among Awdawms

Psychic races – the races who use powers based on the mind including the Neyeb, Machat, Bealorns, and Tiablos; not just strictly the mindreaders

Psychic stones - small stones that are sensitive to imprinting when subjected to certain procedures by those with telepathic, prophetic, foreseeing, illusionist, and other similar abilities

Seyal Vawtrian - a Vawtrian who is particularly gifted in becoming any living creature that primarily lives on land. Has added strength and weight. Often the broadest and having more aggressive or tenacious temperaments.

Separated Worlds – worlds that were created but not yet connected to the Tue-Rah for general access; typically believed to be uninhabited; forbidden for anyone to visit without permission.

Sikalt - someone who creates a problem and then leaves without dealing with it or someone who avoids a problem they are making worse

Sodiwa – a Tiablo community that pursues a particular focus of skills and works toward a common goal; usually exclusively Tiablo because of risks undertaken through the improvement of the various Tiablo skills

Tra- a blue perpetual renewing energy source from Ecekom

Tue-Rah - an interdimensional portal that connects the worlds through time and space. Every world has one primary Tue-Rah formation and a number of smaller sub Tue-Rahs. It is alive in one sense and capable of making its own decisions, but it can be controlled through the temples and certain devices

Veskaro/Veskare - a Vawtrian term for the spouse of a Vawtrian. It is used after the locking has completed or when an arrangement has been made, and essentially means "most beloved one" or some variation of most beloved as adapted by the individual

Vestov – the process of providing sexual pleasure and climax to one's mate and self; a deeper and more emotionally connected sexually practice

Waste - a Vawtrian term for destroying an individual at the cellular level and turning that individual into dust

ACKNOWLEDGMENTS

In one sense, I always feel as if I repeat myself in these acknowledgments. But that's really because I am so incredibly blessed to have such a strong foundation of support. Just like children, it takes a village to create a book.

I am especially grateful to Clare Sager for inviting me into this multi-author set. In addition to being a generally incredible person, she put a tremendous amount of work into this, and the concept was one that had me excited from the start.

I am also so very thankful for all the people who helped me whip this story into shape. Katherine Bennet's advice in the development and finetuning of the plots and character arcs was, as always, exceptional. Even when I start off telling her what I think the problem is, she is always able to work through my muddled information to realize what the real issue is and help me come up with solutions to fix it in a way that honors the creative vision.

Huge thanks as well to Maggie Myers who stepped in to help me with edits at the last minute. Her thoughtful expertise in finetuning this manuscript took it to a new level.

And such tremendous thanks to my proofreaders Nic Page, Cassie G., Rachel Cass, and Nicole Zoltak. These incredible women have really stepped up especially as I have dealt with worsening dyslexia and other challenges. Their insight and commentary also encourage me to keep going and makes me want to be a stronger author with each story I complete.

Natalie Bernard designed the illustrated cover in a way that exceeded my every hope. The way that she captured the intensity of the movement between Tengrii and Rhea as well as the palette made me so happy. And she was exceptionally polite when I sent her my remarkably rough and childlike sketch of what I wanted it to look like.

Saint Jupit3r Graphics likewise did such incredible work on the underjacket design. I wasn't really certain what to expect other than knowing what color I wanted it to be as well as a few elements. And they turned out gold. I could stare at all the elements in that cover for hours.

In addition to all this, I am enormously grateful to Clare Sager for her formatting skills. She turned this beauty into something next level. And I am so very thankful to Carissa Broadbent for handling the cover formatting and typography. Utterly gorgeous work, as you can see.

So much gratitude and thanks to my author friends who helped me. This includes everyone listed above as well as Catharine Glen and Janeen Ippolito for their consistent encouragement as well as checking in on me and reminding me to do things like drink water and take walks.

A great big thank you also to my Books, Gowns, and Crowns ARC readers: Iris, Summer, Katelyn, Danielle, Sarah, Lauren, Sydney, Elizabeth, Krysti, Kenya, Sarah, Amy, and those of you who just wanted a hello but not your name included. It was such a pleasure to get to meet you all, and I look forward to seeing you again soon, you magnificent darlings. You were all utterly fabulous.

Enormous thanks to my family for their consistent support even when they aren't always certain what I'm up to. Special props to my husband, James, in particular who despite being uneasy about snakes supported this story and helped with cleaning kitchen and keeping the cats off my keyboard.

And a very special thank you to you the reader who has gone on this journey with me. You make all this possible in so many ways. Whether this is our first time meeting or one of many, thank you. I hope you're doing well and that your year just gets better from here.

I am an exceptionally blessed and fortunate woman to have such wonderful people in my life. I could not do it without you all.

ALSO BY JESSICA M. BUTLER

The Tue-Rah Chronicles

Identity Revealed

Enemy Known

Princess Reviled

Wilderness Untamed

Shifter King

Empire Undone

Tue-Rah Tales

Locked

Alone

Cursed

Standalones

The Mermaid Bride

Bound By Blood

Through the Paintings Dimly

The Celebrity

Little Scapegoat

Vellas

Fae Rose Bride

Anthologies

Once Upon Now

Vices and Virtues

Fierce Hearts

Adamant Spirits

About the Author

Jessica M. Butler is an adventurer, author, and attorney who never outgrew her love for telling stories and playing in imaginary worlds. She is the author of the epic fantasy romance series *Tue-Rah Chronicles* including *Identity Revealed, Enemy Known,* and *Princess Reviled, Wilderness Untamed, Shifter King* along with independent novellas *Locked, Cursed,* and *Alone,* set in the same world. She has also written numerous fantasy tales such as *Mermaid Bride, Little Scapegoat, Through the Paintings Dimly, Why Yes, Bluebeard, I'd Love To,* and more. For the most part, she writes speculative fiction with a heavy focus on multicultural high fantasy and suspenseful adventures and passionate romances. She lives with her husband and law partner, James Fry, in rural Indiana where they are quite happy with their five cats: Thor, Loptr, Fenrir, Hela, and Herne.

For more books or updates:
www.jmbutlerauthor.com

facebook.com/jmbutler1728

twitter.com/jessicabfry

instagram.com/jessicambutlerauthor

Printed in Great Britain
by Amazon

42445816R00263